Addison Blakely:
CONFESSIONS
OF A PK

Addison Blakely:
CONFESSIONS
OF A PK

Kimberley,
Many blessings to a
fellow writer! ☺

Betsy St. Amant

♥ *Betsy St. Amant*

BARBOUR
PUBLISHING

Published by Barbour Publishing, Inc., P.O. Box 719, Uhrichsville, Ohio 44683, www.barbourbooks.com

Our mission is to publish and distribute inspirational products offering exceptional value and biblical encouragement to the masses.

 Member of the
Evangelical Christian
Publishers Association

Printed in the United States of America.

Dedication

To Lori—and not just for the T-shirt.

Acknowledgments

Special thanks to all the girls who helped me remember my high school days—and kept me up to speed on all that has changed since! Mallory, Andrea, and Julianne—you girls are the best! Sarah, thanks for sharing your high school teacher expertise and cheering me on, and Georgiana, for being the world's best crit-partner. Also thanks to my spectacular agent, Tamela Hancock Murray, for always believing in me, and my editor, Kelly McIntosh, for seeing everything in Addison that I did. As always, I couldn't do anything without the support of my hubby—Brandon, I love you! And last but never least, thank You, Jesus, for blessing me with the opportunity to do what I love—and shine a light for You.

Chapter One

He looked good in those jeans, and he knew it.

There was no other explanation for the way Wes stood on the sidewalk across the street, one arm braced against the light post, his back to me as he chatted up a curly haired blond in a midriff-baring top. I'd always hated those shirts. It's like, are you that proud of your belly button? Really?

I still think he only pretended to care about the poodle-ish waif who lived a few streets over. In fact, I was as sure of that as I was sure his favorite song was "Free Bird" and his favorite color was green—well, okay, I assumed that because he wears it the most often, and it does ridiculous things for his eyes. I'd almost told him before, but every time I got that close I froze and could only stare at his crooked grin that had a tendency to melt my legs like a 3 Musketeers bar in the sun. So, to avoid the risk of babbling incoherently and dishonoring my 4.0 reputation, I'd mumble some excuse to head home before I leaped into his arms like the dozens of ska—sorry, there's no other word for it—skanks that willingly did just that. I definitely wasn't the only one who found Wes charming.

But I was the only one who didn't have a clue why.

He turned and caught me watching, and I quickly looked down at my book bag, wishing I hadn't stopped to rearrange the contents before heading home from school. If I'd kept going, then I wouldn't have seen Wes and Poodle Girl making out in front of my house, and I could have naively slipped inside the front door like any other weekday. But my English book had been digging its hard corner into my ribs for the last block, and enough was enough. I grimaced as I tugged the straps of my tote around my shoulder.

I had teased Wes once that his black leather jacket was cliché, and he replied that he needed it for his motorcycle. I didn't even go there. Besides, if leather made him stereotypical, then what did that make me, a bookworm carrying a book bag? Whatever. I loved my books—fiction more than textbooks, of course, though I was never without a variety of both—and they needed a bag, so what was the harm? At least there wasn't an actual picture of a worm on the front. My tote was solid beige, a blank canvas.

Sort of like my love life.

My traitorous gaze darted back to Wes. He winked before redirecting his attention to the blond. Did she notice that he'd noticed me? Did she care? My grip tightened around the strap, and I breathed a loud sigh through my nose, fighting the violent green monster that always threatened to lop off Wes's head.

Though, really, it was my fault she was there with him and I was here, on the outside looking into the mystery of Wes Keegan. It wasn't like Wes hadn't shown interest when he first moved to my hometown of Crooked Hollow, Kansas, four months ago—and how well I remembered that day. I'd been walking home from the library on a breezy Saturday afternoon when a motorcycle blazed down the street beside me. I'd looked up long enough to catch dark eyes with equally dark lashes staring at me from beneath a helmet, and suddenly it was as if my entire world ceased to exist. Yeah, I know—that's corny—but seriously, even the wind stopped whistling through the trees, and the birds hesitated midchorus like in a Disney movie. Then with a grin, he roared away, and I didn't hear about him again until the following week, when the entire town buzzed with rumors of "the new guy." At first, word was he rode a motorcycle and had a few tattoos—then, according to the good ol' gossip mill's churning power, he shoved old ladies into traffic, frightened children with his knife collection, and stole food from the homeless. The rumors got more ridiculous from there—we don't even *have* homeless people in our tiny town—until I finally stopped listening.

But somehow, I couldn't stop caring.

I'm a sucker for an underdog, and while everything about Wes—the bike, the jacket, the tattoos—screamed power and danger, I saw something else. Something that lingered in his dark eyes, something that made me think the outer layer was just that—a facade. A thin, superficial surface.

Anyone with a tattoo of a bird on his forearm couldn't be that bad, huh?

Wes's eyes cut over to me again, and I realized how long I'd been staring. Great. That wasn't obvious. I headed toward my front-porch steps, cheeks flushed, but not fast enough to avoid seeing Poodle Girl take Wes's face in her hands and initiate Kissing Session Round Two. Or was it three? I'd seen them out there several times in the last week, and the fact that the light post they preferred to stand under is stationed directly across from my house didn't go unnoticed. Again, he did it on purpose—same with the jeans.

I just wish I could figure out why. Apparently Poodle Girl was a willing enough cohort—what could he want with me? Was one woman not enough?

Not that it mattered. With a few quick steps, I turned

the knob of the renovated, two-story farmhouse I'd shared
with Dad all of my sixteen years, slightly out of breath, and
blamed the four powdered doughnuts I'd had for breakfast
that morning. I'd made Dad wheat toast again, and I pulled
the doughnuts out (he'd probably eat half the package), so the
pastries were stashed incognito between two slices of bread as
I'd hurried out the door for school. I'd then spent the entire first
period wondering how Wes's lips tasted and annoyed at my
active imagination.

PKs aren't supposed to think about such things. Yeah,
did I mention I'm a pastor's kid? Sounds like it should be a
confession. *Hello, my name is Addison Blakely, and I'm a PK.*
Just like my native status of Crooked Hollow, Kansas—some
things are unfortunately predetermined. (Trust me, unless you
have a passion for cornfields, there's not much to living in a
small town in the heart of the Midwest.)

Maybe *unfortunate* isn't the right word. It's not like I have a
problem with God or anything. He's been there through a lot—
like the death of my mother when I was five. It's just that lately
my prayers don't seem to be getting farther than my bedroom
ceiling.

And I can't help but wonder what living outside of the
fishbowl labeled "PK" would look like.

I let myself inside, grateful Dad was still at the church on
this September Wednesday afternoon and wouldn't be home
until dinner. Maybe somehow I could avoid the inevitable litany
of how's-the-second-week-of-school-going type of questions I
didn't want to answer, and truly, Dad didn't want to hear. What
was I supposed to say? *Going great, Dad. Had to borrow a
tampon from a stranger in history class, then I not only dropped
my books in the hallway but kicked them when I tried to pick
them up, and yes, that happened right in front of a group of*

cheerleaders who were already whispering about my book bag, and oh yeah, I was offered a hit of marijuana—all before lunch. No thanks. Dad wasn't ready for that level of honesty. Sometimes I think in his mind my classmates and I wore ankle-length uniforms and played Maypole during recess.

I dropped my bag on the table and snagged a Coke from the fridge. Despite his own love for sugar, Dad used to allow me only one pop a day, and to him, that rule hasn't changed even though I had my sixteenth birthday almost nine months ago. I usually saved my pop for dinner, but this tiny piece of rebellion was all I allowed myself.

A girl's gotta have *something*.

Fighting the urge to look out the window to see if Wes was still outside, I turned my back to the living room and instead flipped through the cherry-print recipe box on the counter. Wednesday was my night to make dinner (along with Monday and Friday), and I knew Dad would expect something hot and covered in gravy after a long day at work before rushing back to the church for the evening prayer service. At least my attendance wasn't required on Wednesday nights during the school year. It gave me a few hours of peace and quiet at home by myself, not to mention the rare right to the remote control.

People seem to think pastors have it easy. That they go to the office, play a few games of solitaire, field a few phone calls, work on their sermon, and head out early to catch a round of golf. Not my dad. He's invested in his congregation—to a fault. And trust me, that list of faults is long. Half of those people don't deserve an ounce of the patience and attention Dad devotes to them. They form committees and complain about the worship music or protest his assigned parking space in the lot that's been in effect for twenty years. After all the hours my father puts into that church, is it really that big a deal for the parishioners to walk an extra ten feet to the front door? But no one asks my opinion.

And trust me, I have a lot of them.

Most people would be stunned to know I have the thoughts I do. That sometimes I question God. I question myself. That I long to do one wild, reckless, daring move just for the shock factor of it all. I know my mom didn't mean to die and that my father didn't mean to turn overprotective and old-fashioned in her absence. It was how he survived, so I played along. I'd already lost my mom. . . . I couldn't lose my father, too.

Even if it does seem like actually pleasing him is a bar set higher than the one at the summer Olympics.

I plucked a card from the box and slapped it on the counter. Hamburger steaks and gravy. That would make him happy for tonight, if nothing else. I finished the rest of my pop and carefully buried the can in the wastebasket, under yesterday's discarded mail. I turned toward the fridge then hesitated, my fingers locked around the handle as I stared through the window. Wes was still outside, leaning against the light post, but Poodle Girl was nowhere to be seen. My stomach morphed into a butterfly farm.

He was waiting for me.

I closed my eyes, imagining the different scenarios—what would happen if I went outside. What would happen if I didn't. A shiver raced up my spine, and my eyes opened. I couldn't. I wouldn't.

Would I?

BANG.

The front door slammed. Dad was home early.

And once again, the biggest decisions in my life were made for me.

Chapter Two

He's so into you, Addison." Claire Pierson swabbed a french fry through a puddle of ketchup and gestured over my shoulder. "Everyone knows it."

"And I don't care." I sipped from a Coke, taking way too much joy in the fact that I planned on having three that day. The cafeteria food at Crooked Hollow High was too hard to stomach without carbonated assistance.

Can you tell I've become a master at justification?

Claire wouldn't give up. "Austin is hot. A senior. Captain of the varsity football team. Muscles from here to there. What else could you want?"

Hmm, let's see. Brains. A sense of humor. General human decency. I shrugged. "He's not my type." Besides, who wanted to date someone who bragged about sleeping with the majority of the cheerleading squad last year? I could just see Austin checking names off a list he kept under his pillow. No thanks. Besides, I was still a little queasy at having just assisted in dissecting a frog. Attending biology before lunch should be illegal, especially when it involved animal intestines. My food rolled in my stomach. I still couldn't believe Mr. Black had made us dive into dissection in the second week of school.

"Well, Austin sure could be my type." Claire leaned back

in her chair, tucking her blond hair behind one ear, eyes narrowing on her prey some fifteen yards ahead. She said this like she'd just decided, but something in her gaze made me think he'd been in her sights for much longer.

"Then go for it." I stabbed my fork into my pile of cold macaroni noodles and grimaced as it stuck fast. I dropped my fork on my tray. Forget it. I couldn't do it, not when the froggy memories lingered.

"I would, but he doesn't seem interested yet." Claire chewed on her lower lip, oblivious to my upset stomach. "I need to get his attention. Hey, we could double-date then switch at the end of the night." She smirked. "You know I wouldn't need long to convince him."

"Did you really just suggest that?" I arched one eyebrow, a favorite trick I saved for special occasions. If you do it just right, and in the perfect moment, you can actually quiet a room.

"You're right." Claire rolled her eyes. "You, Ms. Prude, date? What was I thinking?" She shoved her tray away from her, her glossy pink fingernails catching the fluorescent lights in the cafeteria. Sometimes I think blood red would be a better color for her.

I counted to five before I answered—rarely do I get to ten with Claire anymore. "I'm not a prude; I'm just not easy. There's a difference." I bit my tongue before something sarcastic could follow that statement about her own current sense of morals. "Besides, you know my dad. He gets full approval of dates, and well—two sentences into a conversation with Austin would nix that one." That is assuming Austin had two full sentences in his vocabulary. I watched as a fellow football player tossed a fry into Austin's mouth from across the table and cheered as if they'd just won the state championship.

Man, I couldn't wait for college.

"Better you than me. Seriously, Addison, I don't see how you put up with all those rules." Claire stood and shouldered her purse. "I'm going in." She flounced over to the jocks' table, where Austin held court with his french-fry jesters, leaving me to once again ponder why I considered Claire my best—and most days, only—friend. People might not be able to help their natural good looks or spoiled backgrounds, but they were still responsible for their attitude—and lately Claire's seemed to be getting more and more negative. But we'd made it through grade school together, so it seemed a waste to part ways now. At least I could count on Claire to always share exactly what she was thinking.

Even if I'd rather not hear it.

I played with the tab on my pop can. So what if Claire thought my dad was strict? Okay, so I thought that, too. But he did it out of love—and probably from sheer naivete of how to raise a teenager alone. That wasn't his fault any more than it was mine. Thankfully none of the guys around town had caught my eye anyway, so it wasn't like we fought about it.

Yet.

At this point, I just hoped Dad would be so grateful of all the headaches I spared him over the years that when I finally found the right guy, he'd like him as much as I did.

A fleeting image of Wes filled my mind, and I rolled in my bottom lip.

And then again, maybe not.

★ ★ ★

My usual desk in my honors English class was taken. That irked me. This was only the second week of school, but hey, a routine is easily created in two weeks. I thrived on my habits. But I kept my mouth shut and took a seat near the back—directly in front of Austin. I cursed my misfortune and pretended to ignore him. I'd heard rumors he'd gotten into the enriched class because the general was full and his uncle, Coach Thompson, pulled some strings. It sure wasn't because of his academic aspirations.

I set my bag under my desk and retrieved my English book and spiral notebook.

"In honor of Shakespeare Week, we'll be picking up *Romeo and Juliet* at act four, scene one. There's no better way to start a school year, in my opinion." Ms. Hawthorne, a pretty, middle-aged woman with a penchant for leather boots, stood at the podium near her desk. She was new to Crooked Hollow this year, but I could already tell she wasn't going to be a typical teacher. How could she be when I coveted her footwear?

She smiled. "Who wants to read first?"

I sort of did, but wasn't about to volunteer two days in a row. The redheaded girl beside me slipped her hand in the air, and I breathed a sigh of relief as she began to read.

I followed along, mouthing the words with Juliet, when Austin kicked the back of my chair. I paused, hoping it was a spasm. He kicked again, and my fingers tightened around my pen in disgust. Why didn't he just pull my hair while he was at it? I ignored him. What exactly did Claire see in this loser? He kicked a third time.

I spun around, my jeans sliding on the desk chair and providing extra momentum. "What?" I tried not to let how proud I was of my hiss show on my face. Even Claire would have approved of that one. She's always harping on me to be more aggressive.

He leaned in with a loud whisper. "What page are we on?"

"Two sixty-eight."

"What book?"

I rolled my eyes. "Get a clue."

"Get a miniskirt." He wiggled his eyebrows suggestively.

"Dude, lay off." The guy to my right chimed in, his tone low and borderline threatening. I blinked at my sudden rescuer. No white horse or shining armor to give away his hero status. Just sandy-blond hair that draped a little long near his eyes—in a cute sort of way, not the please-get-a-haircut kind of way. He seemed vaguely familiar, like maybe we'd had a class together last year.

Before Wes came into the picture and muddled my memory.

Austin leaned back in his chair, but I could tell by the challenge in his eyes that he wasn't done. Oh well, I could handle that later. I offered a small smile to my defender. "Thanks."

"He's a jerk." The guy tossed his hair out of his eyes, and the gesture drew my attention to his startling blue gaze. "I've wanted to tell him off for days."

"What took you so long?" I joked.

Ms. Hawthorne cleared her throat from the front of the class, and immediately my cheeks flushed. "Sorry," I mouthed to her. She nodded with a slight smile before turning her gaze to her teacher's guide. Hmmm. Yesterday when another pair of girls had been caught talking, she wrote them up. Oh well, count my blessings.

I looked back at my new friend, wondering if I should risk Teacher Wrath. He grinned, and I darted a cautious glance up front. "I'm Addison."

"Luke." He lowered his voice to a whisper. "No relation to Darth Vader."

I snorted back a laugh.

"We had a class together first semester last year. Geometry."

That explained it. I nodded, though I truly didn't remember him. Then again, I'd sat on the front row of all my classes and pretty much kept to myself.

The girl beside me finished reading the scene, and Ms. Hawthorne wrote some discussion questions on the board for us to answer. As I was halfway through copying down the third question, she called me to her desk.

Heart in my throat, I tried to keep my chin up as I made my way down the aisle, ignoring the muffled, sarcastic "ooohs" that followed in my wake.

She smiled, her teeth nice and straight without a smidgen of lipstick stain. "Hi, Addison. I hope I'm not embarrassing you."

Oh, not at all. I love feeling like the entire class is staring at my butt. I forced my lips upward. "No problem." *Hurry up, hurry up*. . . .

"I just wanted to ask if you'd mind staying after class for a minute." She was talking softly, but not softly enough. The front row behind me buzzed with rumors. I nodded, even though my chest tightened. What could I have done, besides talk to Luke? Surely this wasn't about that. But I had to know. I'd never gotten detention before, and trust me, I didn't want to start now. "Listen, I'm really sorry for talking during the reading—"

"Oh, that's no big deal." Ms. Hawthorne waved one hand in the air, brushing off the idea as if she hadn't just busted two other girls for the same offense yesterday. "Don't worry. I just received some rave reports from your teachers last year and thought you might want to hear them. I'm very glad you're in my class, Addison. I'm expecting big things from you."

Oh goody, no pressure. I exhaled slowly, hoping my smile seemed less contrived than it felt. No reason to be afraid of pressure, right? It's just that this year would not be a good time to let my grade-point average, not to mention my reputation, slip. College was close—too close.

And yet at other times, much too far away.

"Thanks." I hesitated, not wanting to sound rude. "Um, is

that all?" Not that it wasn't enough. My stomach cramped.

Ms. Hawthorne nodded, shuffling some papers on her desk—probably feeling the same awkward factor that threatened to choke me around the neck. "Yes, go ahead with the assignment, and I'll see you after class."

That last statement wasn't whispered at all, and a few students smirked as I made a beeline back to my chair. Perfect. I sank into my seat, glad to be out of the line of fire, and spotted Luke from the corner of my eye. He was busy scribbling on a sheet of notebook paper, and I was reminded of the assignment I was now behind in completing.

Then he held up the paper with a grin.

Meet me at the water fountain on the second floor after class.

I gestured toward Ms. Hawthorne, implying she wanted me to stay, and he nodded. "I know. After that," he mouthed.

Slowly, I picked up my pen and hovered it above my notebook. Did I really want to get into this? Another chair kick from Austin relinquished my doubts and fired my nerve. I wrote my response and discreetly held it for Luke to see.

Okay.

At least it would shut Claire up for a while.

Luke was leaning against the water fountain as promised, one ankle hooked over the other. It was like a scene from a *90210* rerun, and the corny factor of this entire rendezvous hit me full force.

I stopped in front of him, my textbook held defensively across my chest. "Hi." I wanted to crack a hero joke about his rescue earlier but couldn't think of one fast enough.

"Hi there." He grinned, slow, and it fluttered my stomach a little.

But not as much as Wes's smile. I tried to tamp down

my disappointment. It wasn't Luke's fault. Speaking of Wes, I couldn't help but wonder what he was doing. He was eighteen, according to the folks at the church, so he obviously had graduated before moving here—or maybe dropped out. He didn't look like the college type, and I didn't think he had a job—not by the way he always seemed to show up at the used bookstore or coffee shop every time I did. His dad, Mr. Keegan, had been in our church congregation several years. All that time of nodding and smiling hello on Sunday mornings, and I never knew he had a son. How was that possible?

"Need an escort to your next class?" Luke straightened, moving a step closer to me and jerking me out of my long-lashed, leather-scented daydream.

I blinked. Did he really just say *escort*? I bit my lower lip, instincts torn between accepting his offer—which was sweet in a Disney Channel movie sort of way—and getting the heck out of Dodge before this sudden friendship took a wrong assumption. Slowly, I shook my head. "Luke, I really don't—"

He eased my book from my white-knuckled grip, and before I could argue, shouldered my tote bag. "Where to?" He started walking before I could answer.

I watched helplessly as my books went without me. "Wrong way." I pointed over my shoulder to the west bank of classrooms. "Spanish."

"Thanks for clarifying." Luke smiled as he turned and passed me, now heading toward my next class. "Are you coming, or am I just taking your books for a walk?"

I laughed, despite the knot forming in my gut. Nothing wrong with being—what had he said? escorted?—to class. Besides, if Austin was lurking somewhere, at least this would ward off another immature mating-ritual attempt on his part. I caught up to Luke in a few quick strides and led the way to Spanish.

The look on Claire's face as we passed the open door of her history class made the entire ordeal worth it.

★ ★ ★

"How was school?" Dad asked his most-overused question between mouthfuls of spaghetti. He always chose pasta on his nights to cook, the cheater. Even bachelors can boil water.

I twirled a few noodles onto my fork, wishing he'd taken the time to make real sauce instead of the jarred variety. The spices were never as good bottled. "It was fine."

"Get any test scores back?" He picked up a second piece of garlic bread, and I fought the urge to remind him he was watching his carbs.

"An A on a quiz in English." Thankfully, after Ms. Hawthorne's glowing reviews from last year's teachers. Anything less would have been awkward.

Dad nodded in approval. "Congratulations. Who is your teacher this year?"

"Ms. Hawthorne. She's new this year. I think her name is Karen. No, wait. Kathy."

He coughed violently into his napkin.

"You okay, Dad?" I rose halfway from my chair, unsure if I should pound him on the back or call 911. What was that rule about if they're coughing, they're breathing?

Dad cleared his throat, lowering his napkin to his lap. "Fine, fine. Just went down the wrong pipe." He sipped from his water glass. "Well, congratulations on the A."

"You already said that." I thought about raising my eyebrow at him, but he was already absorbed in sprinkling what looked like the rest of the parmesan cheese onto his plate. So much for his diet.

A sudden *tink* sounded at the living-room window. I glanced over my shoulder then back. Dad frowned, setting the empty cheese canister on the table. "That better not be those neigh-borhood kids again." He started to stand, but I beat him to it.

"I'll handle it, Dad. Finish your dinner." Maybe by the time I came back, he'd find a topic to discuss other than school. I edged into the living room and peered behind the curtains out the front window. Darkness peered back, save for a shadow under the street lamp across the road.

A lone shadow.

The spaghetti flipped in my stomach, and it had nothing to do with the bland sauce. "It's a stray dog, Dad. I'm gonna run it off." Not a complete lie. I pulled open the front door and stepped onto the porch before he could answer.

The cool night air chilled my arms, and I rubbed them with my hands as I crossed the street, my heart pounding so loud I was sure the entire neighborhood would hear it and call the police on charges of disturbance. Wes waited just outside the circle of light pooling on the concrete under the lamp.

"Took you long enough." He straightened from his slouched position beside the pole but didn't take his hands from his jacket pockets. Still, I felt his imagined embrace with the same intensity I did most nights in my dreams. And from the look in his eyes, he was thinking the same.

But it didn't matter. I wasn't blond, I wasn't a skank, and my belly button was safely tucked away under my thick purple sweater.

"What'd you do, throw a rock from twenty yards?" I snorted like I wasn't flattered. It shouldn't matter what he did for me or thought of me.

But it did.

A lot.

He shrugged. "I've got a good arm."

"Then why are you slumming around Crooked Hollow

instead of playing for the pros?" It was sarcasm, my usual defense against Wes's see-right-through-me gaze, but this time it didn't bounce off the chip on his shoulder as usual. Instead, his eyes flickered, like it ricocheted right into his heart.

The flicker disappeared as quickly as it'd happened, and he shrugged again, a flirty light replacing the uncertainty of moments ago. This time my stomach twitched, and I wished for the safety of the flicker. It didn't do nearly the same to my poor insides. Good thing I hadn't gone for the second helping of noodles.

"Professional sports teams tend to frown on jail records."

"What? You've never—" The words froze on my tongue, and I swallowed them, cold and hard. I had no idea if he'd been arrested before. Actually, the things I truly knew about Wes could be counted on maybe one and a half hands—and that was if he was telling the truth about the number of his tattoos. I sort of figured he was lying about that one.

He took a step toward me, his jacket opening slightly at the neck and revealing a hunter-green pullover. "Never what?"

"Nev—never mind." I hated that I stuttered. Poodle Girl probably never stuttered. Then again, she might not have all the motor skills I did, so it could be a poor comparison.

He laughed, the sound husky and warm. "You really think I've been to jail? Give me some credit here, PK."

I hated that label, but the nickname he'd twisted it into somehow caused more flutters than aggravation. I shrugged. "How was I supposed to know? You've only been here a few months." More like four months and three days, almost to the hour, but who was counting? "Anything is possible."

"You're easy to tease." He reached and tweaked my hair, and the nerves on the back of my neck tingled as if I'd been electrocuted. "What else do you believe about me?"

That you're not anything like what you seem. But I couldn't say that out loud, so I rolled my lower lip beneath my teeth and shrugged like I couldn't care in the least.

His eyes sparkled beneath the lamplight, and he tilted his head, a strand of dark hair falling across his forehead. "Here's a secret, Addison. It's not all true." He took a step closer.

I edged backward away from him, my heart screaming at me to go the other way into his arms. Somehow I just knew if I made that first step, they'd open welcomingly, like they did for Poodle Girl. *Stop it, Addison. Wes is trouble. You're not that girl.* But something in his eyes convinced me I could be.

"Addison!"

In the time it took me to look toward my father bellowing from our front door, Wes sidestepped out of the light puddling on the sidewalk and into the shadows.

"Coming, Dad!" I turned back to Wes to say good-bye, but he was gone. Poof. Only the subtle hint of leather and aftershave teasing the wind convinced me I hadn't dreamed the entire encounter in the first place. I stood there like an idiot, searching the darkness for proof I wasn't crazy, until my dad's persistence beckoned me home.

I trudged up the front walk with my hands hooked in my jeans pockets, positive Wes's gaze burned into my back with every step. I refused to reward him with the amusement of a backward glance—wherever he was. It was okay. He'd be back. The thought brought equal parts relief and anxiety.

Dad held the screen door open for me as I hurried inside. "You shouldn't mess with strays, Addison. It's dangerous."

Don't I know it.

Chapter Three

"You're still going to meet me at the library during study hall, right?" I pinched the bridge of my nose against the headache pounding at my temples as I waited for Claire to finish applying her lip gloss in the bathroom mirror. No amount of caffeine seemed to help me wake up today.

After my impromptu, clandestine meeting in the street last night, I couldn't sleep. Thoughts of Wes swirled through my mind, and no matter how many times I tried to count sheep, I ended up counting motorcycles and tattoos. What was wrong with me? Was it possible to have a midlife crisis at sixteen? Guys like Wes had never appealed to me before. They just made me want to hand them a button-down shirt and a bottle of hair gel and tell them to get over themselves and lose the drama.

But Wes was different. Something about his outer persona and his eyes didn't match. The difference screamed "faker," but not in the obnoxious, plastic way of someone trying to be something they weren't. No, Wes's image shouted something else, but I couldn't make out exactly what.

Not with my legs turning to mush beneath me every time he smiled. Talk about hard to focus.

"Yes, for the tenth time, I'll be there." Claire smacked her lips twice before putting her tube of gloss back in her purse.

"And you know where the library is?"

"Addison." The raking of the zipper on her purse punctuated her frustration.

"Sorry, just making sure."

"You underestimate me." She swept past, and the bathroom door nearly hit me in the shoulder as I followed her toward her locker.

"I know. But that project is due for Mr. Black's class Monday, and we've barely made a dent in it." Biology, ugh. Not my favorite subject and usually the messiest. What teacher assigned such a big project that was due so soon after the start of school anyway? It should be illegal—and this coming from a girl who actually enjoyed school most days. I could only imagine what the less-than-studious types were thinking. Probably nothing PG.

"You've never even made a B in your entire life. What's the big deal?" Claire wiggled her fingers in a wave as we passed Austin's locker, and he nodded at her but winked at me. I turned my head the other direction and continued, ignoring Claire's pout.

"Yes, I have." I think. It would have been in elementary school, but it still counted. I wasn't perfect—regardless of what my dad thought.

A shadow nestled on her face. "I said I'd be there."

"I hope so because you know I can't come up with a cell model by myself in time—"

Claire held up one hand so fast she almost hit me in the nose. "I'll be there." She fiddled with her combination and yanked open the door. Someone had taped a flyer advertising the annual end-of-the-semester talent show on her locker, and already a penciled mustache and devil horns adorned the photo of last year's winner.

I pulled it down and handed it to her, knowing she wouldn't want that on her door. She barely even glanced at it as she shoved it inside her locker. "I'll bring you a pop, okay?" A little extra bribe couldn't hurt. I didn't trust Claire's motivation much these days. A fact, sad but true. High school had changed my friend, and I missed the middle-school girl who used to invite me over for sleepovers and always gave me the biggest brownie. I couldn't even picture Claire baking anymore, not without a designer apron tied around her waist and her manicured hands protected by plastic gloves. My sandbox buddy was long gone, lost somewhere beneath two layers of makeup and freshly waxed eyebrows.

"Sure. Whatever. See you in a bit." She banged the door shut and left without a wave.

I rolled in my lower lip as she sauntered off. I hoped the 'tude wasn't because of Austin. Claire knew I wasn't interested in him, and until she recently discovered his supposed interest in me, she had never seemed to be attracted to him either. So what was the big deal? Maybe we'd get a chance to talk during study hall while brainstorming for our project, and I could find out what was bothering her.

Claire's bottled Coke I'd snagged from the vending machine after two dollars and fifty cents' worth of attempts formed a cold layer of condensation on the bottom of my tote bag. Here I was breaking a rule for her—no food or drinks allowed in the library—and she was twenty-five minutes late. We only had an hour before our next class started.

If she was doing her makeup again, I'd kill her.

I tapped my fingers against the open textbook on the table, trying to focus. But frustration toward Claire overwhelmed any creative thought. She knew this project was important to me—

we were partners in the class, and this was a shared effort *and* grade—and she couldn't even be considerate enough of my feelings to be on time?

"I'm gonna kill her." This time I said it out loud, and a freshman at a corner table by the fiction bookshelf shot me a nervous glance.

"Problems?" A voice, thick with accent, sounded over my shoulder, and I turned to see a pretty blond with a bob haircut smiling at me. Her table was loaded with textbooks and an English-German dictionary.

"Nothing new, unfortunately." I hesitated. "You're the exchange student from Germany, aren't you?"

"*Ja*, Marta." She stood and came to my table, sliding into the chair I'd saved for Claire. "I'd tell you my last name, but it wouldn't matter. You wouldn't be able to repeat it or spell it." Her grin widened, revealing an even row of white teeth and lighting her pale-blue eyes.

"In that case, *guten Morgen*." I smiled a greeting.

Marta's accent thickened as she rattled off in German and, I assumed, asked if I spoke the language. Oops. I shook my head. "Sorry, I'm in my second year of Spanish. I'm Addison." I gestured at the chair she just took. "And you're sitting on my imaginary friend Claire, who is apparently standing me up for our study date."

"I see." Marta nodded, her hair swinging against her jawline. "Can I help instead?"

"It's just a project for Mr. Black's biology class. Claire's my partner, and I'm clueless where to start." Inspiration lately had been a dry well. I tried not to blame Wes, but at the moment, it seemed like everything was his fault. If he hadn't ridden into my life a few months ago, this school year would be predictable and boring just like I'd hoped. Now here I was, all ditzy and

unfocused like the girls who hung around him that I made
fun of. The realization burned my stomach, and I turned my
attention back to Marta, determined to focus. "We're supposed
to be making a model of the different parts of a cell, something
simple enough that could be taught to elementary-aged kids."
I sighed. "But there's a bunch of extra points awarded for
creativity, so I'd hoped to do something sort of outside the box."

"Fun. Science is my best subject." Marta slid the book,
which was open to the chart, toward her. "May I?"

"Knock yourself out."

She tilted her head, pale eyebrows bunched in confusion.

"American slang. Sorry." I waved my hand in an effort to
brush off my embarrassment. "I meant, please continue."

"Ja." Marta bent over the text, and her lips pursed as she
read. She looked up after a moment, and I could almost see the
wheels turning in her head. "You wanted creative?"

I nodded.

"What if you made the model of your cell edible? With candy?"

"A candy cell?" Talk about my kind of assignment. There
was a bag of SweeTarts in my purse right now, and I wasn't
even a fifth grader.

Marta continued. "It'd be great for children. How better to
learn than with candy?"

I knew I'd liked this girl. I nodded slowly, liking the idea
more and more the longer it sank in. "Wow, that's totally
perfect." There was only one potential problem. I hesitated.
"Are you taking Mr. Black's class this semester?" I hated to
use her idea if she needed it for herself—though I was sort of
tempted, in this unfamiliar stage of last-minute desperation.
Man, how did slackers do it?

She shook her head, and relief draped over my shoulders
like a fuzzy blanket. I reveled in the warmth, and with a burst

of generosity, reached into my tote and pulled out Claire's pop. "Here. You've earned it." I handed over the bottle.

Marta took it with a puzzled smile.

"It was for Claire, sort of a bribe to get her here on time. We see how well that worked." I gestured to the drink. "Enjoy." Might as well bribe a new friend instead, although on second thought, everything about Marta seemed genuine. It was nice not to have to try to stay one step ahead of catty Claire and her mind games. I almost felt guilty for the realization, but truth was truth.

Marta stole a glance over her shoulder for the librarian before twisting off the cap and taking a few quick sips. I bit back a smile. Looked like the language of rule breaking remained universal.

"Is Claire a friend or just a classmate?" Marta hid the closed bottle on the ground at her feet and leaned forward, as if truly interested.

I shrugged, hating that my hesitation pretty much answered for me. I tried to backpedal at the knowing look in Marta's eyes. "We've grown up together, but lately things are different." I didn't want to spill my entire life story there on the library table, but who do you vent to about your only friend? "We're going in opposite directions, it seems."

"Friendships are hard," Marta agreed. "I know. My sister and I struggled recently, and you can't escape your family." She snorted.

"Do you have a big family?" I uncapped my pen and scribbled some thoughts about the different candies I could use for our cell while I waited for her answer. "I'm an only child."

"Two sisters and a brother."

Wow. What would it be like to have so many siblings? I'd have to quiz her on that later. "So are you the first to participate in an exchange program?"

Marta shook her head, and her hair brushed back to reveal a beautiful pearl earring. Pearls. . .at school? She really was different.

"My brother did the program a few years back. He loved it and taught me a little about the American culture before I came overseas. But some things were still, shall we say, surprising." She laughed. "I learn something new every day."

I could only imagine. I'd heard before that the English language was the most confusing to learn out of all others, with our tendencies for slang—which I'd already proven. Looked like I'd have to watch what I said for a while—that is, if Marta stuck around long enough to become a friend.

And from the smile she offered as she rattled on about her family and home country, entertaining me as I worked on my project, it seemed like she might.

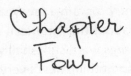

Chapter Four

"Those are too sour, PK."

I jumped at the voice that suddenly spoke over my shoulder, dropping the bag of dollar candy I held in my hand. Wes smirked behind me, and my heart lurched before I could control it.

"What do you mean?" I prided myself on keeping my voice steady, despite his effect on me, and stooped to grab the candy from the floor. Somehow I knew he wouldn't have picked it up for me. If chivalry is dead, then it's flat-out extinct in Crooked Hollow.

"I didn't stutter. I meant just what I said—it's sour." He reached around me, snagging a discounted bag of gummi bears and my heart in one fluid motion. The subtle aroma of leather wafted around me, and I steeled my emotions against it. "You'd like this better. Nice and sweet." He smirked before tossing the bag into the red basket on the floor at my feet.

Something about that smirk told me we weren't talking about just gummi bears anymore. "What if I like sour?" I grabbed the candy and threw it back on the shelf. I didn't, much. Actually, gummi bears *were* my favorite. But that wasn't the battle I apparently fought here.

He crossed his arms over his chest and shrugged as if he

couldn't care less. And he probably didn't. But then why was he here, discussing the pros and cons of candy in aisle three of Crooked Hollow General Grocery?

I made a show of looking behind him. "Speaking of sour, where's your girlfriend?" I swallowed the bitterness rising in my throat and tried to match his nonchalant expression. How did he do that? Years of actually not caring about anything? Or had he simply perfected the mask? "She trying to calculate how much it will cost if mascara is half off?"

Amusement danced in his eyes. "I'm not her keeper."

"Careful. You know what happened to the last guy who said that."

A flicker of confusion replaced the humor in his expression. I started to explain my reference to Cain and Abel from the Bible but decided not to waste my breath. As surely as I knew Wes couldn't care less about Poodle Girl, I knew he hadn't exactly grown up in church.

"Forget it. I'm sure Poodle—"—I swallowed the rest of her secret nickname before I embarrassed myself further—"your friend will be back shortly." If I were with Wes, I sure wouldn't leave him alone for long. But there I went again, mixing fiction with reality.

Like an actor taking her cue, Poodle Girl sauntered up, stage left. "Did you find the powdered doughnuts, baby?"

So much for my favorite breakfast.

She wrapped her arm around Wes's, her hot-pink fingernails neon against his black leather sleeve. She smiled, but her eyes quickly narrowed to overly mascara-ed slits as she flitted her gaze over me. I snorted at the thought that she actually considered me competition.

But as the spider led her willing prey off to find doughnuts, Wes sent me a wink over his shoulder—and for a brief moment, I wondered if maybe I was.

I slammed the door of my house then opened it and slammed it again. Immature, but Dad wasn't home, and because of Wes and my stupid inability to think logically around him, I'd forgotten to actually pay for all the candy for my cell presentation Monday. I got halfway home before realizing I still clutched a bag of sour lemon drops in my hand that I didn't even like—all because I was too stubborn to accept the gummi bears Wes presented and move on. Too sweet? Ha. Wes obviously hadn't seen me PMS-y yet. I could go toe-to-toe with Poodle Girl and still come out swinging.

Too bad that Addison only existed once a month. The rest of the time I was more gummi bear than I wanted to admit. And, if I was honest, way too gummi bear for Wes. Of course he preferred sour. Poodle Girl was as lemon drop as they got.

I threw the bags of redeemed candies on the couch and glared at them. After going back to the store, paying, and apologizing for my sudden bout of kleptomania, I now had about thirty minutes to get started on the assignment before needing to cook dinner for Dad. Thank goodness Marta had shown up with her genius idea this afternoon, or I'd be staring down a big fat zero on our project Monday—well, make that *my* project. I was done covering for Claire. If she couldn't even return my text messages with an explanation about where she'd been today, forget it. I'd tell Mr. Black the truth and let Claire handle the consequences on her own—for once. Let her learn that designer brands and makeup couldn't get her out of this one.

I grabbed the index cards from my backpack, my favorite ballpoint pen, and the candy, then sat at the table and began tearing apart pieces of licorice and lemon drops like my life depended on it. My grade did, at least. Probably not my friendship with Claire. Who knew where that would end up going—assuming I had the guts to actually bail on her as she had me. Though in this case, I wasn't bailing, just being honest. She stood me up—I was simply going to take credit where credit was due.

So why did the thought make me feel like a rat?

Thirty minutes passed with not nearly enough progress— my cell looked more like a cow—and while I threw together a chicken and rice casserole, I lamented the fact I'd be working on this all day Saturday. Somehow that seemed even more pitiful than doing homework on a Friday night.

I could guarantee you Poodle Girl and Wes weren't doing homework. My stomach churned at the thought of what they might be doing instead, and I drew a deep breath. *You don't care. You don't care.* I tried to think about Luke instead and the attention he'd shown me at school, but it was like comparing the attention of Taylor Lautner with that of a nerdy third cousin. Not quite the same.

The front door opened and closed, and Dad's heavy footsteps shrugged across the carpet as he made his way to the kitchen. "Hey, honey. What are you making?" He drew a deep breath. "Needs more salt." He dropped his briefcase on the table and made a beeline for the stove.

"You can tell by the smell? Dad, that's pathetic. I'd prefer you to live past fifty." I intercepted the saltshaker from his threat against my casserole.

"Which isn't too far away."

"Exactly." I appeased him by adding more pepper before sliding the casserole into the oven then had an idea. I casually shut the oven door. "You know, if *you* cooked three nights a week instead of two then you could decide how much—"

"Nice try." He actually smiled, and I found myself relaxing at his lack of pinched brow.

He must have had a good day. Certainly better than mine. It was probably wise not to tell him about my near run-in with the law at the grocery store. Although really, I doubt they'd have even noticed it if I hadn't come back. Sometimes a high moral code is more hassle than benefit. However, being a PK busted for theft is not a scandal I wanted to experience personally.

But dating the local bad boy is?

My conscience taunted me, and I slapped the oven mitt on the counter to drown it out. "Who wants brownies?" My falsetto sounded unconvincing even to my own ears as my dad enthusiastically raised his hand. I hid my burning face in the refrigerator, pretending to search for the eggs that sat on the top shelf directly in front of me.

Too bad the answers I craved weren't as easily accessible.

Sunday morning came way too quickly, but I guess that's what happens when one spends her entire weekend preparing a group project solo. I buttoned the top button of my purple cardigan, knowing I'd be more likely to get away with wearing my above-the-knee skirt and knee-high brown boots if my top half screamed conservatism. It was either pure genius how well I'd pegged my dad's radar over the years—or pitiful.

The birds greeted me with a chorus as I stepped outside and locked the door behind me. Dad had given up long ago on convincing me to go to church as early as he did on Sunday mornings. I made him late—which to him meant showing up one hour before service started instead of two—enough times that I wiggled off that particular hook.

I adjusted my purse on my shoulder, heavy with Jane

Austen's *Pride and Prejudice*, which was silly since I knew I wouldn't read in church even if I could get away with it. Mrs. Vanderford, the lady who always sat in the second pew to my third, had big hair all right, but not that big. Still, I felt lonely without a book in my constant possession.

Likely yet another reason I was sixteen and without a boyfriend.

The birds' song grew slightly more bitter than pretty as I huffed up the corner to Victoria Street, already regretting my choice of pinching footwear. The bad thing about living in a small town—okay, one of the many bad things about living in a small town—was that since everywhere I had legitimate reason to go was in walking distance, it was pointless to have my own car. Or so Dad said. Frankly, I thought he just used that as an excuse not to have to up our insurance plan, but whatever. Pipe dream not to walk the tips or soles off at least one pair of my shoes.

I turned right onto Georgiana Drive and caught movement from the corner of my eye. I did a double take. Poodle Girl—wow, I really needed to learn her name—was getting a newspaper from the end of her driveway, dressed in a fluffy pink robe with curlers in her hair and a cigarette dangling from her mouth. She hesitated as she saw me, and I wished I had the guts to snap a picture on my cell phone. Wouldn't Wes like to see what his Barbie-doll girlfriend looked like in real color?

She straightened, the plastic bag dangling from her hand as she inhaled on her cigarette. "What are you looking at?" The hard stare returned, replacing the previous moment of vulnerability. Her gaze dropped to the Bible in my left hand, and her eyebrow twitched.

"Nothing." I shrugged. "Nice robe."

"Nice boots." She studied me so intently I couldn't decide if she meant the reply as a genuine compliment or insult. Since they were clearance rack, probably the latter. I started to walk again, unwilling to engage in a verbal showdown before church. What was the point?

"He talks about you, you know."

I stopped and slowly turned to meet her gaze, my heart pounding in my chest. "Who?" But we both knew I knew exactly who she meant.

She blew out a puff of smoke. "He says you're cute." She smirked, and this time I knew without a doubt it was an insult. Lemon drops versus gummi bears.

I was too sweet.

My chest heated under my sweater, and I abruptly kept walking without reply, hearing only her haughty laughter trailing in my wake. The birds' treetop melody once again pierced the morning as I hurried up the street toward the church.

This time they sounded downright angry.

I wasn't supposed to be that bored at church. But the beauty of it was I'd learned to hide it over the years. Everywhere else you looked, teenagers popped their gum, scribbled notes on their bulletin about where they wanted to eat lunch (actually, the deacons did that sometimes, too), and whispered as if the pulpit wasn't ten yards away. I guess that's why they didn't sit by me anymore. I'd had a bunch of church friends in elementary school, then once we all became teenagers and realized there were actual consequences for our choices, I was unofficially shunned. I guess they thought I'd tattle on their gossiping during the hymns and flirting during the sermons. Ridiculous, as Dad could easily see all that for himself. Though maybe part of me wanted to join them some mornings, just for the entertainment value.

Don't get me wrong, my dad wasn't a bad preacher. He was good, as far as that went. He had the composition down right, the presentation. But lately he lacked passion. I tried to pinpoint a point in time, tried to figure out exactly when his zeal had dissipated, but I couldn't be sure.

I couldn't even be sure I'd ever felt it for myself in the first place.

Across the aisle, tall, dark-haired Mr. Keegan shifted positions, tugging his almost-too-short pant leg down over his black dress socks and nearly knocking his Bible from his lap. I quickly looked away before he caught me staring. Mr. Keegan had been in the congregation for at least five years, yet I'd never spoken more than two words to him until I met Wes and realized they were father and son. Actually, we spoke the same two words, followed by a polite nod. *Good morning.* That's about it. It was sort of awkward looking him in the eye, knowing how I felt about his son.

And knowing what would happen if anyone else knew.

I tuned back in as Dad wrapped up his extended sermon on David, running for his life from his numerous enemies. Once a king in a palace, now hiding away in a cave in the wilderness. Funny how things change.

In front of me, Mrs. Vanderford shifted positions, temporarily blocking my view of Dad with her big, dark hair.

And funny how they don't.

The organ played a closing chorus to the invitation down the aisle, and I gathered my Bible and purse, eager to beat the crowd out the front doors and get home. This time I'd take the longer route a block over to avoid Poodle Girl's house. Not that she'd likely be in the driveway again—I didn't exactly peg her for the outdoorsy type—but I wasn't ready for round two. Not while still reeling from round one. I still couldn't figure out why her words had affected me so badly. Was she lying about Wes talking about me? Playing the exchange back over in my mind, I could almost detect a hint of jealousy in her voice. Or was that just wishful thinking?

In my distraction, I nearly mowed over a man making his way down the aisle in front of me. "Whoops, sorry." I patted the person's shoulder in apology before realizing it was Mr. Keegan.

He smiled down at me. "No problem."

I averted my gaze, certain my feelings were welling in my eyes. Could he tell I'd just been daydreaming about his son? Would he care?

Heaven knew my father would.

"Excuse me." I tried to ease around him, but Mr. Keegan stepped to the side, motioning me to join him.

"I'm glad I saw you. I need to ask you a question." Mr. Keegan hesitated, his deep-brown eyes, so like Wes's, troubled. "I'm a little worried about how my son is fitting in here at Crooked Hollow. Have you met Wes?"

I tried to swallow the knot tightening my throat, to no avail. I coughed, eyes watering. Great, I was going to die in the third pew of my church in front of Wes's father. I coughed again and finally managed a nod. "Once or twice." Little did he know I could give him a mental transcript of every word Wes and I had spoken together.

"Good." Mr. Keegan rocked back on his heels. "You grew up in Crooked Hollow. Maybe you could show him around." He leaned closer and lowered his voice, his breath so minty fresh I wondered if he'd downed an entire pack of Altoids. "Help him find some *good* friends." His emphasis on the word *good* made me wonder if he'd seen Wes with Poodle Girl as well. If so, no wonder he looked so tired. She wasn't exactly the type of girl to bring home to the parents.

I hesitated, not sure exactly what I was agreeing to. "You want me to be your son's tour guide?"

"Unofficially. Just make friends with him." He smiled. "You seem like a nice girl. Good influence."

My heart sank, but I forced a smile in return and agreed to give it a try. After all, isn't that what good ol' gummi bears do?

Chapter Five

"I can't believe you sold me out in Mr. Black's class." Claire slammed my locker shut, barely missing my hand as I yanked it out of the way.

I met her venomous stare full-on. Usually I hated conflict—especially on a Monday morning—but Claire had pushed one button too many. "If anyone should be upset, it's me. You never showed up at the library Friday and ignored my six hundred texts all weekend."

Claire flipped her hair and averted her gaze as a group of students shuffled past us. "I had things going on."

"Well, I did, too." I spun the combination and tugged my locker back open, my indignation heating into a boil. "Like getting a decent grade on a joint project that I had to do alone."

"I got an incomplete! That's worse than an F."

Seriously? I was so sick of this. All Claire could think of was herself. Typical. I shook my head as I switched out my books. "I believe that's your own fault."

"You've always covered for me before. What gives?" Claire hitched her Coach bag higher on her shoulder, and I wished I had the guts to grab it from her and throw it into my locker. Her expression would be priceless. But that wouldn't be very PK of me.

Though today it was hard to care.

"I'm just tired of being the fallback plan, okay?" I grabbed my English text and slammed my locker closed, even harder than she had. "You took advantage of me. If it hadn't been for Marta, I'd have been sunk. You know my grades are important to me."

Claire frowned. "Who the heck is Marta?"

"A foreign-exchange student from Germany who saved my behind helping me think of the edible cell idea for our project. Since you ditched me." I crossed my arms, hugging my textbook against my flushed chest.

"Weird."

"Not weird—nice. Considerate. Helpful. All of those things that you aren't exactly being anymore."

"What are you trying to say?" Claire planted one hand on her jean-clad hips, disbelief shading her overly made-up eyes.

"I'm saying that's it. Either you're going to be my friend and act like a friend, or I'm done." I couldn't believe I'd actually said it. Yesterday's exchange with Poodle Girl and my own emotional and mental roller coaster over Wes had put me over the edge. I was tired of being perpetually sweet. There was a fine line between being good and being a doormat. And I think I crossed that line with Claire years ago.

Claire's eyebrow twitched. "You don't want me for an enemy, Addison Blakely."

She was right. But I was too upset to care. "See you around." I brushed past her, accidentally bumping my shoulder against hers.

Or maybe not so accidentally.

★ ★ ★

For once I could honestly say I wasn't in the mood for Shakespeare. But in English class, we were reading various scenes from *Hamlet*, having thankfully finished *Romeo and Juliet* before Austin got any more twisted ideas about love. In his case love was a four-letter word—one that more accurately spelled L-U-S-T.

"You okay?" Luke whispered across the aisle.

I gave him a quick nod before pointing at my textbook and holding my finger in front of my mouth. Ms. Hawthorne might have been forgiving once, but I wasn't one to test a teacher's limits. I'd had about as much conflict today as I could handle. The memory of Claire's shock still rang in my head, and I couldn't help but smile. She'd always tried to get me to be more aggressive. Guess she just didn't mean toward her.

"You seem sort of dazed." Luke obviously didn't get my hint. Apparently one verbal save from an overly testosteroned football player, and Luke now considered himself my best buddy. I guess there were worse things in life, though—he seemed nice enough. Besides, my list of friends seemed to be shrinking drastically.

"Just had some drama with a friend before class. You know how high schoolers can be."

He snorted back a laugh, and Ms. Hawthorne looked up from her desk. Luke quickly turned the chuckle into a cough, and Austin "helped" by jumping up and pounding him on the back—with much more force than necessary. They exchanged hard glances, and for a minute I wondered if this incident would turn into a full-blown fight.

Ms. Hawthorne stood behind her desk. "Everything all right back there, boys?"

I couldn't help but smile at her choice of the word *boys* instead of *guys* or *men*. She called it as she saw it.

They offered mumbled replies before Austin returned to his seat.

"Austin, if someone is coughing, they aren't choking." Ms.

Hawthorne leveled him with a warning gaze as if she knew exactly what he'd been doing, and then she sat back down. "Back to *Hamlet*, everyone. Act five."

I fought the urge to look over at Luke, knowing I'd laugh if I did. But Hamlet blurred on the pages before me, and I sneaked a peek at my former rescuer. He shrugged. "We'll talk later," he mouthed.

Austin must have seen him speak to me because he tapped the back of my chair with his foot. Jealous dork. I couldn't respond without risking Ms. Hawthorne's attention again, so I ignored the thumping and went back to reading. But *Hamlet* wasn't exactly a pick-me-up sort of play. Thankfully Claire wasn't in this class with me, or I had a feeling we'd create our own act 6.

The bell rang, and I shut my book with a grateful snap. "Addison, if you please?" Ms. Hawthorne gestured me forward to her desk. I groaned, the sound thankfully lost in the shuffle of everyone packing up their books and exiting the room. She needed to see me *again*? At least this time it wasn't in front of everyone.

I carried my textbook to the front of the room. "Yes, ma'am?" No small talk today. She was nice enough, but bonding with teachers wasn't my thing. I wanted the good grades, but a suck-up I was not. I liked earning my way.

My gaze dropped to the floor. Even if Ms. Hawthorne was wearing really cute black leather boots.

"I was hoping your parents were coming to the open house next Friday evening." She looked up at me from her seated position, her hands folded together over her grade book.

Now what had I done? My mouth dried. "Um—"

"You're not in trouble, don't worry." Ms. Hawthorne smiled. "I'm just eager to meet them. It's not often I get a student with your scholarly reputation in my class."

Sad that since I didn't get in regular trouble and enjoyed making As, I was considered an oddity worthy of parental meeting. What'd she want to do? Shake my dad's hand on a daughter well done? Thank him for raising me better than the herd of buffoons who didn't care about their future or college?

I forced a smile in return, suddenly realizing I'd been staring at her in silence. "I think my dad will be here." I actually hadn't even planned on telling him, but I supposed now I didn't have much choice.

"Wonderful." Ms. Hawthorne stood up, effectively dismissing me. "I look forward to meeting him."

Grateful she didn't ask me about my mom, I just nodded and slipped out the door.

★ ★ ★

I eased into the second row of desks in my Spanish II class, surprised to see Marta occupying the seat on the aisle. Finally, a chance to thank her in person since our impromptu meeting at the library last Friday.

"*Tausend Dank.*" I slid into the desk beside her and grinned at her delighted expression. Her face lit up like the church congregation's did at the close of a budget meeting.

"*Bitte!* You're welcome. And you've been practicing." She tucked her hair behind her ears. "Dare I ask if you've learned more?"

"It was the least I could do to say thanks, after you helped me in the library. Your idea was great. I think my project will get an A." I set my backpack at my feet. "I'm so relieved."

"Did your friend find you? Claire, was it?" Marta leaned forward in her desk, blue eyes attentive.

I shook my head. "That's a long, bad story."

"I'm so sorry." She looked as if she actually meant it,

despite barely knowing me.

"No biggie." I shrugged. "Hey, I don't remember seeing you in this class before." Not that I'd been paying much attention to anything other than my pathetic attempts at learning a new language I hadn't practiced all summer. Foreign languages didn't come easily to me. In fact, I refused to admit how long it took me to get the pronunciation right for that German thank-you.

"I usually sit in the back. But I did miss the first few classes because of meetings with the principal and different teachers. Apparently exchange students are more of a headache on paperwork than plain ol' Americans." Marta rolled her eyes but smiled as if she were getting used to the drama.

"So this will be your third language?"

"Fourth." Marta ticked off the names on her fingers. "German, English, Spanish, and French. I'm not fluent in French yet, but I know enough to get by."

"That's impressive." She must've been crazy smart—and patient. I had the brains and the discipline to become fluent, I knew I did, but I tended to get distracted by other interests. Hard to want to learn a new language when there were plenty of classic books waiting to be read in English first.

"What can I say? I like to be well versed." She grinned. "Besides, it gives me an excuse to beg my father to send me to a Spanish-speaking country next."

Nice. I opened my mouth to reply, but Señora Martinez stepped in front of her desk at the front of the room and called the class to order. "*Atención*, atención." She clapped her hands, a significant feat seeing how she wore a giant ring on almost every one of her fingers. Her bangle bracelets jangled as she held up a colored flyer—the same one that had been on Claire's locker last week. "The annual school talent show will be held the week before Thanksgiving break. It's time to start signing up."

Half the class groaned while the other half cheered. I just stayed silent and sighed inwardly. Nothing personal, but talent shows were for girls like Jessica Daily, who'd already auditioned for *American Idol,* or for guys like Tripp Larson, who could dance better than even a video-edited Usher. If I sang, it was in the shower, and even then I worried about offending my bar of soap—and dancing, well. . .if I had trouble just walking in a straight line sometimes, it should be obvious that rhythm wasn't my strong suit.

Marta raised her hand, but Jessica slipped her tanned arm in the air first. At Señora Martinez's nod, she lowered her arm. "Do we have to audition? Or does everyone who wants to perform get to perform?" I could tell she wasn't worried about passing an audition so much as sharing the stage with those less worthy.

"It depends on the turnout," Señora said. She perched on the edge of her desk, her flowing blue cape settling around her legs. Did she really dress in Spanish garb 24-7, or was it just part of her role as teacher? Because honestly, I could probably learn Spanish better from someone in jeans.

Señora tapped the flyer. "There are thirty time slots available on Wednesday. If more people show up for the audition, they'll go ahead with tryouts. If not, those who want the slots will get them."

"Not a problem." Jessica flashed her pearly teeth, and I wondered not for the first time this year how often she Crest white-stripped.

"Marta, you had a question as well?" Señora Martinez pointed at Marta.

She nodded. "I was curious what the proceeds from the show went toward."

"Proceeds?" Señora frowned. "I don't understand."

"Proceeds from ticket sales, refreshment sales. . ." Marta's voice trailed off, and she threw me a confused look. Sadly, there was no language barrier here, just plain lack of caring from the people involved.

I leaned over and whispered, "Usually any money earned just gets thrown into the school's general fund or the drama department. It's always more for performance than for a good cause." More accurately, a way for the popular to grow more popular and the ridiculed to become more ridiculed, but that was a point to share another time.

"*Doch!* That's such a waste." Unfortunately, Marta didn't whisper, and now the entire class was all ears. She realized the attention and stood formally to her feet. "Why not charge extra this year and find a good cause to donate funds? That's what we do in Stuttgart. European teenagers are much more involved with their communities and beyond than what I've seen here. I think we should change that."

Señora crossed her arms over her chest and nodded thoughtfully. "Marta, that's a wonderful idea. I'll bring it up to the principal and the school board at our next meeting. I don't see why they would object."

Um, I could—because someone would have to be in charge of picking a good cause, researching it, adding that tidbit of information to the flyers and other means of advertising, helping promote in new ways so we'd actually bring in some decent proceeds, rallying the students to actually care enough to put on a quality performance, and keeping up with the funds raised, as well as getting the money to the charity afterward. Somehow I didn't see any of the staff willing to go to all that trouble without personal or direct school benefit.

I raised my arm to explain the hazards involved, although I hated to contradict Marta. It *was* a good idea. But there would be a lot involved that could backfire on her later.

"Addison, excellent!" Señora clapped her hands with excitement, bangles dancing. "You'll make a perfect leader for this. Thanks for volunteering."

My arm slipped back down to my lap, suddenly numb, as Marta enthusiastically patted my back.

What just happened?

Chapter Six

Still lingering in my post-volunteer shock even as the bell rang an hour later, I shuffled into the hallway with the throng of fellow escaping students. Though there was no escaping this particular mess I'd made.

Marta stuck close to my side in the crowd. "I'm so excited you're going to organize this fund-raiser." Her gentle voice lilted higher as she leaned in to be heard over the slamming of lockers around us. "This will be wonderful."

I stopped at my own locker and just stared, not even sure which class I had next, much less what book I needed. What had I gotten myself into? I replayed the last hour in my mind and tried to figure out what had gone so terribly wrong. Apparently I missed a step—a pretty crucial one—sometime between when Señora Martinez mentioned Marta's idea was a good one and when I raised my hand to argue. Well, maybe not argue. More like inform. A now moot point as I was suddenly a hero—at least in Marta's eyes. I bet the rest of the class could not care less about my volunteering—or worse yet, maybe they realized my blunder from the expression that had surely been on my face and were laughing at me.

Marta continued as if I hadn't totally spaced out. "I'd be happy to help you. I know this is a big task."

I couldn't help but smile at her more formal manner of speech. Is that how I would sound if I ever became fluent in Spanish? Not that there was any danger of that happening soon. Yet another moot point. "I don't even know where to start," I finally said. Oh yes, math was next. Great. This day just kept getting better. I swapped out my books in my locker.

Marta's head tilted to one side as if the answer were obvious. "First, you should choose a charity or good cause to contribute the funds to and get the charity approved by the principal."

"You say that like it's so simple," I argued. "There are a zillion good causes out there. How can I narrow it down?" And if I did, how would I choose something anyone would care enough about to promote or invest in? Something relevant that would appeal not only to the students but more importantly, to their parents and families and to the community. They were the ones needing to be convinced to purchase tickets to our petty little performance in the first place. Despite what Jessica Daily thought, not everyone in the world really wanted to hear her sing.

Suddenly even my calculus textbook looked less intimidating than the looming task I'd just taken on.

"Easy. Just make it personal." Marta tapped my arm, jerking me back from the abyss. "What do *you* care about?"

I stared at the textbook in my hand. Not math, that was for sure. Reading, however. . . I looked up. "Books. I like books." I winced. I sounded like an overeager, desperate parrot. Clearing my throat, I tried again. "I mean, I love reading. That's important to me."

"Why is that?" Marta looked as if she actually cared.

I pulled *Pride and Prejudice* from my purse, just long enough for her to see the cover before concealing it back in the depths of my bag. "I'm never without a novel, usually a classic.

New fiction is good, too, but there's just something about the way those older authors wrote that pulls you into an entirely different world when reading."

I was rambling now but couldn't stop. No one had ever listened to me talk about books before. Marta was even nodding like she agreed. I went on, picking up speed. "It sucks that people don't read as much anymore, you know? It's like video games and technology have completely replaced a good book. And then there are the people out there who want to read but can't because they never even learned how—" I stopped and slowly smiled. "Wait a second."

Marta grinned back. "Congratulations. I think you just found your good cause."

★ ★ ★

If I were a more guilt-driven person, I'd feel bad that Marta had helped me twice now with ideas for school-related projects and I'd done nothing for her in return. But instead I was grateful. She had definitely earned a mocha latte, on me.

I pushed open the heavy wooden door of Got Beans, my favorite coffee shop in Crooked Hollow. It was one of the only places to get coffee in Crooked Hollow, besides Blue's Diner, whose coffee looked like the overdue oil I once watched my dad change in his car. Starbucks it was not, but it was still pretty good as far as small-town coffee went. I inhaled the aroma of freshly ground beans, mingled with a hint of cinnamon and chocolate. Someday I'd have to convince my dad to buy something more advanced than a Mr. Coffee so I could try these concoctions at home—for cheap.

The owner, Bert, nodded at us from behind the counter as he punched some buttons on the cash register, his apron-clad full girth touching the machine even as he stood a foot away. But hey, what's that saying about not trusting a skinny cook?

"Be right with you, girls."

"It smells so good in here." Marta drew an appreciative breath.

"It always does." I stepped up to the counter. "You like mochas?" When Marta didn't answer, I darted a glance over my shoulder at her. Her eyes were big as she took in the many menu options.

She shrugged, still staring at the board. "I'm not sure. At home I don't usually drink coffee."

My jaw hung open. "How do you survive high school without caffeine?"

"Milk?"

Oh boy. I turned to Bert, who waited with pen and pad in hand. "Two medium double chocolate mocha lattes, please."

He scribbled on the paper. "Whipped cream?"

"Of course."

"Sprinkles?"

"Bert, I'm disappointed you have to ask."

He laughed. "Extra sprinkles, then. Coming right up." He turned to the complicated-looking espresso machine and went to work making the magic while I laid a few bills on the counter.

Marta followed me to a table for two in the back of the shop, setting her bag down on the floor between the mismatched chairs. Bert probably chose the random pieces to save money, but the retro decor provided a great atmosphere. Autographed black-and-white posters of Bert's favorite celebrities hung on the red walls, along with movie paraphernalia. A baby grand piano sat in the back corner behind us, atop a zebra-striped rug. As much as I loved this place, I couldn't come here to study often—too loud, and I didn't mean the music playing quietly over the speakers.

"Please don't think I'm a complete tourist." Marta grinned

at me as we settled into our seats. "We have coffee shops in Stuttgart—even Starbucks. My parents just raised me to drink healthy drinks."

"My dad tries to limit my pops, too, but hey, we all have our secret vices." I leaned back as Bert brought our steaming mugs and set them on the table.

Marta frowned at me. "Pops?"

"Sodas. Coke. Whatever you want to call it. In the Midwest, we call everything pop. Dr Pepper, Diet Coke, Sprite, anything carbonated." I breathed in the steam curling like ribbon into the air. "Confusing, isn't it?"

"Not as much as other American slang." Marta winked at me over the top of her mug. "This is good." She sounded surprised.

"I wouldn't lead you astray." I sipped my coffee, my earlier stress about the talent show and fund-raiser nearly forgotten as the chocolate did its thing. "So, do you know of any literary organizations I could contact to get this talent show off the ground?"

"Off the ground?"

I swallowed quickly. Man, I was really going to have to pay more attention to my slang. I had no idea how often I used it. "Sorry. I meant started."

Marta laughed. "I was kidding that time."

"Nice one."

She tapped her fingernails against the scarred wooden tabletop. "There's the Reading Tree, who passes out children's literature to kids and values recycling. They're international."

"That could be good." People typically liked to donate money where children were involved. That would definitely be a good cause and one I could sincerely support. But I couldn't help remembering what had slipped out during my verbal rant to Marta earlier, about people being so consumed with technology that they never even learned how to read. Or never were given a chance because their guardians didn't view it as something vital for them to know. It just didn't feel like the right choice yet.

I leaned forward. "What other organizations do you know about? I guess I could just go home and Google instead of making you think so hard." I winced. Oops. Talk about contradictions. Here I was about to use the Internet to find a way to help people avoid technology. Nice.

"Don't worry, I love this kind of thing." Marta scooted her mug out of the way and braced her forearms on the table. Her eyes sparkled, and I wished I could find the same passion for good causes that she possessed. Were American teenagers really that much more immune to the needs of the world than European kids? It left a bitter taste in my mouth that had nothing to do with the coffee.

"There's the Let Them Read Foundation, which raises funds to aid in illiteracy," Marta continued. "They help inner-city schools and missions learn how to read all over the world. I believe the money goes toward teachers, new books, reading games and programs, things like that. They even teach foreign languages."

Yes! I accidentally bumped the table in my enthusiastic reaction, sending our coffee sloshing in the mugs. "That's it! That's perfect." I felt excited, too, and more pathetically, I was excited about finally being excited. "I'll start the research tonight and talk to Principal Stephens tomorrow."

"They have a website that should have plenty of information for you to get started and prepare your advertising methods." Marta picked up her mug, probably to avoid any more consequences of my happy dance.

"I'm still overwhelmed, but this is a good start." Maybe I could really pull this off.

The front door jingled as it opened behind me. Bert greeted the customer. "Back for more, man?"

"You know it."

The familiar baritone sent electric vibes tingling down my spine, and my stomach churned my coffee like a blender on high speed. "Wes."

"Who?"

I hadn't meant to say his name out loud. Had he heard me? "Uh, just a friend." That was a lie on so many levels. Not only were Wes and I more than friends in my mind, in reality we weren't even up to the level of true friendship yet, much less past it. How messed up was that? I downed a gulp of my latte, the warmth clearing my muddled brain, and listened as Wes chatted with Bert, surprisingly open instead of consumed by his typical sarcasm.

Marta watched over my shoulder. "He's coming this way. Are you all right?"

I coughed and sputtered as my drink went down the wrong pipe. He was coming over here? "I'm fine," I croaked.

Wes passed our table without a glance, heading toward the piano. Then he did a double take and stopped fast just before his booted feet planted on the zebra rug. "Addison?"

"Hi there." I forced a casual smile, as if I hadn't almost died drinking a mocha in his presence. "Wes, this is my friend Marta." It felt good to introduce them, as if I was close enough to Wes to merit passing on information. But I was too busy applauding myself on taking another drink of my coffee without incident to give it much more thought. I carefully set the mug far from my shaking hands.

"Nice to meet you." Marta held out her hand, leaving Wes

no choice but to shake it. Nice trick; I should have tried that when we first met. I wondered how his hands felt. Rough and calloused from gripping the handlebars of that motorcycle all day—

"I'm guessing you're not a Texan." Wes's eyebrows dipped.

"Stuttgart, Germany." Marta wrapped her hands around her mug, and I envied her ability to actually be casual without forcing it. Though that was a good thing because otherwise that meant she was interested in Wes, too, and I couldn't have any more competition. Speaking of competition, I wondered if Poodle Girl had mentioned our little encounter yesterday before church to Wes—

"Welcome to America. Guess I'll be seeing you." Wes abruptly headed back the way he'd come, toward the door.

Weird. He hadn't even ordered a coffee.

I twisted in my seat, partially curious and partially just not wanting him to leave. "Where are you going? You just got here." I gestured over my shoulder toward the piano. "And you were about to run into the piano, as I recall."

"Clumsy me." Wes's dry tone indicated that was exactly the opposite of what he meant, and before I could censor my next thoughts, they became verbal.

"Want to sit with us?"

He actually hesitated, and I saw a flash of something light his eyes—respect, maybe? amusement?—before he shook his head. "Gotta run." Then he was gone.

I swear the boy could host his own magic show with all the speed-of-light disappearances he pulled.

"That was odd." Marta finished off her coffee with a long swallow while I tried to figure out exactly how much to reveal—and how much there even *was* to reveal. With Wes, it was hard to say.

Even harder to admit.

"His dad goes to my church," I finally said. "He sort of asked me to make friends with Wes, so I thought I'd invite him to join us." Honest, yet not vulnerable.

"He can't make friends on his own?" Marta asked.

I snorted. "I'm sure he can, but Wes is a loner." I thought of Poodle Girl and grimaced. "And the company he's chosen so far hasn't exactly been stellar."

"Ja. I see." Marta nodded, but she looked confused. I didn't blame her.

When it came to Wes, I was, too.

Chapter Seven

Judging by the sullen looks from the faces on my left and my right, I determined I was the only person sitting in the principal's office who wasn't actually in trouble.

"Addison Blakely, Principal Stephens will see you now." The school secretary, Ms. Margie, smiled at me before shooting a don't-even-try-it look at my pierced and gothed-out lobby companions. I sort of felt like telling them good luck as I made my way inside Principal Stephens's office. He was a nice man, but I've always been on the right side of the law where he was concerned and had no desire to swap sides now.

"Hello, Addison." Principal Stephens gestured for me to sit in the chair across from his desk. I quickly obeyed, wondering if he realized the plant on his windowsill was near death. Looked like Ms. Margie had slacked on the job.

"Señora Martinez told me you'd be stopping by with some ideas for the talent show this year." The principal steepled his hands above the files crowding his desk. I briefly wondered which file was for the guy with the eyebrow ring outside. Probably the extrathick one.

"I somehow ended up—I mean, I volunteered to help find a fund-raiser for the talent show." I shifted in my seat. Weird that I was nervous when I wasn't even here on negative terms.

How did the bad kids handle that kind of pressure? At least this appointment got me out of calculus for a few minutes. "I think I found a charity everyone can jump on board with. So I hoped to get your approval and get things rolling."

After forcing thoughts of Wes and his mysterious coffee shop appearance from my head, Marta and I had managed to discuss the fund-raiser further and even made a to-do list to start the process—once I secured Principal Stephens's permission. Marta's enthusiasm was contagious, and for the first time in a while, it felt good to take charge and make a difference instead of just blending into the background. Very un–gummi bear of me.

Principal Stephens leaned forward with interest. "Which charity is that?"

"The Let Them Read Foundation." I briefly explained what Marta had told me about the organization and what I had discovered via research the night before.

"I think that's a great idea." Principal Stephens nodded his approval, the fluorescent lights in his office reflecting off his bald head. "I'm happy to leave this in your capable hands."

"You don't want progress reports along the way?"

"No, Addison, that's unnecessary. You've proven yourself to be trustworthy and respectful at Crooked Hollow High, and I have no reason to doubt your ability to see this through."

High compliments, though not entirely shocking. "What about the money?"

He frowned. "Are you planning on keeping it for yourself?"

"Of course not."

"Then what's the problem?"

Wow, he really did trust me.

"The drama teacher, Mrs. Lyons, can help you if you feel you need assistance, but I'm sure she will have her hands full with auditions and organizing the talent show." Principal Stephens frowned as he paused to think. "How about you appoint a temporary treasurer from your class to keep you accountable and help collect the money at the door the night of the show? We can get reports from both of you afterward as to the full amount collected."

"Sounds good. I choose Marta."

Principal Stephens picked up his pen and hovered it over a sticky note. "Marta. . . ?"

Uh-oh. I still didn't actually know her last name. "The foreign-exchange student from Germany. We've gotten to be friends, and she helped me brainstorm this fund-raiser."

"Wonderful. Marta from Germany it is." Principal Stephens stuck the yellow note on top of the overflowing inbox on his desk. "Will that be all, Addison? I'm afraid I have a waiting room of not-as-trustworthy students to attend to next."

"Right." Now I felt like telling Principal Stephens good luck. I let myself out and walked quickly through the miniature lobby to the glass front doors. But I heard the whispers directed at my back. They didn't exactly say goody-goody (I'm too much of a lady to repeat what technically came out of their mouths), but that was the gist. Was that how Wes saw me, too? Was that why Poodle Girl had him and I didn't? Why did it even matter?

And why did being good suddenly seem so bad?

I pushed out of the office into the deserted hallway, wishing I had the courage to skip the rest of my math class and go hide out in the library to collect my thoughts. But those guys were exactly right. I wouldn't do something like that. A risk taker I was not.

So I just headed to class like I was supposed to, the heavy rock of "what-if" in my stomach sinking lower with every step.

★ ★ ★

The fact that I sat inside Got Beans again after school had nothing to do with how I hoped Wes would make another random appearance. And the fact that I sat in the darkest, farthest corner from the piano, as if spying, also had nothing to do with anything other than how I liked coffee, and there was a draft from the air vent at my typical table.

Right. And I was leaving town tomorrow to sing backup for Justin Bieber.

"Just call me glutton for punishment," I muttered to my mocha. "And don't worry, it's not your fault you can't cheer me up today. Some issues even chocolate can't touch."

"Addison, if you don't quit talking to your coffee, I'm not giving you double shots anymore," Bert called from the counter, where he wiped down the display case with a rag.

"Can't a girl have a bad day?" I held up my mug. "Besides, where are my sprinkles?"

"I told you I ran out yesterday."

"And I told you that wasn't acceptable."

Bert scowled then held up his hands in surrender. "Some days I swear, kid, if you weren't the preacher's daughter. . ." His voice trailed off, and he winked to show he was joking—sort of. Not like I hadn't heard it before. People were often scared to say their mind to me, even when joking. (Claire would be an exception.) It's like they thought since Dad was a pastor, I had a more direct line to God than they did. Or maybe they just thought I was a tattletale.

Trust me, neither was true.

I wondered what God thought about this infatuation with Wes that I couldn't seem to shake. Probably the same thing my dad would think about it—abomination. Okay, maybe that was a little extreme, but this was Crooked Hollow, and my dad was my dad, and God was, well—you know. Yet here I was camped out in a corner of a coffee shop hoping to see my piece of forbidden fruit waltz in. If I didn't know better, I'd be keeping a weather eye out for rogue lightning bolts. But God didn't work that way.

Still, I was glad the sun was out.

I went back to staring at my sprinkle-less mocha, and Bert went back to cleaning, now humming as he did so. Great, more punishment on an already-glum day.

The bell jangled, and I looked up with as much pathetic enthusiasm as I had the last six times people came in and out. Too bad James Bond didn't hold private lessons. I was an utter failure as a spy—might as well stamp a blinking neon arrow over my head.

That time it was Bert's wife, Megan, with her weekly ledger book. She waved at me (now you *know* I'm a regular) and headed toward the partition to the employee side of the counter.

Someone caught the front door before it closed completely, and Wes walked inside. This time I managed to keep my head down as my heart rammed in my chest like a drummer on steroids. I followed his black-booted feet from under my lashes as he stopped near the counter, talked in low tones with Bert, and then headed once again to the piano. *Don't look up, don't look up. . . .* Oh, who was I kidding? I lifted my gaze and watched as he turned his back in my direction and slid onto the long piano bench. He shed his leather jacket, tossed it over the bench beside him, and then began to play.

And I don't mean "Chopsticks."

A complicated melody filled the air, and I stared, mesmerized, as his fingers danced over the keys. The muscles in his broad shoulders bunched then stretched beneath his dark-green thermal shirt as his arms moved the span of the keyboard.

Without even fully realizing it, I stood and made my way toward him as if drawn like a magnet. Or more accurately in my case, like a moth to a fire.

Nothing but danger.

I stopped a few feet away and continued to watch. He didn't see me. I was invisible to him, yet again. The fact made me more angry than awestruck, and without thinking, I plopped sideways onto the chair closest to the piano and draped my arms over the top rung.

"So the rebel without a cause has musical ability."

His hands stopped midnote, and he darted a look sideways, his dark hair falling across his forehead. "You might say that." He didn't smile, but he didn't frown. Neutral Wes. The only emotion he ever showed was sarcasm or teasing, and really, were those even emotions? My frustration grew. How dare he flaunt Poodle Girl in my face, on *my* street, act as if he was interested in me, and then run away when I tried to make an effort in return? What kind of player did he think he was?

I wanted to insult him, but his playing had been nothing but praiseworthy. I opened my mouth then shut it.

Wes quirked an eyebrow. "You look like a fish when you do that."

"Oh, shut up."

"Seriously, Addison, just say what you want to say. I think I can take it." He shifted on the bench to face me, his familiar scent of leather and aftershave washing over me like a tidal wave of attraction. I instinctively leaned away.

"I was going to say you play really. . .well."

He smirked. "Way to tell me off, PK."

"That's why I hesitated. I didn't want to give you a compliment."

"Why not?"

"Why?" I met his steady stare and held it until I had to look away or risk never catching my breath.

"You're a piece of work." He shifted over on the bench.

"Can you play, too?"

Was that an invitation? There was enough room for my backside on the bench, but barely. Could I subject myself to that kind of proximity? I gulped. "Not really."

I hesitated, curiosity finally overcoming all other emotion. "Can you read music?" There wasn't any on the empty shelf in front of him, so he either couldn't or didn't need to. Playing by ear or memorization was more impressive anyway. Too bad I could do neither.

"Somewhat." He began to play again, but this time the movements were less fluid, and I could tell I was making him nervous. The fact bolstered my spirits. I smiled.

His fingers slipped off the keys, and he cursed. "Quit grinning at me like a monkey."

"Then give me a banana."

Wes turned once again to face me. "Listen, Addison, let's cut to the chase. Are you going to tell anyone about this or not?" He gestured to the piano.

I feigned deep thinking. "Of course. I was just brainstorming the graphics for the billboard I'm going to put up. Wasn't sure how many tattoos to give you in the caricature, though."

He didn't laugh. "I'm not kidding."

I wanted to say neither was I, but he was actually being serious for the first time since I'd met him, and that had to mean something. A step forward?

I swallowed my smile. "I won't tell."

He studied my eyes, as if determining my trustworthiness, and finally nodded once. "Thanks." He started to play again, this time with more confidence. I leaned against the back of my chair, closed my eyes, and listened.

Today might have been a step forward, but when it came to Wes, I still had no idea which path I was heading down.

Chapter Eight

| still don't see why heading up a fund-raiser means I have to suffer through the auditions," I muttered as Marta linked her arm through mine and literally propelled me down the slightly sloped, dimly lit auditorium floor toward the stage.

"You've got to be at least a little curious." She lowered her voice to a whisper. "I know I am." She muscled me into the tenth or eleventh row and plopped down in the aisle chair, blocking any escape attempts on my part.

I crossed my arms and leaned back in the uncomfortable folding seat, wincing as Tyler Dupree hit the wrong note on his violin. We apparently weren't the only curious souls from the school, as several students filled sporadic chairs across the auditorium. Two or three rows of pathetic—sorry, make that hopeful—teens waiting their turn to try out lined the rows directly in front of the stage.

"Maybe seeing whom you're promoting will help you devise an advertising scheme." Marta leaned close to be heard over the screech of what Tyler was trying—unsuccessfully—to pass off as music. "Although I am not sure how to positively market . . .everyone."

"Don't worry. I doubt he makes it that far." Seemed safe to say, since Mrs. Lyons had both hands clamped over her ears and shook her head at Tyler so wildly her hair swung across her glasses.

Unless there were fewer people trying out than the allotted time slots—then everyone got into the show by default.

Yikes. Tyler might have a chance after all. People could want their money back after his performance. I shook my head at the thought. "Besides, the Foundation said they have a special newsletter they can send out locally to help raise awareness for the show."

"Ja, that will help," Marta agreed. We both stared in silence at the stage, Marta probably thinking the same thing I was— that at this rate, we'd be lucky if even the parents showed up.

Tyler mercifully left with his violin tucked between his legs (not literally), and Jessica Daily took his place with a confident smile. While I wasn't exactly Jessica's biggest fan (she had plenty of those), at least I could count on my ears getting a break.

"She's good," Marta said without a trace of the bitterness that would have tinged my own voice. Not that I was jealous of Jessica, exactly—I had no desire to sing well—but I had to admit, having the courage to get front and center like that in front of a ruthless group of peers, with such confidence, well— it was admirable.

Stupid Wes. If I hadn't run into him in the candy aisle of the grocery store that day, I wouldn't be stuck worrying if being sweet and careful were suddenly bad qualities.

Jessica's song ended, and everyone in the small audience clapped. She took a dramatic bow and waved to her fans. When she blew a kiss into the darkened room, I rolled my eyes. Looked like I would be marketing everything from a "warning, bring your own earplugs" to "warning, diva alert" for the fund-raiser.

I followed Marta's cue, leaning over to whisper. "Surely there's got to be some in-between talent in this school. Isn't there someone who can do something well, yet not flaunt it?"

She laughed. "That might be asking too much. This is high school."

Too true. "We might have to get creative with how we promote this."

"Good job, Jessica." Mrs. Lyons motioned for her to leave the stage, where she appeared to be glued to the center.

"Do you think that's the best song choice for me?" Jessica waited, hands clasped behind her back. Apparently those *American Idol* auditions had brainwashed her.

"It was very nice." Mrs. Lyons flapped her hands sideways, as if trying to fan Jessica down the steps.

She remained standing, feet braced apart. "I also plan on having live accompaniment on the piano the night of the show, for a more dramatic presentation than just that CD sound track."

"That will be lovely, dear." Poor Mrs. Lyons flapped so hard I thought she might take off in flight.

"And I—"

"Next!"

A guy from the football team and his ventriloquist dummy bumped Jessica into the wings. I winced. Those things always freaked me out. Jessica must have agreed, judging by the way she quickly fled the stage.

The football player took his place on a stool and braced the doll on his lap. "Hello, everyone." He used a high voice as he opened the mouth of the doll, but his own lips were clearly moving—obvious even from this distance.

Marta and I exchanged glances. Looked like we were going to have to get *very* creative.

★ ★ ★

Mystery meat again. High school was so cliché. I inched my way up in line at the cafeteria, debating the lesser of two evils. Go with a veggie plate and be hungry later, or risk death by meat loaf?

If that was even meat loaf.

"So I hear you're helping with the talent show." Claire's voice rang out behind me, a mixture of scorn and disbelief.

I refused to turn and give her the satisfaction of my full attention, so I just slid my tray along the rails in front of the protective food covers. "Sort of."

"What do you mean?" She pressed in close behind me, as evidenced by a sudden waft of her designer perfume. Not a pleasant aroma when mixed with the smell of lumpy gravy.

"I'm organizing a fund-raiser so the proceeds this year can go to a good cause."

"How noble of you." Claire snorted.

"Thanks." Treat sarcasm with sarcasm—worked with Wes, anyway. I nodded when the cafeteria server offered me mashed potatoes and shook my head vehemently when she held up a spoonful of steamed spinach. At least here at school I had the freedom to choose what I wanted to eat without worrying about Dad following in my carb-lover's footsteps.

Claire's tray clattered onto the rails behind mine. "I saw you watching the auditions. What did you think?"

"Of what?" If she was fishing for compliments, I wasn't about to bite.

She nodded at the cafeteria lady to load her plate with the mystery meat. Brave soul. "My piece. I'm doing a fashion demonstration."

Why was I not surprised? I shrugged. "Sorry, I didn't see it. We left early." More like Marta and I ran for our lives after suffering through Jack Johnson's bumbled misquoting of "The Raven." I could just picture Edgar Allan Poe rolling in his grave.

"We?" Claire frowned.

"Marta and I."

Claire's nose tilted toward the ceiling at Marta's name as if yanked up by a marionette string. "Oh." Disdain dragged the word out several syllables longer than necessary. "Well, whatever. You should have stuck around for the good stuff." Claire accepted a dollop of congealed mac and cheese from the server.

I bypassed it and went for the fruit cup, debating whether to defend Marta or let it go and avoid yet another showdown at Crooked Hollow High. "I think *good* is relative at this talent show." Best to simply focus on the subject at hand until I could escape with my sorry excuse for a lunch.

"Then it should make choosing the winners all the easier to decide." Claire tossed her hair and smiled with that same overconfidence that used to merely strike a nerve. Now that smirk grated me so badly I wanted to smear it with macaroni.

I picked up my tray with both hands before I could indulge my impulses. "Maybe so. See ya." I headed toward a back table, where Marta had saved me a seat. Lucky girl brought her lunch today. We were supposed to go over our list of what needed to be done and set a date to start painting flyers.

"Addison, wait." Claire's tray nearly knocked into mine as she hurried to catch up beside me. "Exactly how involved are you with the advertising for the talent show?"

I stopped. "I'm writing up the ad copy to give the Foundation for their newsletter and website promo. But why do you care?" Out of patience now, I braced my tray against my hip to support its weight. Claire had never been Miss School Spirit unless there was something in it for her—like the glory of cheerleading or the popularity of running for class office.

"I just—" Claire's jaw clenched as if the words she attempted to say tasted bad. She finally spit them out. "I don't want our little misunderstanding to give me bad publicity."

My eyes narrowed. "You call ditching me and treating your best friend badly a misunderstanding?" Man, she had some nerve! "And don't think I don't notice how you talk about Marta. Leave her out of this. She's just being a good friend to me—something you could stand to learn about."

"Don't be ridiculous, Addison." Claire's voice tightened, and she leaned in closer, our trays touching. "I couldn't care less about your little foreign groupie. But there could be scouts at this show, and I refuse to let a chance to be discovered get ruined because of some grudge you're holding against me."

I couldn't stop the laugh that bubbled out of my mouth. "You really think a talent scout is going to come to a small-town high school talent show? This isn't *America's Next Top Model* or *American Idol*, Claire. Did you or did you not hear Kelly on the accordion?"

Claire's lips pressed into a thin line, and an angry spark lit her eyes. "Just because you—"

"Hey, beautiful." A male voice registered in my ears seconds before something solid knocked against my back. I stumbled forward, my tray colliding hard with Claire's and upsetting her plate, which slid to the edge of her tray and sloshed gravy down the front of her white ruffled top.

Claire shrieked as she held her dripping tray away from her. Austin laughed as he brushed past me, convicting himself as the culprit. "Careful with your tray there, cheerleader." He laughed before high-fiving a football buddy at a nearby table. What a jerk. I grabbed some napkins and offered them to Claire. "I'm so sorry. Austin is such a—"

"Don't. Touch. Me." Claire snatched the napkins from my hand, dropped her tray at my feet, and stalked out of the cafeteria to a chorus of guffaws. I stared down at the mystery meat now clinging to my favorite shoes. Claire's threat about my not wanting her for an enemy rang in my mind like a warning bell.

A little late for that now.

★ ★ ★

"Do not let her get to you." Marta offered me half of her strawberry pie, which I gratefully accepted. No way could I eat my lunch after seeing what it looked like smeared across Claire's shirt. "She was embarrassed. She'll calm down."

"You don't know Claire." I shuddered.

"Doch! I feel I do, after watching the way she's treated you lately."

"Our friendship has always been complicated." I speared a mushy strawberry with my fork. "We used to be close, but now it's more like she's the boot and I'm the doormat. I got sick of it."

"You don't deserve that," Marta agreed. She raked a spoonful of whipped cream from the plate between us.

"Deserve it or not, I saw that look in her eyes. She'll label this incident my fault, not Austin's. Maybe if I had big muscles and a football uniform I'd get out of all responsibility, too." I rolled my eyes.

Marta snorted. "I wouldn't recommend it."

"And she'll never forget it."

"But remember, she can't be too mean to you because she is afraid of your advertising powers." Marta grinned and finished her half of the pie. "So you're safe for now."

"Which is ridiculous because it's not like I planned on spotlighting any of the students in the show anyway. I thought on the flyers we'd just list the time, date, place—you know. The basics." I slid the plate away from me, disappointed that the sugar rush hadn't eliminated my negativity. Too bad Got Beans didn't deliver mochas to school.

"You could." Marta pointed her spoon at me. "And not just to appease Claire. But to garner interest from the public. If they know what to expect, they might be more willing to come."

"But what if the entire show is a joke? You saw the tryouts." I winced. "What am I supposed to write on the flyer? Come see the worst ventriloquist act in history? Experience the vocal delights of the world's most arrogant cheerleader?"

"*Nein.* They can't all be that bad." But Marta frowned as if not convinced. "We'll think of something, don't worry." She waved her hand and changed the subject. "Get back to telling me what happened to you and Claire. You said you used to be close."

I filled her in on the last few years of our lives and all the ways Claire had changed. "Then lately she started getting snippy at me because Austin decided I'm his next conquest." Ew. So not interested. "The more I don't fawn all over him, the more attempts he makes to change my mind, then the more jealous Claire gets of his attention to me." A vicious high school cycle I couldn't wait to escape. Surely college wouldn't be this immature. But I still had to survive senior year. Groan. "But even without Austin interfering, I knew things were changing between me and Claire. We used to have a lot in common, but now she's only interested in appearance and guys and sex."

"Meaning you're not?"

I felt a blush staining my cheeks at Marta's direct question. "I'm a preacher's kid."

Marta frowned. "So?"

"So, those decisions are sort of already made for me. I don't waste a lot of time on makeup and hair, as you can tell." I shook my head so my ponytail swished. "See? I have better things to do."

"Your hair is cute up. What about the guy thing? No

boyfriend?" Marta grinned. "What about that guy in the coffee shop—Wes?"

I couldn't exactly tell her Wes was the one making me suddenly doubt all my previous resolve about dating. I cleared my throat. "My dad doesn't encourage dating. He knows all the issues that come with it, and my reputation is linked to his. I have to be careful." I rattled off the answer I'd given a dozen times in the past few years and suddenly realized how textbook it sounded.

Marta chewed her lower lip before answering. "But you are still you, Addison. You're still your own person. Do not hide behind a label of your father's."

"I'm not hiding," I defended. "His rules make sense—most of the time. I've never been one of those girls to get a hundred crushes a year or freak out when a guy didn't call. Those girls bug me." I shrugged, avoiding her eyes. "And I'm not going to start becoming one of them now because of Wes. Besides, he's got a lemon-drop girlfriend."

Marta laughed. "Lemon drop? Is that more American slang?"

"Not exactly." The bell rang, thankfully saving me from any more awkward revelations of my love life—or lack thereof. I quickly stood and gathered our trash on my tray. "Let's go."

My cheeks still felt flushed, and I wished I could subtly fan myself without drawing attention to the blotches that crept up my neck. I dumped my tray in the return bin and walked out of the cafeteria with Marta, her previous words cycling in my head like an iPod set to SHUFFLE. *Your own person. Don't hide. Labels. You're still you.* They struck a chord with me that had never really been pressed before. As I bypassed Austin's table and ignored the catcall he whistled my way, I wished the entire last half hour had simply never happened.

Chapter Nine

The only thing more pathetic than doing a group project solo on a Friday night is going to your school's open house with your father on a Friday night. Like some sort of really screwed-up date.

I followed Dad out of the crowded auditorium amid a sea of fellow overeager parents and sullen students, the assistant principal's monotone welcome speech still droning in my mind.

Dad held the heavy door leading to the south bank of classrooms open for me. "Which class is first?" He looked almost as uncomfortable as me, and I wished we could just go meet Ms. Hawthorne and then bail. She was the only one who requested to meet my dad, so why go through the agony of parading through my lineup of classrooms just like I'd done every morning for weeks already?

I believed in education. I did not believe in parent-teacher meet-and-greets.

"American history. Then gym." Don't get me started on how unfair it was to have gym within two hours of school starting each day. So far it was just a bunch of sitting around in our uniforms, but eventually we'd get to the sweaty stuff, and that would make the rest of the day interesting to say the least.

"History it is." Dad followed me, and not for the first time that night I thought about how the promised complimentary pops and cookies in each class were simply not worth this kind of hassle. Not to mention the awkward level of Dad having to pretend like he knew anything about my school. Good parent, sure. Involved? Not so much.

Though in this case that wasn't necessarily a bad thing.

Inside my American history classroom, the students bunched around the refreshment table, stuffing their faces with dessert, while the parents bunched around each other on the other side of the room, overdressed in their suits, ties, and business slacks. Husbands and wives stood with linked arms, while the single ones openly flirted with the other bare-ring-fingered adults. Leave it to the parents to turn an open house into an open market.

Dad glanced down at his khakis and polo shirt then hesitated between the two groups, as if not sure where he fit in. A twinge of sympathy flittered through my stomach.

I know, Dad. I wonder the same thing every day.

After suffering through an hour of blah, we finally made it to my English classroom. Maybe Dad would be up for heading home after we met Ms. Hawthorne. I really didn't see the point in him sticking around to meet eccentric Señora Martinez or listen to my calculus teacher drone on about critical numbers or integration methods.

We stepped inside the mostly empty classroom, having beat several of the parents to the room this time, and I inhaled deeply the scent of tangy chocolate. Leave it to Ms. Hawthorne to go to the trouble of baking fresh brownies instead of buying a bulk, multicookie tray like the others. Maybe her class wouldn't be so bad this year after all.

"Hi, Addison." Ms. Hawthorne smiled warmly at me. "Help

yourself to a brownie."

"Thanks, I think I will." I started toward the mini-buffet table she had set up with lemonade and dessert, turning to watch from the corner of my eye as she held out her hand to Dad. "You must be Addison's father. I'm Kathy Haw—" Her voice choked, and she stumbled over the rest of her name. "David?"

My eyebrows went up. Wow, I hadn't heard that name in a while, not without "preacher" in front of it. I glanced at Dad, who was turning a very deep shade of magenta as their hands lingered in each other's polite grip.

Dad looked down then quickly shoved his hands in his pockets. "Kathy. It's—it's been a long time."

I nearly choked on my brownie. Did Dad just stutter?

"A very long time." Ms. Hawthorne looked as if she wanted to say more, but she glanced at me and stopped. "How are those brownies, Addison? I debated for an hour on whether or not to put nuts on them."

"They're good. I'm not a big fan of nuts," I mumbled around my bite, still confused. What had just happened? I swallowed, my mouth mushy, and I wished I had a glass of milk instead of sour lemonade in my paper cup. "You two know each other?"

"In high school. Decades ago." Dad's composure had somewhat returned now, his previous discomfort replaced with what I'd recognized over the years as his "pastoral smile." The role of shepherd leading a flock, not one of flesh-and-blood man with any proof of a life lived previous to his ordination. I resented that mask, though I understood it.

It just stank that he wore it so often with me.

The remaining brownie turned to sawdust in my mouth, and I washed it down with a swig of lemonade. "Small world."

Ms. Hawthorne still looked caught off guard. Guess high school English teachers didn't have readily accessible masks to don. "It's good to see you again, David. What are you doing these days?"

I turned my back to them, feigning interest in the brownie pan. I didn't want to eavesdrop, but it wasn't like I had anywhere to go. Besides, I wasn't stupid. Obviously Ms. Hawthorne and Dad had dated in high school, hence the awkward factor radiating between them like UV rays from a tanning bed.

"I'm the pastor at Crooked Hollow Church of Grace." Dad still had his hands in his pockets, and now he was jingling his change. He was nervous, just trying to hide it. Weird. Rarely did people affect my father like that. During the course of my lifetime, he'd counseled suicidal teens, gone with police to help settle domestic disturbances, and put up with more drama from the stuck-in-the-mud blue-haired women of the church than anyone should be subjected to. Why did a blast from his high school past shake him so badly?

"That's right, I've seen your name on the sign. Lovely church." Ms. Hawthorne smiled, relaxing back into the confident teacher I knew. She rested her weight against her desk, kicking one booted foot out from under the folds of her ankle-length skirt. Brown leather today, with ruched tops. I couldn't help admiring them, even while crunching on a second brownie.

"Thank you. And I suppose it's obvious what you're up to lately." Dad gestured to the classroom, and Ms. Hawthorne giggled.

Oh, this wasn't good. I sidled back up to Dad's side, hoping my imminent presence would curb any potential flirting before it happened. "Great brownies." I smiled, hoping I hadn't left chocolate in my teeth—but really, if I had, it served them right to look at it.

Other families started to filter in, including Luke and what had to be his parents. I returned his wave and tugged at Dad's arm. "We better get a seat." And get this nightmare of an evening over with. At least it appeared Claire hadn't bothered to show up with her mom. That would be the only way the night could get worse. Oh yikes, I hadn't even thought about the possibility of Austin showing up. Better take that back. I cast a nervous glance at the door. Surely he wouldn't act a fool in front of my dad. But with Austin, one never knew. "Come on, Dad."

"Yes, please have a seat." Ms. Hawthorne motioned us toward the front row of desks. "But I have to say first, David, I'm so proud of Addison and am truly looking forward to having her in my class this year. She's a breath of fresh air for a new teacher trying to learn the ropes." Ms. Hawthorne gave me a little wink.

I fought back a snort. Like she needed any fresh air. The students listened to her better than they did Mr. Adger, who had been at Crooked Hollow since the dawn of time.

"Addison has already jumped into organizing a fund-raiser for the school's talent show. She's a great influence for the other students." Ms. Hawthorne patted my arm.

"You're organizing a fund-raiser?" Dad turned to me, surprise highlighting his features. "You didn't mention that."

"It just sort of happened." Better sit down, quick, before Dad had any wrong impressions of me turning into Miss School Spirit. Besides, when was I supposed to tell him about the talent show or the Let Them Read Foundation—during our occasional dinner together on the nights he didn't stay at the church late? But I couldn't say that to his face. Not here— probably not ever. Dad's plate stayed full enough without extra drama from me. I forced a smile. "It's no big deal."

"No big deal? Addison, you're too modest." Ms. Hawthorne shook her head as if she couldn't believe my humility. "This is the first year the school is giving proceeds from the talent show to a good cause, a cause that Addison chose and arranged on her own. That's a big deal in my book."

"That's very good to hear, Addison." Dad's cheeks practically glowed with pride, and I wanted to sink through the dirty floor to the support beams below.

I plopped down in the first row and buried my head in my hands as Ms. Hawthorne and Dad continued their private conversation raving about me, despite the fact that the room was now filled with students and parents happily chomping down on brownies and appearing grateful that the teacher was distracted.

Distracted—by my dad.

I used to wonder what it would be like to run away. I read so much growing up that my vivid imagination could fill in the gaps without me actually having to pack a suitcase. But there were several summer nights, lying under the stars on a blanket in our driveway, that I mentally packed a bag and never came back.

The summer I was ten, I got mad at Dad for refusing to let me pierce my ears and pitched a fit big enough to merit my mom coming back from the grave and hushing me herself. That night I pictured myself stuffing my favorite Snoopy backpack with clothes and snacks and taking the bus to my grandparents' house in Mississippi. Then I remembered how despite Grandma's best intentions, she always smelled like lemon furniture polish, and Grandpa's constant cloud of cigar smoke gave me a headache. I decided waiting a few years to pierce my ears was better than that alternative, so I shook out my beach blanket and went back to my room, not even bothering to slam the door.

The next time I remembered making escape plans was

the summer I had just turned thirteen and started my period. While hormones raged, I missed my mom more than ever and decided I would take a train through the mountains to a remote location and live alone the rest of my days, just me and my novels. That particular mental suitcase held more books than clothes. Then I realized the cost of a train ticket, even one-way, had to be more than I could afford with my five-dollar-a-week allowance. Besides, I had just read *Anna Karenina* and had a temporary fear of trains.

Tonight, after Dad went to bed humming—humming!—I brought out my trusty blanket and lay on our driveway in the dark once again, wishing I was still naive enough to think running away would actually accomplish anything other than giving me blisters.

But even more than that, I wished it was summer again instead of thirty-nine degrees.

I shivered inside my sweatshirt and knit hat. I should have packed on more layers, but my decision to come out here tonight had been as unpredictable as Kansas weather in autumn. I clamped my hands behind my head to cushion against the concrete drive and half mourned the loss of my imagination. When did the reality of high school crowd out my vivid eye for pretty adventures? Getting older sucked.

Getting older without the buffer of a mom sucked even more.

I was one of the lucky ones, though. I was so young when Mom died that I didn't really remember her outside of picture prompts, so my grief wasn't as personal as it was to others. But at the same time, the fact that I had nothing to specifically miss made me miss her even more.

And if she were here, I wouldn't have had to worry about my dad embarrassing me during the school's open house.

"What are you doing?"

I jumped and let out a muffled shriek as a dark figure loomed over me, my heart pounding in my chest as I struggled to sit up. It took a minute for my brain to convince my adrenaline rush that an attacker probably wouldn't have asked a casual question before pouncing.

A familiar scent wafted my direction, and a second rush filled my senses for entirely opposite reasons. "Wes, you scared me to death."

"You don't look dead." He sat down on the other end of my blanket and drew his legs up to his chest, elbows resting on his knees.

"Very funny."

"So what are you doing out here in the dark?" He kicked his booted heel against my tropical-print beach blanket. "Pretending to be at the beach?"

"My mom died."

His smirk disappeared, and his face paled in the shadows. "I'm sorry, I didn't realize—"

"No, not like today." I rubbed my fingers over the soft thread of the fabric beneath us. "I was five. But sometimes I come out here and try to remember her."

Wes remained silent, and his lack of sarcastic response almost made me worry.

"You okay?"

He peered at me from beneath the layer of shaggy hair that had fallen across his eyes. "I should be asking you that."

"I just told you, it's not a fresh situation."

"But you're still sitting outside in the dark. Alone."

"Not anymore," I shot back.

"Want me to leave?"

"I don't care." I was such a liar. I reclined back on my elbows and tilted my face to the sky. The stars had debuted for the evening, tiny pinpricks of light against a velvet night sky. The moon was a perfect crescent, spotlighting the crisp air. I blew out my breath, watching the white cloud of air float away. What was Wes really doing here? Half of me wanted to ask if Poodle Girl was busy for the night; the other half feared the answer. I wanted Wes to *want* to hang out with me.

And that scared me as much as the thought of his rejection.

I bit my lip, keeping my profile to him, not willing to meet his gaze in the moonlight. I felt it, though, his steady stare on my face.

"My mom's gone, too." The quiet admission pierced the night air, the words sharp and coated with bitterness.

"I'm sorry." I didn't know what else to say and didn't dare act on my impulse to touch his arm.

"Your mom didn't choose to die. Mine chose to leave." Wes let out a half laugh, half grunt. "Trust me, you're lucky."

Weird, he used the exact word I'd thought just moments earlier. I shrugged. "I don't feel it."

"My mom acts as if she's dead to me, yet she's very much alive and very much not interested." He hesitated, his voice deepening with emotion I hadn't realized he possessed. "She's somewhere farther across Kansas, last I heard."

Somewhere during the course of his story, Wes had scooted closer to me on the blanket, our shoulders nearly touching, the scent of his leather jacket washing over me like a comforting presence all its own.

I swallowed, trying to ignore his proximity. "Is that why you came here?"

"Trust me—Crooked Hollow wasn't my first choice. But she kicked me out for the last time, and it beat living on the streets."

"You could have tried getting a job, you know." I didn't think he had one now, either, come to think of it. Not with all the lurking about town he did.

He grinned, slow and dangerous. "Why do you say that? Wishing I hadn't come?"

"No, I just meant—"

His fingers grazed mine in the darkness, and I sucked in my breath. Definitely not regretting him coming.

But might be regretting something else if I wasn't careful.

"Don't you have a girlfriend?" I pulled my hand free, cupping them both around my knees instead. The wind picked up, and I instinctively leaned closer to his warmth. His attention was nice, don't get me wrong—actually, way more than nice—but I couldn't dwell on that, or I'd never come out of it.

"I don't know. I don't do labels."

I snorted. "I bet there's one on the inside of that jacket."

He shrugged out of it and draped it across my shoulders. The scent of his cologne embraced me, and I snuggled into its black leather folds, realizing too late I'd taken one step further down a path I couldn't control.

"You care about that label now, PK?"

"Not so much."

The breeze stirred my hair again, this time not leaving the bitter chill behind that it had before. I clenched his jacket closed at my neck, determined not to read more into this than it was. "What's her name?" The words slipped out, and I mentally snatched them back, but it was too late.

"What, Poodle Girl isn't good enough for you now?"

Mortified, my eyes shot to meet his as heat crept up my neck.

Wes laughed, shaking his head. "You let that one slip more times than you realized."

"I'm sorry."

"Quit apologizing. Sonya is as high maintenance as a poodle sometimes, that's for sure."

"Then why are you—" I cut off my own sentence, already knowing the answer. High maintenance or not, with a body like hers, the answer was obvious. Though for me, a quality personality ranked higher than washboard abs, hence my aversion to Austin. Poodle Girl—no, Sonya—must have some decent qualities locked inside her skintight clothes that I hadn't seen yet.

Or maybe Wes was just as shallow as he appeared.

"Why am I with her?" He finished my sentence, the question hovering between us like an anvil ready to crash. Although my heart was the only one in jeopardy. Man, I hated that. Vulnerability didn't exactly seem to lurk in Wes's gene pool.

"It's none of my business." I looked back at the moon, a much safer orb to study than Wes's dark-brown ones.

"I'm not with Sonya, like I said." Wes shrugged. "We have an understanding. It's casual."

Casual. Casual—what? The options sickened my stomach, and I slowly slid out of his jacket. Silently I handed it to him, wrapping my arms around my knees to stay warm. Once again I was brutally reminded that Wes and I played on completely different playing fields, with completely different sets of rules.

If his particular game even had rules at all.

"Thanks for the loan." I nodded at his jacket as he slipped it back on, a puzzled frown creasing his brow.

Wes shifted his cross-legged position to face me, forcing my attention from the sky. "Why does she bother you so much?"

I didn't want to talk about Sonya, didn't want to picture them together. Somehow his giving Poodle Girl a name made her even more real. What kind of game was he playing? If he talked to her about me, as she said he did, then why did he talk to me about her? The whole thing was giving me a headache, and I shouldn't have even cared in the first place. This was definitely one of those moments I wished I knew God was really listening.

I settled for my safety net of choice—denial. "Who?"

Wes scoffed. "Don't be stupid. Sonya."

"Well, why do you think it bothers me?" I stood up quickly, reaching down to gather my blanket and nearly pushing Wes off the corner in the process. "I'm not exactly the stupid one here, Wes." Though the fact that I'd just blurted my feelings out to him pretty much confirmed the opposite. I folded the blanket against my chest, as much for distance between us as for warmth, and turned toward the house.

"Wait." He came up beside me, a step too close and a step too far away all at the same time. "I don't get it, Addison. You're . . .different. With other girls, I get it. I know what they want. I know what I want." He shook his head, squinting at me in the darkness like I was a puzzle he desperately wanted to piece together. "But you're like three different people around me."

"What do you mean?" Curiosity piqued my interest, overriding the warning in my head that kept trying to usher me back inside. Maybe God was trying to talk to me after all.

Wes took a step closer, holding up one finger. "You act as if I'm too far beneath you to even acknowledge. The high and mighty PK." He eased even closer, ticking off his second point on his middle finger. "But other times you act as if I'm a project you're trying to fix."

He was too close now, his breath tickling my neck. My own breath shortened, and warmth flooded my stomach and chest despite the freezing wind stirring the leaves around us.

"Then other times. . ." His voice trailed off, and he lightly touched the side of my cheek with his fingers. "I get the feeling you actually like me." His head dipped, and his lips zeroed in toward mine. I closed my eyes, anticipating the rush of heat, the taste of his lips, the warmth of his embrace.

Until I pictured him pulling a similar move on Sonya.

I jerked backward, relief and regret thudding painfully in equal measures. "Good call." I drew a steadying breath, forcing myself to look him in the eye. "You're right about all three." Then I yanked open the front door and dead-bolted it before my heart could hightail it back outside into his arms.

Chapter Ten

The only good thing about being at the school at ten
o'clock on a Saturday was that there was no way I'd run
into Wes. "Marta, will you pass me the red paint?" I covered a
yawn with my paint-splattered hand.

Marta slid the can across the canvas sheet we had laid
out on the gym floor. "Here you go. And I need the smaller
paintbrush." We traded brushes, and she dipped the small
one into the cup of water to clean it. "These signs are looking
great." She tilted her head to study our poster-board progress,
swiping red-tinged hair out of her eyes. Her hair was too short
for a ponytail. I had learned my lesson about paint the hard
way a few summers back when helping make car-wash posters
for the youth group. My hair was safely up in a bun.

"So far so good." If I kept thoughts of Wes and last night's
near kiss at bay, my hands remained steady enough to outline
properly. But as soon as I remembered the way he'd leaned
toward me, eyes lit with something indefinable, I started trem-
bling. I'd already knocked over the can of blue, which had
thankfully only been halfway full at the time.

"You seem different today." Marta bent over the board and
carefully lined my yellow letters with blue. "Are you well?"

I didn't look at her, just kept carefully filling in the stenciled letters proclaiming TALENT SHOW with red paint. "Late night. I didn't sleep great." Wes had made sure of that. I felt the touch of his hand on my cheek for hours after I'd gone inside. I was mad at myself for not kissing him, but madder still for even wanting to in the first place. I wasn't *that* girl, and I never would be. No matter how complicated life became, I refused to become a curly haired groupie in a belly shirt. That wasn't the answer.

And I didn't need to hear God's audible voice to know that much.

Marta opened the can of green paint. "Maybe tonight will be better."

I mumbled an agreement, though I doubted the memories would vanish in twenty-four hours. Not when they were branded this deeply.

Marta began writing our school's name on the bottom of her poster with careful strokes. "Did you try counting sheep?" She grinned.

More like leather jackets and tattoos. "Has that ever actually worked for anyone?"

"Nein. I doubt it." Marta set her paintbrush on the canvas and twisted one arm to the side in a stretch. "No one who would be willing to admit it, at least."

Wes certainly had admitted plenty last night. I dipped my brush in the red and finished painting the *W* in *SHOW*, thoughts still churning. Was his opening up last night about his family part of a master plan to throw me off guard? Maybe he wasn't any different than Austin. Maybe I was just this uncatchable fish to him, and that was the only appeal. Guys liked a challenge, but in Austin's case, it was a matter of true disgust on my part rather than a game of hard-to-get.

But as hard as I tried to convince myself Wes was like all the other high school boys in my class, I just couldn't. He might be a year or two older than them, but it went way beyond that. He hadn't been making up that stuff about his mom. I saw the pain in his eyes, saw him peeling back several top layers of facade. There was a depth to Wes that went past his leather jacket, a depth I hadn't noticed him sharing with anyone else.

The question remained, why was he showing it to me?

"Um, Addison?"

Marta's voice yanked me back to reality inside the gym. I jerked backward, my brush dripping on my sweatpants. "What?"

She pointed to the *W* on my poster that I'd not only filled in but also added a big *E* and *S* after it. WES. I stared at the painted evidence in front of me and winced. Busted.

Marta's lips twisted to the side as she glanced from me to the ruined poster and then back to me. "I think it's my turn to buy the coffee. We have to talk."

★ ★ ★

We claimed a corner table at Got Beans, ignoring the weekend rush buzzing in for caffeine and pastries. For once I wasn't concerned about seeing Wes there because if the only reason he came to Got Beans was to play the piano incognito, there'd be no way he'd show up on a busy Saturday.

I ran my finger over the lid of my mocha, watching the steam funnel through the tiny spout. My constant awareness of Wes's presence or potential presence everywhere I went gnawed at me, evidence that was even more glaring than the kind I'd painted on the poster board at school. The report was in, there was no more denying it. I had fallen for Wes.

Exactly how hard I'd fallen was yet to be determined.

Marta peered at me over the cup of her latte, having branched out from our previous coffee trip. She'd even asked for extra caramel, and I couldn't help but feel proud, like I'd personally birthed her into the world of caffeinated delights.

"Is it good?"

She nodded, licking foam off her lips. "Yes. But that's not why we're here." She narrowed her eyes pointedly at me, and I took the hint.

"I guess I should have stuck to doodling on a notebook like an average teenager, huh?" I couldn't help but grin, and she laughed.

"That would have been more normal." She tilted her head to one side, studying me with that wise gaze I couldn't get past, the one that said "even though I'm the same age as you, I've seen so much more." It made me jealous, though I could never hold bitterness toward Marta. The saying "good as gold" pretty much summed her up, though it was definitely cliché. I hated clichés.

Wes's leather jacket and motorcycle roared to the front of my memory. Well, maybe not all clichés. I shook my head to clear the image that wouldn't erase.

"At least you painted over it before throwing the poster away."

I exhaled loudly, and relief sagged my shoulders despite the tension knots still lingering. "Good thinking on your part. Definitely not what I'd want the rest of the drama team to see."

"Your secret is safe with me." Marta sipped her latte then folded her hands on the table and leaned forward as if ready to share more secrets. "Now, let's. . .what do they say? Oh yeah. Scoop."

"Scoop?" I stared at her like she'd lost her mind until the language barrier cleared, and I cracked up. "You mean *dish*?"

Marta fluttered one hand in the air. "Dish, scoop, whatever. Tell me what's going on. Why are you doodling Wes's name on anything, much less in red paint?"

"Because you had the blue?"

She glared in mock impatience, and I shifted in my seat, hating the attention. I wasn't the gossipy girlfriend sort, especially not over my love life. I'd never had one to speak of, and sadly enough, still didn't. "I don't know what to say. There's nothing going on." Other than Wes coming to my house and sitting in my driveway and cracking open that bronzed heart of his and revealing wounds from his past. . . . Okay, maybe there was something to tell.

I took a deep breath. "Wes came over last night. When I said we were just friends, we are. His dad wanted me to look out for him, but I sort of had been doing that anyway. I'm drawn to him."

Marta nodded, urging me on. "But?"

"Well, I was lying in my driveway, which I know is weird, but it's this thing I do sometimes, and he showed up and sat with me." My voice cracked, and I cleared my throat. "We talked about parental stuff, and he actually opened up a little. Lost the macho act for once, you know?" I stared at my cup, which was easier than looking into Marta's understanding, encouraging gaze. "We really connected. Until he tried to kiss me."

She gasped, and my eyes darted to her face, which was flushed with excitement as if she'd been the one in danger of losing her heart instead of me. "Did he?"

"I stopped him." Even as I said the words out loud, I mentally smacked my forehead with one hand in regret while proudly patting myself on the back with the other. "It's not right. We're too different." Like night and day. Oil and water.

Gummi bears and lemon drops.

"I thought the rule was opposites attract." Marta smiled, but it faded when I didn't smile back. "Oh, Addison. Do you regret it?"

"Yes. No." I pushed my mocha around the table in a small

circular pattern. "It would have been my first kiss."

Her eyebrows shot up. "Impressive."

"I guess it is sort of rare." Sixteen and never been kissed. I used to be proud of that, like I'd reached some sort of pinnacle of PK success. Avoid temptation, check. Protect virginity at all costs, check. Even then my true-love-waits ring glinted under the lights of Got Beans, a shimmering, solid white-gold band my dad gave me when I was twelve that I hadn't taken off since. I stared at it now, somehow doubting Sonya's father ever got her one. Did they really help? Or was it the fear of God drilled into me working the protective powers instead?

Marta leaned forward, her voice lowering. "If it makes you feel better, I've been kissed, but I'm still a virgin."

"You are?" I wasn't shocked, just somewhat surprised. Marta had such a cultured, adult attitude to her that I could have realistically seen that one going either way. But it did make me feel better. A lot better. Now there were at least two confessing virgins in the eleventh grade. Probably more hiding in the chess team.

I wasn't naive enough to think everyone saying they'd done it had actually done so—I knew the power of peer pressure could lead to embellishments and lies to save face. Thankfully, since I'm a PK, no one ever asked me about it. They assumed, and they assumed correctly, and likely blamed my dad for a lot of my decision. So no persecution for that one. It was like I got a free pass.

Or was that just another wall of my father's I hid behind?

"I made that decision years ago," Marta said. "For personal reasons, for faith-based reasons, for family reasons." She shrugged. "It's the right choice for me."

"I thought European teenagers were more. . .advanced. . .in that area of life." It was hard to say the actual terminology out loud, even to Marta. Sex was a four-letter word in our house. I never got "the talk" from my dad—I got a book and a brochure.

"Statistically, European teens have more experience. But the teen pregnancy rates are lower. We're taught differently about sex education and protection." Marta waved one hand in the air. "All of which is good, but I wish more of my friends would choose abstinence for themselves. It's one thing to protect against an unwanted pregnancy or disease, but you can't protect yourself against the emotional side effects of having that kind of intimate relationship at our age. I've seen what those choices do, the hurt they leave behind." She tapped her finger against her coffee cup. "I decided for myself it wasn't worth it."

"I agree." And I did. Didn't I? Funny, this wouldn't have ever crossed my mind in the first place if not for Wes's random appearance last night. Though I had to admit, the thought of him making out with Sonya and then offering a kiss to me burned my insides up with too many emotions to define.

"Besides, abstinence before marriage is what the Bible instructs, and I figure God has a reason for His rules." Marta winked. "But you know all about that."

Oh, trust me.

She continued. "So why didn't you kiss him? Because you didn't want him to be your first kiss? Or because you think there is no hope for a relationship there?"

"Definitely not the first." My lips twisted to the side as I thought. "Somewhat the latter."

"I'm guessing there's a third reason lurking?"

"He has a girlfriend, who isn't his girlfriend."

Marta just sat back and shook her head like she wasn't even going to try to figure that one out.

"Remember the lemon-drop girlfriend I mentioned last

time we were here and saw Wes?" I gestured around the shop.

Marta nodded. "What is that reference about, again?"

"Long story. But anyway, Wes told me last night when I asked about her that he's not into labels." I took a fortifying sip of my mocha. "And I'm not into knockoffs."

She blew out her breath. "So it's not ideal."

"Not at all."

We stared at our coffees until Marta finally looked up. "Guess we should get back to the gym and paint some posters—ones without boys' names on them."

I couldn't help but laugh at that as we gathered our trash and slipped outside. Too bad it wasn't as easy to paint over the impression Wes left on my heart.

Chapter Eleven

Since I had "volunteered" to organize the fund-raiser for the talent show, everyone assumed I also needed to be at every rehearsal and paint party between now and then. The final list of chosen contestants had been posted earlier in the week, thankfully minus Kelly's accordion and Tyler's violin. I was glad to see a couple of popular names listed under hip-hop group dancers, as well as a ballet solo. Maybe this wouldn't be such an epic fail after all.

I don't know who had the biggest laugh over seeing my name written as assistant director under Mrs. Lyons—me or Marta. But when I realized it wasn't a joke, I stopped laughing.

"It will be a good experience," Marta consoled me as I banged my head against a bank of lockers.

Looking up at the six-foot backdrop we were supposed to paint and my two "volunteers"—two football players playing sword fight with the only available brushes—I could pretty much assure her it wouldn't be. "Hey, guys, can we focus?"

They turned surprised glances my way, as if realizing I was there for the first time. I fought the urge to steal their "swords" and bean them on the head. "The black background goes on first." That should have been common sense, but with these guys, it wasn't worth the risk of assuming. They dutifully got to work, pausing only once to dab each other's T-shirt sleeves with paint. That was probably as good as it would get.

"Just keep it on the canvas, okay? No paint on the floor."

The cavemen grunted what I hoped was an agreement, and I made my way through the wings toward the stage, clutching the clipboard Mrs. Lyons had given me, as if it possessed magical powers that would somehow give these teenagers a sense of decorum.

Jessica Daily struck a high note from where she practiced out of turn on the first row, totally overpowering the less obnoxious singer currently on the stage.

While I was wishing, make that decorum *and* humility.

Claire breezed past me, her arms loaded with material that I could only figure were the clothes for her fashion demonstration. What *was* a fashion demonstration anyway? I checked my clipboard, but it didn't give me a description. I sighed. "Claire, wait."

She stopped, pivoting on four-inch heels to face me. "What do you want?" Now that the first blitz of posters had been hung around the school and the surrounding neighborhoods, she seemed less inclined to be polite. The disaster in the cafeteria a few weeks ago likely had something to do with that. One doesn't get gravy out of a white blouse very easily—or at all.

"I need more info on your talent." I tapped my clipboard, grateful for the protection it put between me and Claire's venomous gaze. "I'm helping Mrs. Lyons arrange the order of events."

She snorted and shifted the load in her arms. "Whatever you do, just don't put me after that stupid ventriloquist act."

"No problem." I still hadn't figured out how he'd passed auditions in the first place, though I guess if his competition had been the accordion or the violin solos, he was golden. I made a quick note. "You'll go after one of the group dance numbers. Does that work?"

"Whatever." She tossed back her hair. "I'm modeling some clothes, including a few of my own designs."

Claire sewed? This was a news flash. Though it was possible she just borrowed Daddy's credit card and hired it out. "Do you need an emcee?"

She stared blankly at me.

"An announcer. You know, someone to talk about the clothes as you come down the runway?"

"No way." She frowned. "I'm going to prerecord it myself. I can't trust something that important to some random person."

Of course. Because reading from note cards into a microphone was impossibly hard. "Fine." I made another note that she would need a CD player.

"Is that all?" She shifted her weight impatiently.

Tension still palpitated between us. I wished I could make her believe I hadn't bumped her tray on purpose. I hated conflict and hated burned bridges even more, but at the same time I wasn't eager to dive back into a faux friendship again, either. Things had changed. We had changed.

One of us for the worst.

I let out a slow breath. "Yeah, Claire. That's all."

She rushed off without another word. I stared at the list in my hands and closed my eyes against the stress headache pounding in my temples. This talent show just kept getting better and better.

★ ★ ★

Wednesday night while my dad was in church and I was supposed to be doing homework in the kitchen, I threw on my denim jacket and snuck out (is it still sneaking out when you're home alone and use the front door?) to grab a coffee from Got Beans. My brain felt fried from the busy week of school and talent-show preparations. I hadn't even had time to read for fun in what felt like forever. Who knew being an assistant director meant so much work?

The scary thing was I sort of enjoyed it.

One thing was certain—caffeine would be the only way I'd hunch back over my English textbook tonight and finish reading that chapter. I opened the door of Got Beans, and piano music immediately washed over me, a soothing ointment to ease the lingering pain of screeching, off-key singers and bass guitars that had assaulted my eardrums this past week.

My heart knew it was Wes before my eyes confirmed the fact. His fingers fairly danced over the keys. He sounded even better than the last time I heard him play. I took a closer look—his eyes weren't even open! How did he do that? Here I'd been suffering through mediocrity at a so-called talent-show rehearsal when real skill lurked a few blocks away.

"We're closing in thirty minutes," Bert warned from the counter, jerking me away from my intense focus on the piano. Okay, more like on Wes. But he didn't need to know that. I snapped to attention, though my words jumbled like I'd never ordered coffee before. "Mocha? Um, big?"

Bert snorted. "Someone's been hitting the books." He snatched the large cup from the towering pile and went to work making my drink. I leaned against the counter while I waited, casually looking back at Wes as I pulled a few one-dollar bills from my jeans pocket. He must not have heard the bell chime on the door when I came in or else he would've quit playing. Should I interrupt? Or just enjoy the music?

The song ended as Bert handed me my steaming paper cup—the paper part being an obvious "to go" suggestion—and answered my dilemma for me. I hesitated, not sure I wanted to face Wes in front of an audience for the first time since our driveway talk nearly two weeks ago.

Even if that audience shucked his stained apron and headed off to the storage room in the back. Oops. We were alone.

Wes caught my eye, and my feet moved toward him before my brain could send an alternate signal. "Hey." Wow, deep. I swear I got an A on my last vocabulary quiz.

"Hey." He didn't stand but swiveled to face me on the bench. I took a chair at the table closest to the piano and tried not to think of it as "our spot." Just because we'd been there once didn't make it official.

With Wes, nothing would ever be official.

"Haven't seen you in a while." His dark brows lifted in silent question. He wanted to know if I'd been avoiding him. Had I?

"Been at school at lot." I sipped my mocha, suddenly remembering I held it. The coffee warmed me and cleared the mush crowding my brain. "I somehow got roped into helping with the end-of-semester talent show."

"You have talent?"

I swatted his arm before I could wonder if contact was a wise idea. "I didn't say I was in it. I'm behind the scenes, trust me."

"I gotcha." He nodded, as if for once out of sarcasm.

I studied him over the rim of my cup, appreciating the way his blue thermal top brightened his complexion and the pushed-up sleeves revealed the corded muscles in his forearms—and that mysterious bird tattoo. His ever-present leather jacket draped over the seat next to mine at the table, and I breathed in. The scent was probably in my imagination, but I enjoyed it anyway. Had it really been two weeks since he draped it over my shoulders in my driveway? Was that Wes the one I sat with tonight, or was this the rebel-without-a-cause Wes? I never could tell until I was too invested to run away.

"Too bad you aren't in our school. We could use some real

talent." I gestured to the piano.

"That's what a GED will get you out of." He ran a finger over the keys, a gentle *plink* breaking the silence.

I knew GEDs were equivalent to a high school diploma now, at least as far as the job force was concerned, but I hadn't realized he'd truly dropped out. Thought that was just another rumor. "Did you really hate school that much?" I knew doing well and actually liking school most of the time wasn't necessarily normal, nor was my love of reading, but that didn't mean I was the only person in my grade. Everyone else was sticking it out. Why hadn't he?

"Wasn't my favorite." He shrugged it off, as if dropping out of high school was a no-big-deal decision. Maybe to him it was.

But somehow I doubted it. I doubted every single layer of that tough-guy act, more so now since our late-night talk than ever before. I persisted like a Labrador sniffing out a doggy biscuit. "But don't you want to work? Get a job? Do something?"

"And give up all this?" He waved his arms over the piano in a grand gesture. There was the sarcasm. That meant I was getting closer to the main issue.

"I'm not buying your defense mechanisms." I crossed my arms, realizing too late it was a defense mechanism of my own.

Wes shut the lid over the piano keys with a snap. "Last time I checked, Dr. Phil didn't need any help. So quit psychoanalyzing me. I get enough of that."

I dropped my arms and leaned forward, unable to change the subject. "Wes, you're eighteen. You have a gift for music. Why waste that? Why not go for something? College or a career."

"What's the point?" His voice rose, and he glanced over his shoulder at the front counter. Thankfully Bert hadn't returned yet, another hint we should leave soon. But I felt glued to my chair. Wes lowered his voice slightly. "My dad is so busy trying to play like he wants me around that he's just glad I stay out of his hair. And my mom is the one who shipped me here so she could live her own life. So why should I care about my future? No one else does."

"I do." The words slipped off my tongue so fast I actually touched my mouth after. But I meant them. And he already knew that.

Wes narrowed his eyes at me. "And you said I was a player? You're the one playing games now."

"No, I'm not. And I never called you a player." I cradled my cup with both hands, wishing there were a coffee that could both wake you up *and* give you the right words for conversations like these. "I just said you had a girlfriend. Or whatever Sonya is." Shudder.

He shook his head. "Things aren't always black and white, Addison."

They were in my world. Drinking, black. Church, white. Boys with motorcycles, black. Christian music in the car, white. It was definite, simple, defined. Easy.

Suffocating.

"Are you with Sonya or not?" I winced. Out of all the things I could have said in that moment, that's what I picked? I mentally poured my coffee over my head.

"Tell me this, PK." Wes scooted to the end of the bench and leaned forward until our knees nearly touched. His breath smelled like peppermint mocha, and his spicy aftershave wafted toward me, drawing me in and nearly consuming me. "Would it even matter if I wasn't?"

My heart pounded like a frontline drummer during a football game, and I knew what he was asking. But I couldn't give an answer. Not an honest one. My mouth dried, and I stared into his eyes, wishing I could nod, say yes, anything in the affirmative. I knew my heart, knew what I wanted. . .but I knew my dad and his rules even better.

My dad. Dad! I checked my watch. He'd be home any minute—and see one kitchen table full of books, minus one daughter. I grabbed my cup and stood up. "I'm so late. I've got to run." Literally.

Wes stood with me. "What's it like to play by the rules all the time?"

What's it like being considered dog poo on society? I opened my mouth to shoot off that creative barb but closed it at the glint in his eyes. This wasn't sarcastic Wes back for more. This was still-serious Wes, despite the rough-around-the-edges tone.

"What's it like?" I asked as I buttoned my jacket. I thought for a moment of all the things I should say, all the things that could possibly witness to him and draw him to the light side.

Then I ditched all the *shoulds* and blurted out the truth instead. "Exhausting."

I turned and left like a good PK, my heart heavier than the boots weighing down my feet as I jogged home, trying not to slosh my coffee. My thoughts churned with each step. Black. White. Black. White.

If that were true, then why was everything suddenly so gray?

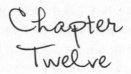

Chapter Twelve

For the first time in my life, I walked into English class with a knot in my stomach. And it had nothing to do with the lukewarm corndog I'd choked down at lunch.

I hadn't finished my homework.

I heard that stereotypical horror-movie sound effect (*reeee! reeee!*) in my head every time I thought about it during the morning. Despite my attempts to complete my discussion questions on chapter 6 during lunch, it just hadn't been possible. Kids kept coming up to me at the table with questions about the talent show, and by the time I realized I should have gone to the library for privacy instead of the cafeteria to eat, it was too late. The bell had rung, signaling my doom.

After racing home last night and sliding into my kitchen chair mere seconds before my dad came in through the garage, I was emotionally spent. Let's just say concentrating became impossible. I tried to finish reading but could only see a replay of my conversation with Wes on the pages, the black letters against the white page a taunt of his earlier words. *"Things aren't always black and white."*

I slipped into my desk chair and opened my book like every other day. Yet my palms were sweaty, and I couldn't look Ms. Hawthorne in the eye. I wasn't sure how to proceed. This was foreign territory. Did I tell her the truth up front? Hope she didn't make her typical rounds collecting assignments? Lie? Beg for mercy? Play it cool?

My corndog bobbed along in a private mosh pit in my stomach. My vision blurred. I was *such* a gummi bear. No doubt Wes would be snickering right now if he saw me. Never mind—Wes was too cool to snicker. He'd guffaw. No, that was worse. Smirk. That's it. He'd smirk. Those gorgeous lips turning up into a half—

"Addison?"

I jumped so hard, my foot jerked across the floor, pushing me back in my seat. Unfortunately, I'd been sitting with one leg curled under me, and the momentum was enough to heave me right over the side. I landed on the floor in an ungraceful heap. My cheeks burned with embarrassment as Ms. Hawthorne stood over me, one hand pressed to her chest as if *I'd* scared *her*. "I'm so sorry, Addison! I didn't mean to startle you."

Around us, the classroom (must have filled up while I'd been lost in my guilt-ridden daydream) of students—ahem—snickered. I closed my eyes briefly, wishing the dirty tile would swallow me whole. But we were on the second floor, and I wasn't sure what classroom lay beneath us. Probably biology, full of dissection trays and formaldehyde. That wouldn't be any better.

"It's okay." I wasn't about to confess that my backside hurt. Besides, the only thing I could think of now was how grateful I was to have worn jeans and not a skirt.

"You all right?" Luke's deep baritone sounded over my left shoulder, and the next thing I knew, his strong grip hauled me to my feet. Ms. Hawthorne hovered over me, a handful of homework assignments tucked under one sweater-clad arm.

Concern pinched her perfectly plucked eyebrows. "Do you need the nurse?"

Only if Nurse Gill had an erase-the-last-fifteen-minutes pill I could take. I shook out of Luke's grasp and slipped back into my chair. "No, I'm fine." Pride bruised. Please leave.

And forget to ask me for my homework.

I held my breath as Ms. Hawthorne continued to hover. "If you're sure, Addison, then I won't embarrass you further." She straightened the collected assignments into a neat stack by tapping them on my desk. I bit my lower lip as she stared right at me, waiting.

This was it. Any minute now I'd get detention or at least a frowny face on my next paper, along with a giant red D for disappointment. Earlier this week Austin had blown off the assignment yet again, and Ms. Hawthorne had sent him to the principal's office to "realign his attitude," as she'd put it. How would it look for me to waltz back into Principal Stephens's office as a flunkie just weeks after I'd been the Mother Teresa of Crooked Hollow High, arranging for money to be sent to illiterate children?

I cleared my throat, determined to handle the unfamiliar situation with grace and elegance to make up for my chair dive. "I, um. I don't—that is, I didn't have a chance to—" Forget it. I flopped my head on my desk and banged it twice. "I suck."

"Addison, are you sure you don't need the nurse?"

I forced myself to look up. Ms. Hawthorne lowered her previously panicked voice as understanding dawned in her eyes. "Do you not have the homework today?"

From my peripheral, I caught Luke covering his smile with his hand. Any minute now I expected to hear a "loser" cough from somewhere in the back of the room. Or maybe a few gasps of shock. I finally managed to shake my head. "No."

Ms. Hawthorne studied my eyes for a moment then nodded once. "All right, then." She moved on to the student behind me and continued taking up the papers.

That was it? I had a stomachache half the day for that? Part of me wanted to call her back and point out the misery I'd been in all day, but the other, smarter part of me hollered to shut up and count my blessings.

Beside me Luke leaned back in his chair and shook his head. "Lucky break."

Maybe so.

The rest of class flew by in a blur, and I became the epitome of the model student, raising my hand to volunteer when no one else would, picking up my neighbor's pen when they dropped it, reading out loud when asked. I copied down the homework assignment twice, just in case I needed proof I'd been paying attention. When the bell rang dismissing us, I took my time gathering my papers, giving Ms. Hawthorne one more time to change her mind and reprimand me. At least this way it'd be privately, though I don't see how any punishment she could have doled out would have been more embarrassing than falling out of my chair. Maybe that's why I'd avoided any consequences—she knew I had put myself through enough.

I stalled at my desk until the classroom almost cleared. Then Austin pushed past me from the back of the room. "Must be nice to be the favorite." He shook his head as he kept going, and at first I was so relieved he hadn't made a pass at me that it took a minute for his words to sink in. The favorite? Like, teacher's pet? Really? Guess he hadn't gotten his attitude "realigned" that day after all.

"See you tomorrow, Addison," Ms. Hawthorne called from her desk with a knowing smile, as if guessing why I continued to stand in the empty room. That was it. Free and clear.

But the whispers and furtive glances my fellow classmates shot my way told me I was anything but.

* * *

After the day I had, ice cream was a must. I stood in line at Screamin' Cones after school and wished Marta were there to share the fat grams and encouragement. I'd invited her on my way home, but she'd had to get back to her host family. Apparently her fill-in mom had planned a shopping spree that she refused to let Marta out of, wanting her to take plenty of "American" clothes with her when she went back home in the spring. I'd secretly envied the opportunity to shop with a real mom figure, but Marta barely tolerated it. "Mrs. Davidson is so nice, but she thinks I need to look like the cover of *Seventeen* magazine." Marta had shaken her head as she closed her locker door. "I don't really see many kids looking like that."

We took a shared glance around the crowded hall of Crooked Hollow High. No verbal agreement on my part had been necessary.

"Next." The harried-looking college student working the ice-cream counter motioned me forward. Apparently I wasn't the only person having a bad day, judging by the way the line now snaked out the door.

"Two scoops of strawberry in a waffle cone." I dug through my coin purse for my money. "With sprinkles."

She keyed in the order on the register then plunged her hand into a plastic glove as she went for the strawberry bucket. "Four thirty-two."

I stared at the dollar bill in my hand and the three pennies in the bottom of my coin purse. "Um, without sprinkles?"

Her eyes narrowed, and she plucked the glove off. Punched more buttons. "Four dollars even."

Odd that sprinkles cost thirty-two cents. I jingled my change, trying to sound confident. "One scoop. Plain cone." I frowned. Good-bye sweet waffle bliss.

She didn't reglove, wisely doubting my financial ability. "Two ninety-five."

I stared at the dollar bill then tried to send her a "have pity, I've had a rough day" vibe. She was a hormonal young woman. Surely she'd understand. I widened my eyes and tried to think of puppies. Lost. In the rain.

She wasn't buying it. "Next!"

Dismissed—unless I wanted to purchase a solo cup of sprinkles. The guy behind me jostled me out of the way as he stepped up in line, clutching a five-dollar bill. Must be nice. Apparently I'd spent more of my meager allowance on mochas lately than I'd realized.

With a growling stomach and rising temper, I stomped outside. My backpack felt heavier now that my afternoon of homework (yes, I was going to do it!) faced me without the assistance of cold, creamy calories.

"Why the long face, PK? You've missed me that much?" Wes fell into step beside me on the sidewalk, and for once I wasn't even surprised at his sudden appearance.

"I'm not in the mood, Keegan." I quickened my pace, unable to bear any more lectures or life analogies from my own personal dark angel. It was his fault I'd had a crappy day anyway. If I hadn't gotten lost in his rare showing of vulnerability inside Got Beans, I'd have done my homework and not been mocked about being the teacher's pet the rest of the afternoon.

Wes increased his stride to match mine. "So the PK has mood swings. Where's all that goodness and light?"

I stopped at a crosswalk and waited for the light to change, determined not to look at him. "There's nothing good about an ice-cream craving denied." I wanted to tell him to leave me alone, but I was tired of lying to myself. Wasn't going to start lying out loud, too. As much as I didn't want him there, I did.

See how complicated life gets without ice cream?

"That's what the attitude's about?" Wes grabbed my arm, preventing me from crossing when the pedestrian light turned white. I shook it free but felt the impression through my sleeve in a wave of heat. "Ice cream?" He looked like he wanted to laugh but wasn't sure if he'd get decked. Smart man.

"Leave me to mourn in peace." It wasn't just about the ice cream, of course, but I wasn't going to spill my guts—heart, whatever—right there on the sidewalk.

Especially not without a little frozen dairy courage.

"Wait here." Wes turned and jogged down the sidewalk without a backward glance, as if he just expected to speak and I'd obey. I snorted and started to walk in the opposite direction. Forget that. Let the poodle girls of the world fall all over his demands. I was independent. I was my own woman. I was—

Was he going inside Screamin' Cones?

I stopped and waited.

He appeared an eternity later, after I'd decided that Hydrangea Street had thirty-seven cracks in the sidewalk from the traffic light all the way to the front door of Screamin' Cones.

He stopped in front of me and handed me a cone. I was so elated that it took me a minute to realize it wasn't strawberry. It was cookies and cream. Black and white.

Nice.

I wanted to shove the cone into his smirk—see, I knew he smirked!—but I really wanted the treat more. I took a bite and my tongue froze over. Bliss. After a third lick, I swallowed. "Thanks."

"You're welcome." He didn't point out his color scheme, and I wasn't about to. Somehow the silent agreement upped my opinion of him another notch—not to mention the fact that he'd even gotten me ice cream in the first place—and we walked together toward my house.

"So what are you doing besides rescuing damsels in distress today?" I thought about offering him a bite, but I thought that might give him the wrong idea. Too intimate, sharing a cone.

Plus, I didn't like to share.

"Hung out at Got Beans for a while. Hit the music store." He shuffled his feet, kicking at a rock on the road before rejoining my steady pace. "Weed-Eated my dad's yard."

I nearly choked. "You mow?" Somehow I couldn't conjure a picture of him wielding the noisy machine, carefully tending a flower bed in his leather jacket.

"Sure." He nodded, straight faced. "Then I read books to some kids at the library for story hour, got a mani-pedi, and knitted my granny a scarf."

Loser. I'd almost fallen for it. "You had me until the scarf."

He laughed out loud, the sound sudden and surprising and—perfect. I'd never heard him laugh like that, had never caught him off guard that way before. I couldn't help but stare at the way his face transformed, all guards down.

I liked it way more than I should have.

Wes stopped walking once we reached my street, his expression carefully arranged into a picture of fake innocence. "Did I mention the condition that came with the ice cream?"

So much for Mr. Nice Guy. "No, somehow you missed that step." I held up my half-eaten cone. "What if I refuse? A little late, don't you think?"

"Oh, it's never too late." He took a step closer to me, and I held my ground despite the shiver that started in my stomach. He tilted his head to one side, the familiar spark I could only describe as Wes now firmly back in his eyes. "Go out with me."

"What?" I nearly dropped my cone but thankfully

recovered before I smeared it across the front of his jacket. Or maybe he needed the wake-up call. Me, go out with Wes?

"I didn't stutter." He shoved his hands in his pockets and waited, rocking slightly back on his heels.

He wasn't kidding. My heart jump-started in my chest, and a hundred different warning signals clanged in my head. I drew a deep breath to regain my composure, to fight back the tiny, niggling feeling inside that was nothing short of desire mixed with victory. Me. Wes wanted me.

Not Sonya.

But it was still impossible. Reality smacked me across the forehead. There was no way. I couldn't even get through a missed homework assignment or stay out past curfew without risking cardiac arrest. No way could I do something this blatantly against my dad's rules. Not without giving myself an ulcer or two. And no way could I ask permission, either. I could just see how that conversation would go. As if.

I took another bite of ice cream, trying to appear cool when really I feared I might hurl on his black boots. "I'm afraid that's going to cost you an entire buffet of ice cream, buddy."

"Not a problem." Wes took another step closer, and I suddenly realized we were standing together—rather closely— in broad daylight on the corner of my street, where all the neighbors could see. And tattle.

Welcome to the fishbowl of PK life.

"You don't have to answer yet." Wes reached out and tucked a stray strand of hair behind my ear before shoving his hands back in his pockets. "Just meet me outside your house tonight after your dad goes to bed. I'll convince you." He winked and then walked away, his casual stroll testifying that this life-changing moment for me was nothing worth breaking a sweat over to him.

I stared at the black-and-white ice cream melting in rivulets down the side of the cone onto my hand, wishing I'd just been able to find another stupid dollar and ninety-two cents in my coin purse.

Chapter Thirteen

"Υou are a lemon drop."

I stared at my reflection in the bathroom mirror and tried to look assured. Confident. Independent. Sour. "You. Are. A. Lemon. Drop."

But my pink polka-dotted pj top pretty much said the opposite.

I rested my forehead against the mirror with a groan. Who was I kidding? I was a gummi bear through and through, and if I didn't quit downing so many mochas and ice-cream cones, I'd be just as jiggly as one.

I looked back at the brown-haired, blue-eyed girl in the mirror, hiding behind flannel pj's and Hello Kitty house-shoe boots, and wondered what a lemon drop would even look like. I gathered my limp hair on top of my head in a messy updo and pursed my lips. Nope. Not helping.

Dropping my hand, I let out a sigh. Dad had finally gone to bed after dozing in his recliner in front of the ten o'clock news, and when I dared to peek out the window, I saw Wes's shadow lurking under the light post and about fainted with nerves. Hence the not-so-helpful pep talk in front of the mirror. But I couldn't go out there. I wasn't what Wes wanted, he wasn't what I needed, and that was that. I'd played by the rules this long; there was no turning back now.

Right?

Meandering my way back into the living room, I peeked through the blinds for the fourteenth time. He was still there. How long would he wait? I tapped my foot, which was harder to do inside a fuzzy boot than I thought, and crossed then uncrossed my arms. Maybe I should just go outside and tell him I wasn't coming. That would have been the responsible thing to do. After all, if I was turning him down, he shouldn't stand on the street all night. It was cold. That wasn't fair.

My actions justified, I slipped a purple hoodie over my pj's and eased open the front door. My boots shuffling across the cold grass, I made my way to the street, where Wes's gaze roamed up and down before landing a double take on my footwear. "Hello Kitty, huh? That's not exactly my definition of sex kitten."

"Didn't realize there'd be a vocabulary quiz." I crossed my arms against the cold and made sure to stand a few feet away and outside of the circle of light. "Listen, I can't stay."

Wes didn't move toward me as I'd expected him to, just studied me with confusion etched in his expression. "Let me get this straight. You came all the way out here, in the cold, to tell me you couldn't come out here?"

"Exactly." Hearing my logic out loud sounded even worse than it had in my head, but there we were.

His lips twisted into a grin, and he reached one arm out to me. I stepped forward on instinct, and his arm caught me around the waist before I could backtrack. "You know, I've never been a fan of polka dots before, but on you, this works."

His loose, barely there embrace stole my breath. I couldn't even fathom the danger I'd be in if he ever held me tight. I concentrated on inhaling and avoiding his eyes. "Like I said, I can't stay. I just didn't want you out here all night."

"A little arrogant, aren't you, thinking I'd wait that long?"

I dared to look up into his eyes, our faces inches apart. "Would you have?"

His gaze clouded over with something indefinable, and his voice turned husky. "I thought I knew."

Dare I believe that I affected him even half as much as he affected me? The thought blew my mind. Impossible. Sonya and those other girls had so much more than me—and I didn't mean just in regard to bra size, though there was definitely that.

He stepped away from me, his hand sliding down the length of my arm until he caught my hand and tugged. "Come with me."

My heart hiccuped. "On a date? Now?"

"I don't date, Addison." Wes pointed over his shoulders to the bushes, where I finally made out the form of his motorcycle stashed in the shadows.

I pulled my hand free of his grasp. "But you asked me out." Pride battled with confusion, and I darted my gaze between him to the death machine lurking behind him. "That was the ice-cream condition." Ice-cream condition? Man, our whole previous conversation sounded so ridiculous when reenacted out loud in the dark.

"Right. I said, 'Go out with me.' As in, go out. On a ride." He threw one leg over the seat of the motorcycle and wheeled it off the sidewalk into the street.

"That's stupid." I hated that I misunderstood him, though I supposed this made a whole lot more sense than picturing Wes across a candlelit table for two. Duh.

"You just said you were going to say no anyway, so why the headache over the particulars?" Wes's grin lit the shadows, and he held out a helmet. His only one. I shook my head. The hand holding the helmet dropped to his lap. "Come on, PK."

The nickname tugged at my stomach, and for a moment everything inside me wanted to jump on the bike. Forget the rules. Forget black and white. I wanted to hug gray. I wanted to ride the line between responsibility and fun and not worry about falling off on the wrong side.

If God wasn't listening anyway. . .

I chewed on my lower lip. Hmmm. Maybe falling off wasn't the best analogy to use when referring to a motorcycle.

He revved the engine. "Last chance."

I squeezed my eyes shut. Sonya wouldn't have hesitated. But was she really the role model I wanted for my life? I was tired of role models. Tired of being one. Tired of living in a fishbowl.

Tired of wondering if Mrs. Kilgore was peering through her curtains right now with a video camera to document all these scandalous details for my dad come Sunday.

I shifted my weight, waves churning in my stomach. The roar of the bike vibrated inside my chest. I didn't ask to be a PK. I didn't ask for a life that meant living like a teenage saint. I didn't ask for any of it, yet it was asked of me every day.

Wes was the only one asking for something tonight, something I for once didn't mind giving.

That did it. Hello Kitty boots and all, I climbed onto the back of the motorcycle and secured the helmet over my hair then wrapped shaking arms around Wes's firm, leather-clad back. He didn't even look at me, just gunned the engine and took off. We soared down the street, my heart riding high above my chest in an adrenaline rush that topped any roller coaster. The wind whipped my hair around my neck, and for a moment I forgot I was wearing my pajamas.

This was life. This was adventure.

This was what it felt like to be a lemon drop.

★ ★ ★

My exhilaration lasted all the way to the first STOP sign, where I frantically pounded Wes on the back and begged to get off. He slowed to a stop at the corner and rested the weight of the bike on one leg as I slid off the side. My legs trembled at the knees, and I hoped my baggy pajama pants covered their obvious knocking. My mind raced faster than his tires had, and I couldn't believe what I'd actually done. I pulled the helmet from my head. "I'm sorry, I just—"

Wes shook his head. "Don't sweat it, PK. I honestly didn't even expect you to get on in the first place."

Somehow, his saying that just made me feel worse instead of better.

I tried to calm my breathing, tried to identify the panic that had coaxed me back onto the safety of the street. The foreign thrill of rebellion. The anxiety over breaking the rules. The fleeting thought of my dad finding my bed empty.

The fear of falling.

I met Wes's steady gaze, and my heart thudded painfully. So much for falling. I was about to crash-land in a heap bigger than the one in English class.

And with much more dire consequences.

"Maybe I could try again." My voice sounded small, timid, and I didn't even believe myself. Wes didn't either. He shot me a look, half contempt, half pity, and it turned my stomach. What did he see when he looked at me—the girl next door? The girl without a life? The girl with the conservative wardrobe? What did he think?

More importantly, when would I stop caring so much?

I tried to lift my chin, tried to act as if his approval or disapproval of my choices meant nothing to me. But my head felt heavier than the helmet still locked in my grip, too many

121

what-ifs weighing it down. "I'm sorry."

He lifted one shoulder in a half shrug. "You apologize too much."

I bit my tongue before I could say "sorry" again. Wes reached out, and my heart skittered before I realized he just wanted his helmet back. I handed it to him, our fingers brushing. The electricity that passed between us did nothing to curb my nerves, and I just wanted to sit on the street and cry.

Why couldn't I be that girl? His girl? What was holding me back? The thought of hurting my dad, yeah. I didn't want to do that. But was that really it? I obviously possessed enough moxie to get on the bike in the first place. Not enough to stay on, but something in me had been strong enough to climb aboard.

Then weak enough to bail.

I shook my head, my conflicting thoughts forming a head-ache in my temples. I felt like I was morphing into one of *those girls* right there on the street in front of my house, turning into a person that cared more about what a guy thought about her than she did herself. When did I equate not taking risks with weakness? That wasn't me.

At this rate, I'd be heading inside to turn all my sweaters into belly shirts. All I needed was some bubble gum to pop.

"You gonna be okay?" Wes's voice broke through the cacophony in my head. He sounded impatient now, like he just wanted to leave. Like I'd had my chance.

And blown it.

"I'd give you a ride back to your house, but, you know. . ." His voice trailed off as he gestured to the motorcycle in silent explanation.

"Right. No, of course. I'm fine." My heart screamed *liar*, but I wasn't going to turn further into someone I wasn't. The last thing I wanted—or that Wes wanted to see—was for me to shrivel up even more. Wounded pride fought for domain over potent embarrassment, and I straightened my shoulders in an attempt to look controlled. Together. Unaffected.

I'd have been able to pull off "aloof" a whole lot better if I hadn't been wearing pajamas and house boots.

Wes brushed his knuckles against my cheek, and the gentle touch was almost my undoing. "Hey, I tried." His fingers lingered for a moment. I closed my eyes, and then they were gone, replaced by a gust of cold air. He revved the engine again and called over the noise. "See ya, PK." He roared away, his parting words sounding more like a final benediction than a casual good-bye.

I stood on the street, hugging my arms across my chest. The wind teased my hair, gently now instead of the wild whipping it'd doled out when I was on the bike. Weird how I missed that already. I watched Wes turn the corner at the next block and felt something break inside me as his image faded into the night.

There weren't enough mochas in the world to drown this ache.

Chapter Fourteen

I'd dodged a bullet.

That was the mantra that kept playing in my head Friday morning at school as I went through the routine of attending classes, taking notes, and trying to scrounge up interest in my bland, undersalted lunch. Last night with Wes had been a war scene, and I'd emerged unscathed. Anything could have happened had I stayed on that motorcycle, and I didn't just mean physical injuries from a potential wreck. I had no business on that death machine, and as much as it pained me to admit it, I had no business with Wes. He was out of my head. Out of my heart. Done. Over.

Gone.

"I know that chicken isn't exactly appealing, but I promise it's already dead." Luke slid into the chair across from me in the cafeteria and grinned.

"Huh?" I stared at him, so lost in my thoughts I'd almost forgotten where I was. I shook my head to clear it, realizing for the first time I had been sitting completely alone. I normally ate with Marta, but she was out this afternoon for a dentist appointment.

Luke took a sip of milk from his carton and motioned to the fisted grip I had on my fork. I followed his gaze from my silverware to the multiple stab marks I'd made in the gravy-covered fowl on my tray and winced. "Busted."

"Bad day?" He started to cut into his own chicken then pushed it aside and went for his Jell-O cup. Smart man.

I twisted the lid off my bottled Coke. "No worse than others. But I think I'm paranoid."

"What about?" He spooned a scoop of red Jell-O into his mouth and looked at me as if he had nothing better to do than hear my conspiracy theories. Sort of a refreshing notion, after my conversation with Dad at breakfast had consisted of deep conversation such as "pass the pepper," "isn't that enough salt already?" and "here's your napkin." I guess that was partially my fault, though. I hadn't exactly tried to talk to Dad about Wes. What was I supposed to say? *Uh, remember the movie* Grease 2? *Just call me Cool Rider.* No thanks.

I fidgeted with the lid from my bottle. "Have people been talking about me?"

"You mean, more than usual?" Luke grinned.

"I'm serious. It mostly seems like people from Ms. Hawthorne's class. Earlier this morning I came up on two girls from English, and they shut up as soon as I got near. Then they walked away before I could even ask for a pen."

"*You* ran out of pens? Ms. Prepared?"

I narrowed my eyes. "I have pens. *They* ran out of ink. Quit avoiding my question."

"Since you insist, there has been some—how should I put it—general discontent about Ms. Hawthorne letting you off the homework hook yesterday." Luke shifted in his seat. "Not from me, of course."

"Of course." I rolled my eyes at him.

"Just seems odd since she came down so hard on Austin recently for the same thing—though that wasn't his first time to miss an assignment."

I nodded slowly, remembering Austin's indirect "teacher's pet" comment. Great. "So people think she's playing favorites with me?"

Luke shrugged. "It's high school, Addison. Everything has to be equal, or people get worked up whether they really care or not." He lifted his chin and lowered his lashes, taking on a mock regal form. "And trust me, I don't care because I do my homework." He sniffed. "Unlike others."

"Cut it out." I couldn't help but laugh. "It was one time. Maybe that's why Ms. Hawthorne gave me a break."

"Maybe." Luke looked quickly back down at his tray.

Too quickly. I frowned. "What are you not telling me?"

He all but whistled with fake innocence. "Nothing."

"This fork can stab your arm as easily as it did my chicken." I wiggled it in front of him. "Talk."

"Fine, but not because I'm scared of your cutlery." Luke leaned forward, bracing his arms on either side of his tray. His sandy-blond hair fell across his forehead. He looked over his shoulder then lowered his voice even though there didn't appear to be any fellow students within hearing distance. "I'll tell you because if these rumors were about me, I'd want to know."

My stomach tightened into a hard ball. "Rumors?" So I wasn't paranoid. I knew it. Of all the things I ever got to be right about, it had to be this. Perfect. No wonder I had been sitting alone when Luke came up.

"Word in the hallway is that your dad and Ms. Hawthorne looked pretty cozy during the open house the other week."

I laughed. "Is that all? That's ridiculous. They're old friends, catching up. Apparently they went to school together or something." I sat back, relieved. That was hardly noteworthy of being labeled a teacher's pet. I took a long sip of Coke.

126

Luke hesitated then slowly reached across the table and took my fork off my plate. What was he doing—?

"They were also seen 'catching up' at Got Beans last weekend."

I sprayed Coke across Luke's tray. "That's impossible."

He blinked at me and made a show of wiping his napkin across his damp forearms. "Then a modern miracle occurred because apparently several of Austin's buddies from our class went there to study together for that big test coming up and saw them laughing over some lattes."

"My dad would never go on a date and not tell me." But the words sounded hollow even to my own ears. I normally knew Dad's schedule better than I knew the U.S. states in alphabetical order, but with all the time I'd spent at school, after hours working on the talent-show preparations—or stalking Wes at Got Beans—it was actually very possible for him to have squeezed in a life without my knowing it.

But why the secrecy? My stomach turned. Dad would think nothing of having coffee with an old friend on the weekend, taking a much-needed break from sermon preparations. He'd done it before, though it was usually with a deacon. If this coffee date—no, not date, *meeting*—was not a big deal, then why didn't he mention it to me? Or did he just not mention it because it wasn't a big deal? My head swam, and I pushed my fingers against my temples.

"Just don't shoot the messenger, okay?" Luke handed my fork back.

I started to say something sarcastic then realized he was still dripping and slid some napkins his way. "Looks like you already bore the brunt of my surprise."

"Next time I have news, I'll bring an umbrella." He smiled, and when I didn't return it, he reached across the table and touched my hand. "You all right?"

I nodded then shook my head instead. Tears burned the back of my throat and I coughed, embarrassed at the sudden emotion. Even if Dad really did have coffee with Ms. Hawthorne, why did it bother me? She was my teacher, so yeah that sort of sucked, but it went deeper than that. Dad had never dated. I always figured it was because he kept my mom on such a pedestal—where she belonged.

Was she losing her place?

Luke's hand gently squeezed my fingers. "It was just coffee, Addison."

"I know." For now. I forced a smile at Luke, took in his steady, sympathetic eyes, his brow pinched in concern. I lowered my gaze and stared at the place where our hands met, wishing Luke's touch sent even half the shiver up my arm that Wes's did. Yet all the contact did was remind me how much Luke wasn't Wes.

The emotion built in my chest, and fresh tears crowded my eyes. Wes. My dad dating. It was too much. I pulled my hand away and stood so fast my chair tipped backward. "I've got to go." Now, before I cried in the middle of the cafeteria and gave everyone even more gossip for the ugly mill. I tossed my trash onto my tray, my vision blurring.

Luke held out his hand, the one I'd just let go of. "Stop, I've got it. Go on." He nodded his head toward the cafeteria door. His compassionate expression hinted that he understood I needed to be alone to process.

I nodded my thanks, still not trusting my voice, and bolted for the girls' room. Once again, Luke was my hero, the knight in shining armor coming to my rescue.

And all I could think about was the dark villain breaking my heart.

★ ★ ★

I recovered with only minor blotching from crying and breathed a long sigh of relief when the final bell of the day rang. At least now I could go home and avoid any more whispers or hints of rumors—both the real and the imagined.

Until I remembered there was a talent-show practice this afternoon, and I had promised Mrs. Lyons I'd be there to help. The poor woman was getting so frazzled about the show and the lack of seriousness the students were giving it that she'd started talking to herself. I caught her in the hallway yesterday muttering phrases like *lack of respect*, *bunch of monkeys*, and *the Bahamas*.

I trudged to the auditorium, dropped my backpack on the aisle seat in the front row, and grabbed my clipboard from Mrs. Lyons's outstretched hand. She had two pencils shoved in her hair, and her eyes were wide behind her glasses.

"The backdrop needs salvaging. Let's just say Tweedle Dee and Tweedle—I mean, the football players lost their painting privileges." Mrs. Lyons swiped her hair out of her face and pointed to the next item on the list in my hands. "Jessica's pianist has yet to show up for a practice, but she swears she's still on board. Try to confirm that for me. And Michael from the hip-hop dance group thinks that not changing socks between now and the night of the performance is going to make him 'lucky.' For everyone's sake, can you try to change his mind?"

I flinched. "Uh, sure."

"You're an angel." Mrs. Lyons flitted back to her seat.

I'm glad she didn't see the face I made. Angels probably felt a little more compassionate and cherubic than I did at the moment, but then again, how many angels were in charge of sweaty footwear? I'd read the entire Bible (usually once a year to please my dad) and that wasn't anywhere in their job descriptions that I'd ever found.

I stared at my list, debating which item to check off first. Michael would be last, that was for sure. Looked like Jessica would be the less evil option. I waited, listening, and sure enough heard her practicing from stage left even though it wasn't her turn yet. I made my way up the stairs, ducked behind the curtain, and pasted on a smile that hopefully looked more sincere than it felt.

She stopped midchorus. "What?"

"Mrs. Lyons is a little worried about your piano player. Is she definitely going to make it?" I hovered my pen over my list, trying to appear professional. Jessica just looked bummed I didn't compliment her on her song.

"She's been sick lately. She'll be here for our next rehearsal." Jessica flapped the sheet music in her hand and turned hopeful eyes on me. "Do you want to hear me practice this next verse? I'm totally not good singing a cappella."

Tapping my clipboard with my pencil, I shook my head. "Sorry, long to-do list." I left out the fact that I'd hear her anyway. I headed for the production room behind the stage, where we'd painted and stored the backdrop, hoping that "salvage" was an overly dramatic term. Mrs. Lyons was the drama teacher, after all, so maybe it wasn't as bad as she'd implied.

On my way, I passed the closed door to the single-stall bathroom and stopped at the sound of retching. Someone was sick. I hesitated and then tapped twice on the door. "Everything okay in there?" Ew. I hoped they'd say yes. I didn't know what I wanted to major in when I got to college, but nursing was definitely last on the list.

Water ran in the sink, and then the door opened. Claire stood framed inside, drying her hands on a paper towel. "Do you always check on people when they have to pee?"

"It sounded like you were puking up your guts." A distinctive odor drifted from behind her, proving my point. "Claire, you can't deny that smell."

"I didn't deny it. I had a bad lunch, that's all. Food poisoning." She tossed the towel in the trash and grabbed the can of air freshener on the counter by the sink. With liberal sprays, the smell morphed into a field of flowers.

By a garbage dump.

"Whatever. Sorry I cared." Too bad the posters for the show were already hung. Otherwise someone's name might have gotten left off the list. I turned to leave.

"No problem." Claire loudly cleared her throat. "And by the way, next time your dad goes out with Ms. Hawthorne, get him to tell her Austin needs an A on his next quiz. For the football team, you understand." She smirked and sauntered away before I could reply.

Not that there was anything I could say.

Chapter Fifteen

I let the front door slam and didn't feel even an ounce of remorse. "Dad!" I hollered up the stairs before realizing he sat at the kitchen table with his Bible and a variety of commentaries. Nice. Hard to play the angst-driven, angered teen when confronted with a Bible. I stopped in the middle of the entryway, unsure how to proceed.

"Something on your mind?" Hearing his rare use of dry wit almost made me change my mind. But I slid into the chair he scooted out for me, averting my gaze from the Bible. Preacher or not, he was still my dad.

And he was dating my teacher.

My temper flared again. "Is there anything you'd like to tell me?"

His eyebrow rose—just one, which is where I'd learned the trick. "I'm assuming so, from your tone. But I don't know what it is."

"Think hard." I crossed my arms over my chest and waited.

"Did you get a haircut?" His eyes flitted over my hair, which was the same as always.

My hands fell to my lap in surrender. "Do you really think I'd stomp in the house yelling because you didn't notice my haircut?"

"It looks nice."

I slumped forward until my head hit the table. Good grief. I couldn't even act like a normal, hormonal teenager without feeling sorry for my clueless father. My anger subsided, and I rolled my head sideways and peered at him from under my curtain of hair. Come to think of it, it probably did need a trim. "It's not about my hair, Dad."

"Then can you please point it out for me? I have a lot of studying to get done tonight." He tapped his books. "The sermon Sunday is on Job. I'll probably be up for a while."

"Why don't you get some coffee at Got Beans, then?" I held my breath.

A shadow passed over his face then disappeared. "I don't need caffeine this late." He squinted at me. "You're still limiting your pop intake, aren't you?"

"As much as you're limiting your carbs."

"You're a growing teenager—you don't need a lot of caffeine at your age."

I sat up straight. "Tell me this. Did you *need* caffeine when you took my teacher for lattes?"

He slowly closed the Bible in front of him, understanding dawning in his expression. "So that's what this is about."

Frustration washed over me in a wave. "No, Dad, it's about the fact that everyone at school thinks Ms. Hawthorne is playing favorites with me because you're dating her." My voice rose, and I struggled to tamp it down despite the emotion once again clogging my throat. "I work hard for my grades, and the one time I don't finish a homework assignment—the one time in my entire life—I get away with it. But not because I'm a good student, oh no. It's because I'm suddenly the teacher's pet." I took my first breath in a full minute before continuing my rant. "And you know the worst part? I had to hear about it from Luke!"

Dad bristled. "Who's Luke? Not your boyfriend." It wasn't a question so much as a statement. Great, *now* Dad wanted to get involved in my life? After years of living through silent meals, passing each other on the way to the bathroom, and helping him lint-brush his suit jacket every Sunday? I played by the rules, to a fault, and his even remotely thinking that I didn't made me want to throw them all out the front door.

"No, Luke is not my boyfriend." And neither was Wes, thanks to Dad and my overly worked conscience. I gritted my teeth. "He's just a guy in my English class, and that's so not the point." I swallowed hard. "Why didn't you tell me?"

"There's nothing to tell, Addison." He let out a weary sigh, and for the first time in a while I noticed how drawn his face seemed, how slumped his shoulders were. Was that gray hair on his temples new?

"I don't know what this Luke person told you, but I am not dating Ms. Hawthorne." He ran his hand down the length of his face. "Yet."

I bolted upright, a wave of heat flushing my throat. "Yet?" No, no, no.

"I ran into Kathy at Got Beans last weekend when I went to study my sermon notes. We started chatting, and I invited her to sit with me. We had a lovely discussion." Dad traced the worn letters of his name on the cover of his King James. "I'd like to do it again."

What about Mom? But my voice refused to ask that question out loud. I pressed my lips together, trying to find the right way to speak my mind—and not cry. "If you're ready to date, Dad, I can try to support that." The words tasted funny in my mouth. "But why Ms. Hawthorne? Just because you knew her a long time ago doesn't mean she's the only woman out there. Why not someone from church?"

Dad just shook his head, and even I saw the dangers of that scenario. Dating a church member would be like someone dating their boss or counselor. Typically not a good idea.

"It's not like I'm suddenly flinging myself on the dating train, Addison." Dad scooted his books aside so he could brace his arms on the table. He held my gaze steady with his. "I don't want to date just anyone. Kathy and I. . ." He looked down then back at me. "When you came home from school several weeks ago and told me your English teacher was Kathy Hawthorne, I wasn't sure if it was the same woman I knew before. I went to your open house hoping it was, and also hoping it wasn't."

I frowned. "Dad, that doesn't make sense."

He exhaled loudly. "Kathy and I dated in high school. You might say we were high school sweethearts."

My stomach dropped. *Oh.* That made sense.

And made my life a whole lot more complicated.

"We considered getting engaged after graduation, but our parents discouraged it. We were so young." Dad slowly shook his head, his eyes lost in the past as he stared somewhere over my shoulder. "We went to different colleges, and I met your mother, and well, you know the rest." He lifted one weary shoulder in a half shrug. "I never thought Kathy would end up back in Crooked Hollow."

As my teacher. I wanted to tattoo that on his forehead, but I had the distinct impression it honestly didn't matter. Dad might get along with the youth group at church, but he wasn't exactly up to date on how the teenage world operated. I might as well paint a giant red target on my chest and pass out arrows.

"Is this all right with you?"

I started to shake my head, started to say, *Of course it's not—are you crazy?* But as I watched my Dad's hopeful expression and the way he held his breath at my answer, I knew anything other than yes would be the most selfish thing I'd ever done.

So once again, I folded my hands in my lap, pasted on a smile, and did what every self-surviving PK learned to do from day one.

Lie.

★ ★ ★

"I heard you needed an artist, little lady."

I looked up from my clipboard of assignments as Luke swaggered across the production room toward me. He had paintbrushes tucked into the waistband of his jeans, his voice dramatically deep. "Just point me to the nearest watering hole, and I'll get these here brushes ready." He tipped an imaginary hat. "That is, unless you'd like to come riding with me." He shot me an exaggerated, corny wink.

Shaking my head, I laughed. If Luke knew how many times I'd thought of him lately as my hero, he'd swagger for real. The past almost two weeks had flown by, what with my being so busy with talent-show prep and pretending I didn't care that Wes had left me on the street corner in my pj's. Not to mention the tiny task of adapting to the thought of my dad dating. Ugh.

I shook off the image. "Unless you have a stick horse tucked away in the wings, cowboy, fat chance." I gently pushed him toward the giant backdrop. Unfortunately, Mrs. Lyons hadn't been exaggerating when she said it needed to be salvaged. "See those blobs at the top?"

Luke squinted up at the backdrop, his performance over. "Sort of."

"Yeah, those are supposed to be stars."

"Oh, wow."

"Exactly." I sighed. "And these stick things over here are supposed to be trees, and Mrs. Lyons wanted this middle space

swirled to look like fog. You know, for the theme of the show—
'A Night with the Stars.' "

"Clever."

I watched his expression as he glanced back at the sorry
excuses for stars the football players had painted. "Still feeling
confident, cowpoke?"

Luke scratched his head. "Um. Yes?"

"Very funny. Now get to work. Call me when it looks like it's
supposed to."

"Just so you know, I charge extra for every sarcastic
comment."

"Put it on my tab." I swept past him toward the stage
entrance, wishing I could stay and joke around. But that would
mean no one would be around to call the newspaper to find
out why our ad didn't run, explain to the dance team why they
couldn't use explicit lyrics during their performance, or bring
Mrs. Lyons water to take with her anxiety meds.

I'd given up on Michael and his socks and invested in nose
plugs instead.

"Need some help?" Marta appeared before me, dropping
her backpack on a chair away from the paint-splattered canvas.

"You're here!" I actually hugged her. Between her
appointments and shopping dates with her host mom lately, I
felt like I hadn't seen her in forever.

Luke fake-pouted across the room. "Hey, I didn't get that
same kind of greeting."

"Marta didn't pretend to be a cowboy," I shot back.

She frowned as she pulled away from me. "Did I miss
something?" Then she shook her head. "Never mind. I don't
want to know. Sorry I missed the last practice. I know I told you
I'd help, but my host mom is on a rampage." She lifted her shirt
an inch above her jeans. "Like my new belt?"

It was turquoise and covered in rhinestones. I bit my lip. "I do if you do."

"Doch! Don't pretend. It's awful." She giggled. "That's why I didn't tuck my blouse in."

"Trust me, that belt is punishment enough, so I won't yell at you for being absent lately." I showed her my clipboard. "Item one, two, or three?"

She wrinkled her pert nose. "Those are my choices?"

"Welcome to the world of drama. And need I remind you, you talked me into this." I tilted my head to one side. "You know, you could always just take over for me since you were the one so gung-ho about this fund-raiser from the beginning."

Marta's lips twisted to the side. "I don't know what 'gung ho' means, but I know what 'take over' means, so I'm just going to choose item number one."

"Good girl. Have fun." I ripped the paper with the phone number she needed off the board and handed it to her. Now for the dance team.

I found Tripp Larson and some other guys practicing some break-dancing moves in the corner while they waited for their turn onstage. I hesitated to interrupt, not wanting them to snap a bone because of me. "Hey, guys?" The music coming from the portable stereo on the floor clarified the importance of my mission. I cringed. "Tripp? Guys!"

"Addison, the stage props are finally finished." Mrs. Lyons rushed over to me, which was fine since the dance team hadn't so much as even looked up yet. "Would you get some of the boys to move them to the storage closet?"

"The two trees?" Mrs. Lyons had wanted cutout trees built and painted to stand in front of the backdrop onstage, for a "three-dimensional look," as she'd put it. Frankly I thought the whole thing was overkill and wasn't sure why we were using a forest in the first place, though I guess it did go nicely with the stars. "Sure, I'll get them moved."

"You're a doll." She beamed.

I just nodded. "No problem." So far, according to Mrs. Lyons, I'd been an angel, a doll, a sweetie pie, and a blessing in disguise.

Not sure why she'd added the disguise part, but oh well.

"Oh, and someone is sick in the bathroom. Would you check on them?" She rushed off before I could morph from doll into Chucky Doll. Again? Why was the offstage bathroom the "get sick" room of choice for this school? I made my way toward the shut door and tapped twice. Claire opened it from the inside. I reeled back. Talk about déjà vu. "Let me guess. More food poisoning?"

She shrugged, but her face waxed pale. "Think what you want."

I grabbed Claire's arm and tugged her into the hallway, away from the sick smell. "I think you're throwing up on purpose. Are you?"

She shrugged again.

"Claire, that's dangerous. Why would you do that? You're what, a size four?" I jabbed at her skinny waist. "Don't be stupid."

She lifted her chin. "I need to be a size two for the show."

"That's ridiculous, Claire. They're *your* clothes. Just let the seams out."

"Like you'd ever understand." She started to walk away, but I snagged the back of her shirt.

"Then enlighten me, before I go tell Mrs. Lyons that it's you who keeps getting sick in the bathroom. Trust me, if anyone has the right to throw up around here, it's me after dealing with Michael and his stupid lucky socks."

Confusion pinched her bland expression. "Who?"

"Forget it. Just tell me why you think losing weight—especially this way—matters so much."

Claire crossed her arms over her sparkly pink top. "It's the fastest way I know how."

"Um, not eating cheese fries in the cafeteria might help, too."

"Whatever." She rolled her eyes. "This is easier."

"And gross. Not to mention dangerous."

"You said that already."

"Then believe me. What is this really about, Claire?" I clutched my clipboard in front of my chest, wishing I could use it to beat some sense into her. Crash diets were one thing, but bulimia? Crazy.

"We're not even friends anymore. Why do you care?"

I softened at the hardness in her eyes. "Not being friends was your choice. But I still don't want you to hurt yourself."

"How noble. This is your fault anyway."

I reared back. "How is you shoving your finger down your throat my fault, exactly?"

"Austin." Claire's face twisted into a pout. "If you would have just dated him when he wanted to, he'd have moved on by now and wouldn't be ignoring me to chase after you. But you just had to dis him. Now he's obsessed."

"Dis him? What is this, a reality show?" I briefly closed my eyes. The entire school was going crazy. We didn't need a theater department—there was plenty of drama right here offstage. "I don't like Austin. Never have, never will. I still don't see how that makes your eating disorder my fault."

"Simple. I have to work harder to get his attention now because of you." Claire ran her hands over the front of her flat stomach.

"Right, because puking on purpose is so very attractive."

"I just need to look my best on the stage that night, all right? It's the only way I can think of to get him to finally notice me. If I think that means losing five pounds immediately, then why do you care? Just leave me alone. I'll quit after the show." She glared at me. "And don't even think about telling Mrs. Lyons. She'll have me bonding with the school counselor, and rumors about me needing counseling are the last thing I need right now."

"Oh, like rumors about my dad and my English teacher are on my Christmas list?"

We stared at each other, anger sparking between us until Claire slowly wilted. "You're right. I shouldn't have made that worse." She paused. "So are you going to tell on me?"

I hesitated, her apology throwing me off guard. The show was in less than a month. Surely she couldn't do any permanent damage to her body in that time. Besides, Mrs. Lyons didn't need any extra headaches, and this show didn't need any bad publicity. Not that Claire's eating disorders would make the newspapers, but in a small town, people talked. And if word got out that something like this had come up because of a school production, the show would suffer. Funds would suffer. The Let Them Read Foundation would suffer.

"Fine." I sighed. "But if I catch you doing this one more time after the show is over, I'm going straight to Principal Stephens. Or your mom." I shuddered, not sure which would be worse.

"I promise." Claire backed away, her eyes averted. "And, uh. Thanks."

"You're welcome." I watched her go, a mixture of anger, frustration, and regret swirling in my stomach. Anger at her choices, frustration over her pathetic reasons, and regret over the way a lifelong friendship had turned out. Maybe sharing this secret would make things better between us.

Or at least keep her quiet about my dad.

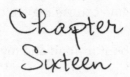
Chapter Sixteen

There was a rose in my mailbox.

I backed up a few feet away from the box and peered cautiously inside, as if the red petals would explode on contact. I'd never gotten flowers before. Somehow I expected my first flowers to accompany a bouquet of balloons or lie in a beautiful basket of greenery—not on top of the latest copy of *Seventeen* magazine and the electric bill.

I instinctively looked over my shoulder, but of course no one was there. Besides, who did I think it was from? Mrs. Kilgore and her PK spy camera? Doubtful. Speaking of spies, I decided I better handle the flower invasion privately before it became official church business.

Careful of the thorns, I plucked the mail and the rose from the box and shut the lid like any other Wednesday afternoon. I casually flipped through the mail as I strolled up the driveway to the house, though I was really checking out the small white envelope pinned through the stem of the rose. JILLIAN'S FLOWERS & GIFTS was embossed across the paper. A store-bought rose—in a mailbox? Obviously whoever sent it was someone who wanted to do something nice but couldn't afford a full bouquet and delivery charges.

Someone who sounded a lot like unemployed Wes.

My stomach cramped, and excitement bubbled in my chest before I could tamp it down. Maybe he was apologizing for riding away and leaving me on the street that Thursday night. Had it already been two weeks? I'd avoided Got Beans like I was allergic to mochas, which only served as double punishment. No Wes sightings, *and* no liquid caffeine. But I couldn't handle running into him, couldn't stand near him after all that had passed between us and pretend like it was all okay, like my heart didn't still have more cracks in it than the sidewalk in front of Screamin' Cones.

Once inside the house, I dropped the mail on the table and ripped open the envelope. My thoughts raced in competition with my heartbeat, and I gave myself a paper cut. I paused to suck my ring finger then shook off the irritating pain and yanked the little card free of the envelope.

> *Dear Addison,*
>
> *Thought you could use a little color in your life with all the stress of the talent show lately. You're doing a great job. Let me know if you need me to confiscate more paintbrushes from football players.*
>
> *Sincerely,*
> *Luke (aka Your Favorite Artist)*

The envelope fluttered slowly to the floor, and I stared down at the rose, its deep red not nearly as vibrant as it'd seemed outside. Sweet gesture, but not from the guy I wanted it to be from. I should have known, though. Wes would be more likely to send a coupon for a discounted tattoo than a single red rose. Why had I even hoped?

I reread the message and smiled. Typical Luke. The perfect

combination of sincerity and humor—with a dash of romance. If I didn't know better, I'd swear the boy read romance novels on a regular basis. Guys his age just didn't believe in chivalry and earning a girl's heart anymore. Instead they overdosed on hair gel and protein shakes and expected us to swoon while they flexed and talked back to teachers as if attitude equaled attractiveness. No, Luke was a rare breed for sure.

But he still wasn't Wes.

I brushed my finger across the soft petals, wondering where this left my growing friendship with Luke. Ignoring his gesture and continuing on with our teasing, half-flirty way of interacting felt wrong. But confronting him and telling him I only considered him a friend felt really aggressive.

Lifting the rose to my face, I inhaled the spicy-sweet scent. *Oh, Luke*. Why couldn't it have been a white rose? Or yellow? Any color other than the in-your-face-I-like-you shade of red that practically bled hope across my kitchen table. I hated to dash his dreams with a big ol' dose of reality.

I knew all too well how it felt.

I stood, tossed the envelope in the trash, and hurried up the stairs to stash the card in my desk drawer with other keepsakes. It seemed wrong to throw it away after he went to so much effort. I dropped the rose on my nightstand and realized the petals had reddened my fingers. Now it was obvious I'd received it. Man, I really hated to risk losing our friendship over something like this. Luke made me laugh. Made me relax. Made me believe not all boys were scum.

But he did it in such a brotherly kind of way.

I stared at the rose, which seemed to be staring back at me, and groaned. Maybe I could just play it off. Take Luke's lead at school tomorrow and see if he talked about it. If he didn't, I would be off the hook, and we could continue as usual—joking, insulting, being friends.

If he did, well, then to make it up to him, I'd have to start a mission to find Luke a woman more wonderful than myself. One more open to a relationship.

I rubbed my red-tinged fingers together in a vain effort to remove the stain. One whose heart didn't bleed hope for another.

★ ★ ★

Enough was enough. If I didn't get a mocha soon, I'd self-destruct. I strode inside Got Beans with my head up, my shoulders back, and my coffee money rubbing a hole in my jeans pocket, begging to be free. I'd just get it to go—that way if Wes was there, I could slip out before he saw me. If he wasn't there, well, I knew better than to sit around and wait. Besides, Dad was at church again, and I didn't want to remember the last time I'd run into Wes on a Wednesday night. My stomach shivered thinking about it. *Black and white. . .rules. . .would it even matter. . .*

Bert blinked twice at me as I walked up to the counter, like I was a mirage. "About time you came back. You get lost?" He laughed at his sorry excuse for a joke as he got to work on my mocha.

"Have you ever considered getting another employee?" My eyes strained to look toward the piano, but I refused. Besides, I didn't hear music other than the faint strains of Aerosmith floating over the speakers, so obviously Wes wasn't playing. "If you didn't work so much, you wouldn't know to miss me."

Bert shrugged as he heaped my mocha with a generous dollop of sprinkles. "If I didn't work here, then I'd be stuck at home with the little lady."

"I heard that," his wife bellowed from the depths of the storage room. Bert grinned and handed me my hot mocha. It smelled so good I tipped him an extra dollar and made my way outside.

The stars were just beginning to prick the night sky. I took a careful sip then tilted my head back to enjoy the view as I strolled down the deserted street. At least there was one good thing about living in a small town—I didn't have to fear walking home alone nearly as much as most girls my age would. There was hardly anyone out this time of—

I collided hard with someone, hot mocha sloshing out of the lid onto my wrist. "Ow!"

"Watch where you're going!" was the angry retort. Male retort. A strong hand gripped my arm. My heart racing frantically, I reared back to launch my only weapon at my attacker—good-bye sweet liquid caffeine—when I realized the hand on my sweatshirt sleeve was attached to Wes.

"Wes?" I lowered my coffee, and he lowered the free hand he'd thrown up for protection from my attempted scalding.

He let go. "Coffee shouldn't be a weapon, PK." He adjusted the collar of his leather jacket and cracked his neck to the side. I couldn't help but appreciate how I'd obviously caught him off guard.

But my elation was short lived at the throbbing of my wrist. I sucked in my breath as I studied the red mark. "Wow, that hurts."

Wes stepped closer and angled my palm toward the streetlight to get a better view. "You need some burn cream on that, or it'll blister up. Come on, my house is closer than yours." He took my elbow and began tugging me down the street.

My mouth opened. Me, in Wes's house? I pulled back. "I'm fine, really."

He stopped. "You want a scar?"

"No."

146

"Then come on." He started walking, not touching me this time, just expecting me to follow. I hesitated. *Not a good idea, Addison. Not a good idea.* But the pain in my wrist was inching toward unbearable. Besides, it might be interesting to see how people lived on the dark side.

I took a sip of mocha for fortification then hurried after Wes. The brisk walk to his house only took a few minutes, but the fiery ache on my hand made the journey feel endless. Wes didn't say much, just unlocked the front door to a split-level house a lot like mine, and let us inside. He didn't holler a warning to his father, and I hoped Mr. Keegan wasn't the type who enjoyed walking around naked.

I kept my eyes partially closed just in case as Wes led me through a living room strewn with coffee cups, paper plates, an open pizza box with half a slice left inside, and several newspapers, down a carpeted hallway and into a bathroom that was surprisingly white and clean. The faint hint of air freshener hung in the air, but this scent was pleasant, unlike Claire's last attempt with wildflowers in the drama room. I sniffed. Vanilla. It made me remember the mocha in my hand, and I set it beside the sink.

Wes opened the medicine cabinet. "Sit." He pointed to the closed toilet lid.

"A little stingy with the words tonight, aren't we?" I couldn't help the sarcasm; it had built in my chest with every angry throb of the burn, every memory that stoked my senses on our rushed walk to his house. His hinting about a date, his showing up with his motorcycle, leaving me in the street after I chickened out.

"What's there to say?" He rattled through the jars and bottles lining the shelves.

I plopped down on the seat. "An apology, maybe?"

"For what? Taking care of your injury?" He plucked a tube from the array of medicines.

"You know what I mean."

Wes exhaled, pausing momentarily in his search to cast an impatient glance at the ceiling. "You wanted off the bike. You got off the bike. End of story."

Chapter one, maybe. This was far from over, and Wes knew it as much as I did. Stupid boy just didn't want to admit it. An entire week had passed, and I'd been unable to convince myself of the same. The question was, how would it actually end?

He shut the cabinet, annoyance creeping into his tone. "I'd have to apologize if I had ignored your endless pounding on my back and kept driving."

Aha. "So you admit you wanted to?"

"I didn't say that."

"You implied it. Like you imply a lot of things."

He silenced me with a look as he sat on the edge of the tub in front of me, our knees brushing. He pushed up the sleeve of my sweatshirt then wiggled the tiny tube of cream in my face. "This might hurt a little."

It hurt worse than he knew, but not so much my wrist. More like the potential. The almost. The what-would-have-beens—they all throbbed much worse than my burn.

Then the reality of his touch on my injury jolted my brain, and I sucked in my breath as the medicine made contact with my jilted nerves.

He screwed the lid back onto the cream. "Told you so."

Not in so many words, but yeah, he'd warned me about himself. So had my father, indirectly. Even I had known not to fall for him.

And yet the sting continued.

Tears welled in my eyes, and I hoped he assumed it was just

from the pain on my hand. "Wes, I—"

"Shh." He picked up my wrist, held it up to his lips, and gently blew. The cool air immediately soothed the burn, but his proximity and compassion did little to ease the ache in my heart. I wanted angry Wes, sarcastic Wes, brooding Wes. The Wes that made me more frustrated than love struck. That Wes I could handle. This sweet guy in front of me was about to be my undoing.

He pressed his lips against my wrist, an inch above the burn, his dark, steady gaze never leaving mine. "That better?"

I couldn't breathe, much less answer. I nodded, searching his expression. We stared at each other, the only sounds my ragged breathing and the steady drip of water in the bathroom sink.

He abruptly released my arm and stood, raking his fingers through his hair and half pivoting away from me. "Dang it, Addison." He turned to face me, his expression a narrow-eyed mixture of grief and surprise. "This is what I didn't want."

"What? Me dumping hot coffee on myself?"

"No." He waved one hand in the air as if my clumsiness didn't surprise him anymore. Too bad he hadn't seen me fall out of my chair in English. Then he'd be convinced. "This. You."

"You didn't want me?" This conversation was starting to hurt worse than my burn. "I sort of figured that out by now, Wes, but thanks for clearing things up. Here, you want to dump some salt on this while you're at it?" I shoved my upturned wrist toward him.

Gently, he reeled me toward him. My breath caught as he pulled me close and tilted my chin. Our gazes locked. "Exactly the opposite." Then he leaned down and kissed me.

My head whirled. I closed my eyes, breathing in the scent of leather and spice and vanilla air freshener. I always thought the heroines in romance novels were pretty ridiculous to have weak knees during such a moment, but I now had a completely new understanding and respect for them. In fact, I'm shocked I kept standing at all. I kissed him back, my thoughts racing almost as fast as my thumping heartbeat.

If my first rose came in a mailbox, it sort of figured my first kiss happened in a bathroom.

Wes pulled away first. "Go out with me."

"We tried that already." I clutched his jacket sleeve with one hand, still feeling off balance. "Remember? Endless pounding?"

"I mean on a date."

"You said you didn't date."

Wes let me go, taking a step back and releasing a long sigh. "I know what I said, PK. This is me changing my mind."

He looked surprisingly vulnerable, standing by a green striped shower curtain with his hands in his pockets, his expression sincere. I tried to think logically and not factor in how my lips still tingled from his kiss. Wes. And me. On a date. A real date. I shook my head, trying to fathom the image of Wes picking me up, taking me to dinner—

Picking me up. My dad. There'd be no way he'd agree to this. What was I supposed to say? *Please, Daddy, he kisses really good?* Not. Happening. Besides the fact that a date with Wes would only be a setup for more heartbreak on my part. I'd rather throw a hot mocha in my own face than have my heart stomped on by a certain pair of black boots again. Dating Wes would be a recipe for disaster, in more ways than one.

I looked at Wes, who remained stoic, still, waiting for my response, and drew in a deep breath for courage. Then I said the only thing I could.

"Okay."

Chapter Seventeen

If I hadn't been reliving Wes's kiss while choosing apples at Crooked Hollow Grocery, I probably would have remembered to pick them from the top of the arrangement instead of the bottom.

I grabbed the fruit rolling around at my feet and winced as a third apple disappeared under the cake display. Hopefully no one had noticed—but no. I looked up and saw two grandmas, a bag boy, a toddler, and my dad staring right at me, mouths agape. I considered bowing, but figured by the bag boy's scowl that probably wasn't a good idea. Instead I delivered the apples quickly to their now-toppled display.

"You missed the one that dropped in the bin of potatoes." Dad pointed, obviously feeling that standing guard next to our shopping cart was more important than helping me rescue the victimized apples. I quickly gathered the last remainders of runaway fruit and joined Dad at our cart. Hopefully the next several people that purchased apples would wash them well before eating.

"What in the world happened there?" Dad scratched the back of his neck.

"Avalanche?" I couldn't exactly confess the truth. Even now my lips tingled at the memory of Wes's kiss, and I quickly pressed them together. "Come on, let's just keep going. Next on the list is milk."

My thoughts raced faster than the apples had rolled as I followed Dad away from the scene of the crime. Somehow I had to find a way to either convince my father to let me go out with Wes, or even more unlikely, convince myself not to care about blatantly breaking the rules for once in my life. One thing was certain: I refused to miss out on my date. Something—or someone—had to give.

"Oh no, step away from the Little Debbies." I snagged Dad's sleeve and tugged him away from the enticing display set up at the end of the bread aisle. "This is why I knew you shouldn't come here alone." Though maybe I was the one who shouldn't be allowed to come while distracted. I looked over my shoulder toward the produce section, but thankfully it appeared that business was now as usual.

"What do you mean? I come here alone all the time." Dad cast a longing glance at the miniature chocolate cupcakes before following me to the dairy section.

I stopped in front of the selection of butter and milk. "Right, and the healthiest thing you come home with is a can of reduced-fat cinnamon rolls."

"Well regardless of how much you trust my shopping skills, at least we're spending time together. Kind of like a father-daughter date." Dad looked as uncomfortable saying those words as I felt hearing them. He coughed and tried to look interested in the rows of refrigerated biscuits.

Spending time together? What was with the sudden urge to bond? Hadn't he avoided that these past sixteen years? A little late now. I shook my head. "No, we're grocery shopping, and I'm here so you will buy something that's not a straight carb. Look in the buggy, Dad." I pointed to the goods inside our cart.

"Wonder bread. Pasta shells. Cheez-Its. You need to eat food that has color sometimes."

"The Cheez-Its are orange."

His logic and his defensive tone sounded so much like mine I just stared at him. How many fun times had we lost over the years because of living separate lives? How many grocery outings and laughs had we skipped because we always just did it by ourselves, whoever had the most time that particular week?

How many experiences did I miss out on because he'd rather be known as Pastor than Father?

Dad bent to restack some fallen items inside our cart. "Besides, I needed to tell you something."

"Right, because everyone knows there's no better place to have a heart-to-heart than next to the dairy case, debating one percent versus two percent milk." I snagged a gallon of one percent, biting back the bitterness creeping up my throat.

Dad chucked a tub of butter into the cart, and I quickly traded it for a reduced-fat version of the same brand. He started pushing the cart. "It's nothing huge. I just wanted to let you know that I'm taking Kathy on a date tomorrow night."

My breath stuck in my throat, and I stopped in the middle of the aisle. Now that the rumors at school had finally died down—partially thanks to my semitruce with Claire after catching her in the bathroom at school—he was going to parade their relationship throughout Crooked Hollow. That would be all the juice the gossip mill would need to run full speed again.

"Is this going to be a problem?"

Dad's voice started my feet moving again, and I quickstepped to keep up with him. He shot me a sidelong glance as he navigated the cart down the row of toiletries. "You said you were supportive of the idea."

I also once said I'd never buy country music, yet Dierks Bentley and Carrie Underwood both lived inside my iPod. "I said I was supportive of you dating." That was true, even though it felt like the words had shredded my lips on their way out.

"But not about dating Kathy?" Dad stopped the cart and frowned at me. I tried to frown back, but it was hard to maintain the seriousness of the moment when Dad had stopped directly in front of the tampons.

"Pastor Blakely!"

My head swiveled to the left as a warm male voice called from down the aisle. Mr. Keegan smiled as he ambled toward us, a full grocery basket dangling from one hand. Uh-oh. I swallowed hard, all urges to laugh completely erased. Did he know I'd been at his house last night? The burn on my wrist, tucked discreetly under a bandage, throbbed in sympathy. I mentally begged Mr. Keegan to keep walking, but he bent to rearrange the contents in his basket—probably adjusting the weight—then stopped directly beside our cart.

"Good to see you." Dad shook his hand then gestured to me. "You've met Addison at church, I'm sure."

Mr. Keegan nodded. "We certainly have." He smiled at me, eyes slightly glazed over as if he'd stayed up late—maybe worrying about his son and me? "I wanted to thank you for taking my request seriously about getting to know Wes. He mentioned you came by the house last night. Something about a burn on your hand?"

Dad's eyes widened, and his face reddened. I spoke quickly. "It's fine. Just needed some cream and a bandage." Funny how Wes suddenly decided to get chatty with his father. *Did he also tell you he kissed me beside your guest bath toilet? And oh yeah, you need a new lightbulb above the sink.*

"I'm glad it's okay. I'm sorry I missed seeing you." Mr.

Keegan shifted his full grocery basket to his other arm.

"You were at the Keegans' last night?" Dad's voice sounded like a cat had jumped down his throat and attempted to strangle him. "With Wes? Alone?"

"Dad, it wasn't like that. I went to get a mocha from Got Beans and burned my hand on my coffee. Wes happened to be outside and wanted to help—that's all." I could feel a flush rising up my chest and knew once the telltale red reached my cheeks, my credibility would be shot.

Dad's eyes went from wide to narrowed slits. "I see."

No, he didn't. But that wasn't the point at the moment. Mr. Keegan darted a look from me to Dad and back again. "Anyway, thanks again, Addison, for all your help. I know it's not easy being a friend to Wes."

It was actually a lot easier than he knew. But I smiled, fighting back my blush. "No problem."

"See you both Sunday." Mr. Keegan lifted his free hand in a wave and headed back the way he'd come, seemingly completely unaware of the bomb he'd just dropped at my feet.

Dad managed to wait until Mr. Keegan cleared the end of the row before leveling a Look at me. I'd only gotten the Look twice before in my entire life. Once, when I was nine and let the neighborhood dog inside our house for a bath and ended up soaping the entire hallway. The second time was when I was twelve and missed curfew by three hours because of losing myself in a book at the public library. Dad had called the police, and I remembered their laughs now as I rushed up the walkway to the front door. *"We've got kids across town pushing drugs, and he's worried because his little girl is studying too hard."*

I cleared my throat, deciding it would be wise to speak first. "Mr. Keegan asked me at church a few weeks back to make friends with Wes. He's worried about him and thinks I'd be a good influence." Odd how the image Wes painted of his dad and the Mr. Keegan I knew at church seemed composed by two different artists. But that was a thought to ponder another time—like when Dad's eyes weren't shooting sparks. I quickly continued. "So, I ran into Wes a few times at Got Beans, and we started talking."

"Talking? Do you mean the literal term of *talking* as in having a conversation, or *talking* as in the weird dating language you teenagers have today?" Dad crossed his arms over his polo.

"The first one." Which was true. Dad didn't ask me if I'd kissed him, and I wasn't about to volunteer that information. But if I had any hopes of going on a real date with Wes, my one opening loomed before me. It was probably the smallest window I'd ever seen, but it was there, and I had to try.

I took a deep breath. "But now that you mention it, Wes has hinted around about wanting to ask me out." Better to ease Dad into the idea than blurt out that Wes already had. "You know, one day. In the future."

Dad lifted one eyebrow, and I had the uncanny urge to raise mine back. "And?"

"And. . .I'd like to go." A glimmer of an idea blazed across my mind, a flash of hope as quick as a lightning bug on a summer night. I schooled my tone back to a disinterested drawl. "Sort of how you'd like to go out with Ms. Hawthorne." I risked a peek at him from under my lowered lashes.

Dad stared at me, and I couldn't help but wonder if he respected my crafty train of thought or just wanted to ground me for life for even implying such a bargain out loud. Probably both.

We stood in a silent stare down as shoppers brushed past us. A woman plucked a box of tampons from behind Dad's right shoulder, yet he never blinked. I could almost see the wheels turning in his head, could sense him weighing his desire to go out with Ms. Hawthorne against his desire to keep me eternally eleven years old and horse crazy instead of boy crazy.

His shoulders slumped slightly. "Okay."

"Okay?" I hadn't meant to sound so surprised, but shocked was an understatement.

Dad tilted his head to one side. "On one condition."

"Fair enough." My heart raced. What condition? That I wear a chastity belt? Polish my promise ring? Never shave my legs again?

"It has to be a double date. I don't trust him alone with you." He rubbed his fingers down the length of his face. "Any boy, for that matter, but especially that one."

I almost didn't even hear the insult directed at Wes. "Double date?" My lips twisted to the side as I thought. Who in the world could Wes and I double with? Definitely not Claire and Austin—assuming he was even giving her the time of day yet. Maybe Marta. Marta and. . .who? My eyes widened. Luke. Marta and Luke. She'd do it for me because she was my friend, and Luke would do it. . .well, Luke would do it because of the rose. I'd have some fast talking to do, but it could work.

I exhaled loudly. "Fine. Double date it is."

"Okay, then." Dad sized me up with another look then nodded once and started pushing the cart down the aisle. I cast a glance up at him as I matched his pace, unable to stop smiling.

I think for the first time in our entire lives, we understood each other.

★ ★ ★

I bounced the basketball under my palm, the feel of the orangey-brown rubber more foreign to me than Taco Bell was to Marta. I was book smart, not sports smart—or even remotely coordinated, for that matter. If my gym teacher had seen the apple incident in the grocery store last night, I could guarantee she'd have removed all sports equipment from my reach.

A few feet across the hard gym floor, Marta held out her hands to catch the ball. "A double date?"

I tossed it to her. It bounced once between us before landing in her manicured hands. Her host mom had insisted they get matching mani-pedis the night before. I avoided looking at my own ragged nails, which could more than stand a coat of clear polish or two. "Have you ever been on one?"

Marta shrugged. "We go out in groups a lot in Stuttgart. Is that the same thing?"

"Sort of. But don't worry, it'll be fun." I had yet to convince Wes of this fact, though, or even see him since our kiss for that matter. I offered my cell number as he walked me home that night, but he just said he'd find me. If this had been any other guy, I'd have feared I was getting the dreaded brush-off. But for some reason, I trusted he'd be around. Maybe it was the look in his eye after our kiss. Or the way he'd said "PK" in that tone that was pure Wes.

I shivered and rubbed my bare arms. Despite the late-October chill outside, the air conditioner in the gym was running, and here we were in the most ugly blue-and-yellow gym outfits known to man. No one else looked cold, though. Probably because they weren't remembering being kissed by a leather-wearing, tattoo-sporting, motorcycle-driving hottie.

Marta threw the ball to me. "I will go. Anything to avoid another shopping trip with my host family. So who is my date?"

"Luke. He's in my English class." I lobbed it back.

The ball stopped abruptly in Marta's grip. "The one who

sent you the rose?"

"That's him."

"And you want *me* to go out with him? Tonight?" She laughed, loudly enough to cause stares from the other students in our class doing this stupid passing exercise. "While you're with another guy?"

"I didn't say it was ideal." Far from ideal, actually. I clapped my hands for the ball, ready to get it over with. The gym exercise. The pending conversation with Luke. This potentially disastrous double date. All of it. Why did my dad have to have his dating rules? If he could go out with my teacher, why couldn't I go out with who I wanted? I'd given my dad about *this* much grief during my entire life, and instead of more trust, I just got more rules.

Although when I was with Wes, I sort of understood why Dad had them.

I shook my head, my frustration peaking. "So are you on board or not? And don't pretend you don't know what the phrase means."

Marta attempted to spin the ball on one finger like our gym teacher had earlier in the period. "Ja, I'm on board. I'm not saying this won't be a sinking ship, though." The ball fell to the ground with a thump, and she scooped it up. "Do you want me to help you convince Luke? You know, smile and bat my eyes?"

She fluttered her lashes at me dramatically, and I couldn't help but laugh. Maybe this date would be okay after all. At least I had my new best friend as backup.

Now to convince Luke he wanted to go with Marta instead of with me.

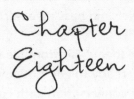

Chapter Eighteen

Ding-dong.

My hand jerked, smearing lip gloss from my mouth to the bottom of my chin in a sticky trail of Think Pink. Wes was here. I darted from my bedroom mirror to my purse to check the time on my cell phone. 6:28 p.m. He was even on time. No, actually, two minutes early.

What had I done to the guy?

I zipped my purse and took one last look at my reflection, my heart hammering so loudly I was surprised the floor didn't vibrate under my feet. Luke and Marta were meeting us at the movie theater in thirty minutes, then we were getting coffee afterward at Got Beans. I figured sitting silently for two hours in the dark before any of us were expected to make conversation would be a smooth way to avoid the awkward factor—especially after Luke's reluctance to the whole arrangement and Marta's pretend, yet exaggerated, offense at his hesitation. Oh, today had held one afternoon I was glad I never had to repeat.

Not that Wes had taken to the idea of a double date any better, but when I'd confirmed that was the only way it would happen, he'd agreed with only three eye rolls. I'd expected more.

The bell chimed again, jolting my feet into action.

Dad and I reached the door at the same time, and I coughed at the sudden wave of Old Spice. "What did you do, shower with that stuff?" I waved my hand in front of my face

His cheeks reddened. "I might have spilled it." His date with Ms. Hawthorne—Kathy? Was there a different protocol when your teacher was dating your father?—was tonight, too, and he was obviously more than a little nervous. "Is it too much?"

I patted his shoulder, so grateful he'd allowed me my (supervised) freedom for the evening that I felt downright compassionate. "It'll be fine. Just drive with the windows down the first ten minutes."

He reached for the doorknob, and I hip-checked him out of the way before realizing that wasn't exactly respectful. "Sorry." I braced my back against the door as the bell chimed a third time. "I was going to get it."

"Then get it already." Dad smoothed his hands down the front of his shirt, and I could swear there was a slight tremble to them.

I yanked open the door, all smiles. Ms. Hawthorne smiled back. "Oh. Hi." Not Wes. I should have known he wouldn't be early. I stepped aside and waved her in. Why hadn't Dad gone to pick her up? Weird.

"Hello, Addison." She entered the foyer and grinned at my father. "David."

"You look nice." He shoved his hands in his pockets, and I grabbed his elbow before he could start nervously jingling his spare change.

"Dad, better hurry. You guys don't want to be late." And if he wasn't there when Wes arrived, even better. I wouldn't have to deal with the overprotective looks and any embarrassing claims about shotguns (that we didn't own).

Too late. Wes appeared over Ms. Hawthorne's shoulder on

the front stoop. "Hey."

I smiled back. "Hey." Then we stood together in the foyer, one truly uncomfortable, awkward group of people.

"Well, we should get going." Dad broke the silence first and motioned for Ms. Hawthorne to step outside. "Addison." He ushered me through the doorway next, pausing momentarily to shake Wes's hand. "Wes."

"Sir." He nodded, reclaiming his hand as quickly as possible. But I could tell it took a lot for Wes to say anything at all, and somehow it just endeared him to me further. He really was trying—for me. *Me*. Not Poodle—er, Sonya.

We all stepped outside in the evening air, the brisk breeze a welcome relief to the nervous sweat breaking out along my hairline. Dad locked the door behind us, and I headed down the driveway toward—oh no. Wes's motorcycle! Group date or not, there would be no way Dad would let me on that thing. My mind conjured and rejected a dozen excuses and justifications before I realized Wes had brought his dad's Jeep instead. Crisis averted. Apparently he'd thought ahead as well.

Or just figured I was still too much of a gummi bear to get on his bike again.

Wes headed for his side of the Jeep, keys in hand. I decided to overlook his lack of opening the door for me. Again, this whole date-night, movie-and-popcorn thing was new to him. He deserved a few breaks. Besides, who really did that anymore?

Dad hesitated on his way to our sedan on the other side of the drive. "Shouldn't we all ride together?"

I froze, one hand on the handle of the passenger door of the Jeep. "Why?" He didn't even trust me in a car alone with Wes for the three minutes it took to drive to Crooked Hollow Theater? What did he think would happen? Good grief, there were only two STOP signs between our house and our destination. *Please don't embarrass me.*

Dad opened the passenger door of the sedan for Ms. Hawthorne, and I felt a random pang of resentment that Wes hadn't done that for me. I shot a sidelong glance at Wes, but he didn't seem to realize my train of thought. He tossed his keys from one hand to the other as he impatiently waited for my dad's explanation. And Dad better have one because if he thought for one minute I would get in that car with him and—

"It makes more sense to ride together." Dad shut the door and walked around to his side. "And it would save Wes the gas money."

"But the movie theater is across town from Got Beans. Isn't that where you're going?" Not that that reason carried much weight, since it literally meant a five-minute difference, but I wasn't going down without a fight.

Dad rubbed his hand over his forehead. "That's where *we're* going."

"Right. You and Ms. Hawthorne."

Dad's brow pinched. "And you and Wes."

A prickle of dread started at my midsection and worked its way up to my chest, stabbing with tiny needles of fear. My mouth dried. I couldn't breathe. Dad and I stared at each other as our conversation in the grocery store slowly replayed in my mind in painful slow motion. *"It has to be a double date. . . . I don't trust him alone with you. . . . Fine, double date it is. . . ."* I had automatically assumed a double date with friends, while Dad obviously meant with him and Ms. Hawthorne.

Oh man. This was worse than going down. This was dive-bombing. This was exploding from the sky in a burst of fire.

Panic gripped my throat in a relentless vise. I glanced at Wes, whose face paled as he widened his eyes at me and shook his head.

This. Was. Not. Happening.

Me and Wes? Going out with my dad and my *teacher*? And on a Friday night, no less? If anyone from school saw us, the rumor mill wouldn't just churn. It'd self-implode.

I clenched my hands into fists. This was a war. I must fight. For my dignity. For my new relationship with Wes that was about to be destroyed before it even got started. For overprotected teenage girls everywhere.

This was my moment.

Clearing my throat, I shoved down the panic and tried for diplomacy. "Dad, I think we misunderstood each other."

He paused, one hand braced on the open door of his car. Inside the vehicle, Ms. Hawthorne twisted in her seat, watching the back-and-forth dialogue with a confused frown. "How so?"

"When you said double date, I thought you meant with my friends. I made plans with Luke and Marta from school." I held up my cell phone, as if it could somehow justify my story.

Dad shrugged, my cell apparently not relying the proper message. "Cancel."

Cancel? After all the grief I went through just getting Luke to agree to go on a double date—with another girl instead of me? I'd embarrassed him enough just by asking. My heart actually hurt. I pressed a hand to my chest. Was this a heart attack? Was I going to fall out in the driveway beside Wes's Jeep? I could hear the teaser news trailer now. *"Teenage girl dies of mortification overload. Details at eleven."*

"Dad, I can't."

"Then I'm afraid Wes has to go home."

I turned to Wes, pleading with my eyes for him to agree. He shook his head, hands raised as if he wasn't touching this with a ten-foot pole. I didn't blame him. I rushed around to his side of the Jeep and stood in front of him, my back to my father.

"This is our only chance. Please."

"I didn't sign up for going out with your dad, Addison. He's my father's pastor." He grimaced. "Do you know how weird that is?"

"Ms. Hawthorne is my English teacher." I laughed, the sound void of any humor. "I could write a manual on weird."

Wes groaned. "Are you really asking me to do this?" He ran a hand over his hair and sighed, glancing down at me and then away. "Don't look at me like that."

"Like what?" I widened my eyes and tried to look even sadder than I had that day at Screamin' Cones. It hadn't worked on the clerk, but maybe Wes cared a little more. He better.

"Like I just kicked your puppy." He tilted his head to one side. "Actually, I'd rather let a dog bite *me* than go out with your dad."

"Very funny." I gripped his arm, willing him to look into my eyes. "Listen, you already agreed to a double date. Let's get this over with. Then next time can be just us."

His eyes said he doubted it, and I sort of did, too, but my arsenal of weapons was rapidly depleting. I squeezed his arm. "Please. For me? I'll even buy your coffee."

He smiled then, and I knew he was budging. "With whip?"

"And sprinkles."

Wes snorted. "You come anywhere near my coffee with sprinkles, and we're going to fight." His eyes smoldered as he looked down at me, and I sort of wished he'd kiss me again. Then I remembered my dad was standing about fifteen feet behind me and changed my mind.

"So, deal?"

"Deal." Wes stepped away from me and exhaled so loud his breath clouded in the evening air.

Victory! "We'll meet you at Got Beans," I called across the driveway to my dad. He shook his head but got in the car without further comment. I slid into the Jeep, exhausted. I'd won a battle, but the biggest war was still to come.

I was determined to reschedule my double date with Luke and Marta.

★ ★ ★

SORRY, DATE'S OFF. WILL RESCHEDULE.

HAHA. U AMERICANS HAVE ODD SENSE OF HUMOR.

NO, 4 REAL. LONG STORY.

BUT WE R ALREADY HERE!

I'M SO SORRY.

LUKE BOUGHT POPCORN AND IS TAKING ALL THE BUTTERED PIECES.

NO SYMPATHY. I'M AT GOT BEANS WITH MY DAD AND ENGLISH TEACHER.

OH.

YEAH.

WILL PRAY 4 U.

I smirked at Marta's last text then turned my phone off and dropped it in my purse. She'd better pray hard because if Wes leaned any farther away from the table, he was going to fall out of his chair. I'd never been more convinced of body language telling a story more so than when I looked at Wes's crossed arms, slumped shoulders, and legs angled toward the door. Everything about him screamed "escape," and I could more than relate.

Dad wasn't helping the entire awkward factor. He alternated frowning at Wes and smiling at Ms. Hawthorne, and the whole thing gave me a headache. I sipped at my mocha, but my mouth was so dry I could barely even taste it. No one had spoken in six minutes. Trust me, I'd timed it.

The soft background music Bert typically played seemed louder than usual, but that was probably because of the quiet hovering like a storm cloud ready to burst. The tension was so thick I'm surprised it didn't become a tangible object dangling over our heads. Like an anvil.

Ms. Hawthorne's coffee cup suddenly toppled over, and a stream of liquid spilled out on the table. "Oh, goodness. David, would you get me a napkin?"

Dad rushed to the counter, and Ms. Hawthorne leaned toward me, voice low. "Addison, I know this is a little weird for you." She nodded at Wes. "And you. But I have some advice."

Wes's eyes flickered in her direction, but his body didn't move. I was going to owe him big for this one. A new tattoo? Free bike wash?

"What's that?" It was only polite to ask, though I had little confidence she could remedy this situation. Come on, I was drinking my favorite mocha with extra sprinkles, and that wasn't even touching my problems.

Ms. Hawthorne glanced over her shoulder at Dad, who was still fumbling to retrieve the napkins from the jammed canister at the front counter. "Just go with it tonight, and the odds of this evening ever being a repeat will significantly diminish."

Wes frowned in confusion, and I even had to think her sentence over twice before catching her meaning. You'd have thought she was a math teacher instead of English. "So you think if we play along, he'll let us go out alone next time?"

"Or at least go out with your friends." She lifted her shoulder in a shrug. "It's worth a try. Fuming and pouting isn't working, though I do understand the motivation behind it."

She was right. Wes and I sitting here silently wouldn't hurry the night along or win any brownie points with my dad. I nudged Wes's leg with my foot, and he slowly straightened in his chair. "What do you think?"

He lifted both hands in surrender. "I'm in—anything to

avoid this version of family fun again." He tipped his head at Ms. Hawthorne. "No offense."

She laughed. "None taken. I wouldn't have wanted to go out with my dad and teacher when I was a teenager either. Of course, he was married, so that would have been even more awkward." She grinned at me.

"Thanks." I flashed her a quick smile, grateful I had at least one ally during this mixed-up night. I leaned forward, lowering my voice to a whisper as Dad approached with a handful of napkins. "Did you spill your coffee on purpose?" I was torn between admiring her ambition and wanting to scold her for wasting even a drop of mocha heaven.

She only winked as Dad slid back into the chair beside her.

I shook my head, thinking I had severely underestimated my English teacher. I should have known she was different if only by her footwear. Any teacher who valued fashion over comfort in the classroom had to be at least a little cool.

"What'd I miss?" Dad looked at each of us with expectation.

I took a long sip of mocha. No one jumped in, so it was up to me. "Wes here was just getting ready to tell Ms. Hawthorne about his favorite novel." Hey, I already owed him, so why not enjoy the show?

I expected him to cough, perhaps even spew coffee, but he just let loose a lazy smile. "That's right. *To Kill a Mockingbird*."

It was my turn to cough. What? Surely he was just joking or trying to show off by pulling a familiar title out of thin air. Time for a trap. I smiled sweetly. "I haven't read that one in years. Why don't you refresh my memory of the plotline?"

Wes shrugged and then went into an animated, lengthy description of Scout and Jem, Atticus Finch, and Boo Radley. My mouth opened wider and wider until I finally clenched it shut. Wes read classics—and enjoyed them. What other secrets lurked behind that stupid leather jacket? (Okay, not stupid, because man, it smelled really good, but you know what I mean.)

When he finished his summary, Wes found my hand under the table and gave it a squeeze. I met his gaze for a moment, Ms. Hawthorne's questions a mere drone in the back of my mind as Got Beans faded into a blur. I forgot about how embarrassing it was to be out with my English teacher on a Friday night, forgot about Luke and Marta sitting awkwardly in a movie theater without me, forgot about Dad's long list of rules. Nothing existed but Wes and his dark-brown gaze, the likes of which held a subtle spark that made my stomach flip-flop.

He'd never seemed more dangerous to me than he did in that moment.

Chapter Nineteen

I still can't believe you convinced your father to let you come." Marta tested the weight of a hot-pink bowling ball then put it back on the shelf. "Especially after all the overprotective horror stories I've heard. I thought my host mom was bad." Marta let loose an exaggerated shudder.

"Wes made a decent impression at Got Beans last night, so maybe Ms. Hawthorne was right in her theory." I picked up a silver ball. Too heavy. I'd throw my shoulder out. "Or maybe Dad was just eager to have an evening with Ms. Hawthorne alone, too, and figured this was the lesser of two evils."

"Or a combination of both."

"You're probably right." Last night couldn't have ended soon enough, even though the entire evening only lasted two hours. We'd all made small talk and downed our coffee then sat around trying to pretend we all wanted to be there while stealing glances at the clock. Thankfully Wes had come around and put in some effort, even drawing Ms. Hawthorne into more conversation about another classic. Who'd have thought Wes read novels? Then again, I'd never have pegged him for a pianist either, and he obviously had great talent there. Not for the first time, I wondered why he felt he had to hide behind the bad-boy vibe when he had so much going for him.

Maybe he'd just never had anyone around to tell him.

Marta gestured to where Luke was typing our names into the computer system on lane 22. Wes stood beside him, hands shoved into his pockets as he surveyed the room. "Is Wes all right? He seemed quiet when we got here."

"That's Wes. He's not exactly a big talker." I nudged her with my hip. "So you never told me—how did things go with Luke at the movie theater?"

Marta rolled her eyes. "Before or after he talked about you all night?"

"After?" I winced.

"Let's just say it was a good thing I already knew he liked you, or I'd have been insulted." She finally chose a purple ball with green lightning bolts and fell into step beside me as we made our way toward the lane.

"I'm really sorry how everything turned out." I lowered my voice as we drew nearer to the boys, even though the nearly deafening slam of balls ricocheting off pins would surely cover my words. "I'd hoped maybe Luke would change his mind about brunettes and go for a blond."

Marta patted her flaxen hair and grinned. "We could always stop at a salon on the way home."

"Don't you dare! Your hair is gorgeous." And natural. Mine was, too, but her butter-colored hair looked like a famous stylist had groomed it, while mine hung plain and brown around my shoulders.

"And yours isn't? Both of those guys over there like you, Addison. I'm pretty sure your hair isn't an issue for them." Marta elbowed me in the ribs. "I was kidding anyway. I'm not interested in Luke that way. Not really. He's a good friend."

"Then I think that's his curse because that's exactly how I feel about him."

"He's got a golden heart to do this for you as a favor." Marta shot me a glance that clearly warned I'd better not forget that, and I couldn't help but smile at her protectiveness of her new "friend." Maybe there was hope for the two of them yet.

"What'd you say?" Luke looked up from the computer screen with a smile as we dropped our balls onto the return conveyor. His gaze lingered slightly longer on me than it did on Marta, and I quickly looked away.

Marta brushed her hands on her jeans. "Girl stuff. You wouldn't be interested."

"That's for sure." Luke wrinkled his nose. "Hey, Wes, you're up first."

Wes headed for the ball return, and I caught his arm. "Please tell me you're not bowling in that jacket."

"Why not? I'm going to suck regardless." But he shrugged out of his jacket and draped it over one of the seats.

"Have you never bowled before?" Marta asked. "I haven't."

"I have." Wes picked up his ball and spun it around in an attempt to find the finger holes. "But it's not exactly my thing."

"Not much of a sports guy?" Luke came to stand beside me, and I tried to tell myself it was just so he could see Wes better as he bowled.

Wes's eyes darted from Luke to me and back again. "Let's just say I'm not into competition." Then he turned and thrust the ball down the lane, where it slammed immediately into the gutter.

"Less force, more strategy." Luke clapped Wes's shoulder. "You're up again."

I winced as Wes's expression darkened, but to his credit he didn't say anything, just waited for his ball to be returned. This time he hesitated at the foul line, lining up his shot before releasing the ball with slightly less strength behind it. The ball arced to the left and made it halfway down the lane before slipping into the gutter.

"Don't worry, I'm sure I'll be worse." Marta slipped past Wes to get her ball. But she made a spare, and Luke a strike. As I picked up my ball from the conveyor, I couldn't help but wonder why Luke had put our names in the order he had, as if Marta and Wes were a team and he and I were a team after them. An accident? Or a subtle hint of his feelings for me? But Luke didn't seem the crafty sort. I was probably just projecting Wes's bad mood and blowing things out of proportion.

I shook off the uneasy feeling looming over me and tried to smile for Wes's sake as he prepared his next shot. Luke was doing us a favor, as Marta had pointed out. He deserved some grace. Hopefully Wes would see that, too.

★ ★ ★

"That guy is a jerk." Wes slammed the door of his dad's Jeep and shoved the key into the ignition.

I buckled my seat belt, my heart pounding beneath the wide strap. "What do you mean?" I knew, though. I knew exactly.

Wes reached for a pack of gum under the console and ripped open a piece before shoving it in his mouth. His words were muffled as he chewed, but his meaning clear. "Luke. Is. A. Jerk."

My thoughts raced, replaying Luke's instructional yet borderline condescending advice to Wes—and every friendly gesture or touch toward me. I swallowed hard. "But what about ice cream?"

Wes turned to face me, head cocked to the side as if he couldn't believe that was my chief concern.

"I'm not saying I need it." Although I sort of did. "I meant we're supposed to meet them at Screamin' Cones. That's the plan."

"Then just text Marta and tell her you're not hungry."

I leveled my gaze at Wes. "And you expect her to believe that?"

Wes turned the keys, and the Jeep sprang to life. "I don't care. If you want ice cream, I'll drive into the next town and get it. I just don't want to be near him again. He's annoying."

"Why do you say that?"

"Are you *that* naive? He's into you." Wes shook his head at me, as if he couldn't believe my ignorance—which really wasn't ignorance so much as it was denial. Luke having feelings for me beyond friendship complicated this delicate quartet we'd all created, and without him and Marta, my chances of seeing Wes in a dating atmosphere again plummeted to nonexistent. Then he'd go running back to Lemon Drop for a good time while this particular Gummi Bear was once again left in her room with nothing but homework assignments and classic novels for company. I'd come so far, I wasn't backing up now. I was on a date with Wes Keegan. *Me.*

As much as I loved my books, they weren't going to make up for losing what I'd finally obtained.

I let out a huff. "Okay, so I might have noticed a little."

"Good job, Sherlock." Wes reached for another piece of gum.

"You do realize you're not supposed to chew a whole pack at a time?" I gestured to the second empty wrapper in his lap.

"Very funny. I chew gum when I want to smoke."

"You smoke?" Funny, I'd never noticed the scent on him before.

"I did. Past tense."

He must have seen my nose wrinkle because he rolled his eyes. "What, PK? Judging another dirty habit of sinners?"

"I didn't say that." Although the whole concept of smoking totally sickened me—and not just the smell, but the whole blackened-lungs thing. Ew. What was the point?

"You thought it. Come on, don't tell me smoking hasn't been condemned from your dad's pulpit before."

I bit my tongue, unable to deny it.

Wes smirked. "Smoking, drinking, sex. Let me guess. Rock 'n' roll, too?"

"Don't be ridiculous. My dad loves Heart."

"Oh brother." Wes closed his eyes. "PK, what do *you* think? Not your dad. And not what you think God thinks. *You.*"

I lifted my chin, unwilling to back down, even though I knew that was his goal. "I think smoking's gross."

"Fair enough." His lips twisted to one side. "What about the rest of the list?"

My mouth opened on instinct, but all potential words froze on my tongue, refusing to slip out. I knew the right answers. I knew what I should say, what my Sunday school teacher had drilled into us since we were kids—how to say no to peer pressure, how to share our faith while politely turning down offers we'd better refuse.

But why?

Wes never dropped my gaze, and by the slight curve of his lips, I knew he'd seen the truth, seen my reluctant yet inevitable answer to his question.

I didn't have a clue.

A car horn honked behind us, and Luke waved from the driver's seat of his car as he gestured for us to pull out of the parking space and lead the way.

"Did I mention I don't like that guy?" Eyes narrowed, Wes jerked the gearshift into REVERSE, his jaw locked. "Where to? And if you say Screamin' Cones, even as a joke, I swear I'll drive this Jeep through that window into the bowling alley."

Grateful the past topic was over, I leaned in his direction, as far as my seat belt would allow, and grinned. "Screamin' Cones?" The words came out in a half whisper, and I honestly had no idea what I'd do if he actually shoved the car into DRIVE and gassed it.

Wes held my gaze, the muscle in his jaw twitching, the storm in his eyes slowly clearing to reveal a spark of humor. He let out a short laugh, and when he met my eyes again, his had all but softened. "Leave it to you to call my bluffs." He trailed a finger down my cheek, and my lips parted automatically, our previous disagreement forgotten. Would he kiss me again, right here in the parking lot?

But he just returned both hands to the steering wheel, and I eased back into my seat, glad I'd cheered him up if nothing else. "You can take me home. I'll text Marta and tell her you're not feeling well."

"So now you're lying, PK? How else am I going to corrupt you?" He backed out of the parking space.

"It's not a lie." My heart raced like it did every time he called me PK, and I quickly reached down and pulled my phone from my purse to hide my reaction. "I think grumpy qualifies as not feeling well."

"Come on, word-girl. You can do better than grumpy. That makes me sound like a cartoon bear." Wes drove onto the street. "Or a dwarf."

"Well you're not Happy, Sleepy, or Bashful, and I doubt you'd want to be Dopey, so. . ." My voice trailed off as I typed out a quick message to Marta. Definitely not Bashful, not with the smoldering glances he kept sending my way. My stomach flip-flopped, and I shut my phone as soon as I received Marta's simple "okay" response. If she had caught even half of Luke's subliminal messages tonight, then she probably could fill in the blanks pretty quickly.

"You forgot Sneezy."

"That's impressive. Can you name all of Santa's reindeer, too?" I twisted in my seat to face him, drawing one leg up underneath me.

Wes stopped at a red light. "Very funny. I happened to watch *Snow White* growing up."

"Happened?" I snorted.

"More like was forced to by my mother. It was her favorite movie, and she always had it playing." Wes's smile dimmed. "She said it reminded her that even when life wasn't fair, there was always a silver lining. Always someone to help us, like the dwarfs."

I smiled. Nice concept. "Always a prince on the way?"

Wes swallowed as he stared straight ahead, his Adam's apple bobbing in his throat. "She never lacked for those. Even when she was still with my dad."

Oh.

I sat quietly, unsure what to say. Apparently Wes had more baggage in his past than I'd realized, but with each tiny revelation, it was like a piece of his leather-coated puzzle slid into place. I wanted to tell him I was sorry, but it sounded so flippant. Sorry for what? It wasn't my fault he'd had a rotten home life, and it wasn't his, either. I wondered how many people knew about his childhood. And how did Mr. Keegan fit into the picture? Wes made him out to be an uncaring monster, but the man at church seemed genuinely concerned about his son. It didn't add up.

I reached over the middle console and laid my hand on Wes's, wishing I had some deep and profound words to offer. Something to heal his past. Something to bring light to his future.

"At least she didn't make you watch *Cinderella*. Because

I can guarantee you I wouldn't know how to walk in glass slippers."

Wes shot me a look, and I held my breath, unsure if joking my way out of this conversation was genius or three-strikes-in-one. Then he smiled and shook his head as the light turned green. He accelerated through the intersection, his smile morphing into a snort and a chuckle. "I'm many things, Addison, but Prince Charming is not one of them."

"Aha! You knew his name!" I bolted upright and pointed my finger at him with an I-caught-you grin. "You did watch it!"

"Let's just say Mom had a penchant for all the Disney movies and leave it at that, okay?" Wes pulled into my driveway and shoved the gear into PARK.

"You sure are asking me to keep a lot of secrets lately." I stared at him, making no move to unbuckle my seat belt. "First your piano-playing ability, now your knowledge of Disney flicks." *And your messed-up childhood that obviously still bothers you more than you want to admit.*

Wes must have heard what I hadn't said because he leaned over toward me, inches from my face. His hand, still holding mine on top of the console, squeezed my fingers. "Is that a problem?"

His breath, hinting of peppermint gum, was warm on my cheeks. I met his gaze, watched his eyes drop from mine to my lips and up again. "Not a problem at all."

He smiled and started to close the distance between us.

The porch light flicked on and off in my peripheral vision. I sat back with a groan as the curtain on the front window fluttered and the lights blinked again. "I get it, Dad."

"Creative." Back behind the wheel now, Wes tilted his chin up at me, his former confidence and borderline cockiness firmly in place. "Don't worry. Next date, it'll be just us."

My stomach shivered in anticipation as I slid out of the Jeep. I hesitated, not wanting to lose the connection we'd made. "When is that?"

Wes shrugged. "It could have been right now if it weren't for someone's curfew."

"Well that's obviously not an option." The porch light punctuated my point with another blink. "Call me?"

Wes pushed the gear into REVERSE, my hint to close the door. "Good night, Addison."

" 'Night." I shut it and stepped back, my mind whirling and replaying the evening as I navigated the walkway to the front door. My lips felt gypped from his near kiss, and it wasn't until I shut the front door behind me and turned off the porch light that I realized he'd never agreed to call me.

Chapter
Twenty

Marta slipped into the pew at the end of my row and sank down beside me with a grin. "I feel like I escaped."

"You made it!" Yay. Now I didn't have to sit alone among Mrs. Vanderford and the blue-haired observers—or worry about any more awkward convos with Mr. Keegan. I passed Marta a bulletin. "I can't believe your host mom let you visit our church." I lowered my voice. "Especially since they're, you know—"

"Catholic?" Marta laughed as she adjusted the hem of her black skirt. "That doesn't mean they refuse to let me sit under a Protestant preacher."

"Hey, after seeing that turquoise belt, I figured I'd better not assume anything." I held up both hands in defense.

"Ha-ha." She stuck her tongue out at me. "Speaking of. . . I'm *assuming* Wes didn't exactly have a good time last night?"

I twisted the bookmark ribbon from my Bible around my finger and shrugged. "He thinks you're cool." As cool as Wes would admit anyone to being, anyway. Maybe Marta wouldn't pick up on how I didn't mention Luke—

"But not Luke."

Rats. I shrugged again, not wanting to get into it. Wes had confided in me last night, and blabbing it seemed wrong—even if it was to my best friend. Especially after all that talk about secrets.

"Addison, it was obvious. If Wes's dislike for Luke was supposed to be a secret, then he should learn to become a better actor." Marta snorted. "He was not being subtle with what he thought."

"Then why'd you ask?" I opened my bulletin, pretending to peruse the contents but really just trying to redirect my attention before my frustration boiled over. I felt extremely defensive about him and annoyed at the fact that I did. Wes and I weren't in this serious relationship—yet. I really had no reason to get all worked up over someone else's opinion of him. Yet there it was regardless—a fierce loyalty shooting through my veins like a drug.

Marta laid a cool hand on my forearm. "I know you care about Wes. I am not trying to insult him. I am simply asking if you knew why he acted the way he did last night."

My bulletin fell to my lap. She was right. We'd both been there, so it was ridiculous to cut corners. I could share with her without revealing too much personal information. "He's jealous." To sum it. Saying the words out loud gave me a tiny thrill, and I couldn't help the pleasure of the moment. Wes, jealous about *me*—after ditching Sonya, of all people, to ask me out. If he felt territorial over me, that must mean we were heading toward some kind of commitment. The thought sent an excited buzz through my stomach.

That is, if my dad would even begin to allow it. The buzz dissipated, and I shot my father, who sat on the first row going over his sermon notes, a look. Fat chance of that—especially when he wouldn't even let us sit in the Jeep for ten seconds without flashing lights. Yet I couldn't come to terms with just sneaking around like my friends did. What was wrong with me?

Why did I have to be so good all the time?

What did I have to lose?

"Jealous of Luke? So Wes knows Luke likes you." Marta's voice pitched, hinting at her disappointment. "Luke and I went to Screamin' Cones after you and Wes went home, and we had a long talk. He knows you're into Wes. But he's bummed about it." She shook her head with a sad smile. "He thinks he can change your mind."

"That's sweet." Sweet, but annoying. I needed Luke on my side. If Dad refused to let me and Wes date alone, then I'd have to keep doubling with Marta and Luke. And if Luke wasn't on board, or was going to make Wes miserable every time we were all together, then the whole arrangement seemed pointless. It wasn't much of a date to constantly have to calm down Wes's temper. Who knew how many packs of gum he'd go through if forced to deal with Luke on a regular basis?

The gum reminded me of him calling me out on my beliefs, and my neck burned with shame. Some witness I was to the bad boy next door. I couldn't even give an honest answer about my choices.

"He'll get over it eventually." Marta crossed her legs, bobbing one booted foot toward me. "Both of them." She hesitated as the choir began filing into place in the choir loft. "But Addison, I'm a little concerned."

"About what?" We stood together, reaching for the hymnal at the same time as our music minister asked us to rise. My fingers rushed to find the right page while my ears begged to hear Marta's fears.

"You and Wes." She leaned closer to me, peering down at the words to "How Great Thou Art." I knew the verses by heart, so I handed her the hymnal so she could see.

Mrs. Vanderford, always in front of me, shot us a look over

the looming shoulder pad of her dress, clearly instructing us to hush. But I had to know what Marta meant. "What are you talking about?"

Marta lowered her voice to a whisper, still staring at the hymnbook. "He doesn't seem right for you."

I jerked away from her in surprise, my blood pressure immediately rising and sending a hot flush through my veins. My heart beat a wild protest. "That's *your* opinion." I didn't even bother to whisper this time and was rewarded with another glare from in front of me. I ignored the woman and turned my searching gaze to Marta.

Marta just shrugged, an apology filling her eyes as she turned the pages to the next hymn number on the PowerPoint screen. "Blessed Assurance." Perfect. I sure could use some of that right now.

"I'm just being honest. He seems kind of. . .rough around the edges." Marta gestured to my dad on the front row. "You're a preacher's daughter."

"And you said not to let that define me." Blood roared in my ears, drowning out the voices of the congregation around me.

"It shouldn't." Marta whispered so softly I could barely hear her. "But you should also know better."

Her last words struck me like a slap, and I reeled backward, away from her. Away from "Blessed Assurance." I stared blindly at the flowers in front of the pulpit, their autumn blooms of orange and burnt red blurring into a kaleidoscope of color.

Know better? Sure, Wes had an attitude about Luke. Sure, he wasn't Mr. Polite or Prince Charming, as he'd admitted himself. Sure, he had a stereotype about him with the motorcycle and the tattoos and the chip on his leather-clad shoulder, but he wasn't dangerous. Marta didn't know him like I did. She didn't know the vulnerable side, the side that confessed to dark childhood memories. The side that sat with me in my driveway at twilight and admitted his world was screwed up. The side that whispered to me, and me alone. I don't know why he'd chosen me, but I wasn't about to slap it all aside because of pretense and assumptions.

And trust me, that choice had nothing to do with—well, okay, a *little* to do with—how he made me feel when he kissed me.

Marta pressed the bulletin in my hands, and I looked down to see a handwritten note she'd scrawled in the border. *Will explain more later. Do not be mad.*

I let out a slow breath and nodded. There was nothing to do now but wait and discuss this further after the service— maybe over something really yummy to distract my own temper, like a cheeseburger and Cajun fries. I angled slightly to drop the bulletin to the pew behind me, and as I straightened I caught Mr. Keegan's eye from across the aisle. He nodded at me as he sang, his eyes dark and haunting—just like Wes's. I returned his smile with my own, my thoughts churning.

Maybe his son wasn't the only one with secrets.

★ ★ ★

My burger practically oozed as I squished it together and leaned in for a big bite. As much grief as I gave my dad about eating healthy, I had to admit, sometimes a girl just needed some beef. And cheese. And pickles and onions and jalapeños.

Across the table, Marta dipped a fry in a pool of ketchup. "It's going to be rough going back home in a few months." She gestured to the meal in front of her. "Mom never lets me eat like this."

"I bug my dad about his cholesterol and carb intake." I took another bite, juice dribbling down my chin, and swiped it with a napkin. "But I don't have health problems, so I figure I can be a hypocrite a few times a week."

"Yet." Marta grinned around her fry. "If you keep this up. . ."

"Let's just say I'm starting to see my dad's argument with food—'but what a way to go.' " I mimicked his deeper voice, earning a laugh from Marta. I reached for my paper cup full of pop and returned her smile. Comfort food was a must, after the whispered yet heated conversation we'd had during the worship service and the follow-up convo I knew was yet to come.

I set my cup down and took a deep breath, needing my food to settle before taking another monster bite. "So, now that we're fat and happy, what else do you need to tell me about Wes?"

Marta wadded up her empty fry container and tossed it on the tray between us. "I don't want to offend you. But basically, the more I'm around Wes, the more I don't see him as your type."

"What do you mean, my type? Is there a certain type I'm supposed to go for as a PK?"

"I didn't mean that." Marta shook her head. "I meant I am afraid he'll get you into trouble."

"Me, in trouble?" I jabbed my chest with my finger. "Yeah right. I can barely even go over my preapproved weekly caffeine limit without feeling guilty. I somehow doubt Wes is going to convince me to go get some ink or hold up a convenience store."

"You know what I mean." Marta fiddled with her straw wrapper. "There's other ways to get in trouble besides breaking the law or getting tattoos."

Oh. *That*. I felt my face burn, and I forced myself to maintain eye contact. "Yes, I know what you mean. But what makes you think Wes sleeps around?"

"I didn't say that." Marta wrinkled her nose.

"Do you honestly think that because he wears a leather jacket and rides a motorcycle that he sleeps around?" But he did, didn't he? I knew he had to have done so with Sonya, and if not, then they probably came pretty close based on the vague comments he'd made a few months ago. But that didn't mean he did that with every girl he met. Marta was judging Wes on his appearance. That wasn't fair.

"It has nothing to do with his clothes. It's just a vibe he gives off."

"No, it's a vibe he hides behind." I straightened on my side of the booth. "You don't know Wes like I do."

Marta leaned forward. "He doesn't go to church, does he? I remember you telling me that his dad talked to you after the service—it seemed like he came alone."

If it hadn't been for the sincerity and lack of judgment in Marta's eyes, I'd have gotten even more defensive. Instead I reminded myself she was my friend and looking out for me. I inhaled a long breath. "Mr. Keegan has been in our church for years. Wes, not so much." But that didn't mean he might not come with me later, once we were committed. Once he cared enough. Right?

Marta squinted. "Do you even know if he's a Christian? If he believes like you do?"

A pang of guilt stabbed my heart, and I squirmed in my seat, wishing I could write it off as heartburn. All the youth lessons I'd sat under these past five years suddenly rang in my mind. Stuff about not dating anyone you wouldn't marry—and not marrying anyone who didn't share your faith. I agreed with that. But I wasn't marrying Wes. We weren't even an official item yet. It seemed a little premature to be upset about details that wouldn't even matter until marriage.

"We haven't talked much about faith stuff yet." Not enough to brag about, anyway. I shrugged. "We're still new as a couple, you know? It's not like I can hand a guy a checklist of requirements every time he asks me out." Although, on second thought, my dad would probably love that.

"Ja, I know. . . ." Marta's voice trailed off. "I just want you to be careful. Extracareful."

"I will. I am. Remember—I'm a virgin and plan to stay that way." But for some reason, the words didn't sound nearly as concrete coming off my lips as they had in the past. I frowned. "You and I already had that particular talk."

"But did you and Wes have that talk?" She held my gaze, her eyes sincere and filled with compassion. "Because if you are going to be dating, you need to know what to expect. What he expects."

"He doesn't expect anything." Then I remembered Wes's kiss and the gentle way he'd touched my face, and the fries in my stomach began to dance the hula. "Wes knows I'm not like Sonya. He would never ask that of me, even if he wanted to."

I didn't think.

"Did he end things with Sonya for you?"

I nodded, still somewhat surprised it'd been that easy to win Wes over. I hadn't even really tried. I'd just been there, listened, hung around. Thrown his sarcasm back in his face. Maybe that's what Wes needed—someone to keep him on the up-and-up. Not someone like Sonya, who would only drag him down into what he didn't need to be anymore. I could change him. I'd do it and prove it to Marta and my dad and everyone else who thought Wes was just a brooding rebel. I'd show them all.

That is, if he actually called me. Why hadn't he just said "okay" when I asked if he would, and then I'd know? Or maybe I shouldn't have even asked. Was that considered clingy and annoying? Man, dating was hard. I almost missed my books.

Marta slurped the end of her drink then tried to shove her straw through the ice in her cup. "I just hope you know what you are doing."

"I'm not doing anything other than trying to date a nice guy. A guy who needs a good influence."

Marta's brow twitched, but to her credit, she didn't argue. "You know, Luke is also a pretty nice guy. And his wardrobe actually involves cotton and jersey knit."

I threw a fry at her and laughed. "You can have Luke and his cotton T-shirts all you want. They don't do anything for me."

Marta propped one elbow on the table, resting her chin in her hands. "Not that he'd look away from you long enough to see me anyway."

"Give him time. I'm not that hard to get over, trust me." I rolled my eyes as I searched for the last fry in my bag. I shouldn't have thrown away the other one. "Or hey, just use your turquoise belt to catch his attention. It practically glows in the dark."

"You are just so hilarious." Marta flung her wadded-up straw paper at me, and I caught it and tossed it back as she giggled and ducked beneath the table. "Maybe I should enter the talent show after all. How to make ugly clothes look good."

"You'd make the top ten for sure." I grinned at her, glad our friendship had survived the disagreement. Once again the differences between Marta and Claire struck me like a sledgehammer. Marta spoke honestly from her heart and invited discussion. Claire always insisted on winning every argument and forcing the issue until you just gave up from sheer exhaustion. She'd actually make a great lawyer. Maybe that should have been her talent instead of fashion.

"When's our next practice, anyway?" Marta pulled her phone from her purse and hit a few keys to access her calendar.

"Tomorrow. Which reminds me, I need to get that ad copy to Debra at the Foundation for the newsletter." I groaned. "I can't believe we only have a few weeks until showtime."

No telling what Mrs. Lyons would have me do next. I'd have to draw the line in the assistant sand eventually. Like if she asked me to give her a pedicure or told me to clean the boys' bathroom.

"I just hope our advertising pays off for the Let Them Read Foundation." Marta slipped her phone back into her purse. "This could end up making a real difference for some kids—assuming everyone gets their act together to make this show something more than a joke."

No kidding. "I hope so, too." I helped gather the trash onto our tray and then carried it to the garbage can by the door. Man, did I hope. I hoped the talent show was a success. I hoped I wouldn't find Claire puking in the bathroom again tomorrow. I hoped Mrs. Lyons didn't get sent to the ER for high blood pressure the night of the dress rehearsal.

Most of all, I just hoped Wes would actually call me.

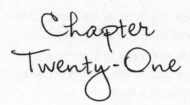

Chapter Twenty-One

"This is for a good cause! Do you people not even care? Have you no respect?"

I winced at the frustration in Marta's rising voice and stood, dropping my clipboard on the stage as I hurried around the heavy velvet curtain. Where was she—and more importantly, why was she yelling about pride and commitment? I stopped short stage left, where Marta actually stood on a cardboard box, hands on her hips as she lectured those poor souls brave enough to stick around and listen.

"This is your school. And if that doesn't make you care, then what about the fact that all the funds received from this show are going to help kids learn how to read?" Marta pointed her finger at Jessica's face, and to her credit, the girl didn't even flinch. "You are supposed to be one of the strongest singers here, but instead of helping someone else, all you do is sing in front of the mirror. It is pathetic."

Oh boy. She'd lost it. "Uh, Marta?" I tugged at her sleeve, but she batted me off. I glared at her, wishing I had the whistle Mrs. Lyons had stolen last week from Coach Thompson. That thing performed miracles when it came to redirecting attention.

"And you." She swung her finger around to point at Tripp, who stood with his arms crossed, leaning against the wall by the electrical outlet. "You're the best dancer here. Why aren't you getting your team ready? Don't think I didn't see Michael's last rehearsal. Your boys have a long way to go before opening night."

Tripp straightened and opened his mouth to protest, but Marta wasn't done. "You should all be helping each other, working together to put on a quality performance. Yet all you're doing is parading around like every act is a solo act, and worse than that, leaving all the hard work to Addison and Mrs. Lyons. Guess what? This is a group project. You might flaunt your specific talent during your time slot, but the final product represents this entire school. You should all be helping make it the best it can be." She crossed her arms over her chest, and I saw a hint of turquoise belt peeking from beneath the hem of her shirt. "You are all ridiculous."

"Okay, show's over, everyone." I grabbed Marta's arm and pulled her from her literal soapbox. "Back to rehearsal."

The majority of the group eagerly dispersed, but Tripp lingered. "Hey, uh, Addison? Is there anything you need me to do before my time spot?"

I stared, my mouth open in what I'm sure was a totally unattractive way. Tripp Larson? Asking to help? After getting railed publicly by a foreign-exchange student? I glanced at Marta. "I think that belt has superpowers."

Marta nudged me, and I turned back to Tripp. "Uh, I mean, yes. That'd be great. Just ask Mrs. Lyons what was next on my list and have at it."

Tripp nodded, and I quickly called him back. "I didn't check this off yet, but I already scanned the copy for the Foundation's advertising. I'll be e-mailing that in to the representative tonight, so don't do that part."

He just lifted one hand in acknowledgment and swaggered

away. Even his walk had rhythm. Then you had guys like Michael. . . . I sighed. One miracle that afternoon was enough. I couldn't be greedy and ask for two.

"What's wrong with you? And by the way, your accent gets thicker when you're mad." I took Marta's elbow and steered her away from the few students who still lingered by the curtain. Some shot her curious glances, but none of the stares carried disdain or anger like I expected.

"Just like I said." Marta cocked her hip to one side, her eyes blazing. "Everyone is acting like a bunch of babies, and I'm tired of it. We—*you* especially—are being worked to death for something you didn't even mean to sign up for. While everyone else jokes their way through rehearsal and expects the final product to magically come together with zero effort. If the town shows up for this, it's going to be, what do you call it? A gigglestock?"

I snorted. "Laughingstock."

"It'll be even worse than that." Marta let out a loud huff. "Then they'll demand their money back or refuse to come next year. Or worse, the school will decide it wasn't worth it, and there will be no more fund-raisers."

"Don't think I'm not grateful. That was downright impressive." I pointed after Tripp. "But seriously, why do you care so much? You won't even be here next year."

Marta's crossed arms dropped to her sides in defeat. "This just isn't what I'm used to. Students in Europe are a lot more universally oriented. They aren't so selfish." She grinned when I raised my eyebrow in disbelief. "Really. They're still teenagers, and they're still divas at times, but they think outside the box."

"I guess I can see that." It didn't take a prescription lens to notice our small-town school wasn't nearly interested enough in worldwide events—or even local charities. Other schools played the morning news in homeroom and discussed current events. We threw spitballs.

Marta brushed her blond hair back from her face and shrugged. "I guess I'm realizing how quickly my year here is going by, and I'd hoped to leave a little of this mind-set when I went home." She wrinkled her nose. "I do not want the only thing I leave behind to be this belt."

I couldn't help but laugh. "You're amazing." I gave Marta an impromptu hug. "Don't think for a minute you haven't done something worthwhile. Just take exhibit A." I stepped back and held out my arms in a wide gesture. "A year ago—no, six months ago—I would have never even considered organizing a fund-raiser or helping direct a school production. And look at me! Coerced, but still kicking." I grinned, and Marta finally smiled back.

"Maybe you are right."

"I'm always right." I nudged her with my elbow. "Now come on, Miss Do-Gooder. Let's see if we can tackle the rest of my clipboard tasks together—assuming Tripp wasn't so motivated by your freak-out back there that he finished the list by himself."

Marta linked her arm through mine as we made our way across the stage to snag my clipboard. "Ja, wouldn't that be something?"

I stopped short. "Speaking of clipboard tasks, I need to make myself a note so I won't forget to e-mail Debra the ad copy for their newsletter. We really need that free advertising. It'll be sent to a bunch of local businesses in Crooked Hollow and the outskirts of town."

"Every little bit will help," Marta agreed. She waited as I pulled up my settings on my phone and began making a notation for a reminder when a familiar voiced sounded from the wings. "Nice set."

Another familiar yet female voice echoed the sentiment. "I agree. Beautiful backdrop. This is really coming together."

No. No. *No.* My fingers froze over the keys on my cell. Marta's soapbox presentation must have gone to my brain. Surely I was imagining things. Surely that wasn't my—

Dad stepped out of the wings, Ms. Hawthorne close on his heels. They smiled when they saw me, though Ms. Hawthorne's grin looked more like an apologetic grimace. A rush of heat flooded my body, and I gripped my phone so hard my knuckles turned white. A spasm of pain bit into my wrist, but I clenched even harder. Better my hands than my teeth.

"Addison, there you are!" Dad practically beamed, as if he'd made a unique discovery. Like *I* was the one out of place in this cozy little scenario.

"What are you doing here?" The words hissed from my lips, and I wished the stage would open up and swallow me whole. I wasn't even in the show, yet this auditorium was about to witness a drama like it'd never seen if my dad didn't exit stage left. *Now.*

"I came to follow Kathy to the mechanic. She's getting her car worked on, so I offered to give her a ride home." Dad shrugged like this made perfect sense.

He couldn't have just met her at the garage instead and spared me this moment? My mouth opened, but words refused to come out. I gaped like the pet goldfish I used to have in elementary school. Bubbles. I sort of wished I could join Bubbles in the ground under the backyard oak tree right about now.

Dad stopped in the middle of the stage and leaned closer to the backdrop for a better glimpse. "Looks like the show is shaping up nicely."

A sudden amused snort from behind garnered my attention.

Claire stood behind me, waiting her turn to go onstage, her arms loaded with clothes. A satisfied smirk danced across her expression, amusement highlighting her eyes. "Wow, Addison. Is your dad going to stick around to help Mr. Adger with his car, too? Or does he only chauffer pretty English teachers?"

If I hadn't still been paralyzed with shock, I'd have slapped her with my clipboard.

Ms. Hawthorne gently tugged at my dad's arm. "I think we should let the kids get back to rehearsal." She pulled harder at my father's reluctance to follow, mouthing "I'm so sorry" to me over his shoulder.

"David, the mechanic will close in fifteen minutes." I recognized the desperate plea in Ms. Hawthorne's voice, and I realized with a start she was on my side. Just like in Got Beans.

"Oh, right. Let's get going, then." He lifted his hand in a wave as they traipsed down the stairs to the auditorium floor. At least he didn't try to hug me. "See you for dinner, Addison. Kathy's staying for meat loaf."

Just get him out, get him out. The stage dipped and bobbed, and I closed my eyes briefly against the flux of dizziness as another wave of mortifying heat washed over my body. The only way this situation could get worse is if I actually fainted. Wouldn't that be just the icing on this cake of nightmares? I inhaled deeply through my nose and let it out slowly through my mouth. Wasn't working.

Staying for meat loaf. There were so many things wrong with that sentence I wasn't even sure where to start. I just nodded weakly, leaning against Marta's supporting arm as my dad and my English teacher marched up the center aisle together.

★ ★ ★

"Amen."

I lifted my bowed head and stared at Ms. Hawthorne across

195

a platter of meat loaf. This. Was. So. Weird. And not just eating together. But praying together? Listening to her quiet murmurs of agreement to my dad's blessing over the meal? I mean, really, we were dealing with runny meat loaf and overly crisped garlic bread. What was there to agree with?

Ms. Hawthorne smiled at my dad, who grinned back like a schoolboy as he passed the pot of canned green beans he'd thrown together. Mondays were typically my day to make dinner, but since I'd been staying late several nights at the school for talent-show prep, he'd taken over some of the cooking. Which was good and bad. Mostly bad.

I reluctantly scooped up the serving spoon and ladled just enough of the meat loaf onto my plate to avoid being questioned about my appetite. To be honest, we could have had filet mignon and loaded baked potatoes and my taste buds still wouldn't have been interested.

And if Dad asked me about my English grade in front of Ms. Hawthorne. . .

"So, Addison." Ms. Hawthorne—Kathy? I still needed to figure that one out—turned her beaming smile toward me like we were all the best of friends and this awkward meal happened every day. "How's the talent show coming along?"

Oh, sure. Bring that up during the few seconds I'd actually managed to forget my dad had mortified me in front of my class. I forced my lips up at the corners, but I'm sure the effort failed miserably. "Pretty good now. Thanks to Marta. She really fired everyone up today." More like blasted them with a Taser.

"Isn't she your foreign-exchange friend?" Dad took a sip from his water glass, peering at me over the rim.

I nodded. "From Germany. She'll be going back after the school year ends." Speaking of Marta. . .I checked the cell phone I'd snuck into my lap, having sent Marta an SOS text she had yet to answer. I needed backup during this meal—moral support to remain seated in this chair like the mature teenager I was, when every instinct inside me wanted to run to my room and blare my music at top volume.

Although, come to think of it, most of the CDs I owned were Christian rock, and somehow they just didn't give off the same effect. Foiled again.

"Marta's a sweet girl. I've heard good things about her." Ms. Hawthorne took a delicate bite of meat loaf, though the consistency was so thin it would barely stay on her fork. Hmm. Maybe Dad's lack of cooking ability would turn her off and send her running back to her own table for one. Again, I had nothing personal against the woman, but meshing school life and home life was about as explosive as teen boys and cherry bombs.

"Naturally. Addison has always made good choices when picking friends."

Dad's sudden comment sent my head jerking in his direction. I narrowed my eyes as he eagerly spooned a bite of overly salted green beans. What happened to our quiet dinners together, just the two of us? Now that we had company, he felt free to compliment me and make pleasant small talk? I wasn't about to be the prize horse he showed off. My grip tightened on my fork.

"Luke is also quite the gem. I see you and Marta hanging out with him at school. He seems to have particularly taken to Marta recently." Ms. Hawthorne set her glass down, sending an amused glance my way. "I try not to pry into my students' personal lives, but some things are a little obvious."

Man, she was way off. I opened my mouth to argue that no, Luke was into *me*. But that would be just the ticket my dad needed to try to steer me away from Wes, and I wasn't up for that particular argument tonight. Not when two hours of homework waited for me upstairs, including English. How unfair was it that I had to go read chapters and write summaries while my English teacher lingered over coffee with my dad downstairs? The very picture churned my stomach, and I set my napkin on the table.

I quickly interrupted their animated chatter about my good grades, my good choices, and my impeccable attendance record at school. "May I be excused?" This trophy daughter needed some privacy, stat.

Dad looked down at my plate, like I was five years old again and he wanted to make sure I ate all my meat before I had dessert. "You didn't eat much."

"Not hungry."

Ms. Hawthorne turned a concerned expression my way. "Are you feeling all right?"

"I'm tired and have a lot of homework." I shot Ms. Hawthorne a pointed glance, which she missed while piercing another piece of meat loaf with her fork. Brave soul. Was she that desperate for a date or for a ride home from the mechanic? From the way she looked at my father, that didn't seem to be the case. No, she was here quite happily by choice.

And it didn't look like she was budging anytime soon.

My stomach rolled again, and I stood up despite not having been excused. If Dad wanted to pretend like we were some *Leave It to Beaver* family, fine. I wasn't going to play the game.

"Don't forget I'll be taking Kathy home after dessert." Dad dabbed his mouth with his napkin then gestured over his shoulder to the oven, where a frozen apple pie heated up.

"Fine. Good night to you both." I dipped my head at Ms. Hawthorne, feeling obligated to include her, despite wishing she'd just leave now. I took my plate to the kitchen sink and then retreated to the stairs.

As I crept up to the second floor, I heard Ms. Hawthorne's soothing voice consoling my father. "I think she's still a little upset about your showing up at the auditorium today."

A few dates with my father and she was suddenly an expert on my feelings? I slammed my door, the harsh sound a welcome respite to the gentle tones below. The worst part was, she was right. I *was* still upset, but not just about that. I'd pay that price tomorrow, especially if Claire followed through with the mischievous gleam in her eye. We might have had a tentative truce, but this kind of gossip would be far too juicy for her to pass up.

But even knowing what was sure to come tomorrow, at the moment I was more upset about Ms. Hawthorne inching her way into our lives—and my dad holding wide the proverbial front door.

I flopped on my bed with a groan and glared at my backpack, wishing for once that homework would just do itself. Any other kid in my position would blow it off and let Ms. Hawthorne figure out why I hadn't done the work. But being forgiven for a missed assignment again wasn't worth being treated differently than the rest of my class.

With a sigh, I lugged my backpack toward me.

Ping.

I glanced at my window. *Ping*. The tiny sound came again. I pulled back the curtain, and there was Wes, throwing rocks. I yanked up the sill and leaned out, careful to keep my voice down. "You do realize I have a cell phone."

"Too modern." He squinted up at me with a grin, the moonlight doing dangerous things to his eyes.

My stomach fluttered. "Right. Because your leather jacket and motorcycle are so vintage."

"You never gave me your number."

"You never took it."

We stared at each other in a silent showdown until Wes finally shrugged. "You coming down or not?" He acted like he was about to lob another rock, and I ducked on instinct.

"Very funny." I leaned my hip against the window frame, letting the brisk night air cool my temper. A gentle breeze rustled the leaves of the oak tree beside my window, a familiar, comforting sound that had put me to sleep many times growing up. "I'm not exactly having a great night."

"So make it better." Wes motioned for me to join him, as if jumping from a second-story window was that easy. "I got the Jeep again, don't worry."

A million excuses and justifications flooded my mind, fighting for top billing. I couldn't just leave with Wes for a few hours, though the idea was much more inviting than hunching over my schoolwork all evening. And Dad was about to take Ms. Hawthorne home, so he wouldn't even miss me for a while— especially since that pie was still in the oven. Still. . .

I closed my eyes, my previous frustration and anger boiling up again. Ms. Hawthorne, spearing green beans like we were all a happy little family. Dad, not even giving a second glance to the framed photo of Mom on the end table. Ms. Hawthorne, whispering secrets to my father about my own thoughts and feelings, like she knew me. Like she belonged.

Like she was my mother.

I opened my eyes and gave Wes a firm nod before I could change my mind. "Do me one favor?"

"What's that?" Wes tilted his head to one side, his dark hair falling across his forehead.

I reached for the closet branch of the oak and took a deep breath. "Catch me."

Chapter Twenty-Two

The stars twinkled above my head through the open roof as the Jeep glided down the two-lane country highway, away from Crooked Hollow. I took a deep breath of the night air and felt myself relax for the first time in days. "I'm glad I came."

"Me, too. You looked like you were about to crack." Wes adjusted his rearview mirror then sent me a quick glance. "You sure you're all right, PK?"

My worries over Wes not having called me all weekend faded away at the concern in his voice. "I'm fine now." Especially since I'd successfully climbed down the tree and not broken my neck.

I hesitantly moved my hand to the console, and Wes twined his fingers through mine. I leaned back against the headrest and closed my eyes, listening to the melody of the open road, the night air, the hum of distant traffic.

The click of a blinker.

"Where are we going?" I asked as Wes turned off the highway onto a tree-lined side street.

He flashed me a smile. "It's a surprise."

"When did you have time to plan a surprise? Thirty minutes ago you didn't even know if I was coming with you." I held on to the roll bar as he made another sharp turn to the left, this time onto a gravel road barely wide enough for one car, much less two.

"I figured you would."

I squinted at him. "A little cocky, are we?"

"Just roll with it, PK. Everything doesn't always have to be scheduled."

Or black and white, if your name was Wes Keegan.

He maneuvered the Jeep around a series of potholes and finally pulled over to the side. An open pasture, covered in autumn's tall grass, spread for miles. The sky, away from streetlights and the city's glare, seemed blacker than ink.

"Come on." He opened his door and climbed out, and I followed suit, trying not to notice how he didn't open mine for me—again. I shut the door behind me and stood silently, drinking in the unobstructed view of the stars. It felt good to get away. Sometimes a girl just needed a moment of peace. Away from English teachers, overprotective, distant fathers, stacks of schoolbooks two feet high. . .

Away from her own conscience.

Wes joined me after a moment, his arms laden with a folded blanket and a picnic basket. "Hungry?"

Wes, with a picnic basket? Somewhere especially warm must have frozen over. I crossed my arms over my chest and grinned. "Hey, Yogi Bear called. He wants his basket back."

"Funny. You hungry or not?"

"Aren't I always?" I followed him to a flat patch of ground several yards away from the Jeep. I'd take a moonlight picnic for two over his opening the door for me any day. "I'm starved, actually. I sort of bailed on dinner."

"Don't blame you." He shook out the blanket and set the basket on top then motioned for me to have a seat. The night air chilled my arms, and he tossed another, lighter blanket my way. "Here, it's colder out than I'd realized."

I draped the quilt around my shoulders and watched, fascinated, as Wes brought out paper plates and several containers from the wooden basket. Who'd have thought this guy had even one romantic bone in his body, much less an entire skeletal structure? After fixing two plates with grapes, sliced strawberries, and cheese squares, he handed me a wine glass. "And for the finishing touch." He uncorked a bottle of red wine and poured us each a glass.

A full glass.

I stared at the burgundy liquid and started to shake my head before I even spoke. "No thanks. I'm good."

"It's just wine, Addison."

"And last time I checked, I wasn't twenty-one. Neither are you."

"I'm old enough to vote; I should be old enough to drink." He took a sip then set the glass on the edge of the blanket away from his plate. "It's relaxing. Takes the edge off."

"Takes the edge off what? Your sense of balance? Your judgment?"

"Don't make this a big deal, PK. If you don't want any, fine. Just don't give me grief, okay?"

"Okay." I bit into a strawberry, not wanting to ruin the night he'd obviously made great effort toward. Besides, as long as he only had one glass, he should be fine to drive me home. I wasn't against taking the keys from him later if need be. Maybe there were some things in my life lately I felt unsure about, but riding around with a drunk driver wasn't one of them.

He leaned back on his elbows, popping a cube of cheese into his mouth. "You're not the only one having a rough night. Or having father issues."

"Oh yeah? So what'd your dad do? Date your old school

principal?" I crossed my legs Indian-style, turning slightly to face him.

Wes snorted. "Hardly." He reached for his glass, taking a sip of the wine and swirling it around absently. "He yells a lot. Stupid stuff."

I shrugged. "Parents yell. It seems common. Not everyone is as quiet as my dad." And not everyone was me, who hardly ever gave cause for yelling. Weird combo.

Pretty boring one, too.

"Oh yeah? Well, is this common?" Wes rolled up his sleeves and revealed a bruise the size of a fist on his arm.

A chill crept over my body that had nothing to do with the breeze. Mr. Keegan? No way. Yet that kind of bruise didn't come from misjudging a door frame or edge of the counter.

Wes must have read my train of thought as he rolled his sleeve down. "Yeah, sweet ol' parishioner Mr. Keegan. There's more where these came from, when he's drunk." He shook his head. "Appearances are deceiving, Addison. Remember that."

Drunk?

Suddenly it all made brutal sense. The glazed-over look in Mr. Keegan's eyes every Sunday. The rearranging of the contents in his basket before he approached my father and me at Crooked Hollow Grocery. The abundance of breath mints.

Finally, I found my voice, and it sounded shaky even to my own ears. "Then why don't you just leave?" I huddled into my blanket, unable to look away from the patch of sleeve covering proof that I was more sheltered than I'd ever realized.

"And go back to my mom, who tossed me here? Said she was sick of me? No thanks. I can handle myself." Wes took a long sip from his glass, his eyes stony.

"Then why not get a job and move out?"

He shot me a "be real" glance over the rim. "This is Crooked

Hollow. Businesses aren't exactly desperate for help. And if it's freezing out or raining, I have to borrow the Jeep when my dad's passed out on the couch with a twelve-pack." He looked away, up at the stars pricking the onyx sky. "Besides, do you really think I'd make enough for my own place shoving mochas across the counter at Got Beans? Or retrieving gutter balls from the bowling alley?"

Not even close. He must have felt as trapped as I often did, just in a more literal sense. I was sixteen—well, almost seventeen. No one expected me to be on my own. After all, I was a junior in high school—I was supposed to live at home, have a curfew, complain about doing homework. But Wes was legal age. He was out in the real world, free to live his own life—just stuck.

Maybe that's where the bird tattoo came in.

Compassion built a solid tower in my chest. I always knew there was more to Wes than initial impressions. If Marta could have heard the pain in his voice, she'd have regretted ever saying anything negative against him.

I studied his profile, heart clenching. "I don't know what to say." Here I was with the perfect opportunity to witness to Wes, to say something encouraging, something to prompt him toward God, toward church, toward changing his current pattern of misbehavior. Something to make him want to be good.

But I had nothing.

God, what do I do? What do I say? But the halfhearted prayer stuck in my throat. Just like in my bedroom at home, my prayers didn't seem to make it past the first layer of the atmosphere.

"It's not your fault. I shouldn't have dumped that on you." Wes tossed his empty glass in the picnic basket and scooted closer to me on the blanket. "I wanted you to relax, not stress you out."

"I'm not stressed." Just hurt for him. I wanted to say that but didn't know how to cross the barrier that still somehow seemed etched between us. I couldn't figure Wes out. One minute he was a lighthearted, witty man playing the piano at Got Beans for my ears only, and the next he was a sullen, angry guy with a the-world-hates-me-sized chip on his shoulder. Where did the real Wes live? It had to be somewhere between those two extremes—somewhere next to where the romantic, picnic-planning Wes resided.

"Enough about me." Wes brushed my hair back from my face, his fingers lightly skimming my cheekbone. "Where did we leave off in your driveway the other night?" He grinned and leaned in for a kiss.

You mean the night when you never agreed to call me and left me waiting all weekend? I wanted to ask, but his lips were already covering mine. The question forgotten, I kissed him back, lost in the enchantment of his spicy leather scent, in the calloused brush of his fingers, in the tantalizing contradiction of cold air and warm breath.

Then his kiss became more urgent, and I might not have even noticed if he hadn't started pushing me back on the blanket. "Wait a second." I jerked my head to the side, breaking contact.

"It's more comfortable down here." Wes tugged at my elbow, and I reluctantly fell down beside him on the blanket. He kissed me again, his hand cupping my shoulder, his knuckles weaving gentle patterns against the tight muscles of my neck, and I forgot my hesitations. My mind blurred in and out, thoughts grasping and fading like a radio trying to tune. How did I go from never-been-kissed to *this*? What had I been missing? Yet somehow I instinctively knew that if I hadn't been kissing Wes specifically, it wouldn't have been nearly as amazing.

I got so lost in the haze of kissing that it took a moment before I realized Wes's hand had left my arm and now prodded at the button of my jeans. *No, no, no. Yes. No.* My body and mind fought a battle as I batted his hand away then allowed him to try again. *No. Yes.*

No. My purity ring suddenly weighed like a boulder on my finger, and with great effort, I broke our kiss and sat up.

Wes stayed reclined on one elbow, a smile on his face but something darker and void of humor in his eyes. "What's the matter, PK?"

All of Marta's warnings about being on the same page with each other swam in my mind, and I struggled for breath, struggled to find a clear thought, something I could hold on to. "I'm a virgin." Oh wow, that totally wasn't what I meant to say.

Cheeks flaming, I wrapped my fingers around my ring, the cold metal biting into my flesh.

"I sort of figured that. It's not a problem, don't worry." Wes sat up beside me, his hands massaging my shoulders that moments ago had been so relaxed. Now they were knotted with tension, and I shrugged away.

His smile disappeared. "Come on, Addison. What's the big deal?"

"The big deal?" I edged away from him, far enough to turn and look him steadily in the eyes. Gone was the flush of embarrassment and in its place, anger. How dare he ignore me all weekend then try this? *And* act like casual sex was completely normal? What was wrong with him? "It's a huge deal." *I'm not Sonya.* But he knew that. It was more than obvious, especially now. My stomach dipped and churned. "Unlike some people, I don't take sex lightly."

"What makes you think I do? And besides, do you even have a reason, or is it just like with all the other forbidden fruits you don't have answers for?" Wes challenged. "Because your dad said not to. . .because your church youth group says it's bad. . ." His voice trailed off as his expectant gaze waited for my answer.

One I still didn't have.

Still, I didn't like the glint in his eye, the one that looked like a cross between amusement and mocking. Who was he to judge? I lifted my chin. "Maybe that's exactly why."

Frustration laced his tone. "You sound real sure."

I *was* sure. Sort of. I mean, something had made me sit up, made me throw on the brakes and say no—and not just to him, but to the alcohol as well. But what was it? My own conscience? God? Common sense?

Why did I suddenly not know the answers to all the questions I grew up reciting?

"Everyone is a virgin at some point, Addison. That's got to change eventually. Why not with me, tonight? I did this for you. For us." Wes gestured to the spread around us, and a sense of understanding sunk in. Wes had gone to a lot of trouble, and he wanted to be with me. *Me.* Addison Blakely, PK. Not to mention he was hurting over his dad. Upset. Broken. My heart caved a little.

But not that much.

"I can't." I pressed my lips together, now raw and swollen. What had felt so good, so right moments ago suddenly just burned. I closed my eyes briefly, taking a steadying breath. When I opened them, Wes shook his head in disappointment.

"So that's that? You're sure?"

I nodded, and he sighed then began to pack up the basket. I remained still, unable to speak, refusing to allow him even one more minute to try and change my mind.

Because I still wasn't entirely convinced he couldn't.

Chapter Twenty-Three

School comes really early in the morning when you toss and turn all night, reliving and rewriting the past.

I stood on the front lawn of Crooked Hollow High, a contraband cup of hot mocha in my hand, shivering as the late-autumn air lifted my hair from my scarf and blew wisps across my face. Good. Maybe it would hide my bloodshot eyes. I shivered but stood my ground, knowing I couldn't take my coffee into the school and refusing to dump even a drop of caffeine into the trash can. Taking another long sip, I ignored the chill and let my inside grow toasty warm while my cheeks chafed in the cold.

"Addison, come inside." Marta bounced on the balls of her feet, rubbing her arms briskly in an effort to keep warm. "Everyone has forgotten about yesterday's talent-show rehearsal. I am sure of it."

"Your accent thickens when you lie." I stubbornly drank another swig, wishing I still had half a cup left to stall with. After yesterday's embarrassment with my father and Ms. Hawthorne replaying in my mind, and the disastrous evening with Wes tugging at my heart, I just wanted to curl up in a ball and hide. Process. Try to make sense of what was swirling around my brain.

She swatted at my arm. "I am not lying."

"Then use contractions."

Marta's brow puckered in confusion.

"You said 'I am' instead of 'I'm.' " I brandished my coffee toward her. "Americans use contractions."

Her eyes narrowed as she crossed her arms over her chest. "How about this one? *You're* crazy."

Great, not only was I being a jerk to my best friend, but now my mocha was gone, and I hadn't even savored the last sip. I tossed the empty cup into a trash can and eyed the school, feeling as if the weary building with its dirty glass-window eyes stared right back. Peering into me, seeing my secrets. Knowing what'd I'd almost done last night.

What I'd wanted to do.

I shivered again, this time not from the cold.

Marta's stance softened, her arms slipping to hang at her sides. "What happened? I get the idea you are upset about more than just your father showing up at school yesterday."

I let her lack of contraction pass that time and offered a shrug instead. I didn't want to lie to her. None of this was her fault. But what could I say? I hated to admit Marta was right, that Wes and I were most definitely not on the same page when it came to expectations, and that after he'd rolled up the picnic blanket and stuffed it in the backseat of the Jeep, he hadn't said another word the entire drive back to my house. Had I failed his test? Were we over? The thought made my stomach churn with disappointment, yet how could I want to stay with someone who asked things of me I couldn't give—wouldn't give?—and then pouted over it? Not one of Wes's best moments.

And definitely not one of my mine.

Still, I couldn't make myself let go. I kept picturing the hurt radiating from his features as he talked about his family, a layer of pain he probably didn't even realize he showed. Wes Keegan, vulnerable? Historic moment.

So why did he have to ruin it by changing the subject so abruptly—and physically?

"Is it Wes?" Marta's prodding voice penetrated my shield, reading my mind. I rolled in my lower lip and nodded. She shuffled a few steps closer, lowering her voice even though we were the only two idiots willing to stand outside in the cold before the warning bell. "Did you see him last night?"

Tears welled in my throat and I coughed, trying to clear the dam. "I snuck out." Saying the words out loud made the guilt roll in like tidal waves, and I couldn't believe I'd been lucky enough to get back inside the house without my dad realizing. After sneaking in once again through the window (and trust me, getting down that tree with help was much easier than getting back up solo), I'd checked on him, and there he sat dozing in front of the TV, his Bible open on his lap like any other night. Seeing the open Bible brought equal measures of guilt and bitterness, and I still had no idea why the contradiction. Guilt, I expected. Resentment? Not so much.

"Did something. . .happen?" Marta's hesitant question spoke volumes louder than her quiet tone.

My chest warmed under my sweater, and I fought the crimson stain I knew had to be rising up my cheeks. "Almost. But no."

Marta tugged the hem of her shirt farther over the top of her jeans, and I realized for the first time she wasn't even wearing a jacket. Yet there she stood with me, discussing my love life in what felt like subzero temps, without a single complaint. Man, this was so screwed up. I didn't deserve her. My dad didn't deserve me treating him with such disrespect for his rules. And I didn't deserve the drama he and Ms. Hawthorne were doling out in my life.

When did everything get so complicated?

Marta's sigh broke my runaway train of thought. "You look confused. Tell me what you're feeling."

"I have no idea." Too much. Not enough. A headache pounded at my temples, and I wished I could wrap my scarf around my face and hide from the world. Not a bad idea, actually. That would solve the problem of going through my day with coffee breath.

"Just try. Whatever this is, you need to get it all out."

I shut my eyes, trying to focus, and pressed my fingers against the bridge of my nose, desperate but unable to fully identify the emotions dancing a conga line inside my head. "Frustration." Ah, there was one, finally. "Anger." Yep, definitely anger over Wes ignoring me the rest of the night. "Confusion." That one in abundance. "Regret."

That last one got me, and I opened my eyes. Marta's widened gaze met mine with shock. "Explain that one."

I opened my mouth then shut it, fear creeping along my spine. Regret that I hadn't pushed the boundaries even further with Wes? Regret that I'd snuck out and deceived my dad? Regret that I hadn't done it all sooner?

Or was it just regret that Wes had initiated the idea of sex, and now I had no idea where our relationship stood?

Before I could decide, Luke strode across the grassy lawn toward us, hands shoved in the pockets of his hooded jacket. "What the heck are you girls doing out here? It's freezing."

"It's actually forty-six degrees." Marta pointed to the digital temperature reading flashing on the school's roadside sign.

"Sarcasm doesn't suit you." He tweaked her chin then rested his propped elbow on my shoulder. "It better suits Addison here."

"Such a comedian."

Luke frowned. "You all right?" He tilted his head, peering down into my face. If he smelled my coffee breath, it served him right for getting so close. Yet somehow his presence didn't annoy me or make me crave distance. He just felt safe. I leaned a little into the warmth his shoulder offered, wishing I could just like Luke instead and ride off into the sunset on a white horse.

But sadly, the only thing I could see myself roaring away on was made of metal and steel, not horseflesh.

I shrugged out from under his arm. "Just having some girl talk."

"Wes was being a jerk," Marta blurted out.

"Thanks a lot." I glared at her, wishing I had a superpower that would allow to me to dole out bad hair days with my eyes. She'd so have a 1980s perm.

"Wes, a jerk? Shocker." Luke bit his lip and winced as he looked back at me. "Sorry, that was rude."

"It's not a secret you guys are not best friends." Marta rolled her eyes. "And Addison, Luke put up with a lot on our double date the other night. He deserves to know the truth."

"Whatever. It's my business." I stalked away from them both, knowing Marta was right and it wasn't that big a deal. But I needed a release, and they were the closest. Better to leave now before I really exploded.

Heavy footsteps jogged after me; then a hand gripped my elbow and tugged me to a stop.

I whirled around. "What, Luke?" I wasn't in the mood for this. If everyone didn't leave me alone, I was going to cry. Not like I bothered to wear makeup today anyway, but still. I had enough crap about to hit me concerning my dad and Ms. Hawthorne without having to worry about blotchy cheeks and red-rimmed eyes, too. Wouldn't that just feed the gossip sharks?

"Look, I'm sorry. I didn't mean to upset you." Luke's blond

hair dipped in his eyes, and he impatiently shoved it back. "I guess this is all just a little complicated."

"You're telling me."

The warning bell rang, piercing the silence of the schoolyard. Perfect. Now we were officially tardy, and Mr. Varland wasn't the most forgiving of history teachers. Probably because my dad wasn't dating him.

Desperate to head to class and get this inevitably awful day over with, I gripped Luke's arm and looked him straight in the eyes. "Do me a favor, okay?"

"Of course. Anything." His eyes lit with anticipation, and I hated to snuff out the puppy-dog eagerness in his eyes. It made me feel even worse. But it had to be done.

"Stop liking me. I'm not worth it." Then I ripped away and rushed into the school.

★ ★ ★

I just thought there had been whispers and stares after Ms. Hawthorne let me off the homework hook a few weeks back. Now I realized that had been nothing. I actually wished for that back. Whispers and stares were much better than pointing fingers, muffled laughter, and out-loud jokes. Pretty sad that I felt grateful toward the students who at least tried to hide what they were talking about.

Staring into the depths of my locker, I glared at my English textbook and hated the fact that class was next. I wanted to go home and start this day over. No, the week. If I had a do-over, I'd have stayed put with my homework and never climbed down that oak tree. Better yet, my dad would have never come to school yesterday, and everyone would be snickering over Lucy McPhee's obvious boob job today rather than hating on my father and my English teacher. Instead, Lucy and her Double-Ds got off scot-free while I faced the torture chamber alone.

I shut my locker and came face-to-face with Claire, flanked by two fellow cheerleaders. "Great. I was wondering how my day could get worse."

Claire smirked, ignoring my comment. "How was the meat loaf?"

"Undercooked. Anything else you want to know?" I shifted my bag higher on my shoulder.

"That depends." Claire shot a look at her plastic friends, who grinned as if they knew what was next. "Is Ms. Hawthorne's car ready, or will she be staying the night at your house again?"

"What?" My defensive act fell useless to my feet, and a fresh wave of anger rushed up my stomach into my chest. "That's ridiculous. You know she didn't stay over."

"Maybe. Maybe not." Claire fluttered her eyelashes dramatically at me. "Why don't we ask Ms. Hawthorne? Maybe she could be convinced to give us some As to keep the rumor mill quiet—like she did for you."

I'd heard the phrase about blood boiling before but never truly understood it until that exact moment. So Claire was out not only to mortify me, but now to ruin both my teacher's and my father's reputations—for the sake of a grade? Like Ms. Hawthorne would ever go for it anyway. She was too good a teacher to fall for bribery or extortion. When had Claire sunk to this level of jerkiness?

Straightening my shoulders, I crossed my arms and stared back. "Fine. Let's ask her, and after that, I'll see if we can sort out your interesting eating habits with the school counselor." I lifted my chin, daring Claire to push me further.

Claire's eyes narrowed to tiny slits, and one of the cheerleaders nudged her. "What's she talking about?"

Elbowing the girl away, Claire kept her hard gaze on me. "Whatever. You're bluffing."

"Last week, yeah, I probably would have been. Today, not so much." I shoved between the group of girls, purposefully bouncing my heavy backpack off Claire. "Guess you'll have to find out." I hurried to class without a backward glance, but I could feel Claire's gaze burrowing into my head the entire way. What was wrong with her? Did she hate me so badly just because of Austin? It had to be more than that. Who cared about a stupid football player? How did we go from lifelong friends to this dirty level of revenge?

I sank into my seat, nodding at Luke in the chair beside mine but refusing to look him in the eye. Turned out it wasn't possible anyway, with the way he slumped across his desk and braced his head on his palm, his hand effectively blocking his profile. Mainly his view of me.

Great. One more enemy to add to my growing list.

And apparently there was room for one more. After class Ms. Hawthorne called me to her desk. Now what? I trudged the aisle to the front of the room like I was taking a death march. My textbook suddenly heavy in my hand, I rested it on the edge of her desk and waited for her to speak first, my mouth dry. I hated the influx of emotions roiling in my chest and didn't dare look at her for fear of erupting.

"Addison, I think we need to talk." Ms. Hawthorne stood so we were on the same level.

I swallowed. "You've heard the rumors, then?"

"It's hard not to." She came around the edge of her desk to lean her weight against the side. She crossed one boot-clad ankle over the other, and I stared at the dot of dirt smudging the toe. Maybe if I focused on that one spot, I could get this conversation over with and leave with as much dignity as I had left. If there was any.

"Are you all right?"

Ms. Hawthorne's soft voice was enough to break the dam, and I crumbled. Literally. I collapsed against her desk, my behind knocking over a pencil organizer and sending pens and highlighters clattering to the floor. "No." My voice broke into a muffled sob, and I buried my face in my hands, mortified.

She didn't even seem to notice the mess I'd made. Instead she patted my shoulder with one hand, enough of a touch to be comforting but not so much that I felt invaded. I appreciated that little gesture more than she'd ever realize and let the tears flow in an incredibly unattractive display.

"It's been a rough week, hasn't it?" Ms. Hawthorne's hand patted a little faster, and I fought back a hiccup as I wiped my eyes with the back of my hands.

"You could say that." I snorted, embarrassed but feeling better for having relieved the pressure behind my eyes.

"A good cry can do wonders." Ms. Hawthorne smiled, drawing back a step to give me a little space now that my freak-out had subsided. Then her eyes grew pensive, and her smile faded. "And single fathers not dating teachers could probably do wonders, too, huh?"

I started to agree, as hope rose in my chest that she could possibly be willing to give up her newfound relationship with my dad for me. Could it be that simple? But the disappointment in her gaze stopped me short, and I pressed my lips together into a thin line. *This is your chance, Addison. Agree with her. End this nightmare already.* But I couldn't. Maybe it was the guilt over knowing what I'd gotten away with last night, or maybe it was just sensing that she truly cared about my father. Whatever it was, I shook my head, the motion feeling a lot less forced than I'd thought it would.

"That's not what I want."

Her eyebrows lifted with surprise, and I talked faster before

I could back down. "I think you're good for my father. It's. . . weird. And the rumors suck." I bit my lower lip then continued. "But that shouldn't stop two adults from being happy."

Ms. Hawthorne's eyes lit with warmth. "I have to admit, I'm a little surprised to hear that. I thought after last night's dinner that things were pretty bad."

"Oh, they are." I grinned to take the edge off my tone I couldn't keep out. I drew a deep breath. "But this is the right decision. Your relationship with my dad is your business." *And if you still want to break up later, that'd be great.* But not because of me. I couldn't do that to either of them, even if the thought of more meat loaf dinners for three did make me want to barf. For multiple reasons.

"How can we make this work then, Addison?" She crossed her arms over her silk blouse and tilted her head toward me. "I don't want you to be a martyr. High school is hard enough. I remember."

Unlikely, but it was nice of her to try. I shrugged. "I guess we can start by agreeing to no special favors. The other students think you're hooking me up with good grades or letting me slack on missed assignments."

"That's preposterous." Ms. Hawthorne shook her head. "I didn't write you up for that homework assignment because it was your first time to miss one. From what I gather from other teachers about your stellar reputation, it was your first time to miss a paper *ever*."

True. Shame coated my insides. She had a point, yet I had been willing to believe Claire and the others because of my own doubt. "You're right. You're fair. I know that." I picked up my book, signaling I hoped this conversation was done. "I'll remember next time."

"And I'll be sure to give you a D on your next quiz just to

even the score." She kept such a straight face my heart skipped a beat in raw panic before I caught the amused glint in her eye.

"Touché." I smiled—genuinely—for the first time all day. The warning bell rang, and students for the next class began shuffling into the room. I backed up a few steps toward the door, raising my voice above the sudden din. "I guess I'll see you later."

She nodded and lifted one hand in a wave before settling back at her desk.

I exited into the hallway, silently finishing the rest of my sentence. *Just hopefully not at my house for dinner.*

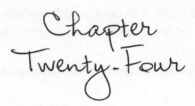

Chapter
Twenty-Four

I squinted at the array of paint samples in front of me on the rack at Crooked Hollow Hardware, totally not seeing how Evergreen Dream differed from Dark Forest. But oh, Mrs. Lyons had been adamant. "We need one small can of paint on hand, in case something happens to the backdrop and it needs touch-ups before the show," she'd said earlier that afternoon after practice. There'd been two pencils stuck in her hair, one with teeth marks, and I couldn't bear to tell her it seemed like a waste of money for a "just in case" scenario.

Oh well, it wasn't my cash. At least hanging out at the hardware store meant I didn't have to go home for dinner right away and face Dad—and pretend I hadn't climbed down a tree the other night to go out with a guy he'd all but forbidden.

I plucked Evergreen Dream from the row of color chips, wishing my conscience would hush already, and turned to the counter to have the paint mixed. A familiar, agitated voice from the next row over stopped me a few feet short of the desk.

"This is all overpriced. What are they trying to do, rob me?"

I frowned. Mr. Keegan? Great, someone else to avoid tonight. I couldn't exactly look him in the eye, knowing what I did about his drinking problem and temper.

That is, if Wes had been telling the truth. I still found it hard to fully believe. Not that being at church every Sunday made someone perfect, but you'd think the truth would have slipped by now if Wes was right. Maybe he'd just been using the story or exaggerating it to get sympathy from me—to get to third base.

Though that bruise had sure looked real enough. And there was the matter of the constant breath mints and the odd behavior at the grocery store. . . .

An even more familiar voice sounded next. "If you hadn't thrown that statue at the coffee table, you wouldn't need to rebuild it."

Wes. My heart stopped then thudded painfully. I clutched the paint chip to my chest, mind racing. What if he wandered down this row next? I couldn't see either of them. Not like this. Not with last night still hanging between us.

"At this point it looks cheaper to just buy another table." Lumber rattled from aisle four.

"I doubt that," Wes argued. "Besides, are you planning on whipping out a pottery wheel to rebuild that statue, too?"

"Who cares? That was your mother's favorite. I don't even know how I ended up with it anyway."

"So it's only okay to throw things you *don't* like?" Wes's egging tone riled my own blood pressure. I could only imagine what it was doing to his dad's. But it seemed like they were a matched pair.

Worse yet, it seemed they were used to this sort of interaction.

"Like you've never broken anything when you've been mad." Mr. Keegan snorted, sarcasm lacing his voice. So *that's* where Wes got his snort. Genetics.

"Whatever." I could almost see Wes rolling his dark eyes. "You were mad and drunk. Fun combo."

"Quit judging me," Mr. Keegan's voice snarled. "At least I go to church and make an effort. You're just content to sit on that stupid bike of yours and sneer down at the rest of the world."

I braced my hand against the counter, trying to steady what felt like the world turning over on its axis. It was true about Mr. Keegan. All of it. Not an emotional ploy by Wes.

More like a cry for help.

A heavy sigh carried over the rack of primer cans, followed by Wes's voice, laced with weariness. "Great. A hungover father and a hardware store. Just what I want to do on a Tuesday night."

"I'm not hungover anymore. And keep your voice down. This isn't exactly public knowledge."

The room dipped as opposite images of Mr. Keegan swirled through my brain. Mr. Keegan, smiling in his pressed slacks at church. Mr. Keegan, asleep with a beer can in hand on his couch. Mr. Keegan, carrying on a carefree conversation with me after the service. Mr. Keegan, using Wes as a punching bag when he'd had one too many.

"What, afraid of running into your beloved pastor and him learning the truth?" Wes laughed, the sound hollow and void.

Mr. Keegan snorted. "At least I try. You're one to talk—you drink as much as me."

My stomach dropped, and I covered my mouth with my hand, my earlier fears realized. I knew that wine last night hadn't just been a special occasion.

Wes's voice rose in aggravation. "I don't drink like that anymore, and you know it!"

Not anymore? I'd just watched him drink a glass. In fact, if I thought about it long enough, I could practically still taste it in his kiss. Was he lying? Or did he used to drink so much he considered a glass of wine nothing at all?

"And I've never broken furniture," Wes continued.

"Help me carry this." Boards clattered against each other. "And before you get high and mighty, remember you put a hole in the wall a month ago."

There was a long pause. "That was an accident."

"Oh so you *accidentally* punched the wall? While ticked off? How convenient."

Wes's voice rose with disgust. "It was either that or punch you back."

I gasped then slapped my hand over my mouth. My stomach churned as my mind desperately tried to mesh what I just heard with what I'd seen over the years. What I'd seen in Wes. I felt like a page opened before me, allowing me to read a few more lines of his story. I knew he felt unwanted with both his parents. Bounced back and forth. Knew he carried a lot of resentment, a ton of anger. But all I could think when I pictured Wes's string of rash behavior was, *No wonder.* And through my shock, one thought resonated louder than the rest.

He didn't hit back.

An elderly man wearing the signature yellow store apron approached me from the side. "Miss? Do you need assistance?"

Boy, did I. I stared at him blankly, my ears still fully focused on the conversation a few yards away. "Yes." Then I realized he meant the paint sample in my hand, not my feeling like I might faint at any moment. "No. I mean, yes. But not right now." I shooed him off, not wanting to miss the rest of what was said.

He frowned, confusion pinching his bushy gray eyebrows. "I'll be right over here when you're ready."

"Fine, thanks." I waved him away, trying to look casual as my ears strained for any hint of tension from the next aisle.

But silence hung as thick as a storm cloud, ready to burst. I halfway felt like peering around the end display to make sure they hadn't somehow killed each other right there in aisle four. But before I could decide, a board clattered to the floor. "Forget it. I'm out of here."

My stomach dropped. Wes. Leaving. I looked around for a hiding place, but the older clerk was now staring at me, probably thinking the crazy girl with the paint chips was about to shoplift. I settled for ducking my head and hiding behind my curtain of hair. Maybe Wes would leave via the other end of aisle four and not this one—

A series of electronic beeps sounded mere feet away as someone dialed on their cell phone. I looked up as Wes turned the corner and spoke into the phone. "Sonya? Yeah. I'm coming. See ya in ten."

He hung up as his eyes locked with mine.

The warm rush of compassion I'd been feeling moments ago froze over with the mention of Sonya's name. I stared, unable to move, though in my heart I was already out the door and halfway down the street at a full run.

I swallowed, looking away, determined not to be the one to speak first. Drumming the paint chip on the counter, I looked impatiently over my shoulder. "Sir? I'm ready to order my paint now." I made a show of checking my watch, as if I'd been a victim of bad customer service instead of eavesdropping.

"Addison." Wes's voice lowered, and he closed the distance between us by a few feet, yet still stopping well away from the counter. "What are you doing here?"

I put a happy falsetto to my voice, hoping to hide the layers of emotion threatening to break free of the dam. "Oh you know, talent-show stuff." Forget happy. I sounded like Minnie Mouse. I coughed, trying to look casual as pain seeped through my chest. "An assistant director's job never ends."

"Uh-huh." Wes nodded, looking unsure if he should continue to make small talk or head for the hills.

Leave, please leave. I forced a smile at the elderly clerk ambling around the counter, who suddenly seemed less than eager to help me check out. "Evergreen Dream, please. One gallon."

He took the chip from me with paint-speckled fingers and eyed me from under his glasses. "Coming right up."

I dared a glance at Wes, who had shoved his cell in his pocket. "How much did you—what did. . ." His voice trailed off as he gestured over his shoulder to aisle four before crossing his arms over his chest. No leather jacket tonight, just a dark-green pullover that made him look achingly approachable. Charming.

Yet somehow more dangerous than ever.

Sympathetic or not, I wasn't about to make this easier on him. Not when he was upset and choosing to turn to Sonya instead of me. "What? Frog in your throat? Cat got your tongue?"

He narrowed his eyes at me, but not before I caught the exhaustion coating his expression. "Neither."

"Well then you should probably hurry." I spoke to Wes, but looked at the clerk, who frowned at me as he continued to mix my order. Great, now he thought I was suspicious *and* rude.

Wes ran a hand through his hair. "Addison, listen. About what happened last night—"

"Just go." I broke him off before the clerk's eyebrows could totally disappear into his receding hairline. Now I was suspicious, rude, and promiscuous. But if he knew what really happened—or rather, didn't happen—he'd be applauding instead of judging. I turned back to Wes, inwardly begging God not to let my tears spill over while he stood there. "It's not important."

The lie burned my tongue, and I felt like the evergreen paint swirling on the machine. Jumbled. Mixed up. How could he connect with me like he did and then seek Sonya out for comfort instead? Because he knew I wouldn't do what she would? Was that all a relationship was to him—physical?

I couldn't do this anymore. I wasn't that girl and never would be, even if I wasn't one hundred percent sure of all the reasons why. I just didn't want to be.

That was enough for now.

I jerked my gaze from the paint and firmly met Wes's stare, willing strength into my knees. "Have fun at Sonya's." *Don't go. Stay. Choose me.* My traitorous thoughts refused to fall into line with my will, and I hoped Wes couldn't see the contradiction in my eyes. Or maybe I hoped he did.

Either way, it didn't matter. He nodded once and strode away, refusing me a backward glance. I watched his retreating figure, relief and disappointment battling for center stage.

But they were both elbowed out of the way by the appearance of a thousand tiny cracks shattering my heart.

Marta showed up with cupcakes exactly seventeen minutes after my SOS text later that night. She nudged open my bedroom door with her foot, toting the box of minicupcakes in one hand and carrying her backpack on her other shoulder. "The junk food has arrived."

I looked up from my position on the bed, surrounded by textbooks I'd opened partially out of necessity, mostly as a disguise. "You brought props. Nice touch." I pointed to the book bag she dropped with a thud to the floor.

"If I am here to study, I have to look the part." She set the box with the familiar red CROOKED HOLLOW BAKERY logo on my desk and pulled two forks wrapped in napkins from her purse. "And we are going to study. No more lies." She shot me a pointed stare.

We told my dad we had a Spanish test coming up, which was true, and that we needed to study, which was also true. We just left out the part about me also needing girl talk and obscene amounts of sugar.

"Technically, I didn't lie to my dad." I held up one finger in defense. "He never specifically asked me if I snuck out the window and went out with Wes last night."

She shook her head. "Weak."

"I know." I sighed and eagerly waved her over. "Comfort food, please."

Marta passed me a cupcake then sat cross-legged on the other end of the bed. I didn't even use the fork or the napkin she offered—just crammed the entire mini–chocolate dessert in my mouth. Peanut butter icing squished between my teeth like a burst of heaven, and I would have sighed in delight if it wouldn't have sent crumbs spraying all over my bedspread.

"So how bad is it?" Marta daintily took a bite of her strawberry cake, napkin spread across her lap.

"The cupcake?" I mumbled with a full mouth. "Not bad at all."

"Nein." She rolled her eyes. "The reason I am here."

I finally used my napkin to wipe the chocolate off my fingers, taking my time. I needed Marta but still wasn't sure how much to reveal. She seemed to have a soft spot for Luke, and I didn't want to offend her by talking down about Wes—even if I needed to vent. What if she told everything to Luke? What if word got around about Wes's family drama? I didn't want that for him, even if he had broken my heart. "It's pretty bad."

"Pretty and bad? How is that possible?" Marta frowned as she took another bite.

"Oh trust me, it's possible." I knew she meant the English phrasing, but Wes had both terms well defined—individually and together. I shook my head before she could grow more confused. "I just meant it's intense."

"So does that mean you finally talked to Wes about what happened the other night?" She quickly corrected herself as I once again held up my finger in protest. "I mean, what *didn't* happen."

"Sort of." I wadded my napkin into a ball. "I was at the hardware store getting paint for Mrs. Lyons and overheard Wes arguing with his father." No need to tell Marta that "arguing" was sort of like saying Lady Gaga wore weird outfits—the understatement of the year. "We ran into each other after. It was awkward."

"Sounds bad, but not, what did you say? Pretty bad?" Marta shrugged. "You have to face him eventually."

"There's more." I swallowed, my mouth dry as the familiar wave of bitterness crept up my throat. I reached for another cupcake, stalling. Even now the memory pounded in my head, a headache that wouldn't leave. I choked the words out. "He was calling Sonya as he was leaving—told her he'd be there in a few minutes."

Marta's eyes bugged. "The lemon-drop girlfriend?"

I just nodded as I popped the cupcake whole into my mouth, my stomach clenching at the thought of what he could have been going to do. Did Sonya know his secrets about his father? Did she even care? Or did she value Wes as lightly as it seemed he valued her? Still, there had to be something to their relationship or else he wouldn't have been heading there in his moment of escape.

"That does change everything." She passed me the entire cupcake box, and I took it without protest. "Do you think they're getting back together?"

"I don't know." I fished a red velvet mini from the package. "The whole conversation was a blur. I was trying to ignore him; he was trying to leave. It was so junior high it was embarrassing."

Marta reached over and patted my pajama-clad knee. "I'm sorry, Addison. I know this is hard. But just think how much worse it would feel right now if you had given in and slept with him."

Her logic made sense. But on the other hand, if I'd slept with him, then we'd have never argued, and he'd never have gone running back to Sonya. "I know you're right. But I don't feel like it right now."

"You said you were a virgin and wanted to stay that way." Marta leaned back, propping herself up on my bed pillows. "So what changed?"

"I think maybe I did." I stared at the cupcake in my hand, my thoughts spinning faster than the ceiling fan whipping above our heads. "Don't get me wrong. I don't regret the decision I made. I'm glad I made it, even though all this happened. And I'd make it again."

I sighed, trying to make sense of the contradictions swirling in my head and in my heart. "But if that's true, why do I feel so awful? I should be mad at Wes—furious, even. Him treating me like this makes him a jerk." Yet the anger I felt in the store was strangely absent. In its place lingered sorrow, regret, and this deep ache that wouldn't go away.

"You've been interested in him for a long time. Maybe it is just hard to let go." Marta adjusted a plaid pillow under her head. "Try to picture him the way he is—the way he acted in the store, the way he acted that night he pressured you. That should make it easier to move on." She waved her hand at me. "Go on, try it."

I closed my eyes in an effort to appease her. But I didn't see the sarcastic, rebellious, I'm-a-jerk-with-a-chip-on-my-shoulder-the-size-of-Mt.-Everest Wes. I saw the hurting, reaching, I'm-acting-out-because-my-family-sucks-and-I-feel-alone Wes.

And despite all he'd done to me, I couldn't make myself give up on him.

"Better?"

Marta's voice brought me back to the present. I opened my eyes, forcing a nod. "A little."

True—just not in the way she'd hoped. Marta was a good friend, wanting me to make wise choices. If our roles had been reversed, I'd probably be giving her the exact same advice. To forget the jerk and find a good guy—a guy like Luke. Someone who brought me flowers just because, who helped out with the things that interested me, who walked me to class at school. Someone with gelled hair and a pressed polo. Someone who could charm my father into his blessing. Someone practical. Logical. Safe.

But I didn't want safe. I'd known safe my entire life. I wanted the guy who would argue with me in the pouring rain, not just stand by carrying the umbrella. I wanted the guy who wore leather and took risks but at the same time made sure I was protected. The guy who possessed a secret passion for classic novels and could play the piano better than Alicia Keys, yet had no idea of his own skills. The guy who made me cry, but also made me *feel*.

I wanted the guy capable of breaking my heart.

Chapter Twenty-Five

I never knew time could drag and fly by at the same time. Every time I thought of my encounter with Wes at Crooked Hollow Hardware, every time I envisioned him knocking on Sonya's front door, my heart plummeted into my stomach, and the hands on the clock all but stilled. Had it really been two weeks since that night at the hardware store? Felt like years.

Yet when I glimpsed my father rushing out the door for yet another coffee date with Ms. Hawthorne, or when I saw how much work the talent show needed before the rapidly approaching opening night, the pages seemed to fly right off my calendar. Not that I was surprised. My heart and mind had yet to sync with each other. It figured time also refused to fall in line.

Mrs. Lyons, however, was all too aware of the clock, and it seemed with each passing moment, she grew even more jittery about the talent show—if that was possible. But hey, she had a prop-room closet full of green paint and a cast that, while they might not shine like the stars on the backdrop behind them, at least wouldn't flat-out embarrass themselves. We'd come a long way.

Now if we just had people show up, all would be well.

"Addison, that Let Them Read Foundation representative

called you again. I don't know why they insist on calling my cell when you're clearly in charge of this." Mrs. Lyons's exasperated voice carried from the first row of theater chairs by the stage, where she'd set up camp for this last rehearsal with her handy-dandy clipboard, a half-eaten cheeseburger, and an unmarked white Styrofoam cup that I couldn't help but wonder had a little something extra mixed into her Diet Coke. "Can you handle this?"

"Sure, I'll call Debra back." Though I couldn't imagine why she'd be calling this close to the show. Everything they needed for advertising had been handled long ago, and since the fund-raiser hadn't actually happened yet, there was nothing to report. A pinch of dread clenched my stomach. This couldn't be good.

Mrs. Lyons rattled off the number I already had programmed in my cell, and I nodded and pretended to write it on my clipboard as I turned my back and hit CALL. I'd learned these past several weeks that with Mrs. Lyons, control was everything—even the appearance of it. If she thought she was handling things—even if handling meant delegating—then she could function. With or without her Diet Coke.

And wasn't that how we all were?

"This is Debra." The brisk voice of the representative carried into my ear, and I made my way into the wings stage right.

"Hey, it's Addison, with Crooked Hollow High. Mrs. Lyons said you'd called?" I forced a smile, hoping my sudden rash of nerves didn't show in my voice. "Were you just checking in with our progress?" *Please, please just be checking in.* Unlikely, however, since I'm sure the entire Let Them Read Foundation had better things to do than make unnecessary phone calls to high school students in Kansas.

But I was desperate for hope. We couldn't handle any more catastrophes. Not when Mrs. Lyons's hair was finally starting to defrizz. Not when Michael had changed his socks, and I hadn't caught Claire throwing up in the bathroom in a solid week. If this fund-raiser didn't go as planned, not only would I be the laughingstock of the school—*again*—but I'd lose the one thing in my life that was actually going positively right now. Concentrating on a bigger picture for once was a nice reminder that the world kept revolving and I really could make a difference somewhere out there.

Even if my own life sucked.

"Once again, we're so grateful your school chose our foundation to donate to," Debra said. Papers shuffled from her end of the connection as I waited for the inevitable "but." "But I'm afraid there's a problem with our advertising agreement."

Marta appeared in the wings, stage left. "Everything all right?" she mouthed across the expanse of stage.

I shook my head, clamping my hand over the mouthpiece of the phone. "Complications." I ducked my head back to the phone. "What sort of problem? Everything was on the paperwork I scanned and e-mailed to you. Just like you asked."

"We never received it."

My heart jump-started. "What? I sent it two weeks ago. The day before the deadline you gave me." My thoughts rushed together. I clearly remembered writing the ad copy, taking it to the school office, and scanning it on the assistant principal's machine.

"I'm sorry, Addison, it's not here."

"But I scanned it at the school office and e-mailed it to you that—" I broke my own sentence with a gasp. That night. The night Wes came to my window. I was supposed to have gone home from the talent show, pulled up my e-mail from my computer, and sent the attachment. I'd even started to put a reminder on my phone until my dad's random appearance at the rehearsal knocked me off balance. "Oh no. Oh no."

"It's not a big deal." Debra's kind voice sounded a million miles away. "I just wanted to let you know it's too late for the newsletter. But I'm sure your other advertising efforts will draw a crowd. Don't worry."

My face grew hot. What other efforts? Besides vague word of mouth and a few posters hung around town and around the school, there were no other efforts, outside of the tiny ad printed in the local newspaper. I'd been counting on this newsletter reaching a venue I couldn't and giving the talent show a prestige it simply didn't have without a foundation's name behind it.

I swallowed my disappointment. It looked like our best chance at success would equal a house full of parents and a money bag full of loose change—at best. I cleared my throat, wishing I were tall enough to actually kick myself in the rear. "I'm sorry, Debra, I remember what happened now. I had a personal crisis that night and—"

"Addison!" Mrs. Lyons's frantic voice nearly knocked me down the stairs. I caught the edge of the heavy velvet curtain just in time, only stumbling over the top step.

Oh, that was professional—there I was on the phone with a respected organization, admitting my failure at responsibility, while being screamed at by a dramatic drama teacher. I bit back the sarcasm threatening to pour out of my mouth and jabbed a finger at the phone, hoping Mrs. Lyons would get the hint and wait. One crisis at a time.

Mrs. Lyons shook her head repeatedly, waving her arms like she wasn't only three yards away, and I shook mine back, trying to catch what Debra was saying. *Go away.*

Mrs. Lyons insisted, and finally I covered the mouthpiece again. "I'm having an emergency here." Debra's voice squawked in my ear, and I quickly moved my hand. "No, Debra, not you. Sorry, my teacher is trying to—"

"The background." Mrs. Lyons's eyes widened behind her glasses, and I swear tears actually shone behind the thick lenses. "The stage background is ruined!"

My lips opened, yet no sound would come out. I clenched the cell in my hand and closed my eyes. I didn't think my heart could sink any lower to the ground. "Debra, I'm going to have to call you back."

★ ★ ★

"I'm so glad you got that extra paint." Mrs. Lyons stood beside me and Marta in the prop room, staring down at the trees that used to stand straight and proud in front of our starry night backdrop but were now mangled and broken.

I raised one eyebrow at my drama teacher. She had no idea what that paint had cost me, money notwithstanding—and obviously had no idea that paint didn't double as superglue. These trees needed a lot more than a coat of Evergreen Dream. They needed a saw, a hammer, and several other tools I had no idea how to use.

Marta patted my shoulder. "We can fix it."

"How?" I stabbed my fingers through my hair as a sudden heat wave of stress built sweat beads along my neck. "Are you secretly a handyman by night? It took the guy who did these for us two weekends to build. I doubt he can work us back in for a redo three nights before the show."

Forget the fact that I had originally thought the trees were pointless. Mrs. Lyons had been right—they'd given the set a dimension, created the feel of an outdoor stage under the stars. Maybe they weren't imperative to the show in general, but in Mrs. Lyons's mind, they were as crucial as any of the performers. I'd have a better chance convincing her to cancel the show altogether than I would encouraging her to toss the props in the Dumpster and move on.

"What happened?" Marta asked. "Everything was fine at the last rehearsal."

"It looks like they broke in half. Like they fell over and then were crushed." I stepped closer to the ruined props, pointing to the wide crack running straight through the middle of each. A blob of brown in the corner of the room caught my attention, and my eyes narrowed as I reached down and plucked a football from the wreckage. "This looks familiar."

Mrs. Lyons gasped. "They wouldn't."

"The same football players who were having sword fights instead of working? I think they would." Probably not on purpose. But they were definitely immature enough to not think about the consequences of playing ball near an open prop-room door. I could just see one of the guys going long, running backward, and crashing into the set.

Then bailing and leaving behind the evidence.

"Well, then, they will just have to fix it." Mrs. Lyons planted her fists on her hips and peered over her glasses, looking every inch the role of an old-fashioned, superintimidating schoolmarm. I almost felt sorry for the guys.

Until I remembered that if they didn't fix the set, it would somehow—as usual—fall on me. Maybe Dad could help. No. I dismissed the idea as quickly as it formed. Not only did I want him far away from this school, but he wasn't exactly Mr. Fix-It. He might be able to coax a sinner down the aisle of the church, but he couldn't unstop a toilet, install a ceiling fan, or build a bookcase to save his life.

"Addison, I trust you'll find the culprits and make sure this set gets fixed?" Mrs. Lyons turned to me, her voice authoritative in tone but her eyes so hopeful I couldn't bear to follow my instincts and run offstage. Screaming. All 300-plus miles to Kansas City.

I just nodded as Marta squeezed my arm in sympathy. Once again I'd somehow volunteered my way into something I had no business doing.

"Oh, I forgot to ask. What did Debra say on the phone?" Mrs. Lyons brushed her hands together, as if ridding herself of the problems before us. I wasn't about to pass over another one, even though at the moment her arms looked pretty empty and mine felt pretty full.

I pasted on a smile. "She was just wishing us good luck on the upcoming performance." Hey, Debra might have said that— after all, I'd missed the last half of the conversation before I'd all but hung up on her. And if she hadn't wished it, she should have.

Because boy, were we going to need it.

"This is a disaster." I stared into my mocha, watching the sprinkles bob along the top of the melting whipped cream like tiny colored boats.

Marta reached across the table and snagged a napkin from the Got Beans canister. "What? Too much chocolate?"

"No. And FYI, that's impossible." I ran my finger around the rim of my mug. "I meant the talent show."

She offered a smile, slightly coated with latte foam. "It will work out."

"You're overly optimistic." Like, to the point it made Taylor Swift seem depressed.

"You don't think God will provide?"

I shrugged, exhaustion weighing on my shoulders. "More like I don't think God is all that interested."

"How can you say that?" Marta frowned, her blond eyebrows

knitting over her eyes. "You know God cares."

"I know He does in general. But this isn't world peace." This was real life. And so far, I hadn't seen much holy intervention. Not when I was the joke of the school because of my father dating my teacher. Not when Wes had made mosaic tiles out of my heart. Not when the talent show was falling apart before my eyes.

How pathetic was it that I couldn't even raise money for a good cause without somehow screwing it up? It was my fault I'd gotten so hung up with Wes that I forgot to send the e-mail on time. That wasn't God's problem. So how could I expect Him to bail me out now? I knew how the game worked. Obey, stay out of His way, and hope to get some blessings for being good—just like with my dad.

Except, well, it hadn't really been working lately.

With either of them.

"You're a preacher's daughter, and you think God is only halfway invested in your life?" Disbelief coated Marta's voice.

Maybe more like *because* I was a preacher's daughter. But she wouldn't get that. I shook my head, trying to dislodge the negativity, but it lingered. "I don't know what I think anymore." I swirled my mocha, watching the sprinkles dance. "Everything is just different." Unexpected tears pricked my eyes, and I ducked my head so Marta wouldn't notice.

"Maybe that's because you finally have to decide for yourself what you think."

Marta's soft tone struck a nerve, and I jerked my gaze to meet hers. My tears instantly dried as a rush of indignation flooded my senses. "What do you mean?"

"You have made comments, Addison, ever since we first met. About what you believe, about why you believe it. About the decisions you make. It sounds like you aren't sure why you decide what you do."

Now she sounded like Wes. "Well, geez. I'm surprised you didn't keep a journal of it all." The sarcasm sprang forth, an immediate defense mechanism I couldn't control. I rolled in my lower lip as reality stung. I was doing exactly what Wes did to me—and everyone else who tried to get close to him. When had he rubbed off on me like that? I'd always had a sarcastic streak, but never out of anger or cruelty. I was practically snapping at Marta, and this wasn't the first time.

I took a long sip of my drink, avoiding Marta's careful gaze. Finally, I set my mug down with a clatter. "Let's just change the subject, okay?" I didn't want to argue, yet I couldn't agree with her, either.

"Ja. Fair enough." She raised both hands as if in surrender. "So, what did the football players say when you confronted them?"

"You mean outside of the grunts of denial?" I rolled my eyes. "They played dumb until one of the guys in the dance group told me he saw two of the football players run into it, just like we thought. But if they won't admit it, it doesn't help me much." I smirked. "If I'd been on the other side of that crash, I'd probably have denied it, too. Mrs. Lyons can be scary."

"Ja. But that means you have to fix it."

"Surprise, surprise." The sprinkles in my drink had finally melted, turning my once-brown mocha into a cloudy, unappetizing gray. It matched my level of motivation. Was this show even worth it now? Who cared if we had a beautiful backdrop on the stage if the audience was only filled with obligatory attendees? Even if every performer had two or three family members show up, we still wouldn't make enough money to give a donation to the Let Them Read Foundation without completely embarrassing the school. Sure, something was better than nothing in theory, but this fund-raiser wore my name. I wanted it to be a success. I wanted to make a difference.

I wanted to prove I wasn't completely invisible.

I chugged back the rest of my mocha and stood, ready to return my mug to the counter and get home. "Guess I'll have to stay late after practice tomorrow and see what I can do about fixing the props myself."

That should be interesting. I cringed at the image of me and a hammer in a silent stare down. I kind of doubted I'd win.

Bert reached across the counter for our mugs. "Thanks." I slid my empty one to him, and he took it with a nod.

"You should buy stock in sprinkles." He whisked the dish into the sink behind the counter.

"Maybe after college." I smiled and turned as Marta shoved her chair under our table and joined me.

"Maybe Luke will stay and help." Marta handed her half-empty mug to Bert, who took it with a disappointed frown at the contents still coating the bottom. "Most guys know a little something about woodworking. And like Mrs. Lyons said, at least we have the extra paint now."

"Do you really think Luke will want to do me any more favors?" I wrinkled my nose at Marta as we waved good-bye to Bert.

Her hesitant silence confirmed my suspicions.

"I'll figure it out. I always do." I jutted my chin out as we headed for the front door, projecting confidence. Too bad I didn't believe myself.

"Ladies, is there a problem?" Bert called us back.

I held the door halfway open with my hip, enjoying the rush of cool night air that flooded my cheeks and neck. "That depends. Are you secretly a whiz at carpentry?" Despite my better judgment, hope rose. Maybe Bert still remembered some aspects of shop class from back in the day. Maybe he'd help us out if I promised to go easy on the sprinkles for the next few weeks—well, days, anyway. Sacrifices could only go so far.

"Carpentry?" He paused, holding Marta's discarded mug over the sink.

My hopes dipped lower at his confusion. "You know. Woodworking. Like, building sets?"

Bert snorted, nearly dropping the cup. He fumbled to catch it as he bent over, laughing. "Wait until the wife hears that one." He hooted. "She'll be cracking up into next Thursday."

Well, at least someone would be.

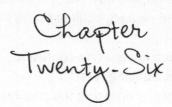

Chapter
Twenty-Six

I can't believe we're at school at five in the morning. On purpose." I blinked sleep from my eyes and squinted at Marta, who looked annoyingly fresh and chipper in her skinny jeans and striped top, hair pulled back and tied in a trendy knot with a scarf.

"You looked so depressed last night leaving Got Beans, I had to do something." She pounded on the side entrance door of the school with her fist, her other hand clutching a bag full of tools she said she scrounged up from her host dad's basement.

"Calling Principal Stephens at home and arranging for the custodian to meet us here at the crack of dawn—make that *before* the crack of dawn—seems like an extreme method." I covered a yawn with my hand. "Why couldn't he have given us the phone number of a handyman instead?" Then I could still be under my warm covers, drifting in and out of sleep and dreams about Wes.

On second thought, maybe it was better to be standing here in the frigid autumn air, begging to be let inside school more than two hours early.

"You know Mrs. Lyons said the budget for this show was maxed." Marta knocked again, louder this time. The sound echoed through the deserted building. I cupped my hands around my eyes and peered through the window. Janitor Todd made his way slowly down the long hall, mop in hand. He didn't seem to be in a hurry, despite the cold that threatened to freeze my eyelashes together.

"Too bad Principal Stephens didn't excuse us from classes today while he was at it." I stepped away from the door and crossed my arms over the wrinkled long-sleeved T-shirt I'd thrown on after my alarm had blared at 4:30 a.m. The hooded sweatshirt I'd added last minute offered little protection against the wind that picked up and stirred the nearly naked tree branches. I hopped on the balls of my feet to get my blood flowing.

"That'd have been nice." Marta smiled and waved at Janitor Todd through the window. Surely he was almost to the door by now.

"I really don't see what good us staring at a heap of broken wood for two hours before class starts is going to do." I bounced again, grumpiness taking over my usually charming personality—along with hunger. I hadn't eaten breakfast before stumbling out the front door. Maybe Janitor Todd had doughnuts stashed somewhere.

"It's better than admitting failure, isn't it?" Marta patted my shoulder. "Have a little faith."

I tried not to cringe at her choice of wording. After our talk at Got Beans, paranoia crept in. Did I not have faith? Was I wrong to think I was bothering God for wanting to be involved in the little things?

Did He even really want to be, or was that just Marta's opinion?

Marta continued, oblivious to my early morning mental drama. "Janitor Todd told the principal he would try to help— even if we have to wrestle the pieces back together with duct tape and paint over it. The stage will be covered in shadow because of the spotlights. Maybe it won't look that bad from the audience."

Sure. And maybe Simon Cowell would show up to judge the talent show.

I hated to burst her happy bubble, but this level of perky was hard to take first thing in the morning—and without a mocha no less. I opened my mouth to argue when the door finally swung open, nearly knocking Marta sideways.

"Come in out of this cold." Janitor Todd stepped back to allow us inside, as if it were our idea to stand out there so long.

The hallway wasn't much warmer, but at least it was free of the wind. I cupped my hands and exhaled into them in a futile attempt to ease the chill. Marta held up her tote bag of tools. "Ready to get started?"

"I need to check on a few things first." Janitor Todd rubbed the gray bristle coating his chin, emitting a sandpaper sound that made me want to cover my ears. "I'll meet you ladies there as soon as I get this building warmed up."

"Deal." Any extra heat would be appreciated. I could pretend to swing a hammer until he got there. I nudged Marta down the hallway. "Let's go."

Marta's low heels clipped a rhythm on the floor as we made our way through the dimly lit hall toward the auditorium. "A little eerie, is it not?" She darted glances into each empty classroom that we passed.

"I'm too sleepy to be scared." I pulled open the door that led into the backstage area of the auditorium. "I'll probably have nightmares about this later once I'm caffeinated." Just add it to the reasons-not-to-sleep list. I'd already tossed and turned last night, dreading the outcome of the talent show. Dreading what the smile on my father's face meant when he hung up from his nightly chat with Ms. Hawthorne. Dreading the inevitable next time I would run into Wes.

Marta led the way to the prop room. The door was open, which was unusual. Mrs. Lyons usually kept it locked unless we were having a rehearsal. I stopped several yards away, suddenly wide awake as the hair on the back of my neck prickled. All thoughts of being too sleepy to be spooked faded away as goose bumps dotted my arms. "Wait."

Marta looked over at me, her scarf swishing against her shoulders. "What is it?"

I rubbed my arms, suddenly chilled again. "That door should be locked." Not that a ghost would break into a theater and leave a door open—and not that I believed in ghosts in the first place. Mostly. But in the wee hours of the morning, with the sun still down and in the silence of the hushed, deserted school, well, logic was a little out of reach.

Marta did a double take at the open door. "The prop room? I am sure Janitor Todd unlocked it for us earlier. He knew we were coming." She offered a grin that on anyone else would have just been condescending, but on Marta it simply leaked amusement.

"Right." Duh. If I hadn't been food and caffeine deprived, I probably could have figured that out on my own. I shook off the lingering heebie-jeebies and joined Marta in the room.

Her shocked gasp made me plow into her back, and it was then I noticed the doorknob had been taken off the prop-room door and sat on the floor by the frame. "What in the world?"

My question hung between us, irrelevant, as we both stared at the two trees standing in the middle of the prop room—the tall, proud, unbroken trees, glistening with a fresh coat of Evergreen Dream.

"Who? What?" Marta's whispered questions also went

unanswered as I stepped gingerly into the room. A paint-speckled sheet covered the floor under the props, the green drips still fresh.

"Looks like someone beat us here." Maybe the school *did* have a ghost—or an elf, like the ones in my favorite childhood fairy tale that repaired shoes for the cobbler. "And obviously someone without a key." I nudged the doorknob on the floor with the toe of my shoe.

"Someone broke into the school in the middle of the night to fix the trees? Why not call and volunteer first?" Marta frowned. "Besides, outside of the talent-show contestants, no one even knew what happened yesterday."

Good point. I sort of doubted Bert had a sudden change of heart.

"There you are! I was hollering for you."

We turned as Janitor Todd's husky voice sounded behind us, breathless like he'd been running—which would be quite the feat for him.

I took one look at his wide eyes and flushed face and fished my cell phone from my pocket. "What's wrong? Are you okay?" He looked like he'd drop from a heart attack at any minute. I posed my finger over the 9 button, ready to call an ambulance.

"I think the school had an intruder last night. The chain on the back door was broken." He braced one arm on the door frame and took a deep breath. "We need to call the police." *Huff. Huff.* "And clear out of here."

My eyes met Marta's, and as one, we looked to the doorknob on the floor by Janitor Todd's feet.

"Come on, girls. It might not be safe." He looked over his shoulder, as if he expected the burglar to leap out at any moment. "We'll call the police from the yard."

"I can assure you, if there was a criminal, he's the most

generous one I've ever met." I gestured to the newly repaired props behind us, and Janitor Todd stared, blinking rapidly. Then he fished glasses out of his uniform pocket, slid them on, and blinked again. "Well, I'll be a tiger's uncle."

"It looks like they broke into this room, too." Marta handed him the loose doorknob.

Janitor Todd turned it over in his hands, frowning. "This will go back on with a few screws. Only takes a minute. Wonder why whoever did this didn't just put it back before they left."

"Apparently they were in a hurry." I looked back at the trees, my mind racing. I was so relieved at least one of the disasters hovering over the talent show was resolved that I almost didn't even care who had pulled off the anonymous good deed. Marta was right—I should have had more faith. Mrs. Lyons was going to freak.

"Still, I'd feel better if we waited outside for the police. I have to file a report, even if the intruder did us a favor." Janitor Todd ushered us forward. "Let's go."

As I followed, I turned to give the room one last glance. A hammer half covered by the canvas caught my eye. I darted back into the room and picked it up then jogged after Marta and fell into step beside her in the hallway.

"Our mysterious handyman left this." I showed her the hammer, keeping my voice low. In case the tool had identification on it, I didn't want Janitor Todd to see it. Despite the fact that someone had broken the law to help us, they'd still saved my hide. I didn't want them to get in trouble.

"Interesting." Marta took the hammer from me, keeping it discreetly at her side as we hurried after Janitor Todd toward the front yard, where he called the cops from a giant phone that looked as old as Zack Morris's from *Saved by the Bell*. "Wait, is that writing?"

She flipped the hammer over in her hands, and big, bold letters jumped out at us from the wooden handle.

KEEGAN.

After Principal Stephens found several twenty-dollar bills slipped under the door in his office, the school decided not to press charges or open an investigation on the intruder. "Obviously whoever did this intended to do a good deed and left money to cover the cost of the broken chain," Principal Stephens had told Janitor Todd and the policemen. "It doesn't seem right to punish them, even if the gesture was a bit unconventional."

The cops had simply shrugged, finished the paperwork, and driven away before the first of the school buses pulled into the parking lot.

Marta and I had stashed the hammer in her locker during the commotion in the school yard, agreeing to keep Wes's secret exactly that. At least until after I talked to him and figured out why he'd done it—and how he even knew about the broken props in the first place.

And I knew where to find him.

The melody filling Got Beans wrapped its chords around my heart and tugged. But not nearly as much as the sight of Wes, sitting on the piano bench, fingers dancing over the keys, eyes closed as he played. His leather jacket draped over the back of the chair at the nearest table, and I automatically inhaled, remembering its smell, its warmth. Would I ever get to wear it again?

Did I even want to?

The conflicting answers to both questions left a bitter taste in my mouth, and I made my way toward the back of the shop, nodding at Bert as I passed the counter. He pointed at his watch with a frown, clearly indicating I should be in school. I just waved the excuse slip Principal Stephens had given me (after much cajoling and blaming of all things talent show related) and sidled up to the piano.

"You forgot this." I held out the hammer, his last name on the handle suddenly seeming even bigger and bolder than before.

Wes stopped playing, his hands sliding off the keys to land in his lap. He twisted toward me, head tilted, lips pursed. "I don't know what you're talking about."

"It says Keegan." I wiggled it in front of him.

"We're not the only Keegans in town." Wes shrugged. "Common name." His eyes flickered with an emotion I could relate to but not quite indentify. Mainly because I was feeling the same thing in the pit of my stomach.

With a sigh, I set the hammer on the table, grabbed his hands, and turned them over, palms up. His fingers curled, revealing flecks of Evergreen Dream staining his fingernails and dotting his calloused skin. "Do I need to call a forensic team to prove anything else, or are you satisfied?"

"Are you?" He jerked his hands away, turning back to the piano. He picked at the keys, the music not nearly as fluent as it had been before he'd seen me. I wasn't sure if I should be insulted or flattered.

"You sure know how to swing a hammer."

"Surprise." He kept playing.

"How'd you even find out about the props in the first place?"

He shrugged again, and from the corner of my eye, I saw Bert wiping down the counter. "Ah, Bert. That's how. You must have come in Got Beans right after Marta and I left last night."

"Ding ding, give the lady a prize." Wes's dry voice didn't miss a beat as he played on.

"Why'd you do it?" I wanted to sit but couldn't commit to staying that long. Not after promising Principal Stephens I'd be back in an hour. Not with the jealousy of knowing Wes had gone to Sonya burning in my gut.

Not with the tears pressing behind my eyes, threatening release with every one of his keystrokes on the piano.

The music continued, jerky and almost amateur. "Do what?"

"Come on, I'm not stupid." A wave of anger pushed back the tears. He had a good enough heart to do me a giant favor, but not enough to confess to it? What game was he playing?

"Never said you were." *Plink, plink.*

Blood pounded in my veins, and my chest grew hot at his indifference. "Just admit it, Wes. Who else in this town would break into a school? You saved me on this."

Plink, plink.

Frustration boiled over, sizzling in my ears, drowning out all sense of reason. "Just admit it!"

He shoved away from the piano and stood, leaning in close to my face. He threw his arms out to his sides in aggravation. "Okay, so I did it. Why do you care?"

"Why do I care?" The tears came then, hot and heavy and out of control, dripping off my cheeks and onto my ratty T-shirt. "Because I thought *you* didn't!"

Without waiting for a reply, I sank into the chair at the table and hid my face in my hands. Great—it figured the meltdown I'd been refusing to have for a week would hit right in front of him. I pressed my palms against my mouth to stifle the sob welling in my chest. I'd said it. It was out there. Maybe now I could move on.

"How can you think that?" Wes sank to the ground at my feet, kneeling in front of me. One hand rested lightly on my jean-clad knee, the impression branding straight through to my soul. "Why would I break into a school and fix those stupid trees if I didn't care?"

"You left." I mumbled into my hands, refusing to look him in the eye, refusing to let him change my mind about him. "You didn't get what you wanted, so you disappeared. And then you went and found it with Sonya."

"Yes, I was upset that night we went for a drive. You shot me down—it bruised my ego. I was embarrassed. But I wasn't mad at you." Wes tugged my hands away from my face, leaving me exposed and vulnerable. I stared at the green on his wrists, avoiding his eyes. "And I didn't disappear."

I allowed my gaze a quick meeting with his and snorted. "You pulled a better vanishing act than David Copperfield."

He smirked. "Hardly. There were no skyscrapers or elephants involved."

"So now you're a magician *and* a comedian?"

"Addison." Wes fairly growled my name, squeezing my hands in his. "You drive me crazy."

I snatched my hands free, wondering what on earth I'd been thinking. "Well you're not exactly a walk in the park yourself."

He slapped one hand on the tabletop. "Would you let me finish?"

"Why? Is Sonya waiting for you?" I bit my lip, but the words had already escaped. Damage done.

The sound of a blender revving up behind the counter made me realize how loud we'd gotten. Since there weren't any other customers for Bert to serve, I figured he probably wasn't even making a drink—just trying to drown out the private conversation we were attempting to have in public. Embarrassment snapped my mouth shut, and I traced the grain in the tabletop with my finger.

Wes exhaled sharply, stood, and pulled the chair out beside me. He sat down, leaning forward and bracing his elbows on his knees. "I'm only going to say this once, so try to listen, PK." His voice lowered, and he waited until I looked up. "I didn't go to Sonya. Not like you think."

My stomach balled into a knot. Now he was going to lie his way out of it? "Whatever. I heard you on the phone. You had that fight with your dad, and you called Sonya. Said you'd be there in ten minutes." There was so much more I wanted to say, so much threatening to spill out of my mouth, but I pressed my lips tightly together. Insulting Sonya wouldn't change what happened, and pointing out how he got what he wanted from her instead of me wouldn't rewrite the past.

And I still didn't think it needed to be rewritten. Not all of it.

Wes shook his head with a little laugh. "I went to her house that night, yeah."

"So you do admit it." The knot tightened until I could barely breathe. "Thanks for finally being honest." I started to stand, but Wes tugged me back down.

"I left my Nickelback CD at her house—weeks ago. She was threatening to throw it away if I didn't come get it."

"A CD, huh?" Right—probably an excuse just to see him again. I bet she opened the door in a silky number from Victoria's Secret, too. Or had he forgotten it on purpose? Neither scenario felt good.

"That's all it was. I got it, and I left." Wes swiped his hand through his hair. "As you probably heard at the store, I had another project I needed to help my dad with."

A hundred detailed questions hovered unasked between us, but I remained determined not to bring them up. Not to be that girl. Besides, did I have the right? I wasn't his girlfriend. He didn't owe me any information.

Funny how I didn't realize that until right then.

I stood abruptly. "Well, I hope you enjoy jamming to Nickelback again."

"That's it?" Wes looked at me from his chair. "You're just going to ask me about Sonya and leave?"

"I have to get back to school." I pointed to the hammer. "And just a thought—next time you want to be secretive, you shouldn't leave your ID lying around."

"It's my dad's hammer." Wes stared at it absently, his eyes darkening, and I wondered if he was imagining his father using the tool to rebuild the coffee table he'd broken while drunk.

My resolve to leave faltered, and I looked toward the door, then at Wes, and back again. My heart twinged, and I gently touched his shoulder. He jumped slightly at the contact then brought his hand up to rest on mine.

I reveled in the warmth of his fingers, my throat closing as more tears begged for release. Why did this feel like good-bye? I coughed in a vain effort to unclog the dam. "Thanks for telling me the truth."

"Guess it's not enough." He stared straight ahead, his fingers sliding off mine to land back in his lap.

Confusion swirled in a sickening vortex in my stomach. "I don't know what would be right now." Too much to process. If Wes was telling the truth, if he wasn't mad at me for refusing to have sex and hadn't gone running back to Sonya, where did that leave us? Where did it leave me?

And why wasn't that answer as obvious as I thought it'd be?

I shrugged away the voices jumbling in my head and clutched the permission slip from the principal in both hands like a lifeline. "Thanks again for fixing the props. Mrs. Lyons is thrilled."

"Then I'm glad I made someone happy." Wes cut his eyes

to me at the word *someone*, and guilt knocked on the door of my heart. But I didn't answer. He'd put me through enough this past week. Good deed today or not, I couldn't pretend like none of it had ever happened. Because even though his sins might not be what I thought they were, I still wasn't convinced we were on the same page.

I made my way to the door, indulging in one last glance back. Wes had already slipped onto the piano bench, fingers running noiselessly over the keys. After a minute, with a bowed head, he began to play again.

The notes flawless and perfect.

I pushed open the door, regret blasting in my stomach like a series of miniature bombs. Same page?

At this point, I'd be okay just knowing we were even in the same book.

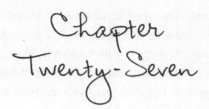

Chapter Twenty-Seven

"What do you mean, you can't find your CD?" I stared at Tripp, my bitten-to-a-nub fingernails digging into my clipboard. "You're on next. Next!"

Tripp just shrugged, fiddling with the zipper on his oversized hooded sweatshirt. From his lack of reaction, you'd think he'd just told me he was having a bad hair day or something equally insignificant.

I closed my eyes and concentrated on breathing, the side seams of my black dress protesting with every inhale. What was it? In through the mouth, out through the nose—or vice versa? Either way, I would hyperventilate if I kept this up. I opened my eyes, forced a smile, and nudged Tripp toward stage right. "Just get your crew ready to go on. I'll find the CD. If they call your name before I get back, stall."

Tripp's eyes widened. "Stall? How?"

"Tell jokes. Stand on your head. I don't care—just stall." I couldn't help the niggle of joy that filled my spirit as I rushed away. Finally, an emotional response—and someone realizing I wasn't necessarily superwoman after all.

If only I could convince Mrs. Lyons of that.

Now, if I were a CD, where would I be?

Claire suddenly stumbled into me from the wings

and caught my arm. "Addison, I'm sick." Her washed-out complexion made the splatter of freckles across her usually tanned nose seem as stark as if someone had drawn them on with a Sharpie.

I gasped. "Wow. You should sit down." She clutched my arm tighter and slowly sank to the floor, nearly pulling me with her.

I wrestled free of her grasp and knelt in front of her, tugging the hem of my dress over my knees. "Were you in the bathroom again?" I stared until she met my eyes, and she slowly nodded.

A sarcastic response filled my mouth, something about her being a genius, but I bit it back. "Wait here." I had to help her—even if she'd made my social life miserable of late. Maybe pulling a Good Samaritan would get her off my back permanently.

Plus, I refused to lose another contestant. Nick and his ventriloquist act had been scratched from the agenda because of a broken dummy—though on second thought, that might actually have been a blessing in disguise.

Walking past the curtains, I vaguely became aware of Melanie Johnson's flute solo from the other side. I hadn't dared to look out at the audience yet. Assuming there even was one. If I peeked out and saw only a small scattering of parents and grandparents, I'd lose it completely. Best not to know.

Focus, Addison. CD and food. CD and food.

And not necessarily in that order.

I picked up my pace backstage. A basket of granola bars and peanut butter crackers sat on a far table against the wall, along with several bottles of water and a punch bowl of lemonade. Shocking, since I hadn't remembered organizing a refreshment table for the cast. Who knew—maybe Mrs. Lyons had actually done something herself.

I grabbed a package of crackers and one of the cereal bars, caught the flash of a silver disk sticking out from behind the stereo in the corner, and plucked Tripp's sound track from the tangle of cords. Yes! Progress.

The remaining strains of Melanie's flute solo faded away, and I jogged past Claire on my way to Tripp. "Here! Eat that. *All* of it." I tossed the food in her lap, ignored her moan of protest, and practically landed on Tripp as I stumbled up the stairs to the stage.

"Here." I shoved the CD at him, and his eyes flooded with relief.

"Cool. Thanks." He stuck his finger through the hole in the center and twirled the disk around.

"Try again. How about, 'I owe you a mocha, thanks'?"

Tripp rolled his eyes but grinned as he gathered his dance team. "We're up!"

A backward glance confirmed Claire was actually eating, so I sagged against the stair rail and allowed a moment of peace. Two catastrophes down. Actually, three down. I'd sent Marta on a sewing-kit emergency twenty minutes ago. Where was she? If we didn't fix the loose strap on Jessica's dress, she'd be singing in a gym uniform.

There were two pieces of good news I kept clinging to, despite the emergencies springing up all around me. One, Austin wasn't in the talent show, and that was reason to celebrate right there. And secondly, regardless of how tonight ended (assuming it ever did), next week was Thanksgiving break. No school for a week, so I could soak in a hot bubble bath and reread my worn copy of *Pride and Prejudice*, or maybe *Emma*, and forget this entire performance ever existed.

My fingers trailed the edge of the heavy velvet curtain as I debated checking out the audience. No, not yet. For a moment, all was well. That could change all too quickly.

"I am back!" Marta's breathless accent had never sounded so good.

I eagerly took the sewing kit from her outstretched hands. "You're an angel." I took in her disheveled appearance and winced. "Did you run all the way to the drugstore?"

She bent over, bracing her hands on her knees and wheezing. "Ja."

"I'll never make fun of your turquoise belt again." I gave her a hug of thanks, nearly knocking her off balance.

"Addison!" A panicked voice filled my ears before I could even straighten. "Addison, this is awful." Jessica's stricken expression didn't bring the typical wave of panic. With Jessica, we could be dealing with a broken nail.

"Relax, I have what we need to fix your dress." I opened the sewing kit and plucked out a needle and a spool of white thread. "Just be still."

"No, it's not that!" She clutched the dangling strap of her dress with one hand, her red fingernails bright against the black of the gown. "My piano player backed out. She's not coming!"

The needle fell to the stage floor. "Not coming?"

Marta stooped down and started feeling for the needle in the dim lights, her hand patting my ankle twice on accident before I had the sense to move out of her way. "So are you going to sing a cappella?"

The horrified look she gave me might have said a lot, but "no" was definitely part of the equation.

It figured. Of all the times during practice that we'd begged Jessica to confirm her pianist. . . I gritted my teeth. No time for lectures on responsibility. As Mrs. Lyons loved to say—over and over and over—the show must go on. I cupped my hands around my mouth and hollered to the students loitering in the wings, waiting their turn. "Can anyone here read music?"

Blank stares were my only response.

A wave of frustration threatened to tug me under. I was so done. I wanted to quit. What did I care about broken dresses and starved contestants and bailing accompanists? I didn't. But I did care about my reputation. And putting on a good performance. And raising money for a worthwhile cause.

I sucked it up. "I'll figure something out. You're not up yet, right?" I searched for my clipboard, which I must have left backstage when I grabbed the refreshments for Claire.

Jessica shook her head, chandelier earrings swaying. "I'm the last of the night."

"Found it!" Marta popped up, holding the needle between two fingers.

"Great." I handed her the kit. "Good luck." She and Jessica both stared warily at the needle while I made a hasty exit. Claire was now standing where I'd left her instead of sitting, and she offered me a shaky smile as I passed. I hesitated, though I truly didn't have time. "Feeling better?"

"I think so." She rubbed her too-skinny stomach with one hand and held the empty package of crackers in the other. A granola bar wrapper lay at her feet.

"Good enough to perform?"

She nodded, her perfectly curled hair swishing around her face. "Addison, listen. I really didn't deserve—"

"Don't worry about it. Just get out there and shine, and eat a Big Mac on the way home, okay?" I smiled back, wondering if this particular truce would stick. Knowing Claire, probably not. But at least my conscience would be clear.

Tripp's dance number wrapped up to a roar of applause, and my pulse thundered almost as loudly. That amount of noise couldn't have come from the group I'd imagined had gathered.

Despite the emergency pressing me forward, I grabbed the curtain, took a deep breath, and pulled it aside just enough to peek out.

At a packed auditorium.

I jerked the curtain closed, eyes wide, staring at the burgundy fabric in front of my face, not daring to believe the truth. How in the world? . . . No way had that crowd shown up from word of mouth and the amateur posters we'd hung around town. Had Debra somehow managed to advertise for us without my participation?

I risked another glance, just to be sure. The panel of judges (Principal Stephens and two unbiased school board members) sat front and center at a separate table near the orchestra pit, pens posed over thick notepads. Mrs. Lyons claimed the aisle seat on the first row nearest to them, having told me she wanted to sit and enjoy the performance after having "worked" so hard.

My gaze flitted over the audience, disbelief still blurring my vision. My dad and Ms. Hawthorne sat in the second row. At least they weren't holding hands. Luke sat behind them with some kids I recognized from our English class. And Bert and his wife took up the last two seats on the fourth row. It looked like not only had families shown up, but most of the town. There were several faces I'd never ever seen before.

The sea of faces farther away faded under the shadows of the dim houselights, yet one slouched position in the last row seemed familiar. I squinted, straining to make out features. Then the back auditorium door opened, allowing a sliver of light to temporarily highlight the person's face.

I stared then blinked twice, certain I was imagining things. I stumbled backward as the curtain swished shut.

Wes.

My palms grew slick, and I clutched the velvet fabric like a life jacket as the stage threatened to dip under my feet. What was he doing here? He probably didn't know anyone in the show, and even if he did, the Wes I knew wouldn't be caught dead at such a performance. No one that snuck into a coffee shop at the slow times of day to secretly play the piano would—

My breath hitched.

Piano.

★ ★ ★

The surprise on Wes's face as I snuck down the main aisle of the auditorium, grabbed his arm, and hauled him to the empty foyer turned to amusement as I voiced my request.

He crossed his arms over his leather jacket. "You've got to be kidding."

My voice pitched like a preteen boy, and I held my arms out to the side, Jessica's sheet music clenched in one hand. "Do I look like I'm kidding?"

He studied me a moment from head to toe, the amusement fading from his chocolate-brown eyes. "No. You look beautiful."

His quiet words stole my next line, and I inhaled sharply, suddenly wishing I'd gone for the updo Marta had suggested— then immediately hating how much I cared what he thought. "Don't."

"Don't what? Tell the truth?"

"Be so nice."

Our gazes locked and held, and Wes ran the back of one finger down my cheek before letting his hand hang at his side. "It's hard not to."

I snorted. "You never used to have trouble."

He shrugged a little. "That was before I realized what an idiot I was."

"Hard to argue with that." We stared at each other. Did my eyes reflect the myriad of thoughts flickering through his own gaze? Regret. Desire. Hope.

Reality.

The sudden rush of air from the heater vents above drowned out the sounds of the muffled performance from inside, and I looked away. "We can't have this conversation right now."

"Then when?" Wes took a step toward me, and I automatically inched away in an all-too-familiar dance.

"I don't know! In case you haven't been listening, I have a lot on my plate tonight. In fact, I can't even see the stinkin' plate anymore." I gestured wildly with the papers in my hand. "So far I've dealt with a wardrobe malfunction to rival Janet Jackson ala Super Bowl 2004, a lost CD, a bulimic contestant, and two last-minute agenda changes. If you don't play for Jessica, I might go insane. And I'm pretty sure she *will* go insane."

Wes tilted his head, looking down at me with an expression I couldn't interpret. Mystery Man, at his finest—and most annoying. He finally spoke. "I don't even know Jessica."

"You know me." I lowered my voice, wishing I didn't need him, wishing I didn't have to beg. "This show is important."

"Why?" Wes scoffed. "It's a bunch of high schoolers, showing off what they think is talent. And trust me, most of it isn't."

"Then why are you here?" I turned his question around, watched a tinge of red crawl up the hint of dark stubble on his cheeks.

I didn't wait for his answer, mostly because I knew he wouldn't have one he'd be willing to share. "I know why you're here, and it's the same reason you're going to march yourself backstage to that piano bench and play for Jessica."

"I don't do high school, PK."

"You're not entering the competition. No one will even be looking at you. The piano is in the back corner of the stage. Trust me, Jessica will make sure all eyes are on her." Judging by her nearly backless gown, Wes's eyes probably would be, too. But I wouldn't think about that. It didn't matter.

Couldn't.

"You don't know what you're asking." Wes ran his hand over his hair, ruffling the dark strands.

I reached up without thinking and brushed it out of his eyes, my bare arms breaking out into a series of goose bumps on contact. "I think I do."

"Trust me." He caught my wrist, holding it with a firm grasp. "You don't."

Tugging free, I shook my head. "I can't fail at this, Wes." I lowered my voice, waiting until a late audience member slipped past us and disappeared through the double doors. Another round of applause washed through the foyer before the doors eased shut. There wasn't time to waste. Jessica would be up soon, and Wes hadn't even glimpsed the sheet music I still held.

"I hate to admit it, but Jessica is the most talented performer of the night—even if she does know it. Without her finale, this show is beyond amateur. Any donations we get will be pity money, and I'll be embarrassed to report back to the Let Them Read Foundation." Embarrassed wouldn't even come close. I'd already shown Debra my shocking level of irresponsibility with deadlines. Handing her fifty dollars in donations would be the arsenic icing on the cupcake of my reputation.

Wes frowned. "If Jessica is so great, why does she even need music?"

"She's terrified to do it a cappella. Who knows, maybe the queen of divas actually has a weak spot." I shrugged. "I don't have time to psychoanalyze the girl. I just need a piano player." I hesitated. "A *good* piano player."

"I'm not that good." He looked away, toward the doors leading to the parking lot.

My heart clenched. I was losing him. This was partly his fault in the first place—if he hadn't dragged me out to the middle of nowhere for a scandalous picnic, I wouldn't have forgotten to send the advertising e-mail in the first place. Who did he think he was?

The lid of my temper clanged in warning then shot off the pot before I could catch it. "Okay, Wes! I know you've done a lot for me already, and I appreciate it—those stupid trees look amazing. But can't you put aside your ego for one night and bail me out when it really matters? Do you really think anyone here cares that you can play an instrument?" My voice shook with anger. "Being talented is not being a nerd. I know you're all about appearances and image, but are you going to be *that* superficial?"

I held his gaze, refusing to look away and make his rejection easier. I hated when women used tears to get their way, but the ones building in my eyes weren't conjured. They were real.

And that just made me even madder.

"You really don't understand." Wes gestured helplessly toward the auditorium. "This isn't image, PK. I haven't—"

"Whatever. No is no; I don't have time for excuses." I flung the sheet music at him and dodged the hand he reached toward me. "Just forget it." I took off down the side hall as paper rained around me.

The drumbeat of all things Wes that played a nonstop beat in my head abruptly stopped, cutting off the rhythm of indecision. I'd made the right choice in backing off, even if he wasn't involved with Sonya. He could break into a school and help me when no one knew, but the minute I needed him in public, all bets were off. I couldn't trust someone like that. I needed someone I could depend on. Someone without excuses. Someone who loved me enough to do whatever it took. I needed the whole package.

And the leather-wrapped one outside those double doors was obviously not it.

★ ★ ★

"Jessica, your dress looks great." I forced a smile as our local diva turned in the backstage room and flashed me a hopeful smile. "Good as new."

She fiddled with the strap on her gown. "Is it straight?"

No. But there wasn't time to care. I grabbed her arm and pulled her toward the stairs. "You're up next, after Claire finishes her fashion presentation." Thankfully my former best friend's voice rang out strong and clear as she narrated each of her designs onstage. Still, I couldn't imagine the pretty ice-blue gown she wore could have possibly been worth starving herself for weeks.

"Who's going to play for me?" Jessica turned expectant eyes toward me, and behind her Marta raised her eyebrows as if wondering the same.

"Actually, I was doing some thinking." I patted Jessica's arm, wishing I were a better actor. My only weapon was that of flattery, and I felt a few rounds short. "You were so great during rehearsals on those afternoons that your friend couldn't make it that I thought you should just do it a cappella." I smiled bigger as Jessica's brows wrinkled into a frown.

"I can't. I can't."

"Yes, you can. You're a rock star. Just like when you

auditioned for *American Idol*, remember?" My stomach churned with all the gushing, but I'd officially reached the end of my fraying rope. "If you can sing without music for those judges, you can do it here." And if she couldn't, well, at least the student body would have an entire week off school to forget any mishaps. Lucky girl.

"What if I choke?" Jessica pressed one hand to the pearls at her neck, and I honestly didn't know if she meant literally or figuratively.

"You won't." I hoped not anyway. Paramedics and stretchers rushing up the main aisle during the middle of Jessica's song somehow wasn't the grand finale I'd pictured. Speaking of choking. . . I squinted at her. "Are you chewing gum?"

She opened her mouth, revealing a hint of bubblegum pink between her teeth.

I cupped my hand under her lips. She spit it out. I handed the gum to Marta, who winced and twirled a slow circle, searching for a trash can. "Listen to me, Jessica. You can do this. Everyone is counting on you. But no pressure, okay?"

"Isn't that an oxymoron or something?" She nibbled her lower lip. "Like jumbo shrimp?"

"Forget the shrimp." I grabbed her shoulders and forced her to focus on me. "Okay, I lied. There's some pressure here. A lot, actually. But honestly, there is no other choice short of scratching your name from the agenda, and I don't think either of us wants to do that. Right?"

She nodded, sparkly earrings catching the fluorescent lights above. "I mean, no. We don't want that."

I shook her a little. "Good. Now go line up in the wings. They're about to call your name." They probably already had, but just like with Tripp, I'd told our volunteer emcee earlier in the evening to stall if needed. Hopefully we still had an audience for Jessica to perform to. The memory of our emcee's eager knock-knock jokes sent a rush of panic through my gut. "And hurry."

Jessica wobbled off in her high heels, head high, shoulders back.

Dress strap dangling.

"Wait!" I grabbed the gum Marta still held, ran to Jessica, stuck the bubblegum on her dress, pressed the strap against it, and then shoved her toward the wings.

I turned back to Marta, who was pouring hand sanitizer into her palms. She looked up with a too-bright, innocent smile. "I do not sew well."

I sank to the floor and covered my face in my hands. "We are so doomed."

Chapter Twenty-Eight

I should have stayed on the backstage drama room floor in the fetal position, but some carnal instinct for conflict took over and propelled me toward the wings. Sort of like those worst-accidents videos they sometimes played on TV. You didn't really want to watch the train smash the car or the stunt biker crash into the lake, but you couldn't help it.

"She will be fine. She is better than she thinks." Marta joined me on the side of the stage, her voice hushed.

I shook my head. "No, trust me, she knows how good she is. Just doesn't seem to realize her voice can be the same with or without music."

"I will pray." Marta took her commitment seriously and closed her eyes right there beside me. I felt inclined to join her, but at this point, a flat-out miracle seemed more necessary and just as out of reach.

Jessica took the stage, and the applause from the audience slowly faded as they waited for her to begin. She cast a nervous look toward me, and I gave her a quick thumbs-up sign. I did pray then, begging God not to let her dress fall apart onstage.

She offered a weak smile, shot a glance toward the empty piano that sat to the left of the stage, then turned toward the audience. I winced, wishing I had remembered to tell the prop guys to forget wheeling the piano onstage for the last number. That empty bench would probably just make her more nervous.

Microphone raised, Jessica opened her mouth and shakily sang the first few words of her song.

Flawless piano music joined her for the second line.

I gasped, and Marta squeezed my arm. We both craned our heads, desperate to look around a surprised Jessica to the piano.

Wes sat on the bench, jacket off, fingers flying over the keys. His dark eyes stared without wavering at the sheet music on the stand before him, brow pinched in concentration.

"Wow." Marta's soft voice said it all, and I couldn't even breathe around the lump in my throat. What had convinced Wes to play? The guilt trip I'd packed his suitcase for? His feelings for me? Obligation? . . .

To her credit, Jessica never missed a beat, despite the sudden change in plans. Confidence high, she engaged the crowd in her up-tempo song, voice effortlessly hitting every note as she performed. She and Wes made a great team, as if they'd been practicing together for months. By the time the song ended perfectly on pitch, the crowd was on their feet, offering a standing ovation. Even the judges had put down their pens and were clapping.

Jessica eagerly dipped into a bow, one hand thankfully protecting her dress strap. She waved and blew a kiss to her adoring fans, and while that once would have made me groan or want to throw up, all I could do was exhale.

Pride, lingering shock, and relief all battled for first in line in my exhausted spirit. I closed my eyes against the fading adrenaline rush, soaking in the moment. It was over. We'd survived. I'd done the best I could. So had Jessica and the other students.

And somehow, so had Wes.

I owed him big-time. I couldn't help but hope this gesture meant what I thought it did. My eyes flitted open, hoping Wes would be able to see my gratitude from across the stage.

But the bench, once again, sat empty.

★ ★ ★

"We did it!" Marta squealed and threw her arms around me, dancing sideways and nearly knocking me against the stage wall, where a large group had gathered to celebrate. I laughed and hugged her back before pulling away to accept the yellow roses my dad presented to me.

"Good job, honey. There should have been an award for best director." He stepped back, one arm around Ms. Hawthorne's shoulders, and for the first time, it didn't bother me. Maybe because I was too giddy with relief that this enormous task was behind me. Or maybe it was because Marta had already gotten a quick tally of the funds collected by our carefully chosen doormen, and the number was double what I'd hoped.

Or maybe because for a moment I'd felt I'd actually done something worthwhile.

"Thanks, Dad." I breathed in the aromatic tang of the roses and buried my face in the soft blooms. He'd never gotten me flowers before. I couldn't help but think Ms. Hawthorne maybe had something to do with the gesture, but I'd take it all the same.

"Excellent work." Ms. Hawthorne smiled, and I shot her an appreciative look that she didn't try to hug me at school in front of all the other kids. Maybe at home—because I was sure Dad had already invited her over.

"We'll clear out of here. . . . Just wanted to say we're proud." Dad offered an awkward hug, and I patted his arm, wishing he hadn't addressed himself as "we." That would take some getting used to, my tentative acceptance of his new dating status or not. "We'll wait for you in the foyer."

Ugh. In front of everyone? No thanks. I bit my lower lip. "I'll walk home."

Dad frowned. "Nonsense. It's getting late."

"Dad, you said yourself, this is Crooked Hollow. Not Chicago." We hadn't had a crime since—well, since Wes broke into the school. I snorted. He'd probably love to add that claim to fame on his growing résumé. Speaking of Wes, I needed to find him. I hadn't seen him anywhere since his sudden disappearance from the stage after Jessica's song. When the judges had awarded Jessica first place, they'd asked who her accompanist had been, and the entire room seemed shocked when she sheepishly announced she didn't know.

"I'll walk her home," Luke offered, stepping up to my side. He smiled hesitantly at me and extended a single red rose surrounded by tufts of baby's breath.

My heart clenched at the sight of the bloom, and I hesitantly took it as Dad nodded his agreement with Luke's offer. "See you at the house, then. We'll have ice cream."

Figures Dad turned all mellow-parent on me now. I just nodded, staring at the rose and then at Luke as a hundred different thoughts roared through my head at once. The one I managed to pluck out as the loudest screamed *NOT NOW!*

But Luke's timing had never been convenient. He wrapped me in a hug, and I indulged him for a moment before pulling away under the pretenses of smelling my second flower arrangement of the night.

I held up the blooms. "Someone's going to think I robbed the florist."

Luke and Marta offered laughs at my weak attempt at humor, but I couldn't stand there and ignore the brimming silence while Luke had *that* look in his eye. Marta must have seen it, too, because her eyes darted from Luke to her black dress sandals and back again. My stomach knotted. Great. And here I thought the drama of the night was over.

Suddenly Bert and his wife, Megan, jostled through the crowd of hugging contestants and parents toward us. "Good show." He draped one arm around Megan's shoulder and offered the biggest grin I'd ever seen on him. "Mochas on the house to celebrate, whenever you stop in next." He smirked at me. "Which, for you, probably means tomorrow."

"Thanks, Bert." I wanted to hug him, but since this was our first conversation ever to be held without the Got Beans counter between us, it seemed more awkward than appropriate. I smiled at Megan instead. "I'm glad you guys came. I honestly didn't expect this big of a turnout. There was a—uh—misunderstanding with some advertising plans."

"We wouldn't have missed it." She patted her husband's arm. "He won't tell you this, so I will. After he heard you and Marta discussing your fears about no one showing up, he decided to help. Sent an e-mail to every coffee shop he knew in a thirty-mile radius and asked them to hang flyers in their stores. Then he told everyone who came in the shop if they showed up, they'd get a coupon for free sprinkles on their drinks."

"Meeegggaan." Bert drew her name out in six syllables, sounding like a petulant child embarrassed by his mom in the school yard.

She dismissed his protests with a flip of her hand. "Whatever. You're a softy, and you know it."

"You did that?" I clutched the flowers to my chest, wondering how many more times I'd be blown off my feet that night.

Bert shrugged, heat flaming in his cheeks. "Well, if you girls are determined to gripe about all your female problems where I can hear you, I figured I might as well help so you'd shut up."

He said *female problems* like all Marta and I talked about

were tampons and Midol. I laughed, relieved the Bert I knew once again stood before me. I couldn't help it. I pulled them both into a hug. "Thank you. You have no idea how much that helped."

"Anytime, kid." Bert tugged at Megan's arm. "Let's go, babe. I've got to open the shop early tomorrow."

It was only nine o'clock, but I let him make his escape without further embarrassing him. I turned around where Marta and Luke stood waiting for me in the dissipating crowd and couldn't contain my smile. "This is turning out to be a pretty good night after all."

"See? I told you prayer works." Marta winked.

Maybe more for some than others, but I'd go with it tonight. "God provided, I won't argue. And I know who He used." I divided the bouquet from my father in half and pressed the flowers into Marta's hand. "I couldn't have done it without you." Even I didn't have to have a flawless connection with God lately to realize she was a total godsend.

"Even though my sewing ability leaves a little to be desired?" She laughed, her eyes lighting up with appreciation.

"Even so. Who knew gum would hold better than thread?"

"Sounds like you ladies have some interesting stories." Luke sidled closer to me and looped an arm around both of our necks. "Why don't we all grab some ice cream on the way home? I want to hear how all this went down."

I opened my mouth to gently turn down his offer when I caught sight of Wes, watching me from the side aisle near the door. He stood shrouded in shadows, his jacket lit with the soft glow of the EMERGENCY EXIT sign above his head.

Luke's arm suddenly weighed a hundred pounds, and I shrugged out of his grasp. "Thanks, but I can't. I have some last-minute business to take care of."

Marta's and Luke's heads swiveled to follow my gaze, and I felt more than heard Luke's disappointed sigh. "But I told your dad I'd walk you home."

"I'll get another escort." I didn't mean to throw the word he'd used on me when we first met back in his face, but it slipped out regardless.

Luke rolled in his lower lip, nodding slowly. "If you're sure."

I wasn't. I had no idea what to say to Wes, but I couldn't leave him in the auditorium after he came through for me like that. He deserved better—even if I did have to knock him down a peg to convince him to help.

Marta gave me a quick hug good-bye. "Text me later and let me know you got home safe." She pulled back, and I caught the rest of her unspoken message loud and clear. She wanted to know what would happen next.

Nodding, I cast a nervous glance toward Wes, who waited patiently for me by the door.

I wanted to know, too.

★ ★ ★

When I'd rushed out of the house earlier this afternoon in a little black dress (that was almost too tight across my hips— better cut back on the whipped cream part of my beloved mochas), I hadn't thought to grab a jacket heavier than a gray, long-sleeved shrug. How could I have known I'd end up walking home with Wes in thirty-degree temps instead of riding in Dad's car with the heat blasting?

Though there was the argument that his proximity still offered a rush of warmth deep inside that easily fought the November chill.

Wes finally broke the quiet that had stretched between us from the school yard halfway down the first block. "Good show tonight."

The compliment warmed me further, especially from him. But I couldn't help wondering if he was just fishing for a compliment back. "Yeah, it was." I hesitated, keeping my eyes on the pavement. "Thanks to you."

He shrugged, his hands shoved in his jacket pockets, elbows out as he slowly shuffled beside me. "What can I say? You needed me."

The fact sent a shiver crawling down the back of my neck, one that had nothing to do with the breeze that ruffled the tree limbs beside us. I didn't like that I needed him any more than I did earlier when having to beg for help. Still, Wes came through for me, even if it wasn't easy—for either of us.

So why did I still feel more frustration than gratitude?

I let out an involuntary shiver.

"Here." Wes shrugged out of his jacket and draped it around my shoulders before I could protest. "Is that okay? Or am I being too nice again?"

I stared at him, unsure at the sincere tone, yet sarcastic phrasing.

"Sorry." Wes sighed and started walking again, urging me forward. "I'm a little keyed up."

I studied him from the corner of my eye as we strolled, his features dancing in and out of passing streetlights. "I thought finally doing something you loved where people could see you would give you an adrenaline rush. Not wear you out."

He shook his head, his profile set in stone. "You still don't get it."

"Then enlighten me!"

We walked the next block, the silence between us louder than anything I've ever heard.

"Wes—"

"Addison—"

Normally that would have made me laugh, but tonight I couldn't dredge up an ounce of humor. Maybe it was the heavy night pressing around me, or maybe it was knowing my dad would have a cow if he saw me walking up the driveway with Wes instead of Luke. Or maybe it was simply that Wes was losing his bad-boy charm. It didn't change my feelings for him, but I finally realized that the romance and mystery of all things Wes, the sarcasm and wit and the brick wall that I had been irrevocably—and unwillingly—drawn to months before, now just felt more like a burden than a puzzle to solve.

Had he changed? Or had I?

And if all I was feeling was true, then why did it hurt so much?

"You first." Wes gestured toward me.

"No, you." I had a feeling Wes wouldn't like what I was about to say—assuming I had the courage to actually say it.

"This sucks." He gestured between us, and I had a feeling he wasn't referring to the physical space that could have hosted a third person.

"I know. But what do you want me to do about it?"

"Forgive me, already." Wes stopped, grabbing the hem of his jacket I wore and tugging me toward him. "I did what you wanted, PK. Even all the crap you never actually said you wanted."

"What are you talking about?" I wanted to wrestle free, knew if I put even an ounce of pressure in the opposite direction, he'd let go of the jacket. But I couldn't. I knew what was coming, knew the script like I was watching a movie I'd written. I couldn't help but think this might be the last time he ever touched me, and I didn't want him to stop.

He leaned close, his breath puffing clouds in the night air. "I tagged along with you on that miserable excuse for a date with your father and teacher—in *public*. Then I took you on a stupid double date to a bowling alley and didn't beat up that idiot who was all over you in front of me." He shook his head as my mind raced to keep up. "I even stopped seeing Sonya. Tried to do the whole 'commitment' thing." He bit off the last words like they'd been dipped in poison.

"Commitment thing?" I laughed, the harsh sound bouncing in the void between us. "Is that what I am to you?"

"No. I didn't mean it to sound so bad." Wes stepped away from me, pushing his hands through his hair. "I'm just saying I've tried. I fixed those trees after Bert went on about how big a deal it was to you. I even played tonight, and you have no idea what that cost me."

"Cost you?" I hated repeating him like a parrot, but I couldn't stop. "You helped me out with those props, yeah, but you broke into a school at the same time, Wes. You fought with your dad in the hardware store, saw me—then went running to Sonya's house for a 'CD.' " I gave the word the air quotes it deserved. "And sure, you played for me tonight, but only after I practically twisted your arm. And it was so last minute, Jessica and I both nearly had heart attacks before you showed up."

A muscle twitched in Wes's jaw. "Everything I just said— that's all you see? The negative?"

I crossed my arms over my chest, lifting my chin. "Not every-thing is black and white."

Wes met my gaze, and we stared at each other for a long moment. I wished I could rip off his jacket and throw it at him, but the moment I expressed my anger, I knew the tears would come. Besides, I couldn't quite figure out why I was mad in the first place.

Maybe because the entire concept of "us" grew more unrealistic with every moment. As I'd just pointed out to him, even the good things Wes did—for me or not for me—were still tinged with gray. He'd never convert into what I needed him to be, what he must become to join me on my side of the religious line. And as much as I was tempted to cross over and join his, I couldn't. I was Addison Blakely, PK.

Whatever that meant.

"Is this about Luke?" Wes started walking again, leaving that ridiculous question in his wake. I had no choice but to hurry after him or shout our business down Victoria Street.

"Don't be crazy." I huffed, trying to match his long stride.

"He's into you, so why is it so crazy? I saw the rose."

"My dad gave me flowers, too."

Wes shot me a sidelong glare. "Don't even."

"Who cares what Luke thinks or feels? This isn't about him."

Wes stopped again, now only half a street from my house. "Then what is it? Why can't you forgive me? I swear to you, nothing happened at Sonya's that night."

"I believe you." Still stung a little, but I did believe him.

"Then is it because I didn't handle your rejection of me that night on our picnic with all the right words? Didn't laugh it off and say 'sorry for trying, pass the grapes'? It hurt, PK. I'm not used to that."

I never knew an apology could hurt worse than the initial offense. "Right. You're used to girls doing whatever you want." The images that popped in my mind made me want to shred his jacket with my fingernails. And he was upset because Luke brought me a rose? The irony of our situation bubbled in my stomach, a fizzy cocktail that made me want to laugh and cry in equal measure.

"So I have a past." Wes threw his arms out to the sides. "I'm not some kind of Disney prince. This is what I am. This is what you get." He lowered his arms, his voice barely louder than a whisper. "If you still want it."

I stared at him, his offer hovering between us, louder than the silence and heavier than the blanket of stars encasing the night sky. This was it, my moment. My choice. What did I want? I used to know. Looking into Wes's open, vulnerable, heartfelt gaze, my heart shouted one answer. My head another. I wanted to fix him. Fix us. Fix this mess between us that had come out of nowhere. I wanted to go back to the night before he pressured me, change his mind.

Change mine.

But there was no going backward, only forward.

I just knew I was tired of running in circles.

Chapter Twenty-Nine

think I've lost my mind." I stared at my bowl of melting chocolate chunk ice cream, too depressed to take another bite. The clock on the kitchen wall ticked a rhythm, a reminder that life inevitably went on despite my desire to crawl under the covers and stay there through spring.

Marta, however, had no problem polishing off her bowl. She helped herself to another spoonful. "Nein. You are starting to realize who you are and what you want."

"I want Wes." I mushed the drippy blob of chocolate with my spoon, watching it ooze. "Or I did. I do. I think. So why couldn't I just say that to him?"

"Because it is obviously not the right choice."

Easy for her to say. Marta was still riding the high from the talent show I'd already forgotten in lieu of my conversation with Wes. I'd come home an hour ago, thankfully without my father noticing the absence of Luke, and asked Dad if he minded if Marta came over for a celebration slumber party. He'd eagerly agreed and scooped up generous servings of ice cream before leaving us alone to take Ms. Hawthorne home. Little did he know that "celebration" was actually code for "SOS."

"I am just glad that every time you have a crisis, there is sugar involved." Marta's eyes twinkled as she licked her spoon.

"Very funny." I shoved my bowl away from me across the kitchen table. "You want mine?"

Marta's lips twisted to one side as she debated then shook her head at the unappealing mass of dairy. "I don't mean to joke. But Addison, you're on a journey."

"To the mental institution?" I folded my arms on the table and laid my head on top of them, unable to erase the image of the disappointment in Wes's eyes when I told him I needed to think about what he asked of me. The scariest part was, I still had no clue what I was supposed to be thinking about.

Maybe I'd thought too much already. Maybe I should just dive back into a relationship with him—whatever *that* would look like—and assume things couldn't possibly go worse than last time. Maybe if I avoided my dad, and Sonya, and the hardware store, and Got Beans, and all things school related, everything would work out this time. No double dates. No unchaperoned picnics. No drama.

But even as I thought it, I knew it wouldn't work. We couldn't avoid reality to be together. Either a relationship worked with all those factors involved, or it didn't.

And right now, it just didn't.

I groaned. "I'm on a journey all right. I'm turning into one of those girls I always made fun of and never understood."

"You understand now?"

"Unfortunately." I sat up straight, dodging the sympathy in Marta's expression. "I know you never liked Wes. You're probably ecstatic."

She frowned. "Ecstatic?"

"Thrilled. Happy. Over the moon." I shot my arm through the air like a rocket.

"I'm not happy you are hurting. But I am happy you are realizing things."

"What things?" I scoffed. "Tell me, because everything is as clear as mud over here."

Marta twirled her spoon in a pattern across her empty bowl, the light tinkling sound almost music-like in quality, the ticking clock above us a drumbeat. I nodded my head to the rhythm then stopped. Either I was more exhausted from the talent show and my emotional meltdown with Wes, or I truly needed a straightjacket.

"How do you feel when you are with Wes?" Marta finally asked. She peered at me with an intense stare that rivaled that of our school counselor.

Wasn't that the sixty-four-million-dollar question? I shrugged. "It's never the same anymore." To put it mildly.

"What did it used to be?"

I thought a moment. "Anticipation. Mystery. Danger. Allure." And chemistry. Oh, the chemistry. But I wasn't going there right now. Besides, Marta already knew that part.

"And what was it tonight?"

I rolled in my lower lip. "Anger. Hurt. Depression. Confusion."

"How did you feel at church as a child?"

"Huh?" I blinked at the sudden one-eighty in conversation. She waved her spoon. "Work with me."

"Church as a kid." I nibbled my lip, thinking way back to my days in Sunday school and children's camp. "I felt excitement at learning. Felt encouraged. Uplifted. Happy."

"What about at church last Sunday?"

The truth struck me like a slap across the face. I actually reached up and touched my cheek. "Hurt. Anger. Boredom. Confusion."

Marta leaned back, crossing her arms, her inquisitive gaze now radiating compassion. "It's a pattern, Addison. It's all connected."

"How?" I shook my head, so close to seeing it, knowing I was on the verge of something big but unable to grasp it. "What does church have to do with Wes?"

"Nein—not church. Your relationship with God."

She'd lost me. "I don't get it."

"Right now you said you feel upset and confused. This has been going on for some time, right?" She shrugged. "Maybe your bad feelings are not so much about Wes as they are about your faith. Maybe you're upset over the wrong thing."

I shook my head rapidly. "We've talked about this, Marta. I'm a PK. I've grown up in church. I know all the—"

"Answers?" She interrupted. "I am not talking about answers. You can quote Bible verses to me all day if you'd like. But that does not have anything to do with your heart and how you feel about God."

"I believe in God." Just saying the words out loud felt ridiculous, like how could I possibly believe anything differently? "I believe He created the earth and believe His son was Jesus and all that."

"I didn't ask what you believed in your head. I asked what you felt with your heart." Marta's voice lowered, despite the fact we were the only ones in the house. "How do you *feel* about God?"

I let out a heavy sigh. "I love God."

"Did that sound as hollow to you as it did to me?"

Indignation rose in my chest. How dare Marta sit there across from me and challenge my faith, the faith I'd possessed literally my entire life? I was on our pew every time the doors were open, except Wednesday nights during homework season. I volunteered every summer for the kids Vacation Bible School program, attended the quarterly Bible studies, and even sang in the youth choir one miserable month when attendance dropped. I'd spooned soup for the homeless, read to the homebound, and wiped more snotty kid noses in the name of Jesus than anyone else in this town—more than Marta had surely ever done. And she wanted to call me out on *my* faith while she spouted easy answers and polished off all the ice cream?

"What do you mean 'hollow'?" I scooted my chair back and stood, ready to leave the table, leave the room, leave this ridiculous conversation. "I meant it." And I did, even if my so-called relationship with Him still felt totally one sided. But hey, I was doing my part.

"Then where is the passion? Where is the emotion? You get very emotional talking about Wes, but when we talk about God, who we are supposed to love the most, you sound like a robot." Marta moved her arms in a mechanical fashion.

If we'd been having any other conversation, I'd have whipped out my cell phone to record the moment for posterity. Instead, all of my frustration from the night—no, the entire month—spilled out. "You don't get it, Marta. Everything I am is church. Faith. God. My whole stinkin' life. Every moment growing up was spent listening to Dad preach on the goodness of God our Heavenly Father then pretending not to care when he came home and practically ignored me—"

I slapped my hand over my mouth, and Marta's eyebrows shot up in surprise. The truth cut a hole into my heart, and I slowly sank back into my chair. No wonder God had been so quiet.

Had I ever really known Him?

Heart racing, I propped my chin in my hands, feeling weaker and more exhausted than I'd felt in months. I opened my mouth, but the plethora of words dancing in my head refused to form a coherent sentence.

"You've gotten your relationship with your *dad* mixed up

with your relationship with your *Father*." Marta pointed a finger to the sky.

"But how do I fix it?" My voice cracked, and I licked my lips, tasting tears I didn't know had fallen as childhood memory after memory rushed at me. Somewhere during the years, the excitement of church and learning about God faded as I began to compare my dad with what I knew about God. Never tangibly, never in a sense that I'd have ever recognized, but the proof was there, straight before me like a road map to the past. I always felt ignored. Loved, yes. But only in the barest of ways. I felt distant. Invisible.

And when Wes saw me, it had been like a door flung open to a dark place aching for light.

"You simply must correct your view of God." Marta gestured with both hands. "Start listening in church instead of waiting for the sermon to be over. Start reading your Bible because you want to, not because you think you have to. Start living out *your* faith—not the faith of your family."

"You make it sound easy." Changing a habit and mind-set I'd possessed the majority of my life wouldn't happen overnight. But a strange urging in my spirit, a sense of excitement that there could be so much more began to seep through my stomach, giving me hope. Making me want to try. *Is that You, God?* I wanted it to be. And that already felt like progress.

I drew a shuddering breath, squeezing my eyes shut. *Okay, God. Let's try this again. For real this time. PK status not withstanding—I'm Yours.*

Marta waited until I opened my eyes to continue. "It will be a process, obviously, and take effort. But it's worth it."

"I feel dumb for missing something so obvious in my own life. How did you see it?" I reached across the table to Marta, sorry that I had ever been angry at her. She'd shone a flashlight into a corner of my soul I hadn't known existed.

And there were more than a few skeletons lurking in the shadows.

"Because I made the same journey years ago." Marta squeezed my hands, lips twisting in a humorless smile. "I'm a PK, too."

The kitchen table seemed to tilt beneath us, and I tightened my grip on her. "What?" But it made sense, even as shock flooded my system. No wonder she understood how I felt, no wonder she had all the right answers and could finish my sentences. She'd lived in the same fishbowl.

Except her water didn't seem nearly as cloudy.

"I had to come to the same conclusion, Addison. I had to embrace faith for myself—not because it'd been thrust upon me since birth." She lifted one shoulder in a half shrug.

My head spun. "This has been quite a night." I let go of her hands and rubbed my temples with my fingers. "I think we're going to need more ice cream."

Marta twisted in her seat to face me as I carried our bowls into the kitchen and rinsed the ice-cream scoop under warm running water. "My dad pastors a large church in Stuttgart. He has for the last decade." She shrugged. "That's part of why I'm here in the States. I needed a change of pace, as you say."

I scooped more ice cream into our bowls then reached into the very back of the fridge where I'd stashed a can of whipped cream Dad would never find—behind a bag of mixed veggies. "But you seem to have it all figured out. What could you possibly need an escape from?"

"Just because I finally chose to embrace my relationship with God rather than push Him away doesn't make the lifestyle easy. I still need the occasional break and space in routine." Marta's voice faded, and she stared absently into the living room, her eyes vacant. Obviously I'd lost her somewhere back in her home country.

I set the full bowl of dessert in front of her, and she snapped out of it. "But that doesn't matter. I'm here to help you because I understand. And I believe God put us together for that very reason."

"Why didn't you say anything before?" I licked my spoon, my appetite slowly returning as I digested the abrupt revelations of the past ten minutes.

Marta dipped her spoon into the cloud of whipped cream and smiled at me. "I didn't want my situation to influence you. You needed to figure things out on your own. And congratulations—you just did."

"Sort of." I stared at my bowl, wishing I had a cherry to put on top. "I don't know where to go from here, though. Especially with my dad. I can't just go up to him and say, 'Hey, I just figured out our crappy relationship is the reason I've never actually realized what it is to be a real Christian.' Can I?"

"Nein." Marta snorted, amusement flickering across her features. "You cannot."

"So?"

She tilted her head, thinking. "I think you need to have an honest talk with your father. Let him know you are interested in changing your relationship, just as you are interested in changing the one you have with God."

Marta was so eloquent, it almost made me jealous. But I was too grateful for her advice to care. "This is going to sound really mushy, but I honestly am so glad you're here." I still felt down about what happened earlier tonight, and I knew nothing was going to be easy about the next few days, but I couldn't help but feel as if a gigantic burden had suddenly evaporated off my shoulders.

"It is a mushy kind of night, ja?" Marta grinned at me, chocolate ice cream smearing the corners of her mouth. She held up her spoon. "A toast. To new chapters."

"To new chapters."

We clinked spoons, and as I scooped up a bite of my dessert, I couldn't help but wonder if my new chapter meant the end for Wes and me.

★ ★ ★

Dad came home a few minutes later while Marta was taking a shower. I met him at the door, hesitant with my approach. As much as I knew we needed to talk, I wondered how much more I could emotionally stand in one night.

Whistling, Dad hung his coat on the rack by the door and dropped his keys on the foyer table, his standard coming-home routine. "You girls sure are up late."

"You sure were out late." I couldn't help the automatic retort, and I bit my lip, not wanting to start this conversation on the wrong foot.

"Touché." Dad smiled, albeit awkwardly. He shoved his hands in his pockets. "How was the ice cream?"

My stomach gurgled on cue, and I pressed my hands against it, grateful I'd changed into sweats before we ate. I doubted my snug black dress could have stood up to that second helping. "Too good."

"I really am proud of your success tonight. I know the Let Them Read Foundation will be very impressed." Dad patted my shoulder and started to move around me. "It's definitely a night of celebration."

"Wait." I swallowed hard. "There's, uh—something you need to know."

He raised one eyebrow at me, and if I hadn't been about to confess a secret, I'd have giggled at his imitation of my signature move. But if I was going to be serious about this for-real Christian thing, I needed to start on the right foot—no more lies or stretching the truth. "I, uh—Luke didn't walk me home tonight."

"You walked alone?" Dad frowned, crossing his arms over his button-down. "That's not a good idea, Addison."

"I wasn't alone. I was with Wes."

A shadow flickered across Dad's face, giving the impression he thought that was worse than walking alone. If he knew what had happened at our so-called picnic last week, he'd have probably come out and said it—along with some other things. But I wasn't going to confess everything. That incident lived in the past, and I wouldn't make that mistake again. Besides, I didn't think Dad could handle that level of honesty in one night.

I watched him carefully, steeling myself for a lecture, a punishment, a disappointed sigh. All the "usuals" that had kept me so well behaved all those years.

"Oh well." Dad waved one hand in the air, brushing off my indiscretion. "You're home safe, and you were honest."

What? No droning talk about danger? No reminder of his list of dating rules? My mouth opened and closed like a fish.

"I don't want to argue. I have some news to share." Dad rubbed his chin, a smile peeking from behind his fingers.

"Okay. I had hoped we could talk, too." I twisted my fingers together, still unsure how to start the conversation that'd been a decade in the making.

"Me first." Dad actually bounced on the balls of his feet a little as a solid grin overtook his features. "I can't hold it in anymore."

"What? Did you get nominated for preacher of the year?" I joked—badly. So much for playing it cool. My stomach twisted in anticipation. Hopefully he'd hurry with his news so I could somehow blurt out this revelation I'd had about church. And God. And Wes. And myself. And him. Okay, so the convo might take longer than I'd thought.

"Don't be silly." He grabbed my shoulders and gave me a happy little shake—the most excitement I'd seen out of him in months. No, years. Wait—ever?

"I asked Kathy to marry me tonight."

All the air rushed out of the room as a bowling ball plopped into my already-full stomach. I reeled backward and would have fallen if Dad hadn't pulled me forward into an impromptu hug.

A million different thoughts and questions—mostly negative—flooded my mind and jammed in my mouth. All I could squeak out was a pathetic, "What?"

Marta appeared at the end of the hallway, a towel wrapped turban-style around her hair. She echoed my sentiment, mumbling in German. Shock radiated in her wide eyes, and she clutched her robe like a life preserver.

I shakily looked back at Dad, who had finally released me and beamed as if he truly had no idea the bomb he'd dropped. "We haven't set a date yet, but she said yes!" His gaze bounced back and forth between me and Marta. "Isn't God good?"

Well, He had a good sense of humor at least.

I steadied myself with one hand against the wall and inhaled deeply, as Dad headed off—still whistling—to the kitchen without waiting for an answer.

"Are you all right?" Marta approached me cautiously, as one might a wild animal stuck in a trap.

I nodded, focusing on my breathing. *This is okay. This is okay.* I repeated the mantra, desperate for a sense of control, a sense of peace. *I can do this. Dad is happy.* That's what mattered, right? And Ms. Hawthorne was nice. Maybe she wore the same size shoe as me, and we could share some of those awesome boots.

Then I saw the framed photo of Mom on the end table by the lamp and burst into tears.

Chapter Thirty

Despite the early morning sunshine streaming through my bedroom window, Saturday looked bleak. I'd tossed and turned for hours the night before while Marta snored on the blow-up mattress beside my bed. But the lack of sleep wasn't my nasally friend's fault—I couldn't stop replaying the past twenty-four hours in my head. Dad's decision to get married. My spiritual revelation I had no clue what to do with. The pending talk with Dad I didn't want to have.

And the inevitable answer to Wes's question that I still couldn't make myself give.

I stuck six powdered doughnuts on a plate and snuck it upstairs to Marta while Dad sipped coffee in front of the TV. This day required fortification, and I was out of mocha money. I waved the plate beneath Marta's nose then thought better of it in case she inhaled the powder and sneezed.

"Get up. I'm having a crisis." I nudged her with my toe.

Marta grunted and rolled over and then sat up and brushed her blond hair out of her face with one hand. "Good morning to you, too." Then she spied the doughnuts and crammed one in her mouth without further comment.

I hid my smile, wondering if Marta's family would blame America for her bad table manners upon her return home.

Then my grin faded. I didn't want Marta to go home. Winter would be over before I knew it, ushering my best friend out with it come spring. Who would I vent to? Who would bring me sugar when I had a bad day?

"What is the crisis this time?" She nibbled her next doughnut. "Haven't you reached your quota?"

I grabbed a doughnut, too, as I sat cross-legged on the other end of her inflatable bed, tucking my Hello Kitty house boots underneath me. The sight of them brought back the night I'd ridden Wes's motorcycle for approximately ten yards, and a knot formed in my throat. "Same stuff. Just more overwhelming in the daylight."

"I thought that was supposed to be the reverse?" She raised flaxen eyebrows at me.

I shrugged as I ate. "In fairy tales and sitcoms, yes. My life? Not so much."

"Is this about your dad? Or Wes?" Marta reached for a third doughnut at the same time I did, leaving behind a sugar-sprinkled plate. "What is it *really* about, Addison?"

"It's everything. But right now. . ." I wrinkled my nose. "Wes." As usual. Would I ever lose the tie he had on me? Would telling him I couldn't be with him even help anything?

"Do you know what you have to tell him?"

I nodded, though how to put my feelings into words was still beyond me. How to look him in the eye while doing so seemed even more out of reach. Time to put my newly solid faith into action. *God, You're listening now, right? It seems like it. So, uh, I'm going to need some advice. And quickly.*

"Then start small." Marta gestured with her doughnut, sending a spray of crumbs across the purple blanket on her lap. "Tell Luke first."

"Luke?" I licked powdered sugar off my lips and frowned.

"What does he have to do with anything?"

"You need to be honest with him. He's still bringing you flowers—often—and while you haven't been encouraging, you still haven't told him you are not interested, either." Marta brushed off her fingers over the empty plate. "It's only fair."

"So you can make a move?" I winked at her, though my heart wasn't in it.

"As if." Marta rolled her eyes then sat up straight. "Hey, I sounded really American then."

"I'm so proud." I pointed at her. "But you like Luke. Admit it."

She nodded slowly. "I do. But it doesn't matter. I will be leaving in a few months, and if we stay friends only, it will be easier. Besides, I doubt he will recover from your rejection that quickly." She smiled. "Ms. Heartbreaker."

"Whatever. He'll be fine." He'd better be. I couldn't handle any more drama right now. But Marta was right—Luke deserved honesty from me, and maybe that conversation would be good practice for the one I needed to have afterward with Wes.

My stomach clenched, and my thoughts backpedaled. Maybe there was still a chance for me and Wes. Maybe he wouldn't distract me from the path I'd set myself on last night. Maybe I'd be a good influence on him, and my dad would come around, and Wes would change—

And maybe Lady Gaga would wear jeans and a T-shirt to the next Grammys.

I pressed my fingers against my forehead and groaned. This had to be done, and the sooner, the better. The holidays were coming—Thanksgiving was next week—and I didn't want all this ugliness looming above me during my favorite time of the year. It'd be weird enough this season with Ms. Hawthorne hanging around—I didn't need any extra tension between the few friends I had. Maybe if I came clean with Luke, we could still be friends. As for Wes. . .

Yeah right. Somehow I knew it would be all or nothing with him.

And I just couldn't make my lips form that dreaded word.

★ ★ ★

CALL ME WHEN U CAN. NO RUSH.

I sent the text to Luke then sat down on the top step of my nearly frozen front porch to wait. Cold seeped through my jeans and jacket, but the chill kept me focused. Determined. The sooner I had this conversation, the sooner I could go inside and warm up with hot chocolate.

My phone blared and I jumped, staring at the caller ID as it flashed Luke's number. That was fast. Too fast. Maybe he wasn't going to take this as easily as I hoped.

I squeezed my eyes shut then pressed the button to answer. "Bored much?"

Luke's warm laugh echoed in my ear. Man, I didn't want to do this. But I couldn't lead him on, and enough flowers had already died for this pathetic attempt at a relationship. Time to spare the rest.

"I just thought calling you back seemed more entertaining than the Cartoon Network." Luke yawned into the phone. "You girls are up early."

Wait a minute. I frowned. "How'd you know Marta was here?"

"She texted me last night on her way over."

Figured. I sort of doubted Marta's whole "long distance" spiel earlier. The sneaky girl was texting him mere hours before her whole "we're just friends" rant. I glanced over my shoulder toward the house, where she was supposedly getting dressed. "Do you have a minute?" I shivered as the cold wrapped around me.

"For you? Of course." Luke turned on the charm, and for the tenth time I wished I could change my feelings and go for the guy who said all the right things and spewed romance like he had cue cards in the wings.

"You're great. And the flower at the show last night was sweet." I hesitated. "All of the flowers you've sent me over the past few weeks, actually. But. . ." I drew a deep breath, unsure how to continue.

Luke filled in my blank. "But you want me to stop."

"Yes. No!" I sucked in my breath. "Yes. You're just. . ."

He let out a sigh. "I'm not Wes."

"Right." My eyes widened, and I slapped my hand over my mouth, my next words muffled. "No! That's not it. I can't be with him either. I mean—" Oh, I needed another doughnut stuffed in my face, pronto. Why was I blabbing my feelings for Wes to Luke? I was the worst breaker-upper ever—and this wasn't even a relationship. Good grief.

"I get it, Addison." Luke laughed, the sound far less cheery than it had been three minutes before. "I knew this was coming. It's nice of you to actually tell me flat out."

Is that what I'd somehow managed to do around all the babbling? I breathed a little easier, though the knot in my stomach had yet to fully unravel. "I'm glad you understand. If I could change things, I would." And I meant that. I hoped he believed me.

"I know." A blaring horn sounded from the cartoon in the background, followed by the familiar *meep meep* of the Looney Tunes Road Runner. "Guess I'll have to end my discount club card at the florist."

Oh my gosh. I sat up straight on the porch stairs, my frozen rear end forgotten. "You didn't."

"I didn't." His laugh sounded more genuine this time. "Got you."

He was going to be fine. I leaned forward, hoping my smile showed in my voice. "As corny as this sounds, can we still—"

"Be friends? We better." The flirty edge to his voice suddenly made me doubt the progress of the entire past five minutes of conversation. Was he thinking if we stayed friends he'd have a better chance of pursuing me later?

No. I shook it off. How conceited was that? He probably just didn't want to let things end badly any more than I did. It seemed a lot easier to save face and move on past the initial awkwardness if we stayed friendly, rather than having to avoid each other at school and make people guess. "Great. So. . .I'll see ya?"

"Yep. See you." Another honk sounded from his end of the line, and I couldn't help but picture the coyote endlessly chasing the road runner.

★ ★ ★

Marta went home an hour later, and I decided to head to the library. Maybe losing myself in a classic novel for a few hours would take the pressure off and let me figure out what to say to Wes. I wasn't stalling—I was preparing.

That was the mantra I repeated to myself, anyway.

I hitched the strap of my book bag higher on my shoulder as I perused the fiction rows, grateful this side of the library offered a sense of peace and quiet for now. The Saturday crowd seemed drawn to the far side of the building, where a local author was signing books and about to lead story hour for children. It was past time I caught up on my to-read list, since the talent show had sucked all my available time the past two months.

Breathing in the familiar, slightly musty smell of my beloved books, I plucked a well-worn volume of *Jane Eyre* off the shelf and let my fingers flip through the frayed pages. How many times had I read that one? Six? I reshelved it and reached for *Wuthering Heights*.

"That one's a bit of a downer."

I jerked so hard at Wes's voice that I dropped the heavy book on my foot. I jumped then bit my lip as pain streamed through my toes. But the rush of awareness at Wes's sudden proximity hurt much more.

"Sorry." He knelt to retrieve the volume then handed it to me, his fingers brushing mine. "Why are you so jumpy?"

"I don't know. What are you doing here?" The words practically hissed from my lips as I scrambled to stick the book back on the shelf. My toe stung, my dignity smarted, and looking into Wes's eyes, my heart broke. I wasn't ready for this.

"Same as you." He grinned as he tugged at the bag on my shoulder, already half-full. "Making up for lost time since the talent show, huh?"

"Something like that." The bag suddenly felt heavy, and I set it on the floor at our feet. "And I've read *Wuthering Heights* already. I don't need a recap."

Wes frowned, leaning against the shelf beside us and crossing his arms over his chest. "What gives, PK? You that upset to see me?"

Yes. But not because of the reason he thought. I shrugged and turned my attention to the row of novels, grazing my thumb along the spines as I pretended to study the titles. I'd practically grown up in this section of the library, and I hated to mar the fond memories with a sad new one. But I couldn't put this off any longer, or my resolve—what little existed—would crumble. *God, help me. I'm trying to do the right thing.*

Wes's hand on my shoulder cut off my silent prayer, and I flinched under his touch. His arm fell slowly to his side. "I'm starting to think you have an answer for me."

I nodded, rolling in my lower lip and refusing to make eye contact. Instead I stared so hard at the spine of *Jane Eyre* the faded text blurred and swam together.

"I get it." Wes's voice cracked a little, and he coughed. "You just can't forgive me, huh?"

"It's not that." I spun to face him then, unwilling to let him think something that wasn't true. "It's where I am right now. Something happened last night that really woke me up—I realized some stuff about my life, and I can't—"

"I see. The old 'it's not you, it's me' line." Wes nodded, the formerly teasing spark in his eye now replaced with a bitter sheen. He snorted. "Guess that's fair. I've used it enough times."

"It's not a line." I drew a shaky breath. "It's a fact. I'm in this process right now, and I can't be distracted." I shook my head. This was even worse than my conversation with Luke—so much for practice. This just sucked. "It's hard to explain."

"Quit being so vague, PK." Wes's arms tightened across his chest. "If you're going to do this, then man up and do it. Tell me the truth. Even if it hurts."

Oh, it hurt all right. Like an eighteen-wheeler parked against my chest. "I am telling you the truth. I don't need a boyfriend right now."

"When does anyone ever *need* a boyfriend?" Wes scoffed. "This isn't about need, Addison. It's about want. What *you* want."

My heart struggled to beat a normal rhythm as the shelves in the library pressed in around me. *I want you, I want you, I want you.* The words pressed against my lips, threatening to spring forth and puddle on the ground between us. Everything in me wanted to wrap myself in his leather jacket and inhale his cologne and believe this would work. Believe that I could find myself while with him, that I could grow and change and finish this journey I started last night fully involved and not distracted in the least. God *and* Wes.

But a still, small voice held me back with a quiet assurance

I couldn't deny. *Wait.*

Tears formed as I met Wes's gaze. "I'm sorry."

He nodded, looking away, his eyes roaming to the shelves of books surrounding us before flitting back to my face and then finally to his shoes. "It's your choice, PK."

Choice. The word sounded so freeing, like I had all these options and privileges. But I didn't. If I wanted to make my life right, really know what it meant to be a Christian, finally allow my prayers to drift higher than my bedroom ceiling, and participate wholeheartedly in a relationship with God for the first time in my church-saturated life, then I couldn't have it all. I couldn't surround myself with the temptation of Wes, the opportunities to sin and pedal backward instead of forward down this new path.

I did have to choose—and it hurt worse than anything else I'd ever felt.

"Nothing about this has been right." I gestured between us, desperate for him to understand, to agree. "We've been off ever since you moved here. First you were with Sonya, and there were all of my dad's rules. Then your issues with your father, and that night in the meadow, and the misunderstanding with Sonya. Our timing is jacked up."

"It doesn't have to be." Wes reached for my hand, and I foolishly allowed him to take it. "You're making it more complicated than it is."

My palm relaxed against the warmth of his grip, and before I knew it, he'd tugged me toward him. I opened my mouth to protest but couldn't speak.

His eyes searched mine as he drew me closer. "This could be our timing, PK. Our moment."

My breath caught in my chest, and automatically my hands snaked around his neck and my fingers tangled in his hair, longer than his jacket collar now in the back. I breathed in his spicy cologne and the scent of leather, my senses dazed as if drugged. My head reeled, the library blurring around us as Wes's eyes dropped to my lips and he leaned in even closer.

I angled my head toward him as if on autopilot, heart racing a frantic beat.

No.

NO!

I jerked backward, my entire body protesting as my mind ordered a rush of adrenaline to separate me from danger. "See!" I couldn't breathe, could only back away and press one hand against my stomach as I sucked air through my lips. "See! I can't."

"You can't date me because you're attracted to me?" Wes's incredulous expression turned to doubt. "Addison, I'm not going to pressure you again. If you're not ready for that step, fine. I'm cool."

But was he? And better yet, was I? I'd just broken up with him, yet at the simple touch of his hand, I was ready to make out in a public library. That didn't bode well for my virtue. I clenched my hands into fists, determined to stay strong. "I *won't* be ready for that. Until I'm married."

A flicker of anxiety darted through his eyes—just a flash, but it lingered long enough for me to see we were definitely not on the same page in that regard. The clarity gave me a rush of assurance that I was making the right choice, and I breathed a silent prayer of thanks.

"If this is about sex, don't let that make up your mind." Wes's voice dropped to a whisper. "I don't care. I can wait."

I somehow doubted that, but the sincerity in his eyes caught me off guard.

"It's not the. . .the sex." I glanced over my shoulder, unable

301

to believe I was having this conversation in public. "It's the whole relationship. It's all tied together, and I can't tie myself to anything else right now."

"What do you mean by 'else'?" Frustration sketched a pattern across Wes's features. "Come on, Addison. The talent show is behind you. You said you forgive me. So what do you have to focus on that's more important than us?"

Aggravation built in my chest at his insistence, and I'd never felt more thankful. Anger was so much easier to bear. Sympathy and compassion? Impossible. Chemistry? Unbearable. "You want the truth?"

"Yes! I've been saying that this whole time."

"Fine." I crossed my arms and tilted my head to one side as I waited for his response. "The answer is God."

Wes's mouth snapped shut as disbelief filled his eyes. He took a step backward.

"I know you don't believe me. I'm a PK. How much more Christian can I get, right?" I snorted. "But it's true. I realized last night that I'm far from where I should be, and I want to make efforts to get there. For real."

Wes continued to stare at me. "God?"

"God." Saying His name out loud brought more assurance of my stand, even though my chest still ached at the crestfallen expression on Wes's face. "I know this is weird. But seriously, why don't you come to church tomorrow?" I reached toward him, my heart cracking into bits as he shook my hand off his arm. "Give it a try. What do you have to lose?"

"Do you know nothing about me, Addison?" Wes's voice rose, and he made no effort to lower it even as a passing librarian shushed us from the end of the row. "Why would I want anything to do with church? For all I know, every person on that pew is a hypocrite just like my dad. Did you know my mom used to sing in the choir when I was a kid?"

I just shook my head as his rant continued, my stomach cramping at the pained glaze in his eyes.

"She did. Second soprano, third seat from the end. Every Sunday. And guess what she was doing every Saturday night? Or should I say, *who*?"

I flinched as the truth of his past slapped me full force.

"So excuse me when I say 'no thanks' to your invitation." He brushed past me then without another word, and once again I was stuck watching him walk away, wondering when it would stop hurting, wondering why God blessed some families so much and others so little, wondering why Wes chose to confide in me.

And wondering what on earth I was supposed to do about it.

Chapter Thirty-One

Staring at my father in the pulpit as he wrapped up his sermon from the book of Acts, one thought played over and over in my mind—louder even than the peppermint wrapper Mrs. Vanderford crinkled from the row in front of me.

I should have told him.

After my completely rotten Saturday afternoon in the library, I'd holed up in the bathtub at home, read almost half of *Wuthering Heights*, and used our entire tank of hot water before facing reality—and my dad—at the dinner table. After a short nap, I felt I was over Wes enough to carry on a conversation about my newly amped faith. (And by enough, I meant not really at all.)

However, instead of Dad and a hot dinner waiting for me at the table, I found a ten-dollar bill and a sticky note informing me he'd gone to Ms. Hawthorne's house while she phoned her family long distance about their engagement, and I should order a pizza—which was wrong for so many reasons; namely, a large pizza cost more than ten dollars, and where did that leave room for cheesy bread?

So I did what any girl in my situation would do when deprived of mochas and allowance money—I'd pocketed the ten dollars, made a turkey sandwich, and gone to bed before he'd come home. Genius, except it left me sitting at church with uncertainty about what to do next churning in my stomach like the giant bubble machine on *Willy Wonka and the Chocolate Factory*. Dad deserved to know the truth about my new commitment—but not so much in the middle of a service. Maybe we could go to lunch afterward and finally talk.

If he didn't already have plans with Ms. Hawthorne, of course.

Dad closed his sermon. As we bowed our heads to pray, my heart climbed into my throat and lodged there like Mrs. Vanderford's peppermint. I could barely hear my father over the roar of blood in my ears as he asked God to lead souls to Him during the invitation.

A quickening of my pulse sent my body on full alert. *Nuh-uh. I'm already Yours, God. We got that worked out. Don't make me walk the aisle, too.* At this close range from the third pew, I'd barely have to cover a few yards before I'd literally be at the altar, but that was so not the point. The preacher's daughter coming to the Lord? What would everyone think? Mrs. Vanderford would choke on her mint, and the entire service would be interrupted with sirens. I couldn't risk it.

I've got to stay put, Lord, for her own good. I eyed the back of her big hair and baggy floral dress and winced. It probably wasn't appropriate to wish Stacy and Clinton from *What Not to Wear* would breeze down the aisle and take the woman away. I'd seen them interrupt performances, plays, and weddings, but never a church service.

You're stalling. My conscience taunted me as Dad's voice droned in what had to be the world's longest prayer. I didn't want it to end, though, because once it did, I had yet another choice to make. My hands grew slick as I fought a private battle.

I wished Marta were here, but she had to attend her host

family's church this week. She'd hold my hand and tug me down the aisle if she thought that's what God wanted. But I didn't need her courage. I had my own.

It just appeared to have been temporarily misplaced.

I lifted my head as Dad said "amen" and subconsciously swayed back and forth to the music as the invitational played.

"Go, Addison."

I didn't really think God spoke audibly, but the pressure urging me forward felt as if He had.

Shaking my head, I gripped the pew in front of me with both hands until my knuckles turned white. *They're gonna freak, Lord. All of them.* I studied the faces around me, feeling nothing but a wave of condemnation that I knew was just my own mind running wild. They'd be happy, not judge me. Most of them anyway. Right? . . . But I couldn't let go of the pew.

"Go, Addison."

"I'm blocked in." Oops, didn't mean to say that out loud. I offered an apologetic smile at the parishioners to my left and right, wishing the carpeted floor would eat me up. *See, God? Boxed in. Trapped. I better stay right here and not interrupt.*

"One more verse," Dad said from the stairs as the piano music continued. He extended his arms wide, a welcoming smile lighting his features. "If anyone desires to know more about the Lord, come now. We won't sing forever."

Hadn't it already been an eternity?

I squeezed the bench harder, the wood warm beneath my hands. A wave of cheap perfume assaulted my nose as Mrs. Vanderford turned and rustled in her purse for another mint. I licked my dry lips, the scuffling of impatient congregation members' feet around me ticking off the seconds like a clock with a bomb attached. Everyone was in a hurry to go home. If no one responded to the invitation, we'd sing a superfast hymn to dismiss, and all these hungry people could go to lunch. I'd be holding up the service if I went now. It was too late.

"Go, Addison."

My chest tightened. *Next week. Okay, God? One more Sunday.*

I didn't really expect an answer, but the sudden silence that loomed in my heart seemed deafening. Here I was finally feeling as if God could hear my prayers, yet I ignored Him when He spoke. A sense of failure swamped my spirit in murky waves, lapping at my soul with regret. I'd been a Christian for one weekend, grown up in the church my entire life, and couldn't obey *one* thing God asked of me? What kind of commitment had I made, exactly? I'd given up an immediate future with Wes for. . .silence? Disobedience? Sin? I wasn't any better off if that was the case.

The closing piano chords faded away, and my stomach lurched. "Wait!"

Without another thought, I hurtled the pew in front of me, pushed past a dazed Mrs. Vanderford, and tripped out of the second row toward the altar.

My dad, standing in front of the pulpit, caught my forearms as I stumbled forward. "Addison?" His face grayed with panic. "Are you okay?"

"I'm—I'm. . ." My words faltered, and I fell into his chest, hiccuping. "I'm a Christian now, Daddy."

My voice echoed across the auditorium, and I pulled away just enough to notice the microphone still clipped to the lapel of his suit.

★ ★ ★

Too bad Mrs. Vanderford didn't share her peppermints because we had a whole slew of parishioners needing fresh breath. Yet as the congregation line filed past me to shake my hand

and congratulate me on my new commitment, my paranoia decreased. No one judged. Oh, I heard a few surprised murmurs, of course, but after that pew vault, I'd have been gossiping, too. Somehow I couldn't help but think God was smiling at that one. It was my own fault—if I'd obeyed when He first called, I wouldn't have had to resort to such drastic measures.

"What a glorious day. I'm so happy for you." One of the blue-haired women who'd taught me in Sunday school when I was younger clasped my warm hands in papery-thin ones, her ring digging into my palm. But I didn't care. I welcomed her sweet smile and even accepted the stiff hug she offered before she ambled away on the arm of her nephew.

Beside me, Dad caught my eye and beamed, and I couldn't help but bask in the attention of his approval. Of course that wasn't why I made my decision, but it felt nice having his attention for once. "We'll get lunch after church, so don't make plans," he whispered before the next parishioner whisked up in line.

As I chatted briefly with old Mr. Davis and his great-grandson, I spied Mr. Keegan slipping out the back doors of the church. My stomach knotted. Maybe he'd realized I'd been at the hardware store that night and overheard his confession of problems. Would Wes have told him I'd been there?

Wes. My heart protested the thought, and I tried to shake him out of my mind, wishing he'd been there with me this morning, wishing he could see the truth about God that I saw so clearly now for the first time in my life. He needed peace. He needed purpose. So why was he letting a couple of hypocrites hold him back from trying to reach either? Somehow I couldn't help but wonder if his secrets went even deeper than I realized.

Mrs. Vanderford stepped up in line then, jerking my thoughts back to reality. She gripped my arm, her hold borderline uncomfortable, and leaned in close. "That was quite the move you made back there." Her lips smiled, but her eyes didn't.

I tried to subtly free my arm. "Sorry about that. I almost waited until it was too late."

"I'll say." Her lined eyebrows rose toward her pouf of hair, and she sniffed. "Sixteen years is quite a while."

My lips pursed into a tight line. Part of me wanted to call her out on what she meant, but the other part of me didn't want the conflict—especially with my dad standing beside me. I collected my thoughts then pasted on an easy smile. "I don't understand." When all else fails, play dumb and put the ball back in the meanie's court.

"I think you do, dear." She glanced at my father, who was involved in conversation with a deacon, then back at me. "He must have had quite the shock this morning. To think he's been leading a church all this time when his own house wasn't even in order."

I sucked in my breath as my back arched. If I'd been a cat, my claws would have been out and scratching. How dare she imply my dad wasn't doing his job? He couldn't make someone change their life or their priorities. He could only encourage, preach, coax. . . . My spiritual life wasn't his responsibility—not directly. It was mine. "Mrs. Vanderford, I don't think—"

She cut me off. "Don't worry, dear. I'm sure everyone will recover from the surprise in due time. And the embarrassment." She tossed a superior smile my way before moving out of the line. "Congratulations again."

I glanced up at Dad as tears pricked my eyes, relieved he was still talking about the upcoming budget meeting with a handful of deacons and didn't notice. The attention finally seemed to be off me, and as I smiled and nodded at the last person in the receiving line, I knew the tears couldn't be restrained any longer.

"I'll meet you in the car, Dad." I didn't wait for an answer, just sped to the third row to collect my purse and Bible and barreled out the back door Mr. Keegan had exited minutes before. My former joy dissipated, I carried my stuff outside to the car before realizing Dad had locked it. I set my bag and Bible on the roof then leaned against the passenger door, whipping out my phone to pretend to text as I let the tears drip down the front of my sweater and black pants.

Maybe Mrs. Vanderford was right. As haughty as the woman was, she had a point in that Dad had to be completely caught off guard by what I did today. And I didn't mean the pew-jumping and the louder-than-life confession into his microphone. What if his smile and look of pride was just a cover for the embarrassment? Maybe he did feel like a failure as a parent, and as a pastor, for not realizing where I'd been all these years. Had I been that good an actor? Or had I been fooling myself, too?

What if nothing had really changed?

The questions swirled through my head like the mix of gray clouds in the sky above. All those years of disconnect between me and Dad, I'd blamed on him. He'd always put so much into the church that he often seemed to put me—us—on the back burner. I knew he prayed for me. I'd seen my name in enough of his prayer journals lying by the recliner to know that much, but had it done any good? Had he even a clue of my struggle? And if today finally broke some ground between us, could it last with the coming distraction of Ms. Hawthorne in our daily lives?

My head throbbed.

"Come on, Dad, let's go," I mumbled under my breath, rubbing my arms to keep warm as I kept one eye on the door to the church. He said we'd go to lunch, but I might turn into a Popsicle first if he didn't hurry. Should I tell him what Mrs.

Vanderford said? Let it go? Hope she wasn't right? Maybe I could gauge Dad's real reaction over a cheeseburger.

I glanced back up at the gloomy weather and cringed. Looked like snow. Perfect.

I'd be left out in the cold once again.

Chapter
Thirty-Two

"Who wants a turkey?" Ms. Hawthorne turned from the stove with a smile, a turkey-shaped sugar cookie balanced on her spatula. If it weren't for her killer black boots, she'd look incredibly too domestic, standing in our kitchen with Dad's EVERYTHING TASTES BETTER WITH GRAVY apron covering her skirt and jade-colored sweater.

"Me!" Marta's hand shot up like we were back in the classroom instead of sitting at my kitchen table, though I knew all too well how easy it was to get confused.

Ms. Hawthorne spooned a cookie onto Marta's plate before turning to me. "Addison?"

I shrugged. "I don't know." This was too weird. Sure, the bowls of different colored icing and the feathers cut from fondant looked like fun, but I wasn't a five-year-old making an edible Thanksgiving craft. I was almost seventeen, being served treats by my English teacher while my dad handled some church business in his home office. Since we were out of school on break, Marta had come over on this windy Monday morning so we could go to Got Beans and vent about yesterday's crazy circumstances. Instead, somehow, we ended up at a table so festive it looked like Thanksgiving had thrown up.

To make matters worse, Dad had invited Ms. Hawthorne

along to lunch yesterday, so we never got to have our talk. I supposed she'd eventually start attending our church instead of her own outside of town, and then she really would be everywhere.

"Come on, girls. Let's get in the holiday spirit." Ms. Hawthorne wiggled her eyebrows at me as she dumped a cookie on my plate. Then she nudged the bowl of icing closer to me and stuck a paintbrush in my hand. "And what better to be thankful for than sugar?"

Good point. There wasn't much to be thankful for about living out the world's most embarrassing Sunday at church, or for giving up a totally hot guy with a penchant for leather, or for realizing how soon Ms. Hawthorne would be living in my house permanently. I just *thought* I'd been invisible before. With her stuffing Dad full of home-cooked meals and wafting her honeysuckle perfume all around the house, I'd downright disappear.

Though I had to admit, the cookie was a nice touch—*and* made from scratch. I'd baked cookies for almost a decade now and had never seen one without a Pillsbury label.

I dipped my brush in the bowl of red icing and began to paint. "All right, why not?" I grinned at Marta and touched her wrist with my brush, leaving a red smear. "I know someone who is always grateful for sugar."

She wiped it off before plunking her brush into the bowl of yellow. "That, too. But I am thankful to be here celebrating my first Thanksgiving." She coated the turkey's golden feathers. "And for new friends."

"And new family." Ms. Hawthorne joined us at the table with her own cookie and offered me a tentative smile.

I forced one back, wondering if it'd always be weird

between us or if eventually we'd find our new normal. Only time would tell.

"David should be joining us soon." Ms. Hawthorne sat down at the chair across from me and began delicately painting her turkey. "He asked us to save him a cookie."

I eyeballed Ms. Hawthorne across the table, another round of doubts assaulting my midsection. After the wedding, would she be careful to keep an eye on Dad's diet and cholesterol like I'd done the past several years? Or would she spoil him with treats and let him get unhealthy in an effort to make him happy? My father was one of the most disciplined men I knew—he could get up at five a.m. like clockwork, even on his days off, and spend a solid hour in prayer and Bible study with zero caffeinated assistance, yet he couldn't turn down a sweet if his life depended on it—and I didn't ever want it to.

I put my brush down. "Ms. Hawthorne?"

"Sweetie, call me Kathy. At least when we're in your own house. Don't you think that makes more sense?"

It did, but still didn't feel natural. I cleared my throat. "About the cookie. I just wanted to—I think we should. . ." My voice trailed off, and I chewed on my lower lip. How did I ask "Do you really have my father's best interests at heart?" without sounding like a total control freak? Or worse yet, a total dork?

But I couldn't ignore my concern—and couldn't let her waltz in and take over as woman of the house without getting a few things straight. My dad and I still had a long way to go with our relationship, and I wanted to make sure he had the chance to get there with me. Carbs or no carbs.

Ms. Hawthorne caught my gaze and straightened in her chair, her eyes taking on a knowing expression. "Marta, would you mind getting the rest of the feathers from the kitchen counter?"

"Sure." Marta pushed her chair back and hurried into the kitchen, leaving us semialone.

"You're worried about your father." Ms. Hawthorne—Kathy? No, not yet—folded her arms across the tabletop, holding my gaze without hesitancy. "I can tell."

"It's not personal. I really—" I coughed. Man, this was awkward. "I really like you. And I know you make my dad happy. I just know a lot of random things about him—things that matter, like his cholesterol and penchant for midnight snacking." I paused. "Things you don't."

"You've done an excellent job taking care of your dad, Addison. I know it hasn't been easy, and I promise I will keep up your efforts. I know you worry about his health." Ms. Hawthorne glanced over my shoulder toward the hallway, where my dad would be coming from any minute, and lowered her voice. "You've probably often felt like a parent yourself around here, having to do more than your share. I'm here to help now." She reached across the table and put her hand over mine. "I love your dad, but I won't take over. I can't replace your mom in your father's life—nor can I replace you."

Her words slid like a balm over my worries, smoothing the bristles that had sprung to life the moment my dad announced their engagement. Feeling generous, I squeezed her hand. "We'll make sure you find your own place here."

She smiled, her eyes softening. "I'd like that."

Silence stretched between us, filling with a different, yet slightly more comfortable level of awkwardness. I tugged my hand free and gestured to our surroundings. "I know you said you won't take over, but feel free to redecorate at will. This place could use it."

Ms. Hawthorne laughed, a soft, cheery sound that warmed me inside and made me think of vanilla candles and lavender laundry detergent and four-course Thanksgiving dinners—all the good parts of having a new mom figure around. Maybe this could work.

Marta returned then with the fondant, and Dad joined us a few moments later from his office. For the next hour, we all decorated turkeys and had an icing war like we were little kids. Dad's usual stress over working from home evaporated every time he grinned at Ms. Hawthorne. While I had to admit I still possessed a tiny spark of jealousy over their closeness and my lack thereof with him, I couldn't help but be glad Dad was finally happy—finally himself. If my actions lately had brought him embarrassment and grief, then at least Ms. Hawthorne was around to bring his smile back.

I tilted my head to one side, studying the blue icing on her nose and the feather Dad had stuck on her cheek that she still hadn't noticed, and something small shifted inside me.

Kathy it was.

★ ★ ★

A few hours later, Marta and I managed to escape the turkey palooza and left to grab coffee and window-shop. The few bucks I had in my pocket were mocha designated, but Marta was hoping to snag a few items of clothing that her host mom hadn't picked out for her.

"I want to try that on." Marta pointed to a fitted cargo-style jacket in the window of Gigi's, a boutique a block down from Got Beans. "Oh! And those jeans, too. Come on." She dragged me inside, and I stood by her closed dressing-room door drinking my coffee as she changed.

"Ms. Hawthorne is really nice." Marta's muffled voice sounded over the partition. "Are you feeling better about the engagement?"

I shrugged before remembering Marta couldn't see me. "A

little. I want my dad to be happy." I ran my fingers down the plaid scarf hanging on a nearby mannequin. "Just kinda stinks that I make him worse."

Marta cracked her door open and frowned at me. "Are you still worried about that lady at your church? I told you to ignore her. That was just rude." She shut the door with a pointed click.

"Rude, yes. But what if she's right?" I let go of the scarf and took a sip of mocha, unable to get Mrs. Vanderford's condescending tone out of my head. I'd even avoided church Sunday night because of her, not able to deal with any more comments with my emotional armor still so severely dented. "What if Dad *is* embarrassed? What if this new faith stuff is just making everything worse?"

"That is ridiculous." Marta swung her door wide and struck a pose. "What do you think?"

The cargo jacket in army green fit perfectly around her narrow torso and came nearly to the pocket of the designer jeans. "Cute. But no rhinestones?"

She stuck her tongue out at me. "I'm getting both." She shut the door again. "Listen, Addison." The jacket flopped over the top of the door, and I set my coffee on the ground before taking it and the hanger she passed me. "You've been in church long enough to know commitments are never easy. You already figured that out concerning Wes. Don't give up now. Just talk to your dad."

Wes. Just hearing his name felt like a sucker punch to my stomach. I slid the jacket onto the hanger, my hands shaking. "I'm not giving up. This is the right choice for me." I hung the jacket on the hook outside the dressing-room door. "I just hate this feeling." Uncertainty. Confusion. Overall *blah*. It's not like I expected sunshine and roses after nailing down my faith, but I had to admit, I didn't expect this many problems so soon.

"Then I repeat." Marta stepped outside wearing her own clothes, her purse slung over her shoulder. "Talk to him. I bet this is just in your head—and Mrs. Vanderford's."

"I'm surprised there's room for anything in her head under all that hair."

"Addison." Marta snorted back a laugh and tried to give me a disapproving look as I grabbed my coffee and we headed to the counter to pay.

"Sorry." Insulting church members probably wasn't what a new-old Christian should do. But I couldn't just drop the negativity she'd shot my way. It embedded in my skin, filling my heart and my mind with its poison. Marta was right. I had to talk to my dad to be free of it.

But what if he agreed with the old bag—I mean, Mrs. Vanderford? *Sorry, Lord. I'm trying. I promise.*

"I'll talk to him after Thanksgiving." I picked up the quarter Marta dropped from her coin purse and handed it to the clerk behind the counter.

"That's three days away." Marta shot me a look as she slipped her receipt into her bag. "Try again."

"Fine. Wednesday."

She shook her head. "Today."

"He's all moony over Ms. Hawthorne today." I sighed as Marta thanked the cashier and we headed outside. "I don't want to ruin their Thanksgiving fun."

Marta clucked. "Rooster."

"I think you mean chicken. And that's not going to work." We stepped outside, and the brisk wind cooled the frustration heating my cheeks. "Okay, tomorrow. I promise."

Marta opened her mouth, probably to argue, but before she could get a word out, we rounded the corner, and I bumped into someone, nearly dropping my half-empty mocha.

"Claire!" I steadied my cup then braced myself for the lecture on watching where I was going—or worse yet, a reminder of the tray incident in the cafeteria last month.

"Sorry." Claire tucked the purse that had fallen off her arm back onto her shoulder and offered me a tentative smile. "I was heading to Gigi's. Heard they have a sale going on."

"We just came from there." Marta held up her bag, as if her statement needed proof.

Claire nodded; then we all looked at each other for a long, awkward moment.

"Well, have fun." I started to edge around my ex–best friend. Short and sweet would be best before Claire's unexpected Dr. Nice morphed into Ms. Snotty.

"Wait. I'm glad I ran into you." Claire hesitated then laughed. "Though I have to admit, I didn't plan on literally."

I offered a quick pity-chuckle, hoping her moment of niceness wasn't about to dissipate in the cold afternoon air.

Claire's smile sobered. "I wanted to say thank you for helping me during the talent show. And for being there even though I was awful to you—about Ms. Hawthorne and everything." She coughed, almost as if she wanted to say more but couldn't make herself. I could understand. Truly shocking she squeezed that much out.

"No problem." I wanted to say that was what friends were for, but since we weren't exactly BFFs anymore, it seemed like a lie. So I didn't.

"I wanted you to know I'm getting help. My mom is shipping me off to a rehab for bulimics." Claire twirled a portion of her hair around her finger, and for the first time I realized how ashy her complexion seemed compared to her usual healthy tan. Dark circles lined her eyes, unmasked even under the layer of makeup she'd caked on. "After I nearly fainted that night before the performance, I realized my—uh, health issue—was worse than I thought. I thought I could stop before it got serious." Regret filled her eyes, and my heart twisted in sympathy. Friends or not, she had a problem. I couldn't help but feel compassion.

"It's mostly thanks to you. If you hadn't caught me all those times. . ." Claire's voice trailed off, and she straightened her shoulders. "Anyway, Mom agrees with the whole rehab thing, of course. She was crying and grounding me all at the same time when I finally confessed."

"That's really good, Claire. I mean, not the grounding part, but you know." My words sounded so trite, but I didn't know what else to say. *Told you so? You're stupid for wanting to hurt yourself to impress a boy or wear a smaller size?* That wouldn't be helpful. At least she had realized the truth now. "I hope the rehab helps."

"Me, too." Claire crossed her arms over her baggy shirt and looked away before finally meeting my eyes again. "I won't be at school next semester. I'm going away after the holidays and hopefully will be back for the summer. Maybe sooner."

I nodded, my tongue feeling suddenly useless in my mouth. Did she expect us to say we'd miss her? I *did* miss the old Claire. The one I grew up with that used to share popcorn and secrets with me while watching *Saved by the Bell* reruns on Saturday mornings. Maybe rehab would bring back a hint of the old Claire. It seemed too much to hope for, but stranger things had happened.

"We wish you the best." Marta finally spoke up, breaking the silence filling the street corner between us. "And we'll pray for you." She nudged my arm, and I nodded.

"Definitely." I meant it—especially now that I believed my prayers actually penetrated my bedroom ceiling.

"Thanks. I just don't know if God would help someone who did something so stupid to themselves." She rolled in her bottom lip. "The sad part is, I still think I'd do it again."

"He'll help you if you truly want to be helped. Trust me, I know." I offered Claire a small smile. "But let rehab hash the rest out with you. You just focus on getting well, okay?" Despite the weird factor, I leaned over and gave Claire a hug, for old time's sake. She hugged me back, and I couldn't help but notice how bony her shoulder blades were beneath her shirt. "E-mail or text me updates, if they let you."

"Thanks, Addison. And thanks to you, too." Claire nodded at Marta then offered a wobbly smile. "I'll see you guys."

I waited until she was out of earshot inside Gigi's before I spoke. "That was sort of like a miracle."

"God still does those, you know." Marta elbowed me, her shopping bag bouncing off my hip. "And He can do another for you and your dad."

"That's probably what it will have to come to." We looked both ways before crossing the street to the next block. As we headed toward the next store, I looked back toward Gigi's. I really hoped Claire would get better. Even if we were never friends again, I wanted her to be okay.

And even if my dad wished he had a stronger Christian for a daughter, I wanted us to be okay, too.

Chapter
Thirty-Three

Dad's office door had never looked so big—or so brown.
I studied the nameplate on the door that read
PASTOR'S OFFICE in chipped gold letters and wondered why
the church had never sprung for engraving his actual name.
Did they not expect him to stay as long as he had? Sometimes
I wondered why he did, especially with people like Mrs.
Vanderford lurking about with their peppermints and harsh
words. But that was Dad—generous to a fault. He truly believed
praying for people like that made them better, or at least made
him stronger.

I had to admit, I had a long way to go before reaching that
level of compassion.

Taking a deep breath, I reached for the doorknob then
slowly lowered my hand as voices sounded through the door.
One of them wasn't my father's.

I stepped back, knowing better than to eavesdrop, and
waited while leaning against the wall. I hadn't told Dad I was
coming, and since his secretary was off this week, he had no
way of knowing I was in the foyer. I contemplated just going
home and waiting to talk to Dad when he came home for
dinner later. Or even waiting until after dinner. Or maybe right
before bedtime.

Technically, I had until 12:01 a.m. before I broke my promise to Marta, and with nerves clenching my stomach and Mrs. Vanderford's voice bruising my mind, waiting sounded better and better.

I made it exactly four steps outside the carpeted foyer when Dad's door swung open and the source of voice #2 emerged.

Mr. Keegan.

Oh man. What if he thought I'd been listening in? As he exited, letting the door shut behind him, he kept his eyes trained on the ground. I had about four seconds before he saw me. I looked around. Maybe I could hide. *Three*. Umbrella stand or coatrack? *Two*. My heart stammered.

One.

Mr. Keegan looked up, catching my gaze. "Addison." He didn't sound very surprised to see me, just tired—and stressed. Wrinkles lined his eyebrows, and I swear his hair seemed grayer than it had in weeks past.

I offered a shaky smile. "Hi. I was just, you know—coming to see my dad."

He nodded, making no move to walk past me. Just stood, arms limp, shoulders low. He held a legal pad under one arm, like he'd been taking notes.

I have no clue why I felt the urge to keep talking. "Not for counseling or anything, you know. Just regular church business. I mean, not church, but personal. Like, father-daughter stuff." I snapped my mouth shut, wishing I could dive inside the umbrella stand after all.

"Addison, I owe you an apology." Mr. Keegan ignored my waterfall of words and gestured to the two armchairs in front of the secretary's vacant desk. He sat down heavily, as if the world weighted upon his shoulders. "Do you mind?"

I perched on the edge of the farthest chair, my mouth dry.

Suddenly I wished I'd heeded my instincts to go home. What in the world did Mr. Keegan have to say to me? And what in the world would I say back? His life was none of my business, especially now that Wes and I were over before we'd even truly begun.

Still, the haunted look in his eyes reminded me of the one in Wes's, and my anxiety lessened. I took a deep breath. "What's up?"

"Wes told me you overheard us that day in the hardware store." Mr. Keegan placed his notepad in his lap, and I glimpsed several Bible verse references scrawled across the pages. "I've lived a lie for so long, being one person inside the church and another at home. One parent inside the church, and another at home." He shook his head. "I can't keep it up any longer."

I shifted in my chair, unsure what to say. The heater clicked on, and a rush of air warmed the room, filling the uncomfortable quiet.

"I have a drinking problem. Wes knows that, and I've denied it. But it's true." Mr. Keegan looked at his lap then at me. "It started when his mother left, at first just a way to ease the pain of the divorce. But then I ran out of excuses and kept drinking anyway."

Whoa, awkward. I straightened in my chair. "Mr. Keegan, you really don't have to—"

He held up both hands. "What I'm trying to say, Addison, is that I've always admired you—the way you carry yourself and represent your father and this church." Mr. Keegan shrugged. "When you made the announcement you did last Sunday about your faith, something clicked. I knew I couldn't keep this up. If you could make such a difficult choice to go down front and announce a change in your life, why couldn't I do the same? So I'm getting help." He pointed to Dad's shut door behind us. "I'm not ready for an official program yet, but I thought counseling could be a first step toward that step, if that makes sense."

I nodded, though I wasn't sure. "That's good." Man, I sucked at this empathy thing. I hadn't done a better job with Claire, though that conversation had to be ten times less weird than this one. I'd never had a grown man confess his multiple failures to me before.

"When I asked you to make friends with my son, it was because I knew you could be a good influence on him, maybe urge him toward a path I knew I couldn't." Mr. Keegan rubbed one hand over his jaw, looking so much like Wes in that moment my heart hurt. "That boy deserves better than what I can give him. Unfortunately, his mom isn't doing him any favors, either. I thought when he came to live with me things would be different this time. But they're not."

Anger began a slow build in my chest then, at the selfishness of these two people. Grief over a divorce or not, how could two parents turn their back on their hurting son? Sure, Wes was responsible for his own actions and choices, but without a stable home, without a safety net or firm foundation, how did he stand a chance?

I leaned forward, my former nerves gone. "It's not too late, you know." I wanted to point out that if things weren't different this time around, it was because Mr. Keegan wasn't any different. But I bit my lip to keep the words inside. "You can make things right with Wes now."

Mr. Keegan shook his head. "Even if that were true, he wouldn't go for it. He's done with me." He stared at a spot over my shoulder, his eyes glazing over with regret. "He said so the other night."

I swallowed, wishing I had the right words, feeling like I finally had a chance to do something good for Wes, and it was slipping right through my fingers. My fists clenched in an effort to catch the opportunity. "Mr. Keegan, with all due respect, Wes doesn't know what he wants."

The words sounded too familiar on my lips as Wes's husky voice rang in my ears. *"This is what I am. This is what you get, if you still want it."* I'd turned him down.

Just like his parents.

"I know what I want for him." Mr. Keegan's voice jerked me back from the memory and the accompanied knife in my gut. He traced a pattern in the carpet with the toe of his loafer. "I want him to be successful. To be happy. To do something productive with his gift for music." He laughed, the sound hollow and lonely. "I was pretty shocked to hear he played at the school talent show the other night. That was the first time he played in public since his mom left. Wished I'd been there to hear him."

"What?" My head snapped up, senses on full alert.

"His mom taught him to play, you know." Mr. Keegan seemed suddenly lost in thought, his head tilted as he continued to stare at the carpet. "She was a natural, just like him. We nicknamed her Songbird."

My breath hitched. Songbird. Wes's tattoo?

Facts seeped through sudden bursts of memories, filling the cracks with truth. It seemed so obvious now. Why hadn't I seen it before? Wes, playing secretly at Got Beans. Wes, refusing to play onstage for Jessica. Wes, begging me in the foyer during the show to understand. *"This isn't about image, PK."* I hadn't let him finish. Just accused him of awful things and left, pouting because I hadn't gotten my way.

Yet he still played.

For me.

My stomach twisted as grief wrung me inside out like a rag. "I didn't realize." I should have. If I cared as much as I thought I did, I should have seen the signs. The clues. Yet all I'd seen was my own agenda—and the one I thought Wes had.

Wrong on both accounts.

"Well, I'd better get going. Your dad gave me homework." Mr. Keegan stood, slapping his legal pad against the palm of his hand with a smile. "I'm glad I ran into you."

His words mirrored Claire's, and I returned his smile even though confusion and regret still had me drugged. Somehow I was more of a mess than ever before, yet God had used me to reach two very different people. Talk about miracles. "Same here."

Mr. Keegan lifted his hand in a wave and slipped outside into the hallway. I stared at my father's door, wishing I could curl up on the carpet in the fetal position and just cry. What was I supposed to do with this new information? I'd always known there was good inside Wes, despite his carefully crafted image of the opposite, had known there was a hurting heart beneath the leather and tattoos. But how could I go to him now after rejecting him twice? Even if he wanted me back, how could I help him as a friend, without crossing the line toward more? Because even if that was what I wanted—and even if that was what *he* still wanted, which was probably a long shot after all the blows to his ego—how could I pursue more than friendship knowing Wes didn't want anything to do with God?

The door to my father's office opened, and Dad walked outside. "Addison! I was just heading out for lunch. What are you doing here?"

I stood up, swiped the tears off my cheeks, and asked the only thing that felt even remotely right at the moment.

"Would you pray with me?"

★ ★ ★

"I can't believe you're not harping on me about this cheese-burger," Dad mumbled around a big bite of juicy beef covered in cheese.

I handed him a napkin with an angelic smile. "That's because I've already decided you're having salad for dinner."

He grinned, wiping his mouth before reaching for another french fry. "At least I opted out of the mayonnaise. Kathy made me read a nutrition chart the other day comparing calories and fat grams of condiments, and I had to admit I was a little surprised."

Since he'd already made such obvious progress, I held my tongue as he reached for the saltshaker, glad Ms. Hawthorne was doing her part as promised. We'd work on him together. For once the thought brought more peace than anguish, but maybe that was just because I'd already been through enough emotional drama for the day.

And it wasn't over yet.

After his fries were severely salted, Dad looked at me. "I appreciate your telling me what Wes's father said earlier. I know you have a lot to process right now. But it seems like there's more on your mind."

This was it, my blinking neon opportunity to share my fears. If I didn't take this chance, Marta would kill me. I took a fortifying sip of Coke then set my cup on the table between us. "There is." I hesitated, searching for the right words, before realizing there really weren't any. "Someone at church said something sort of—mean—Sunday."

Dad's eyebrows rose, but he kept chomping, allowing me the chance to continue.

"She implied that you were embarrassed about my decision. You know, about committing my life to God and all after having grown up in the church." I drew a deep breath. "That you were ashamed of me."

Dad choked, snorting and coughing into his napkin.

"I knew I should have taken that saltshaker away from

you!" I jumped out of our booth and pounded him on the back, drawing the stares of more than a few fellow patrons.

"I'm okay, I'm okay." Voice raspy, Dad held up one hand to stop me as he sucked down a long sip of pop. "It's not the food. I'm just really shocked someone in my congregation said such a thing. Are you sure you didn't misunderstand?"

"I'm sure." I didn't want to name names, didn't want to put Mrs. Vanderford in a negative light in front of my father, even if she did deserve it. It wasn't my place. Besides, the point wasn't the *who*—it was the *what*. And I had to know if she was right.

Dad lowered his voice as he realized we still had an audience from his near-choking episode. "Is that why you stayed home Sunday night? To avoid this person?"

I nodded slowly. "And you."

Dad's expression grayed, and he reached across the table toward me, dragging his sleeve through his puddle of ketchup and not even noticing. "Why, Addison?"

Emotion pricked my throat. "Because I don't know if she's right."

His grip on my hand tightened, and grief filled his gaze. "That's the craziest thing I've ever heard. And trust me, I've heard some whoppers."

I couldn't help but smile, even as tears threatened my eyes.

"I know we've had our struggles and that I haven't been a perfect parent. The Lord knows I've tried." Dad finally pulled his arm out of the ketchup and began dabbing his sleeve with a napkin. "But if for one minute I've ever given you reason to think this woman's words could be true, I apologize."

"So you're. . .happy?" My voice sounded so little-girl small, but I couldn't help it. I casually handed him another napkin, as if his next response didn't matter in the least.

"Am I happy that my daughter made a decision about her

faith from her heart? Of course I am." Dad grinned at me across the table. "I couldn't have been happier Sunday morning. Probably couldn't have been more surprised, either, but that's partly because of your altar-call methods."

"I was boxed in. And the song was almost over." I couldn't help but giggle at the memory, wishing I could have seen my pew vault from my father's point of view. "And I totally didn't realize your microphone was still on."

"That was the sound guy's fault. He usually turns it off during invitations so any altar prayers won't be broadcasted." Dad laughed as he wadded up his trash. "I'll tell him he owes you a mocha."

"That works." I helped Dad load the tray with our wrappings, feeling lighter than I had in weeks. Months. Maybe ever. Who cared what Mrs. Vanderford thought if her negativity was hers alone? Maybe I had embarrassed Dad a little with my methods, as he'd put it, but I'd eventually live down the details of that morning, and the important part—the heart part— would live on. And that was what mattered.

For me and for Dad.

"I wish you'd have come Sunday night." Dad leaned back in his seat, draping one arm around the back of the booth. "There was a certain young man in the back row who might have caught your attention."

I picked up my drink for one last sip. "Who?" If he said Luke, I might just have had to throw my french fry holder at him.

"Wes."

I spit Coke onto my lap. "What? Wes? At church?" I parroted on like an idiot, unable to stop. "Our church? Wes Keegan?"

"That's right. I saw him myself from the pulpit." Now it was Dad's turn to hand me a napkin, and I took it, mind racing.

What did this mean? Had Wes shown up for me? What about all the stuff he had said about his parents and hypocrites?

"Did he ask about me?" My voice sounded tiny again—and far away. I coughed, my pop still lingering in my throat. Only Wes could choke me up while not even being in the same room.

"I didn't get to speak with him. He slipped out during the invitation."

Equal parts relief and regret filled me with those words. Relief Dad hadn't embarrassed Wes by singling him out, regret that I didn't know more about why he was there. Would he have talked to me if I'd come? Would I have even seen him in the back row?

Ha. The rate I was going, I'd probably have felt his presence from the parking lot.

Dad stood and picked up our tray. "Who knows, maybe he'll be back."

I followed Dad to the trash cans, absently tossing my empty cup before we stepped outside to the parking lot. Secret hopes warred for attention, battling reality and logic with fantasy. Maybe Wes would be back. Maybe he'd decided to make an effort for me. Maybe I'd somehow reached him like I'd somehow reached Mr. Keegan and Claire.

Maybe this wasn't "the end" after all.

Chapter Thirty-Four

Marta sashayed toward the lit three-way mirror, bouquet in hand. "Here comes the bride. . . ." She whipped around at the foot of the makeshift stage and tossed the bouquet to me.

I quickly caught it and tucked the flowers behind my back as the bridal consultant shot us a dark look—one almost as snooty as the giant sign on the door proclaiming NO FOOD OR DRINKS in a font bigger than the store name. I couldn't imagine how this place did business. Here it was almost Christmas, yet not a single garland or berry graced the entire place. Everything remained white, crisp, clean—practically sterile.

I was almost afraid to sit down in the viewing area for fear of wrinkling the fabric on the love seat.

Marta giggled as the woman turned away, and I thrust the bouquet back into her hands. "Will you give this to Ms. Hawthorne already before you get us kicked out?" Not that I'd mind going home. Obviously Crooked Hollow didn't have a bridal store, so we'd ridden an hour outside of town with Ms. Hawthorne and Marta singing show tunes the entire way.

Scratch that. Maybe the snobby boutique was the lesser of two evils after all.

"Sorry. I just love weddings." Marta tapped on the door of Ms. Hawthorne's dressing room. "Here you go!" She passed the bouquet over the top. "Almost ready to model?"

"Not quite. This is one stubborn zipper." My teacher's muffled voice grunted from the other side of the door.

I carefully sat back on the plush sofa where I'd suffered through six other dress showings and crossed my arms. I *so* wasn't in the mood for this. As much progress as I'd made with my dad and Ms. Hawthorne—er, Kathy—I just couldn't totally jump on board with this wedding yet. Not when she and my dad spent every waking moment at our house going over plans for the Big Day this summer. Not when I, in a moment of insanity, agreed to be the maid of honor.

And not when every stupid piece of lace and tulle in the bridal store made me wonder where the heck Wes had been the past three weeks.

Ever since my talk with Dad at the diner, I'd been trying to find Wes. I spent more than half of my Thanksgiving break inside Got Beans at random hours of the day, trying to catch him playing the piano, to no avail. I'd staked out the music shop, almost accidentally stole a Christmas CD I'd carried around the store for an hour while stalling, and spent hours walking casually around the block, hoping to find him cruising on his motorcycle among the holiday traffic.

Nothing.

It was like he vanished, riding out of my life as quickly as he rode into it. And why wouldn't he? I'd given him no reasons to stay and far too many to leave. If he really meant he was done with his dad, he could have easily left town. But wouldn't I have heard about it? And where would he go? Certainly not back to his mom.

"Maybe this is the one." The dressing-room door finally swung open, and Kathy emerged. I had to admit, she looked beautiful in the fitted dress with a subtle shimmer of sequins lining the sheer sleeves.

But beautiful or not, I couldn't get used to the idea of a grown woman having a full-fledged wedding with a white dress and the works. Since it was Kathy's first wedding—and only, Dad joked—he insisted she do it right. In my opinion, *right* was in the eye of the beholder—and at the moment, I envisioned a clearance-rack purchase from the mall and a justice of the peace.

Hoping my hesitancy didn't show on my face, I joined the two in the front of the mirror, ready to perform my reluctant duties of maid of honor—whatever that meant.

"Ja. But maybe not long sleeves in the summer." Marta tapped her chin with her finger as she studied Ms. Hawthorne's reflection in the mirror. "Though it is an evening wedding, right?"

"Oh my." The bridal consultant popped back up like a bad dream and immediately began fussing over the full skirt. "This one is ravishing."

Sure she thought so—the price tag dangling from Ms. Hawthorne's hip was five hundred dollars more than the two dresses before it. The suit-clad saleswoman might as well have had a giant commission sign on her forehead. I might not know where to stand or what to do during the ceremony as maid of honor, but I *could* handle some things.

"Excuse me." I smiled politely at the worker exclaiming over Ms. Hawthorne's dress. "Can you tell me where I could get a supersized fountain drink like the one that girl just walked in with?"

I didn't know saleswomen could fly.

"Thank you." Ms. Hawthorne shot me a grateful look in the mirror as she smoothed the front of her gown. "They like to hover, don't they?"

"Like a UFO." I joined her in the reflection. "What do you think?"

She nibbled on her lower lip, the most indecisive movement I'd ever seen my teacher make. "I'm not sure. What would your father think?"

Ew. This conversation was heading down a path I had no interest in venturing. I opened my mouth to mumble some sort of response but was thankfully saved by Marta.

"It's lovely." Marta grinned as she took the bouquet from Ms. Hawthorne and posed in front of the mirror. "But I am a wedding—what do you call them?—fanatic! Maybe my opinion is biased. I actually want you to buy all six dresses."

Oh good grief. "If you want my opinion, I think this shop isn't you." I plucked at the yards of fabric and wrinkled my nose. "You have great taste in clothes, Ms. Haw—Kathy. I think you could find something better for yourself back at home without busybody customer service and elaborate props distracting you." I snatched the bouquet from Marta's hand, ignoring her whine of protest. "I've always heard when it's the right dress, you just know." At least that's what they said on TLC.

"That's a great point." Ms. Hawthorne smiled, her features relaxing for the first time in an hour. "Sort of like with love. When it's the right man, you just know." She nodded at her reflection, having obviously come to some sort of conclusion for herself, then disappeared back inside the dressing room.

Leaving me alone with her words rattling around in my brain. *"When it's the right man, you just know."*

I wouldn't be seventeen for another thirty days. I had no business trying to figure out who I loved or if I loved anyone. I should be focusing on me—on my schoolwork, on the fact that college was only a year and a half away. On figuring out how to live my faith for the first time. On my dad's upcoming marriage and all these major life changes barreling toward me.

So why wouldn't Wes's image go away?

"What do you say we ditch this place, snag one of those holiday milkshakes from Sonic, and head home?" Ms. Hawthorne called over the dressing-room door.

Marta and I grinned and slapped each other high fives.

Now *that* was the teacher I knew and loved.

★ ★ ★

This was the first year Christmas didn't hold nearly the amount of magic I'd remembered. Maybe it was the pile of wedding-planning books stacked beside the nativity set on the coffee table, or maybe it was the gifts labeled "Kathy" under the tree for the first time, or maybe it was the dining room table set for three.

Or maybe I just missed my mom.

I curled up on the couch in the dark, inhaling the steam from my cup of hot chocolate, and drank in the sight of the lit Christmas tree. The stacks of presents were long gone from that morning. The bracelet my dad had given me dangled from my wrist, and I watched the jewels catch the light of the tree.

It'd been a fun day, full of homemade cookies, juicy turkey, and torn wrapping paper. Yet something just didn't quite resonate, despite my earlier attempt at having a quiet time in my room reading the Christmas story from the Bible.

I couldn't stop thinking about Wes, wondering what he was doing with his dad, if they were celebrating the holiday or avoiding each other. Wondering if they had anyone to cook Christmas dinner, if they'd bothered to put up a tree or buy presents.

If Wes had stopped by Sonya's house again.

The lamp by the door suddenly clicked on, illuminating Dad standing in his new monogrammed robe. "You're up late." He yawned. "Can't sleep?"

"Too much sugar, I guess." I gestured with my mug. "So I

had to get more."

He chuckled and joined me on the couch. "You sure were quiet today."

He noticed? I pulled my feet up to make room, not really up for a deep conversation but unwilling to lie about my feelings anymore. We'd never make progress with each other if I refused to talk.

I drew a deep breath. "I miss Mom." I didn't add that Kathy's presence just made Mom's absence even starker. There was honesty, and then there was cruelty.

Dad stared toward the tree, his expression morphing into shadow. "I do, too."

"You do?" I couldn't help the incredulous tone of my voice. "I mean, I know you did. As in, past tense. But I thought now, since the engagement. . ." My voice trailed off as the hole I'd talked myself into opened wider. *Way to ruin Christmas, Addison.*

"I will always love your mother." Dad finally met my gaze, tears glazing his eyes. "I'm thankful the Lord brought Kathy back into my life. But no one will ever replace my first love."

How could such depressing words make me feel better? I was the worst daughter on the planet. I scooted sideways on the couch and leaned against his arm in a half hug. "I like Kathy. This is just—weird. And not because she's my teacher, though that definitely ups the weirdness factor." To put it mildly.

"I know it is." Dad opened his arm and wrapped it around me, his familiar Dad smell enveloping me like a second pair of arms. "There will be a lot of changes for all of us. But I'd like to think they'll be good ones."

"They will be. I'm just melancholy tonight." I sipped my now lukewarm chocolate then set the mug on the coffee table. My bracelet jingled, and I held it up for Dad to see. "Did you pick this out? Be honest."

"I did." Dad beamed. "I can promise you, Kathy wasn't even in the same store."

"It'd be okay if she had helped." Still, I was glad Dad did that one himself. It showed me he was trying just like I was. I eyed him. Though on second thought, maybe I should have bought his robe one size bigger.

"Did you know Kathy almost broke up with me a few months ago? Before the engagement?"

I was glad I'd set my mug down already because I surely would have dropped it. "What? Why?"

"Because of you." Dad shook his head with a little smile. "She told me she didn't think you were having an easy time adjusting to the idea of us being serious, and she refused to be the reason our relationship suffered or your life at school suffered."

"Wow." Speechless, I fingered the beads on my bracelet, suddenly wishing I'd gotten Kathy something more personal than candles for Christmas.

"She really cares about you, Addison. She's also the reason we're waiting until the summer to get married—so she won't be your stepmother and teacher at the same time." Dad let out a small laugh. "Those were her conditions immediately after I proposed, before she'd even say yes."

I couldn't help but smile at that mental image of Dad down on one knee, holding out a ring while Ms. Hawthorne ticked off conditions on her fingers—conditions about me. Maybe I'd been too hard on her. It'd been two steps forward, one step back between us ever since they started dating. If she was going to be so considerate of me, I should return the favor.

Wholeheartedly.

"So, now that Christmas is over, what do you want for your

birthday?" Dad stood up, effectively ending our too-heavy conversation, and walked to the tree. "Besides your annual discounted Christmas ornament, of course."

I groaned, though I secretly loved the tradition. Apparently my mother had bought me a new ornament at the after-Christmas sales every year while she was alive. My dad kept it up until our tree practically sagged under the weight of all the birthday ornaments designated to me alone. "I don't know. A pony?"

"Maybe when you're eighteen." Dad winked, something I hadn't seen him do in years.

"Okay, then a mustang." I grinned. "And I'm not talking about the kind that eats hay and lives in the wild."

Dad's lips twitched to the side. "I still don't see a reason for you to have a car. This is a small town. It's good exercise to walk."

We'd only had this conversation ten times during the past two years. "What if I break my ankle and can't walk everywhere?"

Dad crossed his arms. "Then you wouldn't be able to drive, either."

"I could if it was my left ankle."

We stared at each other, Dad's eyebrows wrinkled as he tried to think of a way around my logic. "I'm not sure that's an expense we need right now, regardless. Insurance would skyrocket."

Weren't we about to become a two-income family? I wasn't going to say that, though, not on Christmas night after such a positive heart-to-heart. So I admitted defeat as I picked up my coffee mug and headed to the sink. "I was kidding. Sort of. I'll just take the pony." I grinned, though my heart wasn't in it. Truth be told, I'd rather have Wes than a pony *and* a car. *Two* cars.

But I was probably more likely to get a Lamborghini for every day of the week than I was to get that secret birthday wish.

Chapter Thirty-Five

think you should have a carnival for your birthday." Marta shut her locker door, brow furrowed as she contemplated the options. "Or the circus! We could make it a tribute to childhood and visit all the traditional birthday themes. Have *Trink-Kakao*! And maybe *ein Haufen Dreck*."

"*Ich spreche kein Deutsch*." I snarkily reminded Marta I didn't speak German—in German.

"It is just chocolate milk and what we call a pile of dirt—you know, chocolate pudding with Gummi worms on top."

Gummi worms. Great. Just the reminder I needed.

"I really, really hope you're kidding." I hitched my book bag on my shoulder, already eager to get home and take a load off. Homework had kicked back after the holiday breaks with a vengeance, and truly, the last thing I wanted to deal with today was birthday talk.

Sad that calculus homework seemed more appealing.

"Why not? It'd be fun." Marta fell into step beside me as we fought the throng of students rushing to head home after a long school day.

"A circus?" I snorted. "You must want an excuse to wear your rhinestone belt again."

"Very funny." Marta pushed open one of the heavy double

doors leading into the parking lot. "Your seventeenth birthday is this upcoming weekend. You can't just ignore it."

"I'm not ignoring it. I just don't want a big party." With the holidays barely behind us and the wedding looming before us, I didn't feel up for celebrating. Sure, I was adjusting slowly to the idea of my dad getting married, and so far I'd kept my commitment to be more considerate of Ms. Hawthorne, but I remained stuck in my melancholy mood. *God, I just want to keep things about us right now. Dad is doing his own thing, and Wes is—well, not in the picture. Is a little solitude too much to ask?* The only time I didn't feel bummed lately was when I woke up early to read my Bible before school. I'd never understood how Dad could do it day after day, but after the first week, it'd been a lot easier than I thought.

Marta dodged a guy running to catch his bus. "Then let's have a sleepover. You have to do something."

"We'll see." I hoped she'd take the hint and drop it, but I'd learned this past semester that subtlety and Marta just didn't blend.

"Is this about Wes?" She stopped walking and tugged at my arm so I'd do the same.

I squinted, lifting one hand against the winter afternoon sun so I could see her face. "He was at church yesterday."

"That's great!" Marta bounced twice on the balls of her feet. Then she must have registered my expression and stopped. "Isn't it?"

"He doesn't talk to me. He comes in late, sits in the back by himself, leaves five minutes before it's over, and disappears on his motorcycle before I can even make it outside." At least I knew he hadn't left town. But at the moment, the fact offered little comfort. I blew a strand of hair out of my eyes and started walking, leaving Marta no choice but to follow. "He's avoiding me."

Not that I blamed him after that painful conversation in the library more than a month ago. I'd rejected him for the second time—or was it the third?—and admitted to choosing my religion over him. Of course I knew it was more than just religion, but to Wes looking from the outside in, that's how it would seem.

But I'd been in church long enough—and felt the sizzling chemistry between me and Wes long enough—to know I couldn't missionary date without getting myself into some serious trouble. If we weren't on the same page with morals, goals, and God, then we didn't stand a chance.

But did that mean I couldn't be his friend? Stay in his life from a distance? He was coming to church for a reason—was it because of me? Or because of something deeper?

Suddenly I wanted to know more than I wanted my next breath.

"Maybe you should talk to him." Marta huffed after me, trying to keep up. "And get closure so you can move on."

Moving on was exactly the opposite of what I *wanted* to do, but her suggestion of talking to him felt right. I'd actually had a hundred conversations with Wes in my mind during the past month, ranging from heated arguments to whispered promises. Still, there was one problem. "I've tried. I've stalked the guy all over town for weeks. I can't find him outside of church, and he obviously isn't interested in talking there."

"Go to his house. He hasn't moved out, has he?"

"Not that I know of." But I didn't know much of anything about him anymore, other than what my nightly dreams reminded me of in the past. "Maybe I should try."

"Go. Now. I'll even take your book bag to your house for you." Marta held out her hand, and I willingly handed over the bulging bag. She stumbled momentarily before hiking it onto her shoulder.

"You're a real friend." I gave her a brief hug before taking off down the sidewalk, my hopes rising for the first time in weeks. If I couldn't have Wes the way I wanted to, I could at least keep a friendship. Any relationship with him was better than none.

I just hoped he'd agree.

I banged on Wes's front door then braced one arm against the frame before my shaky knees gave out completely. What if no one was home and I came over here for nothing? Or worse, what if Mr. Keegan answered the door? He should be at work on a Monday afternoon, but with all the counseling he'd been doing lately with my dad, who knew his schedule anymore.

Standing on his porch brought back memories of the night Wes had doctored my burn. I rubbed my wrist, remembering the light pressure of his touch, the way he'd spoken his heart for the first time before kissing me.

Oh boy. This was *so* not the train of thought I needed to have for a pending "let's be friends" convo.

Peering through the curtained window, I couldn't make out anything inside the house—not even lights. Heart sinking, I knocked one more time then turned my back to the silence and began a slow descent down the stairs. I should have known better than to get my hopes up. Maybe I'd try again tomorrow—if my nerves lasted that long.

Or maybe this was just a sign for me to leave things alone and accept the fact that we were through—on all accounts. *God, a little wisdom?*

The door opened behind me.

I spun around, adrenaline flooding my body as Wes

appeared in front of the screen door. He stepped outside, his expression somewhere between a smile and a question.

Wishing I still had my book bag so I had something to do with my hands, I settled for clasping them behind my back. "Hi." Oh, that was brilliant. If I commented on the weather next, I'd kick myself in the rear.

"Hey." The screen clicked shut behind him, and he met me halfway at the top of the stairs. "You lost?"

He shook his dark hair out of his eyes, and my fingers itched to move it for him. I squeezed my hands together until I almost lost circulation. "Just in the neighborhood." Oh, good grief. This kept getting worse.

His eyebrow twitched, but he didn't laugh, to his credit.

Oh well, I had nothing to lose for being honest. I climbed the stairs until I stood directly in front of him, close enough to breathe in the familiar scent of his aftershave. The leather jacket was absent, and the hunter-green thermal he wore with jeans only highlighted the tone of his muscles. I wanted to hug him but knew better than to get that close. "I wanted to see you."

He tilted his head to one side, eyes studying me, but didn't speak.

"I hate how things ended. I've been looking for you all over town—you just disappeared." My voice shook and I coughed, wishing I could be one of those girls who knew the right words, had the right tone, the right attitude, who knew how to get what she wanted.

Well, I might have been tempted once, but I wouldn't play those games, not anymore. I was just me. Just Addison. The most un-Lemon-Drop girl in Crooked Hollow.

And I was okay with that.

Still, I wished he'd say something.

"I've been around." He leaned casually against the porch

post, just out of reach.

"Around where, exactly? I've spent more hours in the music store and Got Beans than I have at home, trying to find you."

Wes's expression didn't change. "Not around there."

He didn't offer further explanation, and for some reason it made me mad. Did he care or not? What was I even doing there? "You've been at church."

Something flickered in his eyes, but his neutral mask remained. "So I have."

"Why?"

He straightened, arms still crossed. "Do you think I'm coming for you?"

"I don't know what to think." I mirrored his defensive stance, my heart climbing into my throat and refusing to dislodge. "I invited you, but every time you've been there, you've avoided me."

He shrugged. "Then maybe you thought wrong."

"What are you doing?" I wanted to grab him by the shoulders and shake him, but I knew any physical contact would probably end in self-combustion. "Why are you being this way? I came over to apologize. To tell you I wanted to be your friend. I—I miss you." I choked on the emotion building in my chest. "Forget it." I turned to leave, and Wes caught my arm.

"I'm not trying to be a jerk, PK. I'm just confused." Wes's fingers slid down my arm to my hand, his touch burning through the sleeve of my jacket. "I don't know why you're here."

"I'm here for you." I stared at our joined hands, unable to make eye contact. "I can't stand the thought of us never talking again."

"Then talk." He pulled me toward him, and my feet shuffled slowly his direction as if stuck in quicksand.

"I know about your mom." I met his gaze then, his eyes

darkening before the shadow passed. "About the sacrifice you made playing for Jessica—for me—the night of the talent show." I drew a ragged breath. "I never said thank you. Not really."

His grip on my hand tightened. "It was all for you. I couldn't care less about Jessica." He let go of my hand and wrapped one arm loosely around my waist, leaning forward until his forehead touched mine. "It's always been about you."

I breathed in the heady aroma of his cologne, wishing I had the right to lean into his embrace and never leave. But I'd been down that path before, and nothing had changed. Danger was danger, no matter how attractive the package. I pulled away enough to see his eyes.

He touched my cheek with the back of his hand. "How'd you find out?"

"Your dad."

Wes stiffened, his hand freezing on my face. "You talked to my dad?"

I nodded as his arm fell to his side. "I saw him at the church office a few weeks ago. He's getting counseling." That was private information, but if Wes didn't already know, he should. Maybe it would help things between them if he knew his father was trying to get help. "He seems to be making progress."

"He's good with appearances."

I threaded our fingers back together. "Isn't recognizing a problem the first step?"

"Of many." Wes snorted. "I'm not buying into anything yet. He's gone through programs before."

"I realize you know your father better than I do, but he seems sincere about changing. He even admitted that all of his problems were the reason he asked me to be friends with you."

I felt Wes slipping away even before he physically stepped back. "He what?"

"He asked me to be friends with you one day at church. This was months ago, like, back in September." I tried to hold on to his hand, but Wes moved across the porch, pacing, his back rigid.

"My dad asked you to be friends with me?" He ran his hands down the length of his face, eyes narrowed. "Let me guess. Because you'd be a good influence?"

I licked my suddenly dry lips. "Yes, but we were already talking before then. That's not the reason I—"

"All this time, Addison, we were set up by my dad?" Wes paced another lap around the porch, reminding me of a caged tiger ready to strike. "Do you not see the irony of this?"

The wooden boards creaked under his booted feet. I shook my head, helpless, unsure what just happened.

"I really was just a project to you." Wes stopped in front of me, and despite his warm proximity, a cold chill swept over my body. "I said that to you once before, never really thinking it to be accurate. But it's true."

I started to argue, but he didn't give me the chance.

"That's why you broke things off—you realized your project failed." He pointed at me, and the pain in his eyes clenched my stomach in a vice. "You've never been very appreciative of what I've done for you. Breaking up with Sonya, fixing those stupid trees, coming to your show and saving Jessica's solo. It's never going to be enough." He stared at me, his eyes darkening with despair. "I'm never going to be enough."

"That's not true." My voice cracked, and I reached toward him.

He turned away.

"Wes, I swear. I never thought of you as a project." But even as the words left my lips, I knew they weren't completely honest. How many times had I wondered if I could get Wes

to change? How many times had I considered dating him
a missionary project? How many times had I nudged and
prodded, trying to form him into my idea of the dad-pleasing,
perfect boyfriend?

Wes was Wes.

And I never fully accepted that.

He must have read the indecision in my eyes because
his features hardened. "I came to church for you, Addison.
I wanted to see what the heck was so great about it all that
you'd give up what we had going." Wes jammed his hands into
his jeans pockets, shoulders tense. "And you know what? I sort
of liked it. I thought maybe there was something to it after all."
He inhaled deeply. "It made me feel. . .safe. Made me think
maybe some Christians could be different than my parents."

His words tore into me like tiny pellets of truth, opening my
eyes to the plethora of sins I didn't even know I had. Here I'd
been thinking God had used me to reach Claire and Mr. Keegan,
thinking I'd finally arrived as a Christian, thinking I'd done my
duty by sacrificing my deepest desire for the Lord.

Yet the one person I wanted to reach the most, I'd shoved
the furthest away.

"But now I know." Wes opened the screen door before
firing his last shot. "You're all the same."

★ ★ ★

I trudged home, the walk giving me more time to think than I
wanted and even more time to silently berate my dad for being
so adamant about not getting me a car. If I had wheels, I could
have been home by now, diving into my schoolwork instead
of reliving every harsh word with Wes that still rendered me
helpless.

But there was no Lamborghini, or even a fifteen-year-
old, scratched, multipainted hoopty. So on I walked, the

wind singing through the treetops, brushing the winter-bare branches and whistling a reminder that I had totally failed. I hadn't been a good influence on Wes. If anything, I'd turned him further from the direction I'd hoped he'd go.

Who was I to try to convert him into what I thought was a Christian? I'd barely just started figuring it out for myself. Being a Christian wasn't sitting in your designated pew every Sunday or volunteering in the nursery or helping the secretary fold bulletins during the week. Sure, those were good things to do, but as I'd found out, they had no bearing on the status of your heart.

So why did I think Wes had to do those things to prove himself "good enough" for me? Despite his mistakes and rough edges, Wes already had a good heart. He'd had more than his share of knocks, but he'd proven his true character to me time and again. He'd been on a journey himself, searching for worth, searching for his identity outside of his screwed-up home life.

And instead of gently coaxing him toward the God I knew could give him just that, I'd flung ultimatums and stuck my nose in the air.

I'd ruined it.

God, I'm so sorry. Maybe I'm not ready for this whole witnessing thing after all. Pretty sad confession for a PK. I might have done the right thing when I invited Wes to church, but before that I'd been inconsistent. Confusing. Unsure of what I believed.

How did that look to someone who had only seen the more difficult parts of Christianity? To someone who'd only seen hypocrisy and sin and superficial smiles? To someone who never experienced grace and mercy and unconditional love?

Now, because of me, Wes might never have the chance.

If I hadn't seen Marta standing on my front porch with my

book bag, I might have sat on the sidewalk and bawled. Instead I rallied my scattered emotions, already encouraged just by the sight of her. How had I existed without a best friend to dump all these dramas on before? I'd had Claire, but we'd never talked about anything serious. Marta had been a lifesaver—looking back, truly a gift from God.

I joined her by the front door, where my book bag rested on the ground. It'd been a nice gesture for her to bring it home for me—she couldn't have realized I'd come home with a new burden much heavier than my stupid tote.

Marta's typical smiling face was ashen as she looked at me. "I have bad news." She clutched her cell phone to her chest like a life preserver, and my already-sinking heart fell straight to my shoes.

"What is it?" I tried to swallow around the knot in my throat and failed.

"My mom called. There's been some trouble with our family." She sniffed and looked away. "I have to go home early."

"When?" My heart pounded a whining protest. "Not until May, right? Right after school's out?" *No, not now. Don't let her leave now, God. Let her stay at least until March. I can't deal with Wes alone.*

The look on her face told me otherwise before she even shook her head.

"I leave in one week."

Chapter Thirty-Six

On Saturday my birthday dawned exactly how I felt inside—gray, dreary, and bitterly cold. I took one look at the calendar on the wall, today's date circled in purple marker, and then a second look out the window, and pulled the covers over my head. Maybe if I stayed in bed, today would pass without consequence, and I could keep on being sixteen. Then my best friend wouldn't be leaving in a matter of days, I wouldn't have totally lost the first guy I ever pictured myself loving, and my home life wouldn't be that much closer to going up in a puff of wedding smoke.

Turning seventeen with your entire life in shambles didn't seem very celebratory. I'd try again another month.

"Addison, honey, time to wake up!" My dad pounded on my closed bedroom door, something he'd done maybe twice in my entire life.

"Go away," I mumbled into my pillow, even though I knew he couldn't hear.

I heard the door crack open and knew he'd poked his head around the frame. "It's already ten o'clock. Kathy and I are taking you for birthday brunch at Denny's, so you need to get dressed."

My first day being seventeen, and it'd be spent sitting across the table from my father and his fiancée while they giggled and fed each other strawberries off their pancakes. Perfect.

I moaned and burrowed deeper under the covers, praying for a time warp that would make this day simply end and tomorrow begin.

"You have one hour." Dad's cheerful voice rocked me back to reality before my door shut.

After wallowing for another ten minutes, I decided the only thing worse than a birthday brunch out with Dad and Kathy would be a birthday brunch with Dad and Kathy in my room. So I dragged myself to the shower and slapped on some makeup before staring into my abyss of a closet. My clothes stared back at me, mocking, daring to let any of them cheer me up. Why even try? I settled for a sweater with a hole in the elbow and my fat-day jeans, took one look at my hair, kinked from wallowing in bed, and shrugged. What was the point?

I headed downstairs.

"SURPRISE!"

I reeled backward, my sock-clad foot slipping on the bottom step. Grabbing the railing, I barely caught my balance as I gaped at our dining room full of family and friends. Luke and Marta stood under a bouquet of balloons so big they barely cleared the chandelier. Dad and Kathy stood by the table next to a punch bowl and a cake proclaiming my age in sparkly glitter icing. My dad's church secretary, two deacons, and my Sunday school teacher smiled back at me beside a gift table loaded down with ribbons and bows.

My mouth slowly opened, and I said the only thing I possibly could.

"I'll be right back."

I turned on my heel and pounded back up the stairs. *Stupid, stupid, stupid.* I should have known Dad would never take me to Denny's for my birthday. Somehow I managed to yank off the holey sweater and jeans at the same time and slipped into my favorite purple sweaterdress and boots instead. Then I ran the straightener through my hair, added a layer of lip gloss, and strolled competently back downstairs as if, yes, I always looked this good.

"I think you surprised us as much as we did you." Marta linked her arm through mine and giggled. "Where were you going looking so messy? Your dad said he tricked you with brunch."

"That's what I get for choosing comfort clothes on my birthday—utter humiliation." I leaned close so no one would hear. "You're a little stinker. I said I didn't want a party."

"No, you said 'we'll see.' " Marta grinned. "That sounded like yes to me."

I rolled my eyes. "I'll have to remember that."

"Besides, your dad did most of this." Marta gestured around the house. "I just helped him brainstorm."

I hugged her. "It's awesome." Even though I'd been totally caught off guard, I couldn't help but be touched by their joint effort. The entire downstairs had been transformed into party central, the furniture moved aside to make room for games—childhood games, as Marta had envisioned. Pin the tail on the donkey, board games, and musical chairs sat ready and waiting on the carpeted floor. Even a piñata dangled outside the back window. Streamers in bold primary colors hung from the ceiling and wrapped the border of the room. It was the perfect tribute to childhood.

And today, with so much gloom in my immediate forecast, I couldn't think of anything better to celebrate than the carefree days of being a kid.

"Happy birthday, Addison." Luke sidled up to us and handed

Marta and me a glass of red punch. "I plan on beating you both in Chutes and Ladders today."

"Game on." I slapped him a high five, grateful that so far no awkwardness existed between us. Though from the sidelong glances Marta kept shooting his way, I couldn't help but wonder if she was more upset about leaving than she currently let on.

But I couldn't think about that right now. No sense in taking the whole "it's my party, and I'll cry if I want to" theory literally.

I spent the next few minutes greeting guests, thanking people for coming, and promising to play musical chairs ASAP.

"Are you surprised?" Dad finally broke through the throng and hugged me, barely letting go before Kathy did the same.

"Of course she was. David, you should have given her better warning of what to wear." Kathy patted my shoulder. "Don't worry, sweetie. Next surprise party, I'll be here to make sure you know the ropes."

That actually didn't sound too bad. I hugged her back. "Thanks, to both of you. Marta said this was all your idea, Dad."

"Then your best friend is a little bit of a liar." Dad tugged at Marta's hair, and she grinned. "This was teamwork, through and through."

Warmth spread over me, healing some of the open wounds I'd carried this week. Regardless of who had the idea, I was loved. I was celebrated. It couldn't get much better than that.

"Let's have cake." Marta eyed the dessert sitting on the table. "Then you can open your gifts."

"No, I can't wait anymore." Dad ushered me toward the gift table. "Presents first."

"But this will take all day." I couldn't stop staring at the tower of gifts covering the end table. What had Dad done, called in favors from everyone at the church to send a present?

I could only imagine how many gifts would be at his and Kathy's wedding.

"Then at least this one." Dad plucked a small yellow box with a pink bow from the top of the stack and pressed it into my hands. "Here, honey. Happy birthday."

A crowd had gathered, and several people smiled behind their hands as if they already knew what was inside. Cheeks burning, I quickly untied the wrapping, wishing Dad had just waited to give me my gift later in private. If it was a gift card to an underwear store, I'd kill him.

I opened the lid and gaped at a single black key lying on a bed of tissue paper.

"You didn't." I started to touch the key then pulled my finger back as if it might bite.

I looked up at Dad, repeating my question. "You didn't. Did you? No, you didn't."

"I did." His smile beamed so brightly it was a wonder the cake icing didn't melt. "Why don't you look outside?"

Key clenched in my palm, I squealed and ran to the front door, nearly knocking my head against it as I struggled to get it open. I burst onto the front porch, and there in the driveway sat an older model, yet adorable, silver two-door car.

With a motorcycle parked directly behind it.

The next two minutes flew by in a blur. I stared at my car and then at Wes and didn't know whether to laugh or cry or both. Marta, bless her heart, had taken one look at Wes astride his idling bike and immediately ushered everyone back inside the house with bribes of cake and ice cream. I thanked Dad profusely for the car and promised I'd be inside soon.

I couldn't imagine that anything Wes had to say at this point would take long.

"What are you doing here?" My breath puffed in the cold air, and I couldn't keep the tension from my voice as I slowly made my way down the driveway.

He killed the engine and climbed off his bike, setting the kickstand and pocketing his keys before offering me a half smile. "Happy birthday." I noticed a bulge in his leather jacket pocket. A birthday gift? Unlikely. He owed me nothing.

"Sweet ride." Wes nodded toward my car, and I turned toward it with pride, grateful even more for the distraction.

"Yeah, Dad didn't do too bad." I ran my hand over the shiny, clean bumper, exhilaration at my newfound freedom threatening to burst through my skin.

"Have you sat in it yet?"

"No. What, you don't have something manly to prove by looking under the hood first?"

Wes smirked. "Hardly. Come on. Get in."

He actually opened the driver's door for me before walking around to the other side, something he'd never done before. Probably all the birthday gift I'd get from him.

I nestled back against the seat—not leather, but at least they were clean—and rested my hands on the steering wheel. A slow smile seeped across my face. My car. *My* car. No more buses or worn-out shoes or carrying heavy book bags for a mile. No more walking everywhere under the sun.

Oops. Note to self—would *definitely* have to cut back on the mochas now.

Wes slid into the passenger seat, and my car-euphoria bubble popped. "How did you know about the party?"

He leaned his head against the seat, allowing me a full view of his profile, and my stomach fluttered. "Marta invited me."

I didn't know whether to kick her or hug her. "I'm surprised you came."

"Why? Because I freaked out on you the other day, overreacted, and said things I shouldn't have?"

I bit my lower lip. "Uh, yeah. Basically."

"That was sarcasm." He inhaled deeply and exhaled with a short puff of air. "Listen, PK. I'm sorry. When it comes to my dad, I have some hot buttons." He finally looked over at me, and the sincerity in his eyes almost did me in. "You pushed them. But it's just because I don't want him to have anything to do with you. With us."

"Is there an 'us'?" The words slipped out before I could decide if they were worthy. I didn't have anything to offer. I was still a mess myself—I had no business trying to help someone else. And a relationship with Wes—now, just as he was, with all his drama and pain and hurts—would be impossible if he didn't allow God some kind of foothold first. But how could I say that without it sounding like an ultimatum again, without it coming across as if he wasn't on my level?

A level that right about now felt like rock bottom.

"I hope so." Wes took my hand, which I'd rested on the gearshift, and folded his fingers against mine. "But once again, that's really up to you."

I twisted in my seat to face him as the tears built, sensing this was about to become the worst birthday in the history of the world. How many more times could we hurt each other before this—this *thing* between us—would finally end?

Apparently one more time.

I shivered, a chill that had nothing to do with the low temps outside the car. "Wes, nothing has changed."

He pressed one finger to my lips, drawing me to silence. "Do you want to know where I've been the past month?"

I tried to play it off, but in all honesty I was dying to know. "If you want to tell me."

"At school."

I stared at him, blinking, sure I'd missed a step. "Come again?"

"I enrolled at the local university outside of town. I started last week." He brushed one hand in the air as if ridding the car of a pesky fly. "There was a bunch of paperwork and forms to fill out and some financial aid stuff to process, so I practically lived up there for a while. But I'm all set."

"You're going to college?" I stared at Wes, unsure if I should make a big deal out of this incredible news or not. "On a scholarship?"

"Don't look so surprised." He snorted. "It's your fault. All that talk you gave me about wasting my talent." He shrugged. "Thought I'd give it a try."

"That's. . .great." I licked my lips, faltering for the right words. I wanted him to know how proud I was, but at the same time I had no claim on him to really express it. I settled for neutral. For safety. Careful to control the pitch of my voice, I nodded stiffly. "I'm happy for you."

He squeezed my hand. "Addison, what I said on my porch is still true—I really did like your church. And I don't really think you're a hypocrite." He winced. "I was just ticked."

"No, it's true. I am." I wrestled my hand away, all thoughts of control and neutrality flying out the window. "Everyone is a hypocrite, in a sense, because no one is perfect. But being a Christian isn't about being perfect. It's not about the rules and black and white like I once thought. It's just being real and honest before God. Letting Him take over and lead you. Prompt you toward good decisions. And—" I stopped short and groaned. "Oh gosh, I can't even talk about it without preaching a sermon. You must think I'm awful."

"No, PK." Wes reached out and tucked a strand of hair

behind my ear, the back of his knuckles brushing gently across my cheek. "All those times you tried to talk to me before, it wasn't authentic." His hand slowly drew away from my face. "But this is real. This is you."

"But I'm never going to be the girl who can ride on the back of your motorcycle or get matching tattoos." I gestured around my car. "I'm cloth interior to your leather." I let out a half chuckle. "I'm the girl who *wants* to be in the third row at church every week."

Wes leaned in toward me, eyes dancing like he had a secret. "Sounds like my kind of girl."

I reeled back. "So what are you saying? Are you ready to give church another try?" I swallowed hard. "And not just church, but God? Because the former really isn't important when compared."

Wes let out a sigh. "I'm not saying I'm ready to sing 'Kumbaya' and sway around a campfire. But I think I can handle sitting on a pew with you. And listen with an open mind." A slow smile built across his features, one that coated my stomach with butterflies and dared to let me hope I might get my birthday wish after all.

And I don't mean the Lamborghinis.

"Let's just take it from there, okay?" Wes's voice dropped, his husky whisper filling the space between us. "I'm trying, PK. And not *for* you, but because of you."

"That's all I can ask," I whispered back, unable to stop the smile that surely matched his. He eased toward me, and my heart jump-started in anticipation of his kiss. I tilted my head, meeting him halfway, lips parted, ready for. . .

A chaste kiss across my cheek.

"I almost forgot your birthday present." Wes reached into his jacket pocket, leaving me in the driver's seat completely confused. "Here. Happy birthday."

He handed me a box of movie-theater-sized candy, a big orange bow on top covering the letters.

I took it slowly, adrenaline still flooding my body from the kiss-that-wasn't, and numbly pulled off the bow to reveal. . .

Gummi bears.

I snorted. Then snickered. Then tossed my head back and laughed so hard, tears filled my eyes.

"What's so funny?" Wes took the box from me and studied it as if it held the answers to my hysteria. "Isn't this your favorite candy? That day in the store—"

My guffaw broke him off, and his obvious confusion only made me laugh harder. I clutched my stomach as tears fell down my cheeks. If he only knew. Oh, if he only knew.

"Sorry." I hiccuped, finally trying to get control of myself. "It's just a long story." To put it mildly. I knew better than to ask God for a sign, but this one seemed a little too coincidental to be a coincidence, if you know what I mean.

"Whatever. I'd rather make you laugh than cry." He knuckled away a rogue tear still dotting my cheek.

I sobered. "You've done your share of both so far."

"Today's your birthday—a fresh start. How about as your real gift I promise to only do the former?"

His hand cradled my face, and I offered a tentative smile. "Deal." Only time would tell if he could keep such a promise. But I was more than interested in waiting around and finding out.

He edged toward me, pressing his forehead against mine. Once again I eagerly awaited a kiss that didn't come.

I pulled back slightly to see his eyes. "I promise I won't get hysterical again. I'm done laughing."

"No. It's not that." Wes reached up and tangled a strand of my hair around his finger, drawing me close but still not kissing me. He closed his eyes and gently pressed his cheek against mine as if I were breakable. "Things are going to be different this time."

The disappointment over the lack of kiss faded as respect and a little bit of awe filled the gap. Wes wasn't kidding. He really had changed. He really was trying. This wasn't the same boy who'd tried to push me into something I wasn't ready for that night at the impromptu picnic.

This was a man.

"We should get back inside to your party." Wes finally pulled away, letting out a ragged breath that proved he wanted to kiss me as much as I'd wanted him to. My respect grew.

"There's plenty of time for partying. I haven't even opened my gifts yet." I tore open the box of gummi bears and poured a few out. "Speaking of gifts, do you want one?"

"Sure." He plucked a green and a yellow bear from my palm. "I never told you this, but they're my favorite, too."

The red gummi bear froze halfway to my mouth as I stared at Wes in surprise. His favorite. After all this time. . . I popped the candy in my mouth and chewed quickly to hide my smile. *Thanks, God.* There were signs, and then there were *signs.* Regardless, this was one PK who finally knew what she wanted and, most importantly, who she was.

And suddenly lemon drops didn't hold nearly the appeal.

Betsy St. Amant lives and writes in Louisiana. This multi-published author is a wife, mother, former youth Sunday school teacher, and avid reader who has a heart for teenagers and enjoys sharing the wonders of God's grace through her stories.

If You Enjoyed
Confessions of a PK,
be sure to read

DIAMOND ESTATE SERIES
by Nicole O'Dell

THE WISHING PEARL
Book 1

Sixteen-year-old Olivia Mansfield can't
wait to escape the confines of her home,
which promises nothing but perpetual
torment and abuse from her stepfather.
When poor choices lead her to the
brink of a complete breakdown. Olivia
comes to a crossroads. Will she find the
path to ultimate hope and healing that her heart longs for?